D1108675

THE FIXER

A LANCE SPECTOR THRILLER
BOOK 6

SAUL HERZOG

AUTHORCONTACT

1

Craig Ritter pulled his rented Škoda Octavia into the lay-by and yanked the handbrake. He'd had his doubts about the car when he first saw it, but so far, it had served well enough. It offered decent power, decent acceleration, and had the added benefit of not drawing attention. It was as anonymous a car as he could have hoped to find in that part of Russia.

It was a frigidly cold night, well below negative twenty, and he kept the engine running and the heat blowing while he stepped outside. He went to the back of the car and popped the trunk. Inside was a long, polymer gun case. He flipped it open to reveal one L115A3 Long Range Sniper Rifle. Chambered in the 338 Lapua Magnum, it was the preferred rifle of British snipers. Its accuracy was unparalleled. In the right hands, and Ritter's were certainly that, it was capable of taking out targets at distances in excess of one mile. Next to the rifle, enclosed in a segment of the case's protective foam that had been cut out to its precise shape, was a Schmidt & Bender 5-25x56 PM II 25x magnification day scope.

He removed the scope carefully, as well as a Qioptiq Thermal Imager, and screwed the two pieces of equipment together. As a pair, they allowed him to make out human targets at night at ranges beyond even that of the gun.

He breathed on his hands, something he'd been trained not to, and got back into the car. "Phew," he muttered, slamming the door and putting his fingers in front of the hot air blowing from the vent.

The lay-by was about a mile from the farm, on a rise in the road that gave a good vantage over the compound. He raised the scope to his eye like a miniature telescope, something he did before every one of his visits, and immediately lowered it.

"Fuck me," he said aloud.

He didn't need a piece of precision optics to make out what he'd just seen. There was a light on in the house. It was faint, and he couldn't be certain, but it seemed to be coming from the kitchen at the back. He'd been in that room multiple times and could clearly picture its bare bulb dangling from the ceiling. Not once had he seen it switched on.

"Not good, Craigy boy," he muttered. "Not good at all."

He knew, of course, what he was supposed to do next —what the protocol said to do. Release the handbrake, put his foot down, and hightail it out of there as fast as the Škoda's decently powered engine could go. It would mean cutting loose, missing a meet, breaking contact. If contact were not re-established very quickly, that would be it for the mission. He had no other way of passing intel back to Langley.

He bit his lip. He did not want to lose the mission.

There was a procedure, of course, for re-establishing

broken contact. If either party missed a meet, they were both to go to the concession stand at Nikolai Ostrovsky Park at noon the following day. There, they could pass a message, warn of danger, or, if everything was okay, resume contact at the farm. If either party didn't show up at the park, the worst would be assumed, and the plug pulled.

That was all well and good, Ritter thought, but this was not a case of a missed meet, this was a problem with the venue—a light was on that wasn't supposed to be.

"Think, think, think," he muttered, rapping his fingers on the steering wheel in a steady thrum. He did another pass with the scope.

The compound was laid out in the traditional homestead pattern of the region. There was the farmhouse with its pitched roof—squat, solid, hand-built of stone and plaster. Across the cobbled courtyard was a large wooden barn. There were a few other outbuildings—a water well, a cart shed, a rusted-out shipping container used for storage—and the whole lot was enclosed inside a high wooden fence. There were two gates in the fence—one, always open, that led to the driveway, and a larger one, always shut, that led to the fields.

Apart from the light, everything was as it always was— no noise, no people, no animals in the barn, no vehicles in the courtyard. The surrounding fields, which stretched uninterrupted for miles in every direction, were unplowed beneath their covering of snow. The whole place was silent, still, devoid of movement or life of any kind. Just as it was supposed to be.

He wondered briefly if the glow could be coming from something other than a bulb—a small fire perhaps. Maybe they'd needed to burn something. He shook his head. "Not bloody likely," he muttered. The men he was there to meet were even bigger sticklers for protocol than he was. He'd gotten the impression they'd been using the location for a long time, and they certainly didn't want it compromised. They'd made that point abundantly clear.

The first night he met them, he'd made the mistake of lighting a cigarette. The bigger of the two men, Vilgotsky, knocked it clear out of his mouth with a swat of his hand.

"What do you think you're doing?" Ritter said, squaring up to him.

Ritter was not a small man, but this guy would have looked at home on an NFL defensive line. He was a burly, dark-haired Rostov native, six-and-a-half feet tall, and built like a contestant on one of those lumberjack gameshows. According to the brief note Langley had given Ritter prior, the CIA operative in Rostov, a man named Yuriy Volga, had recruited him four years ago on his own initiative. The two had been working together ever since. Ritter noticed that the note did not vouch for Vilgotsky—he'd never been to the United States, or even out of Russia for that matter—and Langley had never had any direct dealings with him. They'd run a background check, and he was paid out of operational funds, but apart from that, he was Volga's man and Volga's responsibility. Given that nothing bad had happened to Volga in the four years since his recruitment, the note concluded, 'Vilgotsky is probably loyal, but treat with extreme caution.'

"You know you can't smoke here," Vilgotsky said in his gruff, heavily-accented English.

"Why not?" Ritter said.

"Because I say."

"I don't tell you not to chew gum," Ritter said. Vilgotsky had been chewing since Ritter's arrival, it seemed a permanent state with him, and he made no effort to do it quietly.

"The ember," Vilgotsky said. "Someone could see it."

"See it?" Ritter said, defiantly putting a fresh cigarette in his mouth. "There's no one out there."

Vilgotsky sniffled loudly, another thing he had a habit of doing, and glanced at the window. Outside, in the immense stillness of the night, there likely wasn't another soul for twenty miles. "Someone could see," he said again, giving the statement an air of finality.

Ritter should have dropped the issue, but he wanted to get a read on this lumbering oaf. He turned to the CIA guy, Volga, and said, "He's kidding, right?"

Volga only shrugged.

Vilgotsky then reached inside his coat pocket—for a moment, Ritter actually thought he was going to draw a gun—but what he pulled was not a weapon, but a wallet. He threw it on the table, and it opened at the fold to reveal a tattered photo of a corpulent woman in a white dress. She was holding a baby on her hip, and a slightly older child was standing next to her.

Ritter glanced at the picture, then back at Vilgotsky. His meaning was clear. He was a local, his family was on the line, and he wasn't about to see things get sloppy because of some British prick foisted on him by Langley.

Ritter's family, meanwhile, was a thousand miles away, safe and sound in their beds in merry England. Who was he to say what was and wasn't a risk? "All right," he said, putting the cigarette back in its pack.

"Better," Vilgotsky said with a nod. "We have our way of doing things here. We prefer to take precaution."

"Fine," Ritter said. "It's gone. Forget about it."

There was a brief silence then until Volga spoke up. "If

you two ladies are done dancing," he said, "maybe I could explain to our new friend how things are going to work." He spoke with a New York accent, or what Ritter assumed was one, the CIA note being quite light on personal details. What it did say was that Volga had been born in Rostov and became a US citizen by naturalization at age three. He spoke fluent Russian, could pass seamlessly as a local, and had been stationed in Rostov for over a decade. It also said he was *reliable*. That wasn't the worst descriptor Ritter had ever seen for an operative of his type. Not the best, but not the worst. He was short and sinewy, in his forties, possibly fifties, with darting eyes and quick gestures. Something about him gave Ritter the impression of a cat that was always about to pounce.

In the early years of Volga's posting, prior to the invasion of Crimea, Rostov was a very low priority on the CIA's map of the world. During that time, Ritter imagined Volga had probably been quite neglected. His posting in the city was unusually long, and while that had its advantages in terms of the connections he could make, it was also a lot of time to develop bad habits. He pictured Volga during those years as the CIA equivalent of Kevin Costner's character in *Dances with Wolves*—just him and the natives, for a very long time, a very long way from home, with very little oversight or support.

Perhaps that was why he'd brought on Vilgotsky—for the company. The CIA, unusually, had allowed it. Asterix and Obelix, one analyst called them in the note Ritter had been given, 'an odd couple, but a productive one.' The partnership had been productive, with most of the progress coming in the years since Vilgotsky's arrival. In that time, Volga had succeeded in insinuating himself very deeply into the local political landscape. The note described him as "a firm fixture in the Rostov social hierarchy, with deep contacts and a multi-dimensional intelligence gathering capability," whatever that meant.

He was also a details guy, meticulous, fastidious, even dainty. Ritter had once watched him eat a service station sub he'd picked up on his way out from the city. He'd unpacked the bag on the wooden table in the farmhouse like he was preparing a picnic, setting the sandwich neatly on a napkin and using the plastic knife and fork provided by the gas station to cut it into pieces.

"He always eat like that?" Ritter said to Vilgotsky.

"He has his ways," Vilgotsky said.

And Ritter couldn't argue with that. If two weeks was enough time to get a read on him, Ritter would say he was a little strange, a little squirrelly, but solidly competent. There was a reason he hadn't been mopped up by the city's security services in all that time.

He certainly wasn't the type to leave a light on by mistake, and neither was Vilgotsky.

And they hadn't left it on as a warning either. They'd explicitly agreed on a warning the first night they'd met—to shut the heavy wooden barn doors, which otherwise hung permanently open on their rusted hinges. "Are you listening?" Volga kept saying in his thin, reedy voice. He sounded like someone doing a Woody Allen impersonation. "Are you catching this? This is important." There was no way he'd change the signal for no good reason.

Ritter checked the barn doors through the scope just to be sure—wide open, as always.

He figured Volga met some of his other contacts at the farm. He'd have had to. Any overlap between sources was risky, but Volga had a strong preference for face-to-face communication, and keeping everything separated simply wasn't possible. Had one of those contacts left on the light?

He couldn't picture it—he certainly couldn't picture Vilgotsky allowing it—but nothing was impossible.

He scanned the long driveway that led out from the road. There were no tire tracks on it, but then there wouldn't be, given that it was still snowing. When Ritter came for his meetings, he never used the driveway. The headlights would have been too conspicuous to anyone passing by, and in the morning, the tire tracks would have been another giveaway. Instead, he parked at a distance and covered the last mile or so on foot. "You'll find a spot to park," Volga had said. "It's all forest. Stay out of sight."

"And hike across country?" Ritter said.

"The exercise won't kill you," Vilgotsky said.

Vilgotsky and Volga were always at the farmhouse when he arrived, always sitting at the table in the dark, and he assumed they did the same thing with their vehicle. He'd never seen it out front.

He drummed his fingers on the steering wheel and wondered what was going on. Why was the light on? There was no use kidding himself. It wasn't good. It was not a simple mistake. Volga and Vilgotsky were in trouble.

Perhaps they were already dead.

And that thought stung more than Ritter would have cared to admit. They'd gotten off to a bumpy start, but despite their best efforts to the contrary, something human had managed to seep its way into the relationship.

"Not exactly a wallflower, is he?" Ritter had said about Vilgotsky that first night. It was after Volga had finished rattling through his rules and procedures, and Vilgotsky had just almost knocked over the table while rising to his feet. They'd been sitting in darkness, but the moon suddenly came out, and its light cast a pallid glow over everyone's face. Ritter's briefing note had included no photos, no physical descriptions, and the meeting was their first time getting a look at each other. "Not the type that blends in with the scenery."

"He fits my cover," Volga said.

"Which is what, exactly?"

"Don't say," Vilgotsky grunted. "He doesn't need to know."

Technically, Vilgotsky was correct. Ritter's job was discrete. He was there to play a very specific role, to target a very specific group of men. Most of them had been in the city less than a month, some for only a matter of days, and Volga had no access to them through his network. They weren't from Rostov, were not a part of the "local social hierarchy," as the note put it, and had never heard the name Yuriy Volga. He wouldn't have been able to get within a hundred miles of them.

For that, someone new would be needed, and that was where Ritter came in. "It's got to be a Brit," the CIA recruiter had said to him. "It's got to be you." And so it was.

But that didn't mean it wasn't still Volga's operation. He was the one who knew the lay of the land and how to work it. He told Ritter who he needed to talk to, how to find them, and what he needed to say. He knew who wanted to hear what, who needed what, and who had to be avoided. Ritter was the face of the operation, he was the one sitting the exam, but every single answer he gave was cribbed straight from Volga.

In addition, Volga handled all communications with Langley. Ritter—new in town and eager to befriend the big fish—was certain to attract scrutiny. The Russian government was highly adept at intercepting cross-border communications, and someone, somewhere, would be targeting Ritter's Internet and phone usage. There was no doubt. Volga, on the other hand, had been knocking around since forever. He wasn't on the top of anyone's list of priorities, and his communications would be far less likely to be targeted. He would report Ritter's findings to Langley and take their instructions.

It was a delicate, deeply coordinated operation, but if successful, it would give the CIA a list of targets that could absolutely cripple Moscow's invasion with laser-like precision. "What if you could stop a war by killing ten men?" the recruiter had said.

"What war are you hoping to stop?" Ritter said back. It was still a few weeks before the invasion, and at the time, it wasn't obvious to Ritter, or really anyone, that Russia's troops were going to cross the border.

The recruiter ignored the question and said simply, "The US military will win any war you throw at it. I shit you not."

"Then what do you need me for?" Ritter said.

"Because our job is to make sure they don't have to."

Ritter had been suspicious of the guy, he was suspicious of anyone who would wear Gucci loafers to a war zone, but he'd taken the mission. And one of the repercussions of that decision, and the point Vilgotsky was so ineloquently trying to make, was that while he and Volga needed to know everything about Ritter's mission, Ritter didn't need to know jack shit about theirs. What a man didn't know, he couldn't compromise.

Ritter was in no hurry to hear the deep secrets of Volga's no doubt intricate and fascinating operation, but

Volga was feeling chatty. "When I first got here—" he said before Vilgotsky cut him off.

"What are you saying? He doesn't need to know any of this."

Volga ignored him and continued, "—no one gave a rat's ass about Rostov-on-Don. It was a nothing assignment. A zero. I was posted here as a punishment."

"Just can't keep your mouth shut, can you?" Vilgotksy muttered.

Ritter never found out what Volga's punishment was for, he never asked, but he could easily imagine the type of work he'd been doing in the years prior to the Crimean invasion—keeping track of fuel levels in gasoline depots, railway schedules, warehouse and port staffing numbers —the kind of low-level crap the CIA carried out at literally thousands of locations across the globe. The data would end up on the CIA website as a travel advisory for US diplomats and businesses. Every once in a while, it would uncover something genuinely useful.

"Let's just say," Volga went on, "and I mean this as the biggest insult possible, it was the kind of work the State Department could have done."

Vilgotsky shook his head. "Why don't you just tell him what color panties you're wearing while you're at it?"

Volga waved a dismissive hand. "Before this invasion," he went on, "I was sending Langley shipping schedules and railway timetables photocopied wholesale from the local gazette. Really scraping the bottom of the barrel."

"It helps them form a picture," Ritter said.

"Yeah, sure," Volga said. "I doubt they read half of it. I could have made it up and they wouldn't have noticed."

Ritter wondered what point he was going to make.

"But now," Volga continued, "it's all different, isn't it?"

"I suppose it is," Ritter said.

"He's here," Volga said, nodding at Vilgotsky. "You're here. The world's at war, and we're on the front line. Everyone wants a piece of us."

Ritter shrugged. "I guess that's true," he said, waiting for Volga to continue. But it turned out that was all Volga had to say.

In any case, Vilgotsky needn't have gotten his panties in such a twist. On a social circuit as small as Rostov's, there were only so many places to schmooze the local elites. It was only a matter of time before they ran into each other. As it happened, it was that very night, less than two hours later, that Ritter spotted Volga. It was back in the city, at the nightclub of the Balkan Hotel, and Volga rolled in wearing a skintight white turtleneck and a plethora of gold jewelry. Ritter didn't speak to him, didn't acknowledge him in any way, but saw more than enough to know what his shtick was. Volga played one of those wheeler-dealer types who always seemed to crawl out of the woodwork in Russia when sanctions kicked in—the kind of guy who could get his hands on a case of Veuve Clicquot on twenty-four hours' notice, or a replica Rolex submariner in your choice of color.

Ritter stayed out of his way, did what he was there to do, and left the club. When he got outside, he found Vilgotsky, looking strangely butch in a black leather jacket and white jeans, leaning on the hood of a souped-up Mercedes-AMG G-wagon. It turned out he was Volga's driver while doing double duty as a bodyguard.

"Hey," Ritter said to him in English, slipping him a US five-dollar bill. "Get me a cab, would you."

Vilgotsky looked like he was ready to deck him, but there were too many people watching to break character.

Instead, he did as he was told, hailed the cab, and when it arrived, Ritter gave him a pat on the arm. "Thanks, pal."

A few days later, Ritter walked into the farmhouse for his second meeting, only to find Volga and Vilgotsky sitting at the table in the dark, the two men grinning like idiots and smoking cigarettes with gusto.

"Oh, fuck you guys," Ritter had said.

Vilgotsky, who was simultaneously chewing gum, his lips smacking away like a camel chewing a cud, said, "What? What's the problem?"

"So it's going to be like that?" Ritter said.

"Like what?"

"Fine," Ritter said to Volga, "but I'm not giving my report in front of him."

"What do you mean?"

"He's a liability. He doesn't need to hear it."

"He's part of the operation."

"He's a halfwit."

"He only looks like a halfwit," Volga said, eyeing Vilgotsky.

Vilgotsky shrugged, like he didn't care one way or the other, and said, "No, no, he's right. I'll wait in the barn."

"I dare say you'll be more comfortable there," Ritter said.

Vilgotsky rose deliberately, slid back his chair, and left the room. Volga and Ritter watched him through the window. He crossed the courtyard and stopped in the doorway of the barn to light another cigarette. Volga said, "He's more sensitive than he looks."

"Sensitive?" Ritter said incredulously.

"And worth his weight in gold."

"That's a lot of gold."

"He saved my life."

"And now he's your driver. I've got a meeting tonight with Meretskov. He doesn't need to hear all about it."

"Suit yourself," Volga said, "but if I were you—"

"You're not me."

"—I'd invite him back in."

Ritter nodded at the window. "Look at him," he said. "He's fine. The fresh air is doing him good."

"He was a cop in this city for twenty years."

"Good for him."

"He knows everyone."

"You know everyone."

"I know what I know because of him. I know the key players. He knows their kids, the kids' friends, their wives' friends, what brand of scotch they like, what sort of hooker they'd go for."

"He's a hooker expert."

"He knows where *all* the bodies are buried. I'm not sure if Langley is aware, but he's the reason this operation exists."

Ritter looked out at him. "Was that picture of his family real?"

Volga nodded. "But they're not in Rostov. They live in Turkey."

"Divorced?"

"Now who doesn't need to know?"

Ritter sighed. "Fine," he said. "Bring him back in, but tell him to keep his mouth shut."

Volga went to the door and called Vilgotsky back. Vilgotsky entered a moment later, rubbing his hands vigorously and swearing about the cold.

Ritter ignored him and began filling in Volga about the meeting he'd planned with Meretskov. He wasn't two sentences in before Vilgotsky interrupted. "You might want to stay away from the Balkan Hotel tonight."

"Why's that?" Ritter said. "Won't you be on valet?"

Vilgotsky touched his nose conspiratorially, then wiped it with the back of his sleeve.

"What does that mean?" Ritter said.

"Just trust me," Vilgotsky said. "Tonight, the Balkan...." He shook his head.

Ritter turned to Volga. "I thought he was going to keep his mouth shut."

"You do whatever you want," Vilgotsky said. "I'll shut up."

"I'm going to the meeting," Ritter said. "If I don't show, we lose Meretskov."

"As you like," Vilgotsky said with a shrug.

Ritter shook his head. "Meretskov's buying for Wagner. I'm sure of it." Wagner was a private Russian mercenary group that had been forcibly recruiting fighters in Russian prisons. It was implicated in multiple atrocities in Ukraine, and the CIA still had no idea who was giving it its orders. "If I'm not there, he walks."

"As you like," Vilgotsky said again.

"It's your call," Volga said. "Entirely your call."

It was Ritter's call, and he had exactly zero intention of heeding Vilgotsky's warning. On the way back to the city, he made up his mind. It was a still night, very cold, and particles of moisture had crystalized in the air. They sparkled in his headlights. He exited the highway onto Prospekt Sholokhova and entered the city through a neighborhood of pre-Stalinist low-rises. The dingy bars and restaurants along the thoroughfare seemed quieter than usual. At the intersection to Voroshilovskiy, he stopped at a red light and put on his blinker. The Balkan was to his right, but when the light changed, he didn't move. The image of Vilgotsky touching his bulbous nose kept coming back to him. The car behind honked, then pulled around him, its engine revving aggressively. Ritter watched it take the turn toward the hotel, then pulled out his phone.

He tried to call Meretskov, but there was no answer. Then, he looked up the number of the hotel and called the bar.

"You speak English?" he said when the bartender picked up.

"Yes, sir."

"Is Georgy Meretskov sitting at the bar?"

"Georgy...."

"Meretskov. Fat guy in a suit. He's probably got two whores with him."

"Oh, he's here, sir. Yes."

"Two whores?"

"Only one, sir."

"Can you tell him the person he was supposed to be meeting won't be able to make it? Something's come up."

"Of course, sir."

"And put his tab on Ritter. I've got an account."

He put down the phone, certain he was making a big mistake, and went back to his own hotel in the theater district. The next morning, he went down for breakfast, and on the table by the concierge's desk he saw the same story on the front page of every newspaper. He picked up a copy of *Izvestia* and looked closely at the color photo. There'd been an incident on Voroshilovskiy Prospekt, right outside the Balkan. He recognized the windows of the hotel bar, all shattered. On the street, dozens of people were lying dead. Blood pooled around their bodies. In front of them, police wearing the kevlar armor and black balaclavas of the Center E counter-extremism unit had formed a line. Some were holding batons and riot shields, but others carried PP-19 Bizon submachine guns.

"What on earth happened?" he said to the *maître d'*.

The *maître d'* seemed reluctant to talk about it. He glanced around the dining room, full of wealthy patrons in serious-looking suits, and said, "I'm sure I have no idea, sir."

"Looks like the police opened fire," Ritter said.

The *maître d'* nodded. "Your table is ready, sir."

2

Lance Spector stood on the embankment, watching the snow fall on the frozen expanse in front of him. Another vast Russian river, he thought, looking out at the thick ice sheets that periodically groaned and creaked under their enormous weight. Even there, in the city, the lights on the opposite shore were almost too far away to see through the mist. An icy gust whipped up, and he thought he smelled the briny scent of seawater. He was in Rostov-on-Don, a port city ten miles from the coast, and the water was frozen there too. A short trek across the sea ice would have brought him onto Ukrainian territory.

Now that war had broken out, Rostov sat uneasily in its proximity to the front. The Kremlin had pounced without warning, lunging over the border with all the finesse of a bear fighting a hornet's nest, and the people were waking up to the fact that they lived on a battlefront —a geopolitical fault line. In their parents' day, that line had been a thousand miles away, in far-off places like Berlin, and Prague, and Budapest. Now it was on their doorstep, and they could smell it—an industrial smell like burning rubber, broken concrete, and diesel fume. At night, if it was very still, they could hear the artillery.

It made them skittish, like enclosed sheep that knew there was a wolf outside the fence. Mariupol was not thirty minutes away by car, and everyone had been there to bathe on its beach, walk on its promenade, and eat its ice cream. Their children went there in summer in long convoys of school buses. When they tuned their televisions to the nightly news and saw familiar-looking, fifteen-story, Soviet-era apartment complexes being pounded to rubble by shellfire, they pictured their own homes. War had come for them before. Hitler had brought it. Stalin had brought it. They knew their own president could do it too.

Some responded by rallying to the flag, signing up for reserve duty, and dusting off long-forgotten rifles. Fathers filled jerry cans with gasoline and checked the batteries of flashlights. Mothers practiced rushing the children to the basement, and packed blankets and picture books and boxes of animal crackers. A few took to the streets in protest.

The Kremlin responded by doing what it always did. It cracked down, militarized the city's security services, and poured in FSB, SVR, and even GRU personnel.

The city was a powder keg.

Anything could happen.

Lance breathed on his hands and drew up his collar against the wind. He was there for Klára Issová, a Czech Intelligence officer he'd met only once before. That was in Prague after the embassy attack, and the only thing he really knew about her was that a Russian assassin had been sent to kill her. That was her sole credential, as far as he was concerned, and it was enough. Trust was a strange thing, elusive, like trying to hold water in your hands. He'd made the decision to trust Klára on instinct, without thinking, and had quickly scribbled down a phone number in a place she might find it. She had found it, and he prayed now that his decision hadn't gotten her killed.

He glanced at his watch. She was late.

And she was on her own now, out in the cold. She'd cut her ties to Czech Intelligence. If anything went wrong, no one would come to get her. That kind of pressure made people slip up. He pictured her at a border crossing, standing in line, and a security officer coming up and telling her to follow him. If that had happened, if she disappeared into an interrogation room without backup or cover, no one would ever hear from her again.

He looked down the street anxiously. It was after midnight, and the bars and cafés were all shut. Apart from a few sailors stumbling in the direction of the nearby Radisson, all was deserted. He shifted from one foot to the other to keep his blood flowing. The sailors laughed. They stumbled past the Radisson, likely headed for one of the other hotels on the embankment, and he watched them closely—four guys, well-built, apparently drunk. He'd have preferred if they weren't there.

Beyond them, a car approached. The beams of its headlights rounded the corner ahead of it, and when it came into view, he saw the glow of a taxi sign on its roof. It passed the sailors and came to a halt by the curb, a few feet from where he stood.

He reached into his coat pocket for the cold steel of his pistol, and let go of it when a woman—blonde, early thirties—stepped out of the car. It was her.

"Hey," she said, pulling her long trench coat closer to

her body. She stood by the cab, holding the door to keep it from leaving.

"You're late," he said.

She looked at him, and he wasn't sure how to read the expression on her face.

"Hey!" the cab driver hollered from inside the car. "You staying or not? I don't have all night."

She beckoned him with a nod, and he got into the back seat next to her. "We're going to the port," he said to the driver, "and take it slow. I don't want to end up in a snowbank."

The driver looked back at him over his shoulder. "Not much going on at the port this time of night, if you ask me."

"No one's asking you," Lance said.

"Nothing legal," the driver muttered as they pulled away.

Lance leaned forward in his seat, watching the road. That seemed to bother the driver, who was also leaning forward, peering through the windshield like a man who'd lost his glasses. "I know where I'm going," he said.

Lance ignored him and only took his eyes off the road to look at Klára. "They watch these streets," he said to her in English. "They watch everything now."

She nodded.

The cab brought them through a heavily industrialized part of the city. On either side, sprawling factories rose up around them, their shafts and chimneys stretching into the night sky like a steel forest. The driver said something about helicopter production and steel smelting but no one was listening. They passed a refinery and a long shipyard spanning multiple blocks. It was followed by a locomotive repair yard, where half a dozen train cars sat alone on the tracks waiting to be repaired. In the spill of light from the street lamps, they looked like grazing animals huddled for warmth.

The snow grew heavier and flurried in the light of the high beams. The wipers scraped noisily on the windshield. The taxi slowed to a crawl, then stopped completely at a red light. Lance looked over his shoulder to check that they weren't being followed. He could see nothing.

3

‌

R itter held his lighter, a silver Zippo with a Union Jack etched on the face, and turned it over in his hand. His jaw was clenched tight. "Asterix and Obelix," he said to himself, unaware he was saying anything.

He'd known this would happen, or something like it. "Everything I touch turns to shit," he'd said when the CIA came for him. "This will be the same. Mark my words."

The man from the CIA was older but still very suave-looking with his slicked-back hair, Panama hat, and tan linen suit. He said simply, "You do this for us, or it doesn't happen at all. Simple as that."

"Then it doesn't happen," Ritter said. "And trust me, you wouldn't want it to." No one could say he hadn't tried to warn them.

He'd tried to warn Volga too. "You need to get out," he'd said at their last meeting. "Both of you, while there's still time."

"Not yet," Volga said.

"The net's closing in," Ritter said. "There were helicopters over the highway on my way here. They were scanning license plates. Soon, they'll be requiring identity cards to leave the city."

Volga shook his head. "We're too close," he said. "If we stop now, we lose everything."

"Then we lose everything," Ritter said, surprised Volga was even fighting him on it. "At least we live to fight another day."

Volga had looked almost sad then, as if he wanted to agree with Ritter but couldn't. He said, "No. We fight *this* day. We fight *this* battle."

"It's worth that much to you?" Ritter said. "Worth risking all our lives?"

Volga said nothing.

"What about him?" Ritter said, nodding at Vilgotsky. "You want to risk his life too?"

Ritter didn't know what he'd expected from Vilgotsky, but what he got was, "You worry about your own skin, Beckham. I'll worry about mine." Beckham was one of the many nicknames Vilgotsky had come up with for him. Prince Harry was another. Anything British would do, it seemed.

"You want to risk your life for a couple of names?" Ritter said, looking at them both incredulously. He'd known since day one that they were a little nutty, but this was taking things to a whole new level.

Volga cleared his throat. "They're not just any names, though, are they? They're *the* names."

Ritter shook his head. That was true, as far as it went, but it didn't mean they were worth dying for. "What does it matter now?"

"It matters," Volga said.

"Why? Because you spent twelve years out here,

watching and waiting, tracking every grain shipment and troop transfer, writing it all down in your little notebook?"

"No," Volga said, his voice calm and level, in contrast to Ritter's.

"Are you trying to make up for missing it?"

"Missing what?" Vilgotsky said.

"You were the watchers. You were the early warning system. Only when war finally came, you missed it, didn't you? The biggest land invasion since World War Two, and you missed it. All of NATO missed it."

"We didn't miss anything," Vilgotsky said.

"You missed the whole damn show! Russia marched in on Ukraine with scarcely a shot being fired, and now you two want to make up for it by becoming martyrs." He knew he was the voice of reason—they needed to get out before the GRU strangled the entire city—but they were staring at him as if he was speaking a foreign language. "If we keep going like this," he said, "I'm going to come out here one night and find you both dead."

No one said anything then. They just stared at him in some strange, mute standoff. They had to know he was right—that was why they weren't saying anything. And if he hadn't known them better, he'd have had no choice but to write them off as fruitcakes. He'd met his share of guys like that, the young ones who'd watched too many Hollywood movies and had illusions of going down in a blaze of glory. Only the ones who hadn't seen death up close thought like that. And that wasn't Volga and Vilgotsky. They knew what death was. They'd seen plenty of it. They may not have been the two sanest guys on the CIA's payroll, but they weren't crazy.

Ritter broke the silence first. "I'm going to come out

here and find your bodies hanging from the rafters," he said. "I know it."

"Go ahead and jinx us, why don't you?" Vilgotsky said.

"This isn't the city it was before the war," Ritter said. "Who's running Center E now? Is it even still a police force?"

No answer.

"Everyone's terrified," Ritter continued. "No one's talking. Those that do end up in an alley with a bullet in their skull."

Vilgotsky eyed Volga nervously.

"How many have you lost in the last week, Volga? Three?"

"Four," Volga said, speaking at last.

"And for what? War's here. There's nothing anyone can do about that now. The mission's over. The ship's sailed."

"It's not over," Volga said.

"If the CIA wants to make a move, we've given them more than enough targets."

They'd been sitting at the table in the farmhouse, as usual. In the dark, as usual. Ritter leaned back and lit a smoke. He looked at them in the silver moonlight. From their faces, he had no idea if his words were having any effect. Vilgotsky leaned forward. Ritter thought he was about to say something, but he was just taking the gum out of his mouth. He stuck it to the underside of the table.

"That's a bad habit," Ritter said.

"Well, if it wasn't for bad habits," Vilgotksy said, "I'd have no habits at all."

Ritter turned to Volga. "What about you? Nothing to say?"

Volga shifted in his seat. He cleared his throat but then bought himself time by lighting a cigarette.

"Just say what you're going to say," Ritter said.

"Fine," Volga said. "Last time you were here, you said there were two names. Did you get them?"

"I got one of them."

"Which one?"

Ritter looked at him, thought for a moment, then shook his head. He just couldn't do it. "Why do you still care so much?"

"Which name?" Volga insisted.

"No one's asking us to go down with the ship."

"Which *name*?" Volga said again, his voice growing so taut it was almost trembling.

"Tell me this isn't some mad attempt to salvage your honor," Ritter said.

"It's not about honor," Volga said.

There was a strange look on Volga's face, and for once, Ritter simply had no idea what to make of it. He stubbed out his cigarette on the table and began pulling on his gloves. "If you two want to die for the CIA," he said, rising to his feet, "then be my guest. But that's not what I signed up for."

And that was true. Ritter definitely had not signed up to die. He was a hired gun, a mercenary fighting for a paycheck. When the man from the CIA first came into his room, Ritter took one look at him and thought it was the painkillers messing with his head. They were in a field hospital in Helmand Province, Afghanistan—not the kind of place people tended to dress up for—and this guy walked in looking like he'd just stepped off a luxury cruise liner in the Caribbean.

Ritter tried to speak, but his voice was too parched to get the words out.

The man handed him the plastic cup of water that had been sitting on his bedside table.

Ritter drank the water. "Thanks," he said.

"Don't mention it," the man said.

Ritter tried to sit up to get a better look at the guy.

"Don't," the man said.

Ritter lowered himself back down onto his pillow. He was looking at the ceiling, but the man was close enough to be in his field of view.

"You know what they call this place?" the man said.

Ritter said nothing.

"The Graveyard of Empires," the man said.

Ritter tried to drink some more water. He ended up spilling most of it on his neck. He said, "And here we are, proving them right."

The man shrugged. "Maybe," he said.

Ritter waited, he assumed the man had come in to say something, but the man seemed in no rush to speak. Ritter said to him, "You're American."

"What gave it away?"

"This is an American facility."

The man nodded.

"What am I doing in an American hospital?"

"Looks to me like you're getting your ass put back together."

"I've been here what? Two days?

"Six."

"Six?"

The man nodded.

"Have you notified my unit?"

"As far as Her Majesty's Armed Forces are concerned," the man said, "you're already dead."

"Well, someone better give *Her Majesty* a call then, hadn't they? No use getting her all worked up."

"Ah, very good," the man said. "Very funny."

"I'm not joking."

"Why don't you let me say what I have to say first? Then you can decide whether or not to let your government know you're still alive."

"Why on earth wouldn't I want them to know I'm alive?"

"Well," the man said with a slight shrug, "maybe you're worth more dead."

"More to who?" Ritter said, his mind going suddenly to the estranged family he had back home—a family that was decidedly not awaiting his return. He'd been a lousy husband, an absent father, and the truth was, he wasn't worth much to anyone, dead *or* alive, other than his unit.

"More to everyone," the man said.

Ritter looked at him. He thought he had a good idea of what was going to follow. There was no such thing in life as a free lunch—or free hospital bed—and this guy was going to propose something—probably something harebrained, or dangerous, or illegal. Otherwise, he wouldn't need a Brit for it. Whatever it was, Ritter wasn't interested. He said, "I think you should send in the nurse."

"The nurse," the man said, all saccharine smiles. "You like her, don't you?"

"She's not bad."

"Easy on the eye."

"She beats lying on a hillside, slowly becoming food for vultures."

"I'll send her right in," the man said. "Just as soon as

you hear me out." He had a folder in his hand, cream-colored, with something stenciled on the front in red ink.

"Let me guess?" Ritter said. "That's my file you're holding."

"It is," the man said, "though not the one you'd think." He showed Ritter the front. Embossed on the cover was the gold Excalibur sword of the UK Special Forces. Stamped over the sword in red ink was the Corinthian helmet of the Special Reconnaissance Regiment.

Ritter tried to sit up. "How'd you go and get your hands on that?"

"I thought it would get your attention."

Ritter collapsed back onto the pillow. There was no way on earth this guy should have been able to get his hands on that file. MI6 had buried it so deeply even his own military no longer knew about it.

"It made for some very interesting reading," the man said.

"None of it true."

The man smiled. "You're very modest."

"I'm high as a kite, is what I am," Ritter said, nodding at the IV. "Can you send in the nurse?"

"In a minute. Just hear me out."

"Then cut to the chase, why don't you?"

"I'm looking for someone with a very specific—"

"You're looking for a killer. Just say it."

"A very particular skill set," the man said.

"Skill set?" Ritter said. "Well, that's one way of putting it."

"How would you put it?"

Ritter made to speak, then decided not to.

"Look," the man said, "I didn't just get them to show

me to the nearest bed. I flew a long way to see you, specifically."

"Are you trying to make me feel special?"

"This is a proposition for you alone," the man said, pulling a seat up next to the bed.

"Make yourself at home."

The man took off his hat and hung it on the IV stand. "I want to send you into Russia," he said.

"Russia's a big place."

"A port in the west, near Ukraine. Rostov. Heard of it?"

"Sure. I hear it's really beautiful this time of year."

"Moscow's facing supply issues in the Donbas. Munitions, equipment, shells, even uniforms and field rations."

"So you want me to go in and pose as a sanctions breaker?"

"An arms dealer. Yes."

"And it's got to be me."

"Someone with your skills."

"There's no one on your own side who could do this?"

"You are on our side."

"Sure I am."

"We're allies."

"*We're* not anything."

The man nodded. They were both silent a minute. Then Ritter said, "You're CIA, aren't you?"

The man didn't answer, which was answer enough.

"There's really no one in the CIA who could help you with this?"

"This is a job for a Brit."

Ritter looked up at the ceiling and let out a long breath through his teeth. He knew this guy was somebody. He didn't know who, exactly, but the fact he had the file put him somewhere near the top of the pile. Whatever he was asking him to get involved in was going to get messy. "Why a Brit?" he said.

"Would you trust an American if you were them?"

"I wouldn't trust anyone."

"Right, but you Brits have a track record with this sort of thing."

The way he kept saying the word '*Brit*,' like it was somehow dirty, that starting to get under Ritter's skin. "A track record?" he said.

"With breaking US sanctions."

"You're saying we're all crooks," Ritter said.

"I'm saying the people I'm trying to target are used to working with Brits. They're used to spending time in London."

"There's no shortage of places these guys spend their time."

"Have you ever been to Kensington Palace Gardens?"

"I don't get around as much as I'd like."

"Very nice place. They also call it oligarch's row."

Ritter felt his jaw tighten. He'd seen enough to know how the world worked. He was under no illusions about his country, his government. London had been a virtual clearing house for dirty Russian money ever since the Queen invited Yeltsin to lunch at the palace. Under Molotov, the flow of funds through London's banks had turned into a torrent. "If you've come here to insult—"

"I've come to offer you a job."

"I already have a job."

"You mean the job that just nearly got your ass blown to smithereens."

"I mean the job my *arse* signed up for."

"You didn't sign up to die recovering a couple of Leyland four-ton trucks."

"I signed up to follow orders."

"That was a bad one."

Ritter said nothing. The truth was, he'd said the same thing when they told him the objective. He'd fought the order, told them good men would die. And good men had died—his men. "You'd have done things differently, would you?"

"I'd at least use you for the job you were built for."

"Which is?"

"Taking the fight to the enemy. Going behind their lines. Hitting them where it hurts before things get to this point."

"What point?"

"War."

"War?"

The man said nothing.

"Russia's not at war," Ritter said.

The man took a card from his inside jacket pocket and put it on the bedside table. Then he got up, put his hat on, and left. Ritter never found out who he was, and he didn't look at the card right away, either. He ignored it, as if that somehow marked the strength of his resistance.

When he did look at it, he saw it had only a phone number.

4

<hr>

"Up there," Lance said to the driver as the cab approached a broad intersection, "at the repair yard." He reached into his pocket for some cash and handed it to the driver.

"You sure you want out?" the driver said, eyeing the bleak landscape. "I told you there's nothing here."

"We're sure," Lance said, stepping out of the car into a howling wind.

Klára followed, though she looked no less skeptical than the driver.

"This is it," Lance said, breathing in the laden, grimy air. It was a very different smell from the river, more mechanic's workshop than ocean brine.

Klára watched the taxi drive away like it was the last lifeboat on a sinking ship, then she turned to Lance and said, "What are we doing out here?"

"We're walking," Lance said, pulling his coat tight against the wind.

She looked uncertain but followed as he made his way toward a cluster of old tenement buildings at the far end of the repair yard. He could have had the cab bring them to the door, but the less the driver knew, the better.

"Don't tell me we're staying up there?" Klára said as they neared the buildings.

"All right," Lance said. "I won't."

"We couldn't have risked a hotel?"

He stopped to let her catch up. "Everything's changed, Klára. Forget what you were used to. I know it looks the same—"

"This doesn't look the same as anything," she said pointedly.

"They're watching everything now. You think they had a tight grip before—"

"I know they watch, Lance."

"Then you know we couldn't risk a hotel."

She looked like she was going to say more but didn't.

Lance sighed. He knew he was being hard on her. She'd stepped onto a plane to meet him in this godawful place without any explanation of why or any idea of what she was letting herself in for. She'd put her neck on the line. There were a lot of people who wouldn't have done the same. "Let's just get to the apartment," he said. "Then we'll talk."

They reached the first of the tenements, and he felt her frustration when she realized they had to walk farther into the dingy neighborhood. The buildings were all drab, built originally to house shipyard workers, and were so blackened by decades of soot and smoke that they looked now as if they'd been built from bricks of coal. The ground floor windows were largely boarded up. What light there was spilled only from the upper levels. They rounded a corner to see a building with a small restaurant on the ground floor. Lance walked up to its wooden door and said, "This is it."

"I see," she said flatly.

He inserted the key while Klára looked through the window of the restaurant. It was shut for the night, empty behind the lace curtain.

"Home sweet home," he said, pushing open the door.

She peered into the dark hallway. "How did you find this place?"

"I saw it advertised on a notice board. The landlady runs the restaurant. I paid her cash for a month's rent."

Klára entered, and Lance scanned the street one last time. There wasn't a soul in sight. The only footsteps in the snow were their own. He checked the upper-floor windows of the buildings across the way, as well as the roofline—all clear—then followed her inside.

"It's cold," Klára said.

Lance flicked on the light to reveal a squalid hallway with a dirty wooden floor, raw from decades of heavy use, and a rickety staircase. The air was thick with the smell of boiled cabbage and potatoes. Five of the seven apartments in the building were inhabited, the one on the ground floor by the landlady. "Come on," he said, aware of the impression she was probably forming. "Upstairs, it's not so bad."

She followed him closely, keeping her gloves on to hold the handrail. The stairs were impossible to climb without them creaking and groaning under their weight, a feature Lance saw as an advantage.

Klára said, "We're going to wake the whole neighborhood."

When they got to the top, Lance stopped and stood for a moment, listening to the silence. There was another light bulb to switch on, and this one flickered and quivered as the wind howled down the street, straining the power lines.

"Wait," Lance whispered, raising a hand.

He went silently to the door of the apartment and listened again, then inserted the key and turned it, throwing open the triple bolt he'd installed earlier that day. It gave out a sharp metallic clank, sharper and louder for the silence of the hall, and the door swung open.

"Wait," Lance said again, then did a quick scan of the interior of the apartment—kitchen, one bedroom, bathroom. He came back a moment later. There was a closet by the door, and he opened it and looked inside. "All clear," he said.

"You sure?"

"Very funny."

"You're like a kid at bedtime," she said quietly.

"I like to stay alive."

itter never saw the man in the suit again, never found out who he was, and never tried to. When he called the number from the card a day later, it was a woman who picked up.

"You can call me Laurel," she said.

"All right, Laurel. How's this supposed to work?"

"You've already been notched up as a casualty by the British," she said. "MIA. Presumed dead."

"That's lovely, isn't it?"

"It is what it is," she said dryly.

He was still at the field hospital, calling her on a satellite phone the Americans had given him for the purpose. "I take it you're aware I have a family," he said.

"I'm aware."

"So what's my wife supposed to make of all this?"

"Well, from what I hear, things haven't exactly been a bed of roses in that department."

"What's that supposed to mean?"

"She's your *ex*-wife, for starters," she said, emphasizing the 'ex'. She waited then, presumably for Ritter to speak, but he said nothing. She continued. "You'll be paid for your work. Untraceable payments to a numbered Swiss bank account. No one will ever know—"

"What about my daughter?" he said.

"Of course," the woman said. "I do understand you'd want her taken care of."

"*Do* you?" he said incredulously. "I'm going to go out on a limb and say you're not a mother."

She hesitated a second, flustered, then said, "Let's try to keep this professional."

He had half a mind to hang up the phone on her—if this was the kind of halfwit they intended him to work with, it didn't bode well for the mission—but he wouldn't have come this far if he hadn't already made up his mind. He knew what he wanted. Security. Not for himself but for his family. It was the reason he'd made the call. "Just tell me what happens to my family," he said.

"The US government will guarantee their safety. You'll never have to worry about them again."

"They'll think I'm dead."

"Only for as long as the operation continues."

"I don't want my daughter growing up in some witness protection program."

"Of course not. That's not what we're offering."

"And I don't want her growing up in America."

Another pause, then, "I see."

"Is that a problem?"

"Our programs tend to be resourced in the US."

"My daughter is English. You find a way to keep her safe in England. Understood?"

"Something can be arranged."

"She'll have round-the-clock protection?"

"She'll have what she needs. She'll be safe."

"You guarantee that?"

"That she'll be watched?"

"That she'll be watched, and if something happens to me, she'll be looked after. Her and her mother. That's my price."

"I guarantee that."

"I don't want her growing up alone."

"Of course not."

"I didn't abandon her."

"Understood, Mr Ritter."

"That's why I'm doing this. For her."

"If the British Army ordered you to your death, she'd have nothing."

"You won't order me to my death?"

"If we do," the woman said flatly, "we'll look after her."

Ritter sighed. He'd felt at the time that she was telling the truth, and he knew there was no point playing games. If he was going to accept, he should tell her. "When this is done," he said, "when it's all over, what will be waiting for me on the other side?"

"We'll make payments monthly to an unnumbered—"

"Can I go back to my family?"

"If that's what you decide."

"Why wouldn't I decide that?"

"The future's a strange thing, Mr Ritter. I find it's usually best not to predict it too closely."

He knew what she was telling him, essentially to say goodbye to his family for good. He should have appreciated the honesty—he wasn't the type to enjoy having smoke blown up his ass—but it wasn't easy. "I see," he said.

"The truth of the matter, Mr Ritter, is that when a man

dies, when he's officially been tallied as a casualty, it's often best if he stays that way."

"Best for who?"

"For everyone."

"Let sleeping dogs lie," he said into the receiver.

"No one wants the dead rising from their graves, Mr Ritter."

"You don't sugarcoat things, do you?"

"I want you to trust what I say."

"And what exactly are you saying?"

"I'm offering you a job. A contract. It's dangerous. You might not come back."

"And how much of a commitment are we looking at?"

"Let's take that day by day, shall we?"

"It's not like I can walk away anyway, is it, once you get your hooks in?"

"That's not how we'd put it."

"It's not like you can just give the CIA the finger and walk away. Not if they don't want you to. Not when they're watching your family."

"You'll have to trust us, Mr Ritter."

And there was the rub. Trust. That slippery eel. Ritter was no fool. He'd walked in with his eyes open. He'd known there were no guarantees. He'd accepted that if he took the job, a bullet could well find him. What he hadn't factored, and what Volga and Vilgotsky had, was the risk of that bullet being fired by the CIA.

"We're not the ones with the death wish," Vilgotsky had said.

"I hope you're not suggesting I am," Ritter said. "Because I vote we cut and run now, before it's too late."

"You're the reason we can't," Vilgotsky said. Volga

grabbed his arm to shut him up, but it was too late. He'd said it.

"Reason you can't what?" Ritter said.

"Cut and run," Vilgotsky said. "What you told us, your intel, it's a hand grenade."

"What?"

"So, thank you," Vilgotsky said sarcastically. "A hand grenade, and with its pin pulled."

"What are you talking about?"

"You pulled the pin," Vilgotsky said again, miming the action while exaggerating each syllable of the sentence as if speaking to an imbecile. "So unless you have a way of putting it back in, very, very carefully, it's going to blow up in all our faces."

Ritter looked at Volga. "Are you going to explain to me what he's talking about?"

Volga hesitated. He looked at Vilgotksy, then back at Ritter.

"Someone better start making sense," Ritter said, "or I'm out of here."

"I didn't want to get into this," Volga said. "I wanted to wait until you'd gotten the names."

"I already told you—"

"—Yes. You got one. Which one?"

"What?"

"You said one was Russian and one was American."

"I got the Russian," Ritter said. "Tushonka."

"Tushonka?" Vilgotsky said, eyeing Volga skeptically.

"What?" Ritter said. "You don't like that name?"

"That's not a name. It's a brand of dog food."

"It's a codename," Volga said.

"You've heard of him?" Ritter said.

"What about the American?" Volga said, ignoring his question. "Who's he been dealing with?"

"I already told you. I don't know yet."

"But you're going to?"

"Apparently, there's a photo."

"Who told you that? The same source?"

"Yes."

"The one who won't give you their identity?" Vilgotsky said.

"They're inside the GRU. I've seen proof."

"How have you been communicating with them?"

"You don't need to know that," Ritter said.

"I want to know what reason you have to believe what they're saying."

"You leave source checking to me," Ritter said. "I wasn't born yesterday. I know what I'm doing."

Volga sighed.

Vilgotsky threw his hands up. "Don't you see?" he said.

"See what?"

"You were given very clear instructions, Beckham. All you had to do was stick to the script, do what Langley wanted, and get them their precious kill list. Instead, you went marching off into the wilderness."

Ritter wasn't sure what else he could have done. When he'd spoken to Laurel, she'd been clear enough, that much was true. He was to go after all high-level Russian personnel who had recently arrived from Moscow. Rostov was filling up with Kremlin henchmen of all kinds, and Ritter's cover as an arms trader would put him in the perfect position to get access to them. At the time, there was an awful lot of noise regarding what exactly the Kremlin was planning. NATO had observed Russian troop movements by satellite, they'd seen equipment buildups in Belarus, and near the Ukrainian border in Rostov Oblast, but what exactly was planned was still anyone's guess. What Laurel wanted from Ritter was a master list of precisely who was coming and going into and out of the city, who was flying in from Moscow and spending money, and what exactly they were buying. It would help Langley paint the picture, but more importantly, it would give the CIA a precision *kill list* of names they could go after at short notice if the worst happened. At the time, it wasn't an invasion of Ukraine she'd been worried about, but an all-out war between Russia and NATO. "Sometimes," she'd said to him, "you go after twenty or thirty key guys, and an entire army disintegrates before your eyes."

"I did exactly what they told me to," Ritter said.

Vilgotsky shook his head. "If only you had," he said, "then we wouldn't be in this mess."

"I did what I was told," Ritter said again, "and I kept you informed every step of the way."

Volga cleared his throat. "Who told you to go after the Main Directorate?"

"Is that what he is?" Ritter said. "This Tushonka character?"

"Just answer the question," Vilgotsky said.

"I didn't choose the GRU. The source came to me. I told you that."

"We should have shut this down then," Volga said. "It's too late now. I already told Langley what you told me."

Ritter remembered him scribbling the information in his little spiral-bound notebook to report back later. He translated his messages in his head into some sort of numeric code, and his notebook pages were full of those streams of random numbers. They looked like the scrib-blings of a madman.

"That's what you're supposed to do."

"I shouldn't have told them," Volga said. "I should have followed my better judgment. I thought we had more time."

"Why? Because the intel is false?"

Volga shook his head. "No. Because it's true."

And that was when the penny finally dropped. Volga was right. The moment he'd raised the specter of an American mole, and they'd reported it to Langley, he'd sealed their fate. They couldn't leave Rostov until they found out who it was. Otherwise, the mole could come for them. They'd never be able to sleep soundly again.

He reached for the glovebox and pulled out his cell. He'd turned it off and wrapped it in aluminum foil—a precaution he always took before coming out to the farm —and he unwrapped it now and powered it up. He had a number for Volga. He'd never used it before, they only communicated face to face, but it was there in case of emergency, and this certainly fit that bill. He dialed and waited. There was a dial tone, but no answer. As he waited, he felt the phone buzz with the vibration of incoming messages. He waited for Volga to pick up, "come on, come on, come on," but the call timed out and went to voicemail. He tried a second time, but the same thing happened. He checked quickly to see if any of the messages had come from Volga, but they hadn't. He powered off the phone, wrapped it back up in the foil, and put it back in the glove box. If a timer hadn't been counting down before, it certainly was now.

Valeria Smirnova stepped out of the bar into the biting night air and took a long, deep breath. A quiet night in at her hotel was all she'd wanted —some room service, maybe a glass of wine from the minibar, she was traveling on the Kremlin's dime after all —but the boys at Rostov-on-Don Police Department Number Four had other ideas.

She was an outsider among their ranks, an intruder from the big bad GRU, but that hadn't stopped them from trying to get her drunk every night since her arrival. "Don't you guys have wives to go home to?" she'd said the first night. They'd only laughed. She'd been pacing herself tonight, sneaking soda waters and pretending they had vodka in them, and she was glad she had. It was after midnight, and there was no sign of a letup any time soon. The last thing she wanted was another hangover.

It was Evgeny Zadorov who was the ringleader. She could hear his voice back inside, hollering over the din of the bar. "Drink, comrades, drink," he was bellowing. The man was a complete halfwit, the stereotypical provincial incompetent, riding his desk to retirement while accomplishing as little as possible with the time. So far, it seemed to be going his way. He'd risen to the rank of lieutenant at Center E, no small feat, and had even managed to amass his own portfolio of suspects.

Not that he was doing much with them, as far as she could tell, but then, what should she have expected? And at least he wasn't a complete asshole—a misogynist, sure, but not the worst she'd encountered, and not aggressive. Mostly, he just didn't care. She'd taken control of one of his files just that afternoon, and even that hadn't been enough to rouse his slumbering professional pride.

The man seemed to have one objective, and one objective only, when it came to her—to get inside her pants. That wasn't so surprising, she supposed, allowing herself just a smidge of vanity—of course her ass was more exciting than a GRU jurisdiction slip—but it did make her wonder where else Rostov's finest were shitting the bed. The country was at war, and as far as she could tell, for all the bluster of local civil rights activists, Rostov's Center E officers were still spending more time trying to knock freebies out of the break room vending machine than locking down the city.

The file she'd taken from Zadorov was a case in point. He'd been sitting on the guy for months, assigning himself mountains of surveillance duty, and racking up a corresponding amount of overtime, just to end up with reports that read like a city cab driver's logbook.

- 11.56 - Suspect drove to City Hall
- 14.34 - Suspect drove to Rostov Glavny train station

- 17.14 - Suspect used a pay phone at Rostov Glavny
- 23.46 - Suspect left city on M-4 heading north

On and on the reports went, dozens and dozens of them. Everyone there padded their paycheck, but this was egregious even by Rostov standards. Thirty-one hours in the past month alone, at time-and-a-half pay. It was a wonder he found time to do anything else. And, of course, not a single flag from accounting.

"You must have suspected him of something," Valeria said to Zadorov when she threw the jurisdiction slip on his desk. "Why else would you waste so much time on him?"

Zadorov looked worried, though a lot less than he should have for a man who'd just paid himself a hundred thousand Rubles in false overtime.

"Honestly," he said, "I thought he was one of your guys. That's why I didn't pounce."

"One of our guys? Why would we be talking to train drivers?"

"City Hall said he was sniffing around because of the pilfering. An entire shipment of artillery shells went missing the week he showed up. It was rumored someone sold it to the Azov Battalion. Can you believe that?"

Valeria shook her head.

"Our own shells against our own guys," Zadorov added.

"All right," Valeria said. "Calm down."

Zadorov threw up his hands. "He looked like a Moscow stooge. He smelled like a Moscow stooge. What can I say?"

"You didn't think to find out where he went when he left the city?"

"When?"

"He drives up the M-4 a few times a week like clockwork. Your own reports say as much."

"My job ends at the city line," Zadorov said, as if that were the one rule of the Rostov Police Department that his honor would not allow him to see broken.

She rolled her eyes. "You don't care about the city line."

"I'd have had FSB down on me like a ton of bricks if I stepped on their toes."

"Then why not pass him onto them?"

"And let them clock the hours?" Zadorov said.

Valeria gave up at that point. What else could she do? "GRU's taking the file," she said simply. "We have something of our own on him. We're picking him up."

"What have you got on him?"

"Very funny," she said.

"Can I sit in on the interrogation?"

"Sure. Why don't I arrange for you to have tea with the president while I'm at it?"

"When are you going to pounce?"

She ignored his question. "If he says anything you need to know, I'll pass it down."

"Fine," Zadorov said, as if two-hundred hours of surveillance, two-hundred hours of his life, sitting in a shitty car, eating shitty food, and smoking shitty cigarettes, meant absolutely nothing to him. "Have him then. My paycheck's hit the cap this month anyway."

That was the kind of grift, the kind of nickel-and-dime corruption, she'd been uncovering at every turn since her arrival. It was what was bogging down the entire invasion effort, as far as she was concerned, but it was so common she was beginning to grow numb to it.

And so were men like Zadorov, it seemed.

"We have to stick together now," he'd been slurring into her ear back in the bar, as if she hadn't basically accused him of dereliction of duty just hours earlier. "We're at war! The country's depending on us." That was the attitude of all of them at Center E now. All comrades in arms now that the troops were on the streets and the flags were flying at full mast. There was nothing like a good war to make men in uniforms feel taller. "Now they see what we've been doing all this time," Zadorov had said, his arm wrapped around her like they were old friends, his mouth so close to her face she could smell the vodka. "They thought we were just crooks, writing tickets and taking bribes like a bunch of tsarist pencil pushers, but now they see what's really been going on. We've been preparing the home front. We've been defending the Motherland all along."

Valeria had nodded patiently while simultaneously removing his hand from her thigh. His lax standards extended not just to professional duties but marital vows too. As well as putting a ham-fisted hand on her lap, he'd also slapped her ass quite firmly when she'd climbed off her stool. She'd said she was going to the restroom, and he was still inside waiting for her.

She didn't think she would go back in. She appreciated the offer and all—she was not above a no-strings-attached quickie with a married man—but tonight was not the night. Not with Evgeny Zadorov, at any rate. She had no doubt his performance in the bedroom would prove as limp as his professional standards.

Across Budonnovskiy Prospekt, the police station was

lit up like a department store. For some reason known only to the administrators at regional HQ, Center E was housed in a nineteenth-century art nouveau palace that had originally been commandeered by Stalin for the Weights and Measures Bureau. It was singularly unsuited to the role of police department, especially one like Center E. It had doors connecting every single room, which meant, in addition to making the place permanently drafty, also made it impossible to know if a conversation was being eavesdropped on.

Valeria finished her cigarette and stubbed it out on the ground. Her car was across the street, but she wondered if she should call a cab. She felt like she could drive but would probably blow over, not that anyone would dare test her. Go home, she thought, or go back inside and let Zadorov take another swing at the prize. Despite herself, she was leaning toward the second option when her phone started to vibrate.

She pulled it out of her pocket. "This is Smirnova."

"It's Gazzaev," a deep voice said. Gazzaev was her GRU investigator. She'd brought him all the way from Moscow because she didn't trust the GRU field office in Rostov not to screw up the job. Her mission, unlike theirs, was top priority, straight from the Prime Directorate, and she'd been told to expect CIA involvement. "Your farmhouse," Gazzaev said. "It's got activity."

The farmhouse he was referring to was the place north of the city she'd followed Zadorov's suspect to earlier in the afternoon. She'd spent an hour in the house working the suspect and his bodyguard, then another few in the car with Gazzaev, waiting for something to happen. Eventually, she'd come back to the city and left him to it.

"What is it? Did the contact show?"

"No. He tried the phone."

"I told you he would."

"You did," Gazzaev said flatly. "We triangulated the source of the call to within a few kilometers of the farm."

"And the area's locked down?"

"Not completely," Gazzaev said.

"Why the hell not?"

"That's on Rostov Oblast. They denied our request. They did send a team to assist at the farm, though."

"They'll screw it up."

"Our team's going in first. They know what to do."

"If he shows."

"He'll show."

"Not if his call wasn't answered."

"He'll show," Gazzaev said again. "He's used to the Center E halfwits tailing him like a herd of goats with bells on their necks. He'll think he's clear."

"Well, for the love of God, keep local PD the hell away from him. We need him alive."

"Understood," Gazzaev said, and the line went dead.

Valeria had a bad feeling about local police being involved. They'd screw the pooch for sure. She had no doubt. She hurried across the sidewalk, tottering on her impractically high heels, and straight onto the street. A black sedan jammed on its brakes, its horn blaring.

"Fuck off," she said, flashing her badge.

She got to her car, turned on the blue and red strobe lights issued by Center E, and put her foot down. The streets were quiet, and she tore through intersections without slowing, almost clipping a tram on Sholokhova. She shouldn't have been driving at all, she knew it, but pushed the thought from her mind. When she got to the highway, she really floored it.

This contact was the guy she'd been sent for. She was sure of it. Yuriy Volga had been running dozens of sources across the city, everything from stevedores and truck drivers to city hall security guards and municipal janitors, but it was only this one that he took the extra precaution of leaving the city for.

She tore northward on the M-4 highway, following signs for the airport. As her speed pushed one-forty km/h, she picked up her phone and voice-dialed Moscow. It was late, no one would pick up, but she'd been given specific instructions to leave messages any time something happened. Moscow was watching this one very closely.

A receptionist answered and said, "Prime Directorate."

Valeria cleared her throat. She wasn't used to this level of formality. "I have a clearance code."

"Go ahead."

"Alpha Four Alpha."

There was a click, a pause, and then a young woman's voice. "Darya Kovalchuck."

"Oh," Valeria said, surprised the secretary was there, given the hour. "I have an update. The code is Alpha Four Alpha."

"Go ahead," Darya Kovalchuck said, her voice sounding strangely tense, like she was afraid at any moment of making a huge mistake.

"There's activity at the farmhouse. Yuriy Volga held out under interrogation, but we learned that there's something he was waiting for. Something from one of his sources. A photograph."

There was silence on the other end of the line, and Valeria wasn't sure if she was supposed to just hang up. She'd only made a handful of these calls, and they'd all been equally weird. She'd heard through the grapevine that the girl taking the messages had been a nurse just a week ago. Apparently, the head of the operation, someone high up and very secretive within the Prime Directorate, had taken a shine to her during a hospital visit and compelled her to his service. Valeria didn't know how much of that was true, but the girl certainly didn't sound like much of a secretary. "Can you hold?" she said, and Valeria got the impression that if she refused, the girl would have burst into tears.

Another silence followed, and then the hiss of the line coming back on. What followed was a sound quite unlike anything Valeria had ever heard before. It was a man's voice, older, very low, but there was also something off about it. "Listen very carefully," the man said. "I'm not going to repeat myself." Valeria had some experience with severe burn victims, and she wondered now if the man speaking to her had perhaps been in a fire once. Maybe that was why he'd been in contact with a nurse.

"I'm listening," she found herself saying.

"You can call me Tushonka. You're handling this mission at my behest. It is of the utmost importance to the highest levels of government."

"I understand," Valeria said, wishing that had been made clearer when she was given the jurisdiction slip. The interrogation of Volga could have been a lot more thorough.

"This contact," the man said. "I want him alive, if possible, but more importantly, I want you to recover the photograph."

"Do you know who he is?" Valeria said.

"No," the man said, "but when you get the photograph, seal it in a tamper-proof pouch immediately. Do not show it to anyone. Do not submit it to Center E. Send it to

Moscow immediately, maximum security, under your code. That's very important."

"I understand."

There was another pause on the line, Valeria waited, but then it went dead. She glanced at the phone to make sure, then pushed her foot down even harder on the accelerator. She was driving a BMW six-series with an upgraded engine, the GRU had enraged Center E by requisitioning all of its best cars, and the speedometer crossed one-sixty as she entered a long curve in the road. The M-4 was one of the better roads in the region—two lanes in each direction with a smooth asphalt surface and fresh reflective markings. She suspected that was part of the reason Volga had chosen the location—good access back to the city, or the airport if things got really hairy.

Not that it had worked out that way for him.

His face flashed before her eyes suddenly, his and the other guy's—Vilgotsky, if she recalled correctly. She hadn't conducted the interrogations personally, that was Gazzaev's job, but she'd watched him go about his grisly work. She'd asked the questions. And she'd administered the *coup de grâce* at the end. A simple bullet to the forehead for each of them. They'd held up well, considering, but the images would still come back to haunt her. She knew that. You didn't get to work for Vladimir Molotov's GRU and still get a good night's sleep at the end of the day. It was strictly one or the other, and she had the prescription to prove it, fresh from her GRU shrink. They were anxiety meds, benzodiazepine according to the label on the bottle, and she hadn't taken any of the pills yet. She unscrewed the cap now and put one in her mouth. "*Vashe zdrov'ye,*" she said aloud and swallowed it dry.

Her phone started to ring again, and at the same time,

she saw the two-kilometer marker for her exit approaching. She tapped the brake and felt the car sway slightly, the automatic traction engaging for a split second to correct the drift. Black ice, she thought, pressing the brake again. The car swayed again. She steered into it as she'd been trained to, then jammed the wheel in the other direction as the whole car suddenly veered into a full three-sixty tailspin. She slammed the brake, spun the steering wheel, and the car came terrifyingly close to hitting the central barrier. If there'd been other cars on the road, she'd have been a goner for sure. As it was, she hit the gravel shoulder on the side of the road and almost passed through it into the ditch below. Stones flew all around her, crashing loudly into the side of the car.

"Whoa!" she cried when it came to its final halt. She slapped the steering wheel and cried out again.

The adrenaline was pumping through her body in a torrent. She had to take several deep breaths just to be able to think straight. The phone was still ringing, and she could see it was Gazzaev.

She put a cigarette in her mouth and picked up. "What is it?" she said, flicking her lighter.

"We have visual on the contact. We're going in."

7

E vgeny Zadorov put down his glass and looked around the bar. He'd been watching Valeria like a hawk, and she should have been back already. He rose, slightly unsteadily, from his stool and half-walked, half-stumbled toward the restrooms. He rapped on the door with his knuckles. "Hello? Valeria?"

No answer.

"Anyone in there?"

The place was a cop bar, popular enough, but only with cops. Very few women frequented it. He pushed open the door and glanced inside—a few sinks, three stalls. He checked the stalls—all empty.

He went back out to the bar and looked around frantically. "You guys seen Valeria?"

"Forget about her, hot shot. Way out of your league."

"Hey," he said, playing the fool, pretending to be drunker than he was, "if I need dating advice, I won't be looking for it from you lot."

He looked around again, trying not to look too

anxious, and one of the guys at the bar said, "She went out for a smoke."

Evgeny took out his own pack and put one in his mouth. "I should keep her company," he said.

"You're wasting your time, buddy."

He made his way to the door, ignoring the jeers, but when he got outside, he saw that Valeria was already rushing away across the street. "Watch it!" he cried as a car jammed to a halt, almost killing her. She didn't seem to hear him over the blare of the car horn, and he watched helplessly as she got into her own car and sped off, lights flashing like there was somewhere she needed to be in a hurry.

"Uh oh," he muttered to himself. Something was definitely up. He'd known as much the moment she took the Volga file.

Evgeny had been tailing Volga for months—it had seemed like a no-brainer when he'd first been approached —but he was seriously regretting it now. He had a nasty feeling it was all going to blow up in his face. It had been bad enough when the GRU appeared in the office, guns blazing, ready to turn Rostov into a battlefront, but once Valeria started sniffing around his files, and this one in particular, he really began sweating it.

"Open a file," Volga had said to him, "pretend to have me under surveillance, you get the overtime, and I'll give you a kickback, too, for your trouble. What could go wrong?"

"A lot," it seemed. He didn't know why Valeria had zeroed in on that file, he knew she'd taken over a few others from his other colleagues too, and he'd been doing his best to get her talking, plying her with drinks and unasked for sexual advances, but he was certainly worried. It wasn't the graft that concerned him, it was the fact that he was pretty sure Volga hadn't been on the up-and-up.

"I'm small-time," Volga had said. "I get people things. No one's going to come looking. The politicians in this town are my best clients."

"Then why would you pay a cop to watch you?" Evgeny said.

"Because if you watch me, no one else will."

It had been logical enough, and it had gone according to plan for a while, but as Zadorov learned more about Volga's movements and habits, he started to suspect he was more than the average black marketeer. For one thing, he spent an inordinate amount of time at the docks and rail yards. Zadorov thought it made sense at first, black marketeers needed to get things in and out, they needed to avoid customs officials and random inspections, but some of it didn't add up. He'd been obsessed with large fuel shipments, especially kerosene-based high-octane fuels. That wasn't anything a petty crook needed to be interested in. Then there were the trips out of the city.

"Follow me as far as the M-4, then fall off," Volga had told him.

Which, naturally, had inspired Evgeny to do the exact opposite. He was careful, and he never booked any of it, but he'd followed Volga out to his secret farmhouse in the countryside, just a few times, just to keep tabs. Not that he'd learned much. He met people there. He met the Brit.

Evgeny, thinking he was smart, later approached the Brit and offered him, without mentioning Volga, the exact same service he carried out for Volga. "If I've got a file open on you, no one else will bother. If they do, I'll be able to warn you."

"Why would I care if the police have a file on me?"

"You're a foreigner doing business around town. It's not a matter of if the police open a file on you, it's a matter of when. Wouldn't you rather it be someone you're friends with?"

"You mean someone I'm paying?"

"I'm like you," Evgeny said. "I'm a businessman. Let's get into business together."

The Brit had agreed to it, though he wasn't as casual about things as Volga. He was a lot more cautious. "I don't want you to follow me," Ritter said. "I don't want you to open a file. Just let me know if my name comes up within Center E. Let me know if there's anything I need to be aware of. I'll pay you for that."

And so, he had. Ever since Valeria came over to his desk and threw down the jurisdiction slip, he'd known shit was hitting the fan. He hadn't dared warn Volga, it was too late for him. The fact, too, that he had a file on him meant he could come under suspicion if Volga suddenly got wise to the fact the GRU was coming for him. But the Brit was different. He had no file open on him.

He ran across the street to the office and went up to the third floor, where he kept the burner phone he used for his 'client work,' as he called it. It was in a drawer in his desk, probably not the smartest place to keep it, but he consoled himself by thinking it was also the last place anyone would look. In any case, everyone in that building was on the take, and until today, he hadn't realized how hot the water was that he was swimming in. He looked around to make sure the office was empty, then tried calling Ritter.

No answer. Not even a dial tone. The phone was off.

As a last resort, and being careful not to incriminate himself, he tapped out a text message.

> Traffic awful on M-4 tonight. Don't go near it.

8

Lance and Klára were in the apartment, sitting at the kitchen counter, and the light from a faded velvet shade overhead gave him his first good look at her. He realized he was staring and looked away when she caught him. "Well?" he said, gesturing at the squalid surroundings.

"I see it," Klára said without giving away any clue as to her opinion.

"Right," he said. "Well, we won't be here long."

"You might have done the dishes."

He looked at the sink. He'd heated a can of beans earlier, and the pot was still sitting there, unwashed, along with his plate and fork. "I'll do it now," he said, getting off his seat.

She got up too and went to the window. He was afraid she would open the curtain and was about to say something when she stopped. "Don't worry," she said. "They could be watching. I know."

He filled the tin kettle with water and set it on a burner on the stove. "Coffee?"

"Got anything stronger?"

"Afraid not," he said. "I'd have stocked up if I'd...." He didn't finish the sentence but started washing the things in the sink while she inspected the contents of the refrigerator. "It's empty," he said.

"I see that."

"Sorry."

"I suppose this mission is too dangerous for food."

"We'll get something in the morning."

She came back to the counter and watched him finish the dishes. When the kettle began to whistle, he took it from the stove. There'd been a battered metal cafetière in the apartment when he arrived, it looked like something someone would take camping, and he poured some of the ground coffee he'd purchased earlier into it. Then he opened a cupboard and took out two chipped cups and saucers.

He joined her at the counter but said nothing. She looked at him, then picked up one of the teacups and examined it, the fine porcelain, the little flowers that had been hand-painted around the rim. "These are surprisingly delicate," she said.

"They were here when I got here," he said.

"Really?" she said, pouring the coffee.

He ignored her sarcasm and reached into his pocket for his smokes. He stopped when he saw her face. It was to be a smoke-free apartment, it seemed, while she was in residence. He put the pack back in his pocket, and she picked up her cup, tilting the contents and looking at it as if judging the quality. "You like it strong," she said.

"Strong and black," he said. "Is that okay?"

She shrugged and took a sip. "I've had worse."

"We can pick up milk in the morning, too," he said.

She removed her coat for the first time since their arrival and threw it on the back of the nearby sofa. "How long do you think we'll be here?"

"I don't know," he said, taking another sip.

"I saw there's only one bedroom."

"I hadn't noticed."

She gave him a wry smile. "Very funny."

"I'll take the couch," he said.

She nodded curtly, as if he'd just given the correct answer, and he got up and went to the bedroom to gather a few things. He wasn't doing her as big a favor as she might have thought. The bed was a bare mattress, and its wire coils felt like they'd been salvaged from old car suspensions. His sleeping bag was on the mattress, he'd picked up two at the market by the bus station, and he rolled it up and laid out hers in its place.

There was a single window in the room, small and curtainless. He would have blocked it up, but it was so dirty no one could see in other than to tell a light was on.

He took his bag from the closet and rifled through it. It contained fake Russian IDs for both of them, as well as two Czech-made CZ 75 9mm pistols, and a Russian PYa 9mm. The weapons were standard-issue for Russian police and common enough not to raise any particular alarms if they were used. He picked up one of the CZ 75s, as well as Klára's ID and a packet of black hair dye he'd bought, and brought them back to the kitchen.

She picked up the ID and examined the photo. "You got this very fast."

"I knew where to go."

"The photo's awful."

"It's not that bad."

Again with the wry smile. She picked up the gun

deftly and checked the sights and that it was loaded. She put it back on the counter. "At some point," she said, looking up at him, "I assume you're going to tell me what our plan is."

"We're waiting."

"Waiting?"

He nodded.

She looked at him skeptically. "Have you seen the news? There's a war going on."

"I know there's a war."

"I'm not sure this is the best time to be... *waiting*."

He said nothing.

She took another sip of her coffee, and he thought he noticed her grimace.

"It's too strong," he said. He grabbed the kettle and topped up the cafetière with hot water.

She watched him but didn't replace the coffee she had. She took another sip, another grimace, and said, "Why did no one see this coming?"

"The war?"

"*Yes*, the war."

He wasn't sure what she was asking him. People had seen it coming, of course. Alarm bells had been ringing in Washington and London and Berlin. At NATO headquarters in Brussels, urgent talks were taking place. Klára's own government had ordered its stock of 152mm howitzers, as well as its DANA self-propelled guns, be transported to Kyiv as a matter of urgency. That had been two days before Russia's troops flooded over the border— two days before the embassy in Prague was attacked. People had been watching. They'd been noticing. How could they have failed to?

Troops had been flooding into Rostov Oblast for

weeks. Equipment too. But the Kremlin took measures to screen it. They were at war already in the Donbas, so much of the shipments could be attributed to that. They also began a series of massive war games with Belarus. Training exercises, they called them. Obviously, they'd been menacing, but that's what training exercises were for.

The media liked to portray war as a game, black and white, and played according to simple rules, like football. But those in the trenches knew there were no rules, there were no points, no plays, no referees. Every action was open to interpretation, and nothing was certain, even after it happened. If it was a game, it was played in mud, and fog, and swamp, and the six inches in front of your face were so full of smoke and shrapnel and dirt that it was a miracle anyone saw anything at all.

Molotov had taken steps to add to the confusion. He'd feinted, and misdirected, and bluffed. He'd leaked invasion plans of the Baltics, going so far as to shoot down Latvian forestry planes to sow extra confusion. He'd ramped up the most terrifying strategic weapons program in living memory, detonating a nuke over the Arctic, and leaking a virus from a bioweapons lab in Yekaterinburg that had sent Langley into a tailspin. He'd knocked the White House off balance with three back-to-back embassy attacks, obliterating the US diplomatic presence in Moscow, Beijing, and Prague almost simultaneously. The attack in Prague was timed to the second to line up with the first troop movements into Ukraine, and was designed from the ground up to create the maximum confusion possible, going so far as to target female personnel to add to the noise.

"Nothing to say?" Klára said. "No excuses to make?"

"I'm not going to defend what's happened."

"President Montgomery deserves to be shot," she said. "He should have had the Third Air Force in Ukraine, or at least Poland, not Ramstein, hundreds of miles away."

"I don't disagree with you."

"And the troops he activated, what good were they in the end?"

Montgomery had put the 77th Field Artillery Regiment on high alert but had stopped short of moving them onto Ukrainian territory. He'd also sent a Carrier Strike Group into the Black Sea, but again, not near enough to Ukrainian territorial waters to block Russian intentions.

"He should have moved faster. This could have been prevented," she said.

"I know."

"He pulled down his pants and bent over. That's what he did. And Molotov moved right in for the kill."

Lance agreed with her, but he didn't want to get into a debate. Their job wasn't to talk, it was to act, and that was why he'd brought her there. "There's a contact," he said, switching the subject.

"A contact?"

"Someone the CIA sent in years ago."

"And what's he been up to?"

"He's been gathering information."

"Well, he didn't gather enough to prevent the invasion, did he?"

"No," Lance said, "but he might have figured out who's responsible."

"Molotov's responsible."

"Molotov didn't act alone," Lance said. "According to the contact, it's someone in Molotov's inner circle who brought this upon us."

"Even if it was one of his underlings, Molotov is the one ultimately responsible."

"This is more than an underling," Lance said. "He's the one who planned the attack in Prague. His name is—"

"Osip Shipenko," Klára said, her eyes widening.

Lance looked at her in surprise.

"I've heard the stories," she said. "Some monster in the Kremlin pulling the strings. A man with a deformity, with blisters on his skin and—"

"They're more than blisters," Lance said.

"He's got to pay for what he did," she said.

As if on cue, their gaze turned to the gun on the counter. "It's not going to be easy to get to a man like that," Lance said. "He's been lurking in the shadows for a long time. Decades. The fact we even know he exists, or that he's been involved in these atrocities—"

"I'm ready to do what it takes," she said.

"There will be blood."

"There's already blood."

"There's no telling where it will take us."

"Is that what your source is going to tell us?" she said. "Where to find him?"

Lance shook his head. He was wondering how much to tell her.

"What is it?" she said.

"Nothing." He'd have liked to change the subject, but he could see from her face that wasn't going to happen.

"Don't doubt me," she said, and there was a new fierceness in her voice. "I'll see this through," she said. "I'll see it to the end. What Shipenko did in Prague—"

"What if this doesn't end with Shipenko?"

"What do you mean?"

"The source managed to confirm that Shipenko was

behind this invasion. He didn't refer to him by name. I've seen the message he sent."

"Okay," Klára said. "How did he refer to him?"

"Tushonka."

"Tushonka?"

"It means—"

"Dog food," she said.

"It's Shipenko's name within the Kremlin."

"Okay," she said.

Lance hesitated.

"Come on," she said impatiently. "If I'm going to risk my life for this thing—"

"There's another name," Lance said. "Someone Tushonka's been talking to. Someone in Washington."

She put her cup down and missed the saucer. "Shit," she said, leaning back to stop it from spilling on her. She grabbed a rag from a hook on the stove and mopped up the spill. "I'm a klutz."

"It's fine."

"Who is it?" she said. "In Washington?"

"That's the thing. He didn't know."

"Well, is he going to find out?"

"He's going to try. He's got a meet with one of his sources tonight. A Brit operating in the city known as the Fixer."

"So the Fixer knows?"

"We'll find out."

"Where are they meeting?"

"I don't know. I don't need to know."

"Then how are we supposed to—"

"I meet the local asset at four fifteen a.m."

She looked at her watch.

"I'll go alone," Lance said.

"No, you won't."

"The meet's prearranged," Lance said. "He's expecting me alone."

"I didn't come all this way to sit on my hands."

"You'll get your chance soon enough," he said. "If you come now, you'll spook him."

She leaned back and looked at her watch again. Lance thought she was going to argue the point again, but she didn't. "Fine," she said. "You meet him. You get the name of the American. Then we decide what to do."

Lance nodded.

"Either way, Shipenko pays for what he did."

"He'll pay," Lance said. "I promise."

She sighed, clearly still not a hundred percent satisfied. She brought her cup to the sink and then picked up the packet of hair dye he'd given her. "I guess I should put this in."

He nodded. "Oh, and Klára?"

"Yes?"

"There's no hot water."

9

Ritter put the car into gear and drove a mile farther up the road, turning onto a rutted logging track he'd scoped out some weeks earlier. There was a spot he knew of where the pine and spruce trees were thick enough to conceal a car, and he stopped there, killed the engine, and got out. The snow had stopped, and the cloud seemed to be clearing enough for some moonlight to break through. He listened intently and heard nothing but the rustle of trees in the breeze.

He went to the back of the car and opened the trunk. There was a black canvas duffel bag next to the gun case, and he pulled it out and set it on the ground. He rubbed his arms hurriedly for warmth. The night was the kind of cold that could get you in trouble fast. He'd seen it in Afghanistan more times than he cared to remember, in the mountains, the cold creeping up on a team and killing them faster than any enemy ever could. He was wearing a thermal base layer, and he reached into the trunk for a thick woolen sweater which he pulled on over his head. Over that, he put on a bulletproof vest, and over that, a specially adjusted down parka with fur lining that fit over the vest. He took off his shoes and pulled on a pair of *mukluk* boots that Volga had given him when they first met.

"Am I going ice fishing?" Ritter had said.

Volga only said, "Trust me," and Ritter was glad that he had.

He checked his handgun, a Glock 17, as well as his tactical knife and flashlight. He considered taking the sniper rifle but decided against it. He was two miles from the farmhouse now, and the extra weight wouldn't do him any favors. Instead, he slung an AK-12 over his shoulder. Over his head, he pulled on a balaclava, adjusting the eyeholes to give as wide a field of vision as possible. He also put on some oversized fleece mitts. They were cumbersome and made it virtually impossible to operate equipment, but they were very effective at preventing frostbite.

When he was ready, he packed the bag back into the trunk and ran over his mental checklist one last time. Threats. Probabilities. Oversights. Mistakes. He was acutely aware that the decisions he made now if he wasn't careful, could lead to his death.

Distance to the farmhouse—two miles.

Average speed in snow—seven miles per hour.

Time to hypothermia at negative thirty—ten minutes.

When he was ready, he set off back down the track at a light jog, his mind running through the list of everything that could go wrong, like Dustin Hoffman's character in *Rain Man*. The moonlight was just enough to see by, and he paused at the road to make sure no cars were coming. There was only silence, and he crossed and hopped the fence into the field, where the half-foot of snow on the ground slowed his pace considerably. He recalculated his speed, his distance, his time to the farmhouse. Every few minutes, a gust of wind whipped up from the direction of the sea, and he had to turn his back to it to cut the chill. He constantly readjusted his gloves and balaclava so that no part of his skin was exposed. He had no desire to lose an appendage to frostbite.

As he approached the farmhouse, he knew that his black silhouette against the snow would make an easy target to anyone watching from the upper floor. With a few hundred yards left to cover, he stopped and dropped to one knee. He pulled off a mitt with his teeth and did a quick scan of the compound through the thermal scope, paying particular attention to the second-floor windows.

All was still clear.

He checked the barn.

Nothing.

He readjusted his balaclava—his breath was melting the snow around his mouth, and as it refroze, it stuck to his lips—then pulled back on the mitt and continued toward the barn.

As soon as he got within sprinting range, he increased his pace, running flat out, bracing with every step for the crack of a gunshot. It never came, and when he was close enough, he threw himself up against the back of the barn, gasping for air, his breath billowing in a white cloud before him.

Then he pulled off the balaclava and mitts and let them fall to the ground and drew his Glock. He waited a minute, listening intently for the slightest sound. He heard nothing but his own breath and the intermittent howl of the wind.

Moving slowly to the corner of the barn, he peered

across the courtyard toward the farmhouse. He still couldn't see into the kitchen, but he was sure now that was where the light was coming from. Some of the light spilled into the front rooms, and he watched those windows closely for any sign of movement.

Nothing.

There was a side door leading into the barn, and he checked it. It was unlocked. He opened it slowly, flinching as it creaked. He stopped and listened. Everything remained completely still, completely silent. He opened it the rest of the way very slowly and entered the barn. He dared turn on his flashlight and did a quick scan of the interior. There were tire marks on the ground, and he went to look at them more closely. Dirt had been kicked up by a tire spin. Someone had parked in there, and it looked like they'd pulled out in a hurry. He crouched down and took a closer look at the tire marks, but they told him nothing.

He switched off the flashlight and crept slowly toward the open barn doors. He could clearly see the farmhouse across the yard, as still and silent as ever. It was scarcely sixty feet across the yard to the door of the house. He took out the thermal imager and did one final sweep, then removed his heavy parka and laid it on the ground, placing the AK-12 on top of it.

This was it, he thought—the moment to take a risk, to roll the dice—a mad sixty-foot dash across a cobbled yard. If it was all a trap, if someone was hiding in the attic, it would be the simplest thing in the world to gun him down as he crossed the yard. The simplest thing in the world, he thought, then bolted from the barn, running flat-out for the farmhouse, diving to the ground and sliding the last few feet like a batter stealing first base. He tucked in against the stone wall and waited five seconds, then gasped for air, sucking in as deeply as his lungs allowed.

Still alive, he thought. No gunman in the attic. No bullet in his skull. Just the silence of the night, broken only by the explosive bursts of his own breath and the steady thrum of his heart.

He waited a few more seconds, then rose to his feet and crept toward a small window by the door. He peered into the house through a lace curtain. In the spilled light from the kitchen, he could make out the bare contours of a bathroom—a porcelain toilet bowl, a metal sink, a claw-foot tub.

He ducked beneath the window and continued to the front door, where he stopped again to listen. Hearing nothing, and with the Glock ready in his hand, he turned the door handle slowly, testing for resistance, bracing every second for the door to make a noise. The handle turned, the door slid open, and then it happened—the agonizing creak of a rusty hinge. He froze, his back hard against the wall, the gun clutched tightly against his chest.

Checkmate, he thought, holding his breath.

But nothing came—no crack of gunfire, no muzzle flash.

He waited as long as he dared, then pushed the door with his foot, keeping his body behind the wall as it creaked open. Still nothing. Entering the house was when he would be at his most vulnerable. During training, they'd told him that shooting a man in a doorway was the closest real life got to actually shooting a fish in a barrel. He stepped through the doorway anyway, moving into the hallway in a fluid, silent motion.

He scanned the hall in front of him, the staircase at its

far end, the door to his left that led to the small sitting room.

All clear.

He moved quickly then along the narrow hallway, half at a crouch, hugging the wall. When he reached the kitchen, he peered around the doorframe, gun first, finger on the trigger. He pulled back reflexively, like a child who'd just touched a stove.

Then he peered around again to confirm what his eyes had just seen.

There was no denying it.

Two men, Volga and Vilgotsky, beneath that errant light bulb, both strapped to wooden chairs, slumped over, a single bullet in each of their foreheads. Their noses were crushed, their eyes swollen shut, their faces so bloody and battered as to be almost unrecognizable. Their hands, fixed to the arms of the chairs with cords of electrical wire, were black at the fingertips where the nails had been pulled out with pliers.

They'd been interrogated.

And Ritter knew all too well how those interrogations went. Not one man in a hundred withstood them without squealing like a pig.

"Checkmate," he said aloud.

10

Levi Roth sat comfortably on a leather sofa, a large fire crackling in the hearth before him, dipping a wafer into coffee that had been served to him in a French Second Empire china teacup. He was in the opulent library of one of Washington's first and only palaces, the Eisenhower Building, which for decades had housed the State Department, the War Department, and the Navy Department. He liked to think of it as the building where the myth of American exceptionalism had been born, and he glanced around at the many symbols of power it had accrued—the furniture, imported from London in the 1850s, the twelve-foot-high globe with its continents of gold, surrounded by seas of inlaid opal, the crystal chandeliers from God only knew where.

There'd been a time when Roth and the president had held their meetings in the Oval Office, but given the changing nature of Roth's role, his growing power within the president's inner circle, and the need for ever more secrecy, they'd switched the venue.

Roth glanced at his watch. He did not appreciate being made to wait, even by the president, and secretly suspected that between the two of them, it was his own time that was the more valuable. He was pulled from his thoughts by the president's bellowing New England accent. "Levi, my fellow. Sorry I kept you waiting. Shrader's been losing her shit over this Telegram chatter."

"Not at all," Roth said. "They've taken very good care of me." He raised his teacup to prove the point.

"Good, good," the president said, joining him by the fire. "But I must confess, I was surprised you wanted to go at this again. I think we both made our positions abundantly clear this morning."

"We did," Roth said with a sigh. The fact was, the two men had been at loggerheads not twelve hours earlier, during the President's morning briefing in the White House situation room. Shrader, Schlesinger, Winnefeld, and Cutler were all present, and Roth had argued heatedly for a more aggressive response to Molotov's invasion of Ukraine. Roth was used to being the hawk in the room, but he regretted the direction that meeting had taken. He'd heard afterward that some of the aides in the room had been genuinely afraid the debate would come to blows. "I apologize for my emotion," he said, rising to his feet.

"No need," the president said, waving a dismissive hand. "I pay you for your thoughts, not your manners."

Roth felt genuinely ashamed of his outburst. "Really, sir."

"No, no," the president said, taking his seat. "You want to move in and assassinate the most dangerous, most guarded man on the planet. A man protected by the world's largest nuclear arsenal."

Roth shook his head. "When you put it like that—"

"I know the man's a demon," the president added, his tone conciliatory, "but for as long as he's in power, we at least know what we're dealing with. There's no guarantee that if we tried to replace him, someone better would take his place."

"Understood," Roth said, wishing they could drop the subject and move on. It had been a mistake to express his preference for regime change so openly, to associate himself with it so memorably. Now, if anything were to happen suddenly to Molotov, all eyes would be on him.

"I let my nerves get the better of me," he said.

"I understand that," the president said. "We're closer to a nuclear exchange than any time since the Cold War. Everyone's nerves are close to fraying."

"Well, I've regained my composure. I assure you."

"Good," the president said, in his paternal and irritating tone. "Molotov, if nothing else, knows how to act in his own interest. The embassy attacks took our eyes off the prize. The weapons tests terrified us. And while we were running around like a bunch of headless chickens, he quietly launched the biggest land invasion since the end of World War Two. He knows what he's doing, Roth, and while we might despise him for it, it does, ultimately, mean that the Russian nuclear arsenal is in the hands of a rational actor."

"I hope you're right," Roth said.

"Don't get me wrong," the president continued. "I get where you're coming from. I do. There's war in Europe. Inflation is through the roof. There'll be fuel shortages this winter. Cities people actually heard of before the war are being shelled to rubble. And Molotov's throwing around nuclear rhetoric like a lippy prizefighter before a weigh-in."

"It's not his threats that I'm worried about," Roth said.

"We've been dealing with him for twenty years, Levi. He's an asshole of historic proportions, but he's not about to bet the farm on this thing in Ukraine."

"I'd say he's already bet the farm. Wouldn't you?"

The president shrugged. "Ukraine?" he said. "I mean, don't get me wrong, I'm all for the self-determination of peoples. If they want to join Europe, if they want to join NATO, then in a perfect world, by all means—"

Roth leaned back and tried to hide his frustration. He didn't want a repeat of the morning, but he'd heard all of these arguments before, and frankly, they made his blood boil.

The president wouldn't let up, though. "Ukraine is in his sphere. It was a Soviet Republic. It has the same religion. I mean, it wasn't even an independent country until—"

"I've heard the arguments," Roth said, interrupting him. They were all arguments for appeasement, as far as he was concerned, and he knew if he let the president go on, things would get heated. He needed to change the subject. "What about what Molotov said on state television? Russia's nuclear deterrent is on a hair trigger. The missiles are fully fueled and launch-ready."

"What do you expect from him?" the president said. "The man's losing on the battlefield. It's a humiliation. He's got no other choice than to talk big."

Roth was doing what he'd promised he wouldn't, he was getting dangerously close to being pulled back into an argument, and he forced himself to bite his tongue.

"Look," he said, "we both know where we stand. You're the president. It's your decision."

The president shrugged, as if the whole thing was purely academic, as if he had no stake in the outcome one way or another, and pulled a cigar from his breast pocket. "Can I offer you one?"

"No," Roth said, more bluntly than he'd intended, and he regretted it as soon as the word escaped his lips. The president was offended. Roth clenched his jaw and wondered how on earth he was going to get through the next subject he needed to broach.

The president made a great show of lighting his cigar, holding the flame to it for a long time, and puffing enough smoke to take on a steam engine. When he was satisfied, he said, "I hope you didn't make me miss dinner with Doris just to rehash our morning's argument."

"No," Roth said, shifting uneasily in his seat. He did not relish what he had to do next. If there was one part of the job he disliked more than anything else, it was lying, especially to the president.

"Well?" the president said expectantly.

Roth cleared his throat. "There are rumors going around, sir."

"What sort of rumors?"

"The only kind," Roth said, keeping his voice level and his gaze locked on the president.

"A rat?" the president said.

Roth nodded, glad he didn't have to say the word himself.

The president looked at him hard, then at the fire. "I see," he said quietly.

Roth was silent for a moment. He could feel the sweat running down his back and prayed the president didn't notice his discomfort. He was passing on this information because he had to. He had no other choice. The risk of it getting back to the president by some other channel was too great, and if that happened, serious questions would be raised as to why the director of the CIA had kept the information to himself. "Someone high level," he said, forcing his face to remain blank.

"Are you sure?" the president said.

Roth said nothing but reached into his pocket for the piece of paper that had started the whole blasted thing. If he'd had his way, it would have been set on fire the minute it came out of the printer.

"What's that you have?" the president said.

The paper was thin, thermal paper, like the kind from a receipt machine, and the words were printed very faintly. It was hard to imagine such a flimsy thing having such far-reaching consequences. With his jaw clenched, he handed it to the president.

"Where did you get this?"

"It was sent by one of my sources in Russia."

"Moscow?"

Roth shook his head.

The president looked at him closely, then looked down at the paper.

Tushonka speaking to someone in Washington at highest level. More to follow.

The president read the note, then, instead of handing it back to Roth, he folded it once and put it in the inside pocket of his vest. He said nothing. Roth watched him until he could bear the silence no longer, then said, "Tushonka is Osip Shipenko."

"I know who he is," the president said. "He's public enemy number one, for God's sake."

Roth swallowed, then said, "Correct, sir. He's the suspected mastermind behind the Prague attack."

"*Suspected*?" the president scoffed.

"We also know he's highly trusted by Molotov. The two go back decades. We suspect he's a member of the Dead Hand," Roth said, referring to the Russian president's most secretive and powerful inner circle. The Dead Hand was the group Molotov trusted with his life and with ensuring the continuity of his regime. As such, he gave them almost unlimited power to achieve their objectives. There was no corner of the Russian state that was off-limits to them. "Perhaps he's its most important member."

"He's been active in the run-up to this invasion," the president said.

Roth nodded. "Yes, sir."

"And he has a weird...."

"Face, sir, that's correct."

"Some sort of...."

"Accident, sir. As a child, he lived at the Aralsk-7 bioweapons facility on Vozrozhdeniya Island. He was caught in a smallpox test there."

The president grimaced. "Do we have any theories as to why he's speaking to one of our people?"

Roth made a face like he was racking his brain to think. "It could be a number of things, sir."

"And I take it we haven't authorized anything like this?"

Roth resisted the urge to wipe his brow. "We have not,

sir."

"So we're looking at a real leak?"

"If the report is true."

"At the highest level?"

"I've already started trying to track it down."

"While we're on the brink of war."

Roth had expected the atmosphere to be tense, but that didn't make it any easier to bear. "Shipenko's records in our databases go deep. He's been a player inside the Kremlin for a very long time. If he's had contact with anyone on our side in the past, there'll be clues."

"Tatyana Aleksandrova had contact with him," the president said.

"That's right," Roth said. "She disclosed it, but...."

"I want her watched. If someone on our side has their fingers in both pies...."

Roth nodded.

"She's Russian, after all."

"Of course, sir. She'll be watched very closely."

"We could be looking at treason," the president said, "plain and simple."

"Yes, sir."

"We have the death penalty for that."

"Of course," Roth said, his own falseness gnawing at him like a canker. He knew very well that Tatyana had no dealings with Shipenko—he knew, in fact, that she'd sooner have her eyes gouged out than speak to him—but if the president wanted to be distracted by that route, so much the better for him. The president had always been one for the lewd stories, and from what Roth had heard, there were plenty of details in Tatyana's report of her encounter with Shipenko to keep the pages turning. "I'll get you a copy of her disclosure, sir. It makes for some interesting reading."

"Do that," the president said, wetting his lips before taking another suck of his cigar. "I'll read it very carefully."

11

R itter stared at the two bodies and, almost without noticing, crossed himself. He'd seen this before—victims of Center E—and it was never pretty.

As his eyes adjusted to the light, he scanned the room. He looked at the chairs—their severe straight backs, the dark walnut wood. They'd been in the hallway the last time he was there. He went to the bodies and bent to get a closer look. It was an ugly business, torture, and worse the closer you got, but if you knew what to look for, it told a story. Sometimes, it told more about the torturer than the victim.

He reached for Volga's hand and ran his thumb over the nail beds. He looked on the floor for the discarded nails. He found one and picked it up, a small clump of meat still attached to its base.

Pliers, he thought.

He looked at the two mangled faces, the bullet wounds strangely symmetrical in the center of their fore-heads, and pressed the swollen flesh around their eyes and mouths. The blood had not quite caked dry. He took out his tactical knife and cut open their shirts. There were no marks on their chests. No cigarette burns. With a grimace, he slid two fingers into Volga's mouth and checked the teeth as if checking a horse he was considering buying. None were missing. He did the same with Vilgotsky, fighting back the urge to gag. Vilgotsky's teeth were a disaster, he was missing more than a few at the back, but that was from bad dentists and too much sugar, not an interrogator's pliers. Ritter wondered, as he wiped his hand on his sleeve, why he'd insisted on chewing so much gum.

He looked down at Vilgotsky's lap.

"Fuck me," he muttered, opening the zipper. A quick check. Nothing down there. No funny business. He did the same with Volga.

The house was as cold as a refrigerator, and he leaned in and sniffed the air. No smell. The bodies hadn't been there long. He glanced over his shoulder as if suddenly reminded someone could still be there, but there was no one.

"What happened, boys?" he said quietly. "Who brought a fox back to the coop?"

Three fingernails were missing from Vilgotsky's left hand. None from his right. That didn't suggest the most thorough of interrogations. They'd been tougher on Volga. All ten of his were gone. He'd held out, Ritter thought. Or they'd wanted more from him. In any case, they hadn't taken it further than the fingers, and there were certainly a lot more places they could have gone. Whoever had done this was not a sadist. They hadn't prolonged the procedure. They'd done their job and no more. He was grateful for that much.

What had gone wrong, Ritter thought. He needed to know. Volga was careful, he was a pro, and unless Ritter was mistaken, he'd also arranged protection with Evgeny Zadorov. Had his CIA connection been sniffed out? Had this been the work of the GRU? Or had he been caught up in the general frenzy that had engulfed the city? There was enough of that going on. Two days earlier, a German businessman had been found in his hotel room near the airport with razor cuts all over his arms and legs. The newspaper reported it as a robbery, but everyone saw Center E's hand in it. The day before that, five students from the local university died when their Lada Granta ended up in the Don. All had been members of the university newspaper and had published articles critical of the invasion. That very morning, Ritter had heard of a railway signals operator who was found hanging from a signpost at the Temernik station by his ankles, the word 'traitor' scrawled on a note tacked to his chest.

That had to be it, he thought. Everything he saw pointed to a quick and dirty interrogation, the kind reserved for ordinary locals and carried out by Center E. If Volga's CIA connection had been discovered, if there'd been even a whiff of a Langley connection, he'd have been transferred to the GRU immediately. Zadorov had told him they were in the city, that they'd even set up their own interrogation rooms at Center E headquarters on Budon-novskiy Prospekt. His gut told him this was the work of local police.

Ritter instinctively ran over any personal information he'd ever given Volga. Not his real name. Not his unit or rank in the British army. Certainly not the fact that he had an ex-wife and daughter. All they'd known was what was necessary for the job and whatever they'd managed to pick up during the meetings. He looked again at Volga's hands. All ten, he thought. The poor bastard had held up well.

No one had come looking for Ritter. He'd been at City Hall not two hours before, scarcely a few blocks from Center E HQ on Budonnovskiy Prospekt, and no one had come knocking. Volga hadn't given him up. They'd held out, and they'd saved his life.

But that didn't mean they hadn't given up something. Everyone gave up something, regardless of how tough they were. It wasn't a chance, it was an inevitability. The question was, how much had they given up, and had they kept to the script?

There was always a script. The CIA knew agents would get caught, and it prepared them for it. When the torture started, they used resistance techniques, they held out for as long as they could, but when the time came to talk, and it always did, they had pre-approved information they could spill. It was real information, valuable to the enemy and damaging to the CIA, but it wasn't mission-critical. It wasn't fatal.

Volga's script included a lie—that he worked for the SBU, the Ukrainian intelligence service, and it contained a truth—that he was gathering intel on the invasion, acquiring targets, watching logistics, laying the ground-work for an eventual counteroffensive. It was precisely the kind of thing that Center E was there to unearth, and they'd have swallowed it whole. Eventually, probably after the tenth fingernail, but before they moved on to more exotic regions of the body, Volga would have given up some names. Real names, smaller fish, local contacts—the people who monitored ship departures and train timeta-bles and fed him bits and pieces of intel for cash. In short, the unlucky bastards Langley deemed expendable. They could expect a visit from Center E in their future.

But none had come for Ritter.

He looked down at the floor, covered in debris and dirt. It also told a story. Three or four men, he thought, judging from the boot marks. There'd been no footprints outside, but that told him little. It had been snowing all day. On the table, there was a crumpled pack of smokes, a local brand, and a porcelain mug next to it full of ash and butts. They weren't the brand Volga and Vilgotsky usually smoked, and he picked up the mug and tipped out the contents. Ten butts—about right for three or four Center E guys to get through a quick interrogation, he thought. Nothing out of the ordinary.

But then, something caught his eye. He picked up one of the butts and held it to the light, then rifled through the other butts and picked out two more. There was no mistaking it. Lipstick. Bright red. That narrowed the field. He looked again at the marks on the ground. He'd assumed standard-issue police boots, but he saw now that some of the marks showed the narrow heel of a woman's pump.

"Who was it, boys? Who was here?" he muttered. "And what did you tell her?"

He looked into the two men's cold, lifeless eyes. It was always dark when they'd met, and he noticed for the first time that Vilgotsky had one blue eye and one green. The wind whipped up again, and the front door slammed shut, sending a sudden surge of adrenaline through his veins. He knocked over the mug, and it shattered on the floor.

He looked down the empty hallway toward the door. He needed to leave, every second he lingered was a gamble, but there was still information there. Information that could save his life. A few seconds, he promised himself, then he would leave. He patted down Volga's pants, checking his pockets, expecting to find nothing, which is what he did find. It was the same with Vilgotsky. Not even loose change.

There were some clothes in a pile on the floor, their jackets, their gloves. They'd been searched by the Russians, but Ritter checked them again anyway, pressing the seams between his thumb and forefinger in case something had been sewn into them. Again, nothing.

"Where's your phone?" he muttered to Volga. It was the one he'd tried from the car, and if Center E had it, they'd have seen his call. "Time to go, Craigy boy." If he left now, he would have to flee the country. He knew too little of what had happened to Volga to risk staying. But leaving was not without its risks either. Leaving was problematic. Getting to Ukraine would be easy enough. He could be across the border before sunrise and in Poland within a day. The CIA was in the process of setting up a large field office in Warsaw, and he'd been given an extraction code for situations like this. But there was the issue of that second name, the American name, that was stopping him. He had it now, and Vilgotsky had been right. It was a hand grenade with its pin pulled. He couldn't waltz into Warsaw Station now, with what he had, and expect a warm reception.

Something else caught his eye. The refrigerator. It had been moved. It was a solid machine, a hefty Soviet-era behemoth the size of a wardrobe and weighing at least four hundred pounds, but it had been moved by about two feet if he was not mistaken. Ritter remembered the time Vilgotsky had opened it. The contents were horrifying, old food that hadn't seen daylight in years, and Volga and Ritter both gave him shit for stinking up the place.

"Looking for a snack?" Ritter had said.

"Sorry," Vilgotsky muttered.

It had been next to the counter then, and every other time Ritter had been there. Now there was a two-foot gap.

There were signs everywhere that the house had been searched, open drawers and cupboards, some overturned furniture, but it had all clearly been a hurried affair. No one had expected to find anything, and the search had been half-hearted.

The refrigerator was a different story. It hadn't simply been shoved out of place. Unless someone had deadlifted the thing straight up and plopped it down two feet to the right, they'd gone to the effort of concealing the marks it would have left on the floor when it moved. He looked at the floor and saw that soil and plaster dust had been sprinkled over the marks. He pictured Volga and Vilgotsky doing it. Had they known they were in trouble?

Another howl of wind rattled through the house, and he thought of the field he still had to cross to get to his car. He had to go.

But he couldn't. Not yet.

He went to the fridge and tried to shove it aside. It remained stubbornly in place as if bolted to the ground. He put his gun on the table and tried again, this time throwing more weight into the effort. It budged an inch, and he shoved it again and again until he'd gotten it back where it usually was. He stepped back and looked at the wall. He'd never noticed it before—the light had never been on before—but built into the stone wall, about three feet from the ground, was a solid cast iron safe. Its door was a foot wide and about the same in height, and it was an old Soviet design that used a key rather than a combination.

He looked at it a second, wondering why he'd never noticed it before, then remembered there'd been a framed painting in front of it. He saw the painting now, leaning against the wall by the table. Presumably, Volga and Vilgotksy had decided it was no longer up to the job. He touched the safe, tapping the solid iron with his knuckle, and shook his head. There was no way he was getting inside without the key. He glanced around the floor, then at the rest of the kitchen, trying to think where Volga might have hidden it. The house was small. Apart from old debris and dirt, it was mostly empty. He grabbed his gun and went first to the cabinets, moving rapidly through each one, scanning the interior with his flashlight and running his hand along the inside corners. He did the same with the drawers, pulling them all the way out and checking behind their backs. There was a garbage can near the fridge and he tipped it over. It contained only the packaging for the sub Volga had eaten with his knife and fork. He checked inside the old gas stove, its heavy door opening with a loud creak.

Nothing.

He moved on immediately to the living room, checking the old console and beneath the moth-eaten cushions on the furniture. There was a landscape painting on the wall, and he pulled it down to check along its frame as well as the wall behind it. In the bathroom, he removed the porcelain cover from the back of the toilet and checked the tank. It was empty. In the cupboard, there was nothing but old cleaning supplies.

He looked toward the rickety set of stairs, scanning the steps with his flashlight. He knew there were two bedrooms up there, but also that if he went up, he'd be even more vulnerable to surprise. He should have been well clear of the place already, across the field and back in his car, but he pushed that thought from his mind and dashed up the stairs. He entered the first bedroom and went straight to the window. It gave a good vista over the farm's long driveway toward the road. It was snowing again, and the fields were as desolate as when he'd arrived. There was a lace curtain by the window, and he checked around it before doing a quick search of the rest of the room. He pulled the bare mattress from the bed and checked the closet as well as the drawers in the bedside cabinet. Nothing. He moved on to the second room and did the same. Again, nothing.

He ran back down the stairs and into the kitchen. The bodies were as they had been, sitting in the chairs like sleeping guards, and it felt to Ritter as if their stench had grown stronger in the time he'd been in the house. He looked at them, the pasty white skin beneath their torn open shirts, and it crossed his mind that Volga could have swallowed the key. He did not relish the thought of cutting open the bodies, but his hand reached for his tactical knife nonetheless.

He approached Volga first, bending down and yanking the two sides of his shirt apart to reveal his stomach. The skin was the color of porridge, with thin blue capillaries visible beneath the surface. He pressed the tip of the knife against the flesh, put his arm in front of his mouth, and immediately felt the bile rise to the back of his throat. He ran to the back door and flung it open, then grabbed his knees, doubled over, and threw up into the snow.

"Fuck," he muttered, spitting and wiping his mouth with the back of his sleeve.

He gave himself a moment to recover, then went back to Volga and was about to return to his task when suddenly, as if in slow motion, the front windows of the house shattered in their frames, sending shards of glass to the ground like a curtain of water. He turned toward the sound and, though he was scarcely conscious of the sensation at that moment, felt the heavy thud of a bullet hitting his chest.

It was followed by a second, and he stumbled backward into the kitchen, crashing onto the table, which collapsed beneath his weight.

For a moment, he didn't know what was happening. He didn't know where he was. He blinked, tried to focus, and, looking straight up, saw the high beams of an approaching vehicle tracking across the ceiling.

12

Ritter lay on the ground catching his breath. He put his hand to his chest and felt the rough edges of damaged kevlar where the bullets had struck. Two shots, stopped by the vest. There was another burst of gunfire, and glass and plaster flew everywhere. By some miracle, his Glock was still in his hand, and he raised it up and fired a single shot at the ceiling, taking out the light. The house plunged into darkness, and, for a moment, all was silent. He slowed his breath and listened. Vehicle engines. Men's voices.

He got to his hands and knees and, remaining beneath the level of the windows, crept down the hallway toward the front door. When he was six feet from it, a fresh bout of gunfire rained on the building, and he dropped to his belly to wait it out. It didn't stop. The bullets just kept coming, shattering every window and tearing to shreds the door before him. He backed away and, glancing up, saw through the tattered wood the headlights of two vehicles. They were on the far side of the compound, about a hundred yards away, and had come to a halt at the gate.

Their high beams shone down on the house like spotlights, and clustered around them were the muzzle flashes of automatic weapons. He estimated about eight men and wondered if the woman with the lipstick was with them.

His Glock held seventeen rounds, and he'd already used one on the lightbulb. He held out the gun now and, steadying his arm against the floor, took careful aim through the gaps in the shattered door. He squeezed the trigger four times in rapid succession. Instantly, the four high beams of the SUVs went out, one after the other, and another round of gunfire hailed down on the house like a wave of hornets. He pressed his body hard against the floorboards, his cheek right on the wood, and looked back toward the kitchen. He could feel the bullets fly by overhead, mere inches above him, striking the old refrigerator at the end of the hallway with the staccato clang of metal on metal. They were all coming from the same direction, and they rained sparks as they ricocheted off the fridge as if hitting the armor of a tank.

He felt the sharp bite of a bullet hitting his arm and grunted in surprise, but it was only a graze. He would live.

There was a crash at the front of the house as what remained of the door fell from its hinges. Outside on the porch, so many bullets had struck the front posts that they were beginning to collapse as if mown down by a chainsaw. The overhanging roof lilted and groaned, and the instant it began to fall, Ritter got up and dashed to the kitchen. It was separated from the front room by a solid stone wall, and he was surprised to see it was still relatively unscathed. Even the windows were intact.

The gunfire had momentarily stopped. That meant they were coming for him. He went back out to the hall, ran up the stairs, and crept up to the shattered window of the nearest bedroom. A ragged piece of lace fluttered in the breeze of the shattered window. Peering through it, he saw a team of six men running toward the house in tactical formation. He fired a single shot, striking the lead man in the head, then ducked back as another hail of gunfire ensued. Peering through the debris, he took two more shots, dropping another of the men. The remaining men stopped advancing and fell back to the vehicles, dragging their two casualties with them.

Ritter took a breath. He'd bought himself some time— minutes, maybe less. They wouldn't try another frontal assault, but as soon as they'd regrouped, they'd encircle the house. The Glock wouldn't be enough to hold them off then. Even the AK-12, which he'd left in the barn, wouldn't be enough firepower. His only option was to run. He could leave by the back door in the kitchen and make for the fields. They'd be hot on his heels—he'd be leaving a clear trail in the snow—but there was no helping that. Also, when they realized which way he was headed, they'd go back to the vehicles and cut him off. They'd get to where he'd parked long before him, and he'd make for easy pickings in the open field, but he didn't know what else to do.

He hurried back to the kitchen and looked wistfully one last time at the safe. It held something important. Something vital. He could feel it. But he forced himself to look away. He sniffed again. There was definitely something different in the air, no mistaking it, but it wasn't the corpses. It was gas. A bullet must have struck a pipe. He looked at the old stove and remembered it had never been fully disconnected from the grid. He'd seen it working a few times when Volga, against Vilgotsky's vehement objections, used it to light a cigarette. He ran over to it now and turned on all the dials. Then he opened the heavy oven door and listened for the hiss. There was more than enough flow.

The kitchen had two doors leading to the front of the house, one to the hallway, the other to the living room. Ritter shut them both—they'd been open and had escaped the worst of the gunfire—but they were far from airtight. In particular, there was an inch-high gap between them and the floor. That was a problem.

He looked around for something to block the gap, his eyes darting frantically before coming to rest on the corpses. "Sorry, fellas," he said with a grimace.

He went to Volga first and cut the ties that held him in the chair. Then, grabbing him by the ankles, he yanked firmly, pulling the limp body forward. It fell with a thud, and Volga's skull smacked hard against the floor. Ritter winced but nevertheless dragged the body by the ankles to the first door, blocking the gap. He did the same with Vilgotsky, who weighed quite a bit more, and blocked up the second door.

He needed a flame next, a candle would have been perfect, but there was none. The only fuel he could see was the brown paper bag Volga's gas station sandwich had come in. It was lying on the floor next to the overturned garbage can, and he grabbed it and put it back in the can. He pulled out his lighter and was about to set it aflame— there was a very limited time before the concentration of gas in the room reached its tipping point—but he suddenly stopped. Something had caught his eye. He'd knocked over the table when he fell on it, and he saw now that, stuck to its underside with a piece of Vilgotsky's disgusting chewing gum, was a small, metal key.

He unpicked the key quickly from the gum, then

hurried to the safe and inserted it in the keyhole. There was a click, and the door opened. Ritter reached in and grabbed the only thing it contained—a tattered, spiral-bound notebook, every sheet covered in Volga's curious numeric codes. He stuffed it in his pocket and took out his Zippo. He'd still intended on lighting the paper, but he could smell how laden the air had become with gas. It was too late.

Then he heard the creak of someone's weight coming onto the rickety porch at the front of the house.

His time was up.

13

Ritter slipped out the back door, shut the door firmly behind him, and began sprinting for the back of the compound. As he ran, a man rounded the corner of the farmhouse, and, without breaking stride, Ritter raised his pistol and fired off a shot. The man fell to the ground, and Ritter kept running without watching him fall. The fence was a four-foot high post and rail structure, but just as he was about to leap onto it, the ground grew uneven. He stumbled and had to grab the top rail of the fence to break his fall.

"Freeze," someone yelled in Russian from behind him.

He spun and fired a shot blindly in the direction of the voice. A burst of automatic gunfire came back. The bullets pelted the snow around him, and he dropped to one knee, steadied his grip on the gun with both hands, and fired off another shot. This time, the man collapsed to the ground, but not before another two rounded the other side of the house.

"Stop," one of them yelled, followed by some more words Ritter didn't understand. He didn't need a language degree to see the guns they had trained on him. They were fifty yards from where he stood, and he didn't think they'd miss.

He raised his hands, holding his gun on his thumb by the trigger guard. He didn't speak because he didn't want to give away the fact he was a foreigner.

They yelled some more, and he assumed they were telling him to drop the gun. They were next to the house, just outside the kitchen window, and he waited a moment for more to arrive. They yelled again. He didn't drop the gun, and the man who'd yelled raised his rifle to fire.

"Wait," Ritter said in English. "I don't understand."

Another man emerged from behind the house. In English, he said, "They told you to drop the gun." This man seemed to be the leader of the crew. He glanced at his men, and at that precise moment, Ritter dropped to the ground. Gunfire opened up immediately, pelting the snow all around him, but Ritter returned only a single bullet. He hardly even needed to aim. Holding up the gun, he pointed in the direction of the kitchen window and pulled the trigger. Instantaneously, the room exploded. Glass flew outward with so much force it rained on Ritter's back. An enormous fireball ripped through the house, starting in the kitchen and funneling around the stone structure, sending a shudder through the air like thunder. Flames billowed out of every opening as if someone had just opened the door of a blast furnace, and flames shot sixty feet up into the sky. Ritter braced, laying face down in the snow, but even from that distance, a wave of heat rushed over him so hot that he was worried it would singe his hair.

He waited for it to pass, then looked up at the house and assessed the damage. It was so bright he had to shield his eyes, but as his vision adjusted, he made out what could have been a vision from hell. Two men were running toward him, engulfed in flames, screaming blood-curdling cries as they burned alive. He stared at them a moment, his mind struggling to process what he was seeing, then raised his gun and fired off two more shots, ending their agony.

He remained on the ground a few seconds longer, but no one else emerged from the flames. Whether they'd all been caught in the blast or some were still on the far side of the house with the vehicles, he didn't wait to find out. He climbed the fence and began running across the frozen fields as fast as he could, suffering from his lack of balaclava and mitts. He kept running, stopping only to shield his face when the wind whipped up too strongly to bear. He stopped when he reached the road and looked back. The fire was still billowing from the house, sending a plume of thick black smoke hundreds of feet into the night sky. The roof of the house had caved in, and he could see the two black vehicles still at the front gate where they had been, covered in debris. No survivors, he thought.

He could see the turn-off for the logging track and was about to cross the road when he saw the lights of an approaching vehicle. He crouched out of sight and waited for what turned out to be a single, black BMW with flashing police lights. He watched it pass, waited a moment to make sure no more cars were coming, then crossed the road and hurried back to where he'd parked his Škoda.

He slowed as he approached the clearing, his fingers numb from clenching the Glock, and crouched down in the undergrowth. When he was close enough to see the car, he stopped and waited. He held his breath and listened for any sound. There was none. It was all exactly as he'd left it. He went up to the car and climbed into the driver's seat, shutting the door quietly behind him. Then he fired up the engine and held his hands in front of the heating vent. His fingers swelled up painfully.

He'd memorized the local road network, including the back roads and logging tracks, but he didn't know if he wanted to risk getting stuck in the snow. The car, to avoid attracting attention, didn't have much on it in terms of additional winter equipment, just a good set of tires. He checked his gun, set it on the seat next to him, and drove slowly down the track. As he approached the road, he shut off his lights entirely—he'd disabled the safety feature that usually prevented that—and rolled the last few feet to the road at a crawl.

All was clear.

He pulled onto the road and looked down across the fields toward the farmhouse. It was still burning, and he could see clearly the headlights of the BMW as it approached down the long driveway. He turned the other way and drove very slowly in the dark. When he'd rounded a corner and no longer had a line of sight on the farmhouse, he switched on his lights and picked up speed. He drove cross country and only dared get on the M-4 when he'd reached the suburb of Shakhty. From there, it was a quick run into the city. It was well after midnight, and traffic was extremely sparse. He left the highway at the airport and drove along Aksayskiy Prospekt into the city center to avoid checkpoints.

He drove cautiously, constantly on the lookout for trouble. Everyone felt the heightened security situation in the city, and, while no curfew had officially been called, people no longer drove around at night unless they had to. There were roadblocks everywhere, and people were pulled over constantly and asked to explain themselves. Being innocent was no guarantee that an encounter would go well.

As he approached the theater district, he saw his first roadblock. It was at the far end of a wide stretch of boulevard, a handful of police cruisers with their lights flashing. A cop in the street was flagging down a car with his flashlight. Ritter turned down a side street onto a relatively affluent residential street of older-style apartment buildings and pulled into the first parking spot he found. He sat with his pistol in his lap, the engine off, waiting. Sure enough, a moment later, a cruiser drove by, probably having noticed him turn. It was moving slowly, scanning the street, but didn't spot him. He watched it get to the end of the street and turn, then waited another minute before pulling out of the spot and continuing in its direction.

The car was a liability now, especially at night, and he needed to get rid of it. He considered destroying it. He could light it on fire easily enough or dump it in the river, but he still didn't know what was ahead of him. In the trunk, he had extra clothing, weapons, and a briefcase full of cash in a number of currencies. In the glove box, he had four different passports with his picture inside. He might need them.

He needed some place safe to leave it—some place where it wouldn't attract attention and where he could come back to it safely if he needed. There was an underground parking lot beneath the new shopping center, it was just a few blocks away, but it would attract attention there after a few days.

He also knew he couldn't go back to his own hotel. He

was approaching an intersection and was about to turn left when he saw the blue and red lights of another checkpoint. He instantly turned right instead and found himself on Voroshilovskiy Prospekt, passing the grand entrance to the Balkan Hotel. The ground floor still bore the signs of the explosion that had killed Meretskov two weeks earlier, but it was one of the grandest hotels in the city, and it was already back in full swing inside. Ritter had been there a number of times in the past week. Instinctively, he pulled into the ornate entryway and stopped next to the valet. Dozens of incandescent light bulbs hung over the front of the hotel, and the light made Ritter feel exposed.

He hurriedly tidied up the car, took off his parka and kevlar vest, and threw them on the back seat. There was a small hole in the arm of his sweater, and he hid it by putting on his heavy black civilian coat. He took the phone from the glove box and locked it, then stepped out of the car.

"Good evening, sir," the valet said in Russian.

Ritter handed him the key and an American twenty-dollar bill.

itter walked across the hotel lobby to the check-in desk and asked for a room on the top floor. He was no stranger to the place and assumed the concierge recognized him, but he didn't think it mattered. In any case, he didn't have time to worry about that now. He got his key, paid cash, and left a hefty tip, then took the elevator up to the sixth floor. He knew the building. He'd scoped it out before and knew where the exits were located, where the stairwells led, and how to get to the roof.

When he got to the room, he shut the door firmly behind him and shut his eyes. He took a deep breath, then opened them and scanned the room—a bed, a TV, a side table and lamp, and a desk that was too small to work at. He looked for the smoke alarm on the ceiling, he knew where to find it, but someone had already removed it. He could tell from the round outline on the ceiling where it had been. He checked the drawers of the desk and found it there, opened, with its batteries removed.

He sat on the bed and lit a cigarette. He was tapping

his foot nervously and stopped when he realized he was doing it.

"Think," he muttered, rubbing his eyes. There were a number of threads he needed to untangle, but the most critical now was whether Volga and Vilgotsky's unfortunate demise was the result of CIA treachery. Had the CIA sent someone in to take care of them? Was he paranoid for thinking that? Given the circumstances, a little paranoia seemed in order. "Should have seen this coming," he muttered, rapping his hands on his knee like a drummer practicing. "I should have known. I should have known."

He was yanked from his thoughts by a noise in the corridor. Before he realized what he was doing, he'd raised his gun and was pointing it at the door, his finger on the trigger ready to blow someone's head off.

"Come on," he muttered. "Come and get me, you bastards."

But no one came. The door remained motionless. There was more noise, and he rose to his feet and approached the door, keeping as shielded by the wall as possible. He waited next to the door, his back against the wall, then leaned in front of it and peered through the peephole. There were two people outside, a few feet away, just visible in the convex field of vision of the peephole. One was a man in torn jeans and a jacket. The other was a woman in a skimpy red dress. She'd fallen to the ground and was laughing hysterically, waving her feet in the air, and he was trying in vain to hush her up and get her to the room. Ritter glanced at his watch—he knew the area well, the rhythm of the nightlife, and had himself stumbled back to this very hotel in a similar state. It was about the time the clubs let out.

Outside, he heard a car horn blaring. He went to the

window and pulled back the lace curtain. It was nothing —some kids driving home from the party, almost certainly over the alcohol limit. Someone in a black car seemed to have upset the driver of a white Audi, and the two were getting out of their cars, yelling at each other. Ritter let the curtain fall back into place.

He went back to the bed and pulled the cell phone from his pocket. There'd been messages on it. He'd seen some from Zadorov. He wanted to check them now, but powering up the phone would be too risky. If he did, he would have to leave the hotel immediately, and he wasn't ready to do that.

He needed to get his head straight. He went into the bathroom and wet his face. He checked the wound on his arm and cleaned it up. His clothing was presentable enough. The blood didn't show on the black wool. He sat back on the bed and focused on his breathing. He needed to calm down. His mind was running at a million miles an hour.

There was more noise from the corridor, and he was back on his feet. Through the peephole, he saw the couple at the door across from his, fumbling with their room key. He waited until they got the door open, then watched the empty corridor for a few moments.

"Calm down, Craigy boy," he muttered. He had work to do. But instead of going back to the bed, he opened the door and, gun in hand, slipped out to the corridor. If there was ever a time for paranoia, he told himself, it was now. He looked both ways up and down the empty corridor. There was no one there. He put away the gun and walked toward the fire door at the end of the corridor. He knew it led to a bare, concrete stairwell from which it was possible, with a little force, to gain access to the roof. When he reached the door, he pushed it open and held it with his foot to stop it from locking behind him. He looked up and down the stairwell. There was no one there.

He went back to the corridor and walked toward the elevators at the other end, passing his own room on the way. As he approached, he eyed the downward pointing arrow that indicated when an elevator was approaching. It was unlit. He was about to turn and go back to his room when he heard the click of a gun. He swung around, drawing his pistol in a fluid motion, ready to unload on whoever was there, but there was no one. He realized his mistake. It wasn't the sound of a gun, it was the ice machine. It was in an open vestibule, next to a vending machine and a firehose, and the ice spilled noisily into the bucket.

"Get your shit together," he muttered to himself, putting away the gun. Being alert was one thing, but being jumpy was another. Jumpy people made mistakes. They ended up in coffins.

He checked his pockets for change, then bought some snacks from the vending machine and brought them back to the room. He had a lot of work to do. Volga's notebook wasn't going to decipher itself.

15

Osip Shipenko was not a man built for motion. Indeed, he was a creature hardly built for the ordinary world at all and was reminded of the fact every time his driver took him over another pothole.

"Easy, damn it," he growled from the back of his new Mercedes Pullman Guard limousine. The car was beautiful, easily one of the best production models in the world, and he was glad he'd been able to get it before sanctions kicked in and cut off supply. As well as its luxury features, it came with bullet-proof glass and an upgraded hull, capable of withstanding a bomb, as standard. The world's most powerful corporate executives used them, and the only thing better, as far as Osip was concerned, was the president's Russian-built, twenty-two-foot-long Aurus Senat.

Osip eased himself up from his seat and examined the plush, white leather upholstery. He'd known white was a bad idea, too easily stained by the fluid-filled pustules that covered ninety percent of his body, but he was tired of making decisions based on his condition. He'd spent half his life being poked and prodded by doctors, so if some stained leather was the cost of getting what he wanted, it was a price he was willing to pay. Besides, the Mercedes sales literature had pointed out that the leather was the same color as what the president had. That, of course, had sealed the deal.

Osip's condition was the result of a childhood accident at the Aralsk-7 bioweapons facility on Vozrozhdeniya Island. His parents had been scientists there, and the incident that had altered his life so dramatically was caused by some flagrantly reckless orders from Moscow, a drunk pilot, a low-flying crop duster, and a weaponized strain of the variola virus. It resulted in Osip and his seventeen-year-old, redheaded governess being two of the last Soviet citizens ever to contract smallpox. The governess never emerged from the pressurized isolation chamber they'd been locked in for treatment, but Osip, who was six years old at the time, did. By then, he was so hideously ravaged and deformed that even his own mother couldn't look at him without recoiling in revulsion. He spent the rest of his youth in the All-Union Research Institute of Experimental Virology in Pokrov, east of Moscow, where doctors performed experiments that advanced the Soviet bioweapons program but had the simultaneous effect of depriving Osip of the ability to form meaningful emotional attachments. In any case, relationships would have been difficult for him, with severe maculopapular scarring covering ninety percent of his body and forming a hardened, scaly callous that cracked and bled constantly. The effect was so unsightly that his superiors at the KGB, when he was eventually allowed to join the organization, took to calling him Dog Face, or Meat Face, or Tushonka, after a brand of Soviet-era dog food.

Not wanting to be seen as weak, Osip had recently taken to using the moniker as an internal codename. Reclaiming that name, which had been intended as an insult for so long, was the perfect way to mark his transition from a hidden, faceless servant of the president to arguably the second most powerful man in the country and the head of the highly secretive Dead Hand organization.

He looked out the car window at the dismal morning that was taking shape. He was in the affluent Moscow suburb of Odintovsky, approaching the president's private villa at Novo-Ogaryovo, and low predawn cloud hung over the houses like a poisonous mist.

"Almost there, sir," the driver said, approaching the gates of the presidential villa.

Shipenko had been there dozens of times, indeed, he was one of the few visitors the president still permitted to enter, but that didn't make him feel any more at ease. Nothing about this summons boded well—not the hour, not the fact it was unscheduled, not the president's tone. Certainly not the fact that Osip had no idea what it was regarding.

"Just make sure they know who the hell I am," he said to the driver. "I don't want to be flagged for an inspection."

The driver pulled up slowly to the first checkpoint and handed the guard the security documents Shipenko's office had prepared in advance. The guard waved them through to the second checkpoint, where a small guardhouse overlooked the gate like a hunting blind. Four officious-looking soldiers in the uniform of the president's elite guard came out of the guardhouse and approached the car.

"Tell them to be quick," Osip muttered before raising the divider between himself and the driver.

The process of getting into Novo-Ogaryovo never went smoothly. It seemed to Osip that no amount of preplanning or bureaucratic box-ticking was ever enough. It was true that a rogue CIA asset had recently breached the compound and assassinated the Polar Bear, one of Osip's Dead Hand predecessors, but even before that, getting in had been ridiculously painful. Just one more show of force, Osip thought, one more way of reminding the world who was in charge.

One of the guards was speaking to the driver, and by the amount of time it was taking, Osip could tell it wasn't going smoothly. The guard looked through the window at Osip, then rapped on the tinted glass.

"What is it?" Osip growled, lowering the window.

"Security inspection. Out of the car."

"Go to hell."

"Now," the head guard said, approaching from behind. "Out of the car. No one's excepted."

"Do you have any idea who I am?"

The head guard nodded. He did know who Osip was. Since his promotion, everyone was getting to know who he was. It was a strange feeling for Osip, given the decades he'd spent keeping himself completely invisible, but not without its perks. It didn't make a bit of difference here, though. Not for the president's guard. "You know the drill," the guard said, stepping back from the door.

"I'm the second most powerful man in the federation," Osip spat, wincing as he pulled himself out of the car.

When the guards got their first full view of him, his twisted body, his scabbed and cracking skin, Osip saw the doubt cross their faces. "Do the search," the head guard barked at them, his voice sounding less confident by the second. "And be quick about it."

The men did their check, scanning the undercarriage and trunk extremely hurriedly before giving the head guard the nod.

"All right," the head guard said to the driver. "You're good to go."

The driver got the door, and Osip climbed back into his seat. A moment later, they were through the gates and heading down the long driveway to the villa. The building was palatial, one of the largest residences in all of Russia, but Osip was well used to the place. Indeed, he had a villa of his own not far away, as did most of the Dead Hand members.

"Sir," the driver said as they approached the staff entrance on the east wing of the building, "they're waving us around to the front."

That was unusual. The front entrance was reserved for official visits, such as those from foreign dignitaries and heads of state. Osip had certainly never come or gone that way. He was a creature of shadows, or at least, he had been. He wasn't used to the limelight. A man with a less pessimistic view might have viewed this as a positive signal, a sign of rising prestige, but Osip knew better. "What are they bringing us this way for?" he muttered.

The front of the building had a fine neoclassical entrance, complete with rows of symmetrical Palladian windows and columns. A grand set of thirty-six marble steps in three flights led to the door, and Osip was already wondering if he would be expected to climb them on his own, a thought he did not relish.

As they rounded the corner of the palace, he saw a company of soldiers standing at attention, rifles at their shoulders, near the base of the steps. There were about fifty of them, and they were wearing an old khaki and navy dress uniform that he was sure was reserved for ceremonies.

"This isn't good," he said to the driver. "Who are those men? What are they doing there?"

The driver had no idea and said simply, "Looks like they're waiting for something." He brought the car to a halt at the foot of the steps, and Osip looked up at them with dread. They'd been cleared of snow, but still, they were treacherous things, especially for someone like him. Two members of the president's guard, far away at the very top of the steps, were standing at attention.

"Do you need—" the driver began, but Osip cut him off before he could finish the sentence.

"I'm fine," he growled. "Just get me my stick."

The driver got out and ran around the car. He opened Osip's door and handed him his rosewood cane.

Osip hauled himself out of his seat with a sigh. He wasn't a cripple and refused to think of himself as such, but his afflictions did have an impact, and many ordinary exertions were difficult for him. The president, of course, was well aware of that fact, and as Osip began hobbling up the steps, he wondered if Molotov was watching. His office was in that part of the building, overlooking those very steps, and he was well aware of the president's penchant for making his underlings squirm. He paused for breath at the top of the first flight and stole a glance at the president's window. He couldn't tell.

It was all quite strange, he thought, quite out of the ordinary. He looked back up at the front door and, clenching his jaw, continued his climb. It only took a few minutes to reach the top, but his lungs were burning when he got there, and he was leaning heavily on his cane.

He did muster enough strength to growl, "Back off," at the guard who came forward to offer assistance. "I made it this far," Osip added, looking up at the twenty-foot-tall oaken doors. They were still shut, surely a bad sign, and only now that he was standing right by them did the servants inside begin to pull them open. Osip waited impatiently and said to the guard he'd just sworn at, "What are those soldiers doing there?"

The guard said nothing—speaking to a guest was a breach of protocol—but when Osip rolled his eyes, he said, "They're Sevastopol Brigade, sir."

"Sevastopol Brigade?" Osip said. "That's strange." Sevastopol was the colloquial name for the 27th Guards Motor Rifle Brigade, part of the First Guards Tank Army of the Western Military District. They were an elite unit, though that didn't always mean what it was supposed to mean, and they were ordinarily stationed at Mosrentgen, which was just a few miles away, outside the city's main ring road. "Why are they here?" he said.

"No idea, sir," the guard said.

Osip looked at them again. "They look cold," he said.

16

Lance opened his eyes and checked his watch. It was almost four. He'd slept a few hours on the wiry sofa in the living room, and it was doing a number on his back. He got up and stretched, then, out of habit, checked the street outside. All was as deserted as ever, not even tire tracks in the snow. He went down the hall to the bedroom. At his request, Klára had left the door ajar, and he peered in through the crack. She was asleep. He went into the bathroom and splashed cold water on his face. He looked at his reflection in the mirror —he looked old, he thought. He went back to the living room and put on the clothes he'd been wearing the day before, including his boots and the Russian overcoat he'd bought at the market by the train station. It wasn't the warmest, but it blended in. There was some cold coffee on the counter, and he poured himself a mug and sipped it. He checked his gun, put it in his coat pocket, then let himself quietly out of the apartment, taking the mug of coffee with him. If everything went according to plan, he would have the name of the American traitor by the time he returned.

At the bottom of the stairs, he stopped to pull on his gloves. He drained the rest of the coffee in the mug and stepped out into the biting cold. Before shutting the door, he crouched down and placed the mug just inside. If it had moved when he got back, he'd know the door had been opened.

He checked his watch and walked the few blocks to the nearest tram line, keeping a brisk pace for warmth. The first trams of the morning would be leaving the depot soon and passing the nearby stop. The tramline ran down the center of the street, and he followed it, eying warily every corner, doorway, and vehicle. It was a hundred yards farther down the street to the tram stop, a modest brick three-sided enclosure with a shuttered kiosk on one end and a bank of pay phones at the other. There were a few people already there, factory shifts started early in that part of the city, and he scanned each person as he approached, avoiding eye contact. There was a man in a long coat sitting on a bench, and another in a short gray coat leaning on a signpost and smoking a cigarette. There was a woman in a cleaner's uniform on the bench at the far end of the stop. Lance took up a position near the pay phones and waited. A moment later, the tram pulled in, creaking and screeching on its steel rail. Lance waited for everyone else to board before doing so himself.

In addition to the people from his stop, there were four other riders already on the tram. He eyed each of them in turn, then found a seat near the back where he could keep an eye on them. The tram was electric but rickety, and it picked up speed in clanky, jerky motions.

He thought ahead to where he was headed. It was the

meet with the local CIA asset, a man named Yuriy Volga. Lance wondered what he was going to learn from him. Who's name was he going to give? Who'd been talking to Shipenko?

He didn't like that things had taken this direction. The president had told him to hunt down Osip Shipenko, and that was what he'd agreed to. Now, there was talk of a traitor, and it was making things messy. It would mean more blood.

Lance had been an assassin for a long time, and he was beginning to feel the weight of it. He could remember clearly the face of every person he'd ever killed, and those faces had started to haunt him like old ghosts. Each job added a new face to the choir, a new voice to the chorus, so that they gradually grew louder and louder until they drowned out everything else. Other assassins complained of the same thing, and the shrinks at Langley even had a term for it. They called it blood trauma. It was like mercury in a thermometer that could only go up. Each job, each drop of blood, raised the temperature little by little until, eventually, some invisible line was reached, and the assassin went off the deep end. That was the end of their useful life. There were stories, rumors really, of the CIA going after them then—'retiring' them actively with a bullet to the skull. The truth was such measures were rarely necessary. Assassins were problem solvers, and they solved this particular problem by removing themselves from the equation. There were plenty of ways to do that—getting killed in action, eating a bullet, checking into the looney bin to be obliterated with sedatives and opiates. Crutches—drugs, alcohol, sex—were a given at every stage of the process.

What the shrinks didn't realize, though, was that it

wasn't the violence that kept raising the temperature in the assassin's heads. It wasn't blood that drove them over the edge, it was indignity. If it had been up to Lance, he wouldn't have called it blood trauma, he'd have called it piss trauma, or shit, or snot trauma. Even semen. Because those were the things that got into your soul. He'd once killed six men in a single night in Beirut. It had been many years ago, and the men had deserved to die, no doubt about it, but that didn't stop them from haunting him. To this day, he couldn't eat tabbouleh without picturing someone's head in it, facedown, as if he'd fallen asleep at the table. That same night, another of the men died with his erect cock in his hand. He'd been in the shower, his back to the door, and Lance hadn't realized until the job was already done. He looked down at the corpse and was surprised by how long it took the erection to subside. A lot of people pissed or shat themselves. A lot.

Those details never made it into the reports. No one wanted to know who'd begged for mercy, or cried for their mother, or was having an orgasm when they bit the bullet. Those little treasures were for the assassin to keep, they were his alone, and they grew and grew with each and every job.

Killing was hard. Killing someone you knew was harder.

And if there was a traitor, there was a high chance it was someone Lance knew.

He glanced at his watch—five minutes until the appointment.

The tram lurched to a stop, and more people got on. He looked at them closely as they found seats. None looked out of place, and none sat nearer than eight feet from him. They swayed as the vehicle started back up.

Almost as soon as it had gained speed, it began to slow again.

This was his stop.

He rose from his seat and got off the tram. The station was a raised stretch of concrete built on the median strip of a major arterial road. There was a cloudy, perspex barrier between it and the three lanes of traffic that ran in each direction. He sat down on a bench and glanced at the clock hanging above the platform.

4.15 came and went.

But no one showed. He lit a cigarette and made sure his face was visible. There was no one else at the stop, but someone could have been watching from a distance, from one of the rooftops across the street, maybe. Was Yuriy Volga watching? Was he suspicious? Was he afraid? That was certainly possible. They'd never met before. Lance reached into his pocket and placed his gun discretely on the ground between his feet. It was a gesture of friendship, but nothing happened. Cars drove by in the slush. Someone, not Volga, came onto the platform, and Lance picked up the gun and put it back in his pocket. A tram approached.

It was 4.20.

He flicked away his cigarette and rose to his feet. When the tram arrived, he got on board and headed back in the direction from which he'd come.

17

Once he got inside the presidential palace, Osip was met by a man in a tuxedo who looked like the *maître d'* at a restaurant. He had a sneer on his face as if the job of greeting Osip was something he regarded as beneath him, and he glanced at his watch before speaking. "The president does hate to be kept waiting, Mr Shipenko."

Osip gritted his teeth.

The *maître d'* then turned on his heel and began walking back toward the enormous staircase at the end of the hall. His pace was beyond anything Osip could hope to match, and Osip was forced to hobble after him as fast as he could. They climbed two flights of stairs to the president's executive staff office, which occupied the entire front of the building's third floor. By the time he reached the top of the stairs, Osip's lungs were burning.

"Are you sure you're all right?" the *maître d'* said smugly, tapping his foot.

"I'm fine," Osip growled, hobbling past him. The *maître d'* led him to a windowless, wood-paneled anteroom. The room was large but gloomy, with much of the light coming from the glow of a fire that burned in a marble hearth. There was an old chandelier on the ceiling and on the walls, large oil paintings of long-dead aristocrats and monarchs in ornate gilded frames. It was a well-known fact that Molotov looked on Russia's Tsarist past as a golden age, and he'd even gone so far as to bring back Imperial dress uniforms and titles that hadn't been seen in over a century.

There was a desk in the room, and seated at it was one of the president's personal secretaries, a stolid woman with gray hair and a severe black dress. She winced when she looked up, though she'd seen Osip before, and he let a crooked smile creep across his lips. "Tell him I've arrived," he said.

She picked up the phone receiver, fumbling in her haste and almost knocking it off the desk. "He's here, sir." She nodded then and got up and scurried around the desk to open the heavy double doors that led to the holy of holies, the president's personal office.

When the doors opened, Osip had to raise a hand to shade his eyes. Large windows lined the east-facing wall of the office, and the sun had just begun to rise, sending streams of light through the smoke-laden air of the office.

"You may enter," the secretary said, her soft voice contrasting sharply with the one that followed.

"Come in, Osip," the president bellowed. "Don't dawdle. Get in."

Osip shuffled forward, regretting now that he was still holding the cane—a symbol of his weakness. He entered the room, and the doors shut ominously behind him.

"I take it you've seen the latest reports?" the president growled, not bothering to look up from the document in his hand. He was seated behind his enormous mahogany desk, a crystal rocks glass in his hand, and the slur in his voice suggested he'd been drinking for a while. Osip wondered if he'd been up all night. There was a fire in this room also, larger than the one outside, and the president flung the file in its direction. The papers scattered, and only a few of them found their way to the flames. "This is a disaster," the president said. "An unmitigated disaster."

"Mr President—" Osip started, but the president cut him off immediately.

"It will be the end of me."

"Mr President!" Osip gasped as if the very thought of the president's demise was too great to bear. "There's a very long path from where we are now to that."

The president said nothing, his gaze fixed on the flames of the fire, then he nodded his head. "Aye, Osip. It is a long path, but we're surely on it."

"We've suffered setbacks—"

"I was told," the president said, "that this invasion would be a cakewalk."

Osip watched him carefully. He was well aware of the intelligence the president had been given. Indeed, he'd been doing his damnedest to distance himself from it ever since the first engagements hadn't gone their way.

"The intelligence compiled by the SVR—" Osip began, but the president cut him off again.

"I was told we'd be in Kyiv in a day," the president said, slamming his fist on his desk. Osip unintentionally stepped back, and the president regarded him closely through his beady eyes. A silence grew.

Osip looked down at the floor. "Yes, sir," he said at last, just to break the silence.

"They said the Ukrainians would welcome us with

open arms. That they'd shower us in flowers, and the women would run into the street to kiss our soldiers."

"My office said from the beginning—"

"The largest intelligence apparatus on the globe, Osip. The Main Directorate, the Prime Directorate, the SVR, the FSO, the FSB—"

"Mr President—"

"How could they lead me so astray?"

"The analysis was colored from the outset with an optimism that just—"

"Optimism? More like delusion."

"They overestimated our combat readiness."

"They sold me on a lie."

"They based the reports on certain assumptions—"

"They lied, Osip!" the president said, his voice rising. "They lied."

Osip looked around the room. He was getting worried. Everyone was on shaky ground now. No agency was safe. He would have to choose his words carefully. "The Ukrainians," he started slowly, "are rallying around the flag."

"They're fighting for their lives," the president growled. "For their fucking lives, Osip. Did no one foresee that they would be motivated? Did no one think that shells landing on their homes, on their families, would give them something to fight for?"

"They're motivated, but their resources—"

"Their resources are limitless. The Americans, the Brits, even the Germans and French have gotten out the checkbooks. They're sending more equipment than Kyiv ever dreamed of."

"Their manpower—"

"They've got an entire nation to pull from. Every man

and boy in that cursed country is going to fight to the death. Even the women are rising up."

"The setbacks, sir."

"Don't you *dare* speak to me of setbacks," the president hissed. "Don't you dare."

"I wouldn't presume to make excuses, sir, but—"

"We're *losing!*" the president bellowed. "We're losing! The greatest land power on the planet, the army that drove back Napoleon, that drove back Hitler, and we're losing to the *Ukrainians*."

"It's not the Ukrainians, it's NATO that we're fighting."

"Don't give me that horseshit, Osip. We're fighting *Ukraine*. They're not even a real nation. We gave them their army. We trained them on how to use it. We gave them their damn country, for Christ's sake. They should have fallen over like a house of straw."

"They're on home turf."

"They're on *our* turf. Ours. Do you hear me? Their country doesn't exist. It's a myth. A lie. An aberration."

Osip didn't know what to say. The president was on a knife edge. It didn't look like he'd slept. The enormous ashtray on his desk was so full that the ash had begun to spill over the edge. Osip wondered how long he'd been sitting there, brooding, nursing these grievances. The president leaned back. He looked like he was about to speak again, but he didn't. He took a breath instead, then raised his glass to his lips and drained the contents. He was looking at Osip, watching him with a strange intensity that Osip wasn't sure how to interpret.

Osip shifted on his feet uncomfortably, putting his weight on the cane. What was the president thinking, he wondered. What was going on in his mind? The two men had known each other a very long time, since long before the president had ascended the throne, and if there was anyone he still trusted in the Kremlin, it was Osip. Osip was well aware of the fact and tried to remind himself of it now.

He should have held his tongue and waited for what was coming, but as the president rose to his feet, he lost his nerve. "The bad intelligence, sir. It originated with the SVR."

"Don't you dare pass the buck, Osip. Not now."

"Everything I said was measured."

"So this is my fault?"

"Of course not."

"You said we could *win*."

"I said it was *possible*."

"You said that with the right tactics, the right leadership—"

"I thought the generals would execute—"

"You recommended this path, Osip. You were the one who pushed for it. You said annexing the Donbas, taking provinces, taking land, would put me in the history books."

"I never said success was guaranteed."

The president shook his head. "In this very room, Osip, over this very desk, you told me that if I took Kyiv, I could take the world. You planted the seed."

"And then I told you not to try, sir. I told you it was too great a risk."

"And I called you a cowardly cripple."

Osip looked down at the desk.

"I even had them add it to your file. *Cowardly cripple. Advised against Ukraine invasion.*"

Osip nodded. "I wasn't aware you had a file—"

"Don't be coy, Osip."

Osip looked up at him. "We could still win this, sir."

"*We?*"

Osip realized his mistake immediately. "*You,* sir. *You* could win."

The president sighed. He got up from his seat and went to the bar cart, where he picked up another of the crystal glasses. He brought it to the desk and sat back down. "Come," he said, nodding toward the empty seat facing him. "Sit."

Osip limped forward, uncertain where this change in tone would lead. The president reached down to a drawer beneath the desk and brought up a crystal decanter. There was a coat of arms cut intricately into the glass. "Your seal?" he said, hoping to alter the president's mood.

The question only seemed to annoy the president. "Not quite," he said, shoving the bottle forward. "They screwed it up."

Osip took a closer look but couldn't see what was wrong. Ivan the Great's two-headed eagle was there, intricately etched in the glass in excruciating detail, as was the horseman slaying the dragon. "It looks correct to me, sir."

"That's the problem, Osip. This is the old seal. I'm having it changed."

"Oh," Osip said. "I hadn't heard."

"I was going to announce it at the victory speech. The eagle's heads. They were no longer to be crowned."

"I see, sir," Osip said, nodding. He cared little for heraldry, it was a vestige of the Middle Ages, about as relevant to the present state of affairs as the patterns on a butterfly wing. The president, however, cared for such things a great deal, which meant they couldn't be completely ignored. Traditionally, or at least since the days of the Tsar, the Russian coat of arms contained three crowns—one above each of the eagle's two heads and a third, usually larger, at the center.

"Forgive me, Mr President, but I have forgotten the significance of the three crowns."

"You and everyone else," the president said, "which is part of the problem."

Osip nodded.

"Kazan, Astrakhan, and Siberia," the president then said.

"I beg your pardon, sir."

"That's what the three crowns stood for. Originally."

"Ah," Osip said, beginning to wonder if the stress of war was affecting the president's brain.

"Three conquered kingdoms."

"Of course, sir."

"That is to say, Great Russia, Little Russia, and White Russia."

Osip nodded guardedly. He disliked situations he couldn't predict, and this discussion was one. It could go anywhere. "Russia, Ukraine, and Belarus," he said.

"I told the men at the Baccarat crystal company to redo the crest with a single crown. Not three."

"Quite right, sir."

"There is only one crown in this kingdom, Osip. Mine." Russia was no longer a monarchy, but that had never stopped Molotov from pursuing everything possible that tended to suggest it might become one again. "I ordered a thousand of them," he said, raising the bottle. "I was going to present them at a grand ceremony to celebrate our victory."

"That victory will yet come, sir."

The president shook his head. "It's almost as if they predicted our failure."

Osip nodded. He was used to these delusional bouts. He was not surprised in the least that the president was focusing on this, even as soldiers were being killed in their thousands. "One crown," the president said again. "Mine." He leaned forward and poured some of the viscous amber fluid into Osip's glass and slid it across the table. "Drink."

Osip picked up the glass and sniffed. It was a scotch, an obscure single malt, no doubt, and it nauseated him. It was too early in the morning for that much smoke and peat, but he was not about to say as much. He took a sip, as the president did the same, and put down his glass only when the president did so.

The president then cleared his throat, and from the way he did it, Osip knew he was going to say something momentous. "You know," the president said, leaning back in his seat, "that the thought crossed my mind, before the war started, before we were enmeshed in this quagmire...." He let the words trail off, and Osip wondered what it was he'd been in the process of saying.

The president again sipped his scotch. Osip again did the same and said, "Something crossed your mind, sir?"

"I thought," the president said, "that the time had finally come for you to bite the hand that fed you."

"Sir!" Osip gasped.

"Stab me in the back!"

"Absolutely not, Vladimir. On my soul—"

"Spare me the histrionics, Osip. Everyone does it sooner or—"

"I am loyal as a dog," Osip growled, surprising even himself with his vehemence. "As loyal as a *dog*, sir!"

The president sipped more scotch. "When you advised against the war," he said, "I thought, this mutt. This ungrateful mutt. He wants to rob me of my legacy."

"I never thought that for an instant."

"He wants to deprive me of the greatest accomplishment of my entire reign. My eternal gift to the Russian people."

"I swear to you—"

"You're next in line, after all."

"Please, sir!" Osip gasped.

"Make the president look weak. That's what I thought you were doing. Make him appear too timid to march on his own doorstep."

"That was never my intention, sir."

"I thought you'd started gunning for yourself."

"I assure you, sir! You have to believe me."

"It wouldn't be the first time a prince set his eyes on the throne."

"I am not a prince."

"Aren't you?"

"I'm a soldier, sir. A foot soldier."

"You're more than that, Osip."

"A hound to be ordered."

"You're the second most powerful man in this country, Osip Shipenko. You're number two on the list, and you know it."

"There is no list."

"Don't think I can't see the danger."

"Mr President! Please!"

The president's tone was soft, his voice was calm, but the words were deadly serious. Osip knew he was paranoid, seeing threats in every shadow, but never, in all the decades of their friendship, had his suspicions turned on Osip.

A silence filled the air. Osip didn't know what to say. This was the end, he thought. His turn to be sacrificed at the altar of Molotov's paranoia had come. Neither of them said anything for a long time. The president didn't even sip from his glass. He just sat there, staring at Osip, then staring toward the window overlooking the front steps of the palace.

"I think—" Osip hazarded at last, but the president merely raised a hand.

Osip stopped speaking, and the president picked up the phone on his desk and called in the secretary. She appeared at the door instantly.

"Tell the officer of the squad to be ready," the president said.

She left, and the president glanced again toward the window.

"Squad?" Osip said.

The president didn't respond but rummaged in a drawer in the desk. He brought out a cigar and bit off the end before lighting it. He spat the butt into the overflowing ashtray.

Osip looked around the room, and suddenly, with a dawning sense of horror, he realized what was happening. "This isn't the first time tonight you've had this conversation, is it?" he said.

"I've been having meetings all night, Osip."

Osip followed the president's gaze to the window. "How many meetings, sir?"

"Like I said," the president said, "when you advised against the war, I thought you were gunning for my job. I thought your time had arrived. I'd put you on a countdown, so to speak." He took a puff of the cigar. "But then, we failed to take Kyiv, didn't we? Your advice, out of all the reports I'd been given, you were the only one."

Osip remained silent.

"I started to think, Osip's a good dog. He's always been a good dog. A loyal dog."

"I am a loyal dog, sir."

"It's all you *can* be, isn't it, Osip."

Osip said nothing.

"I mean," the president continued, "*look* at you. You're hideous. You're a monster. Who, in your shoes, could aspire to be a leader of men?"

Osip said nothing, aware that he was on the edge of a trap.

"A freak of nature," the president continued. Then, "No, not nature. Nothing about you is natural."

"That's true, sir."

"Unfortunate, of course. Regrettable, certainly."

"I'm aware of the effect my appearance has on people."

"They could never love you, could they, Osip? The people, I mean. They would never follow you."

"Sir?"

"The public couldn't look at a man whose appearance was so unnaturally deformed and think that was a man they could follow."

"I'm sure not, sir."

"But there's still a power in that, isn't there, Osip? Don't think I haven't noticed. You've adapted, haven't you? You've learned that the people's love isn't the only path to power."

"Sir, I've spent my life in the shadows. Not for one second have I sought to step into the limelight."

"What is it that Machiavelli said? It is better to be feared than loved?"

"I don't know, sir."

"Love is fickle. It comes and goes so easily."

"I know nothing of love, Mr President."

The president took a sip of his scotch and regarded Osip closely. "I want to win this war," he said.

"Of course, Mr President."

"That means no more talk of compromise, no talk of cutting a deal with the Ukrainians, no talk of making peace. It's time to bring the Little Russia back to the Motherland." The president looked again to the window, then rose to his feet and went over to it. He pulled back the lace curtain, then turned to Osip and beckoned him with his hand as if summoning a dog.

Osip got up slowly. He had already guessed what he was about to witness. The president had been there all night. He hadn't slept. It was dawn, and he was still there, still having meetings, still passing his judgments on who was loyal and who was not, who was responsible for the quagmire in Ukraine and who was innocent.

"Do you see?" the president said as Osip peered out through the window.

Osip looked out on the grand steps he'd entered by. His car was gone, but the soldiers from the Sevastopol Brigade were still there, standing in a line at the foot of the steps, and their purpose was now clear. Twenty paces in front of them was a second row, but this time of prisoners.

"What is this?" Osip said softly.

The prisoner's hands were bound behind their backs, and white hoods, like pillowcases, had been pulled over their heads. For the most part, they were still, their bearing giving them a strange dignity.

The president turned to him. "This is all for you, Osip."

"For me?"

"I want this invasion turned around."

"I don't know if I have the authority—"

"Do you see the uniforms the men are wearing?"

Osip looked again at the row of prisoners. There were about thirty of them, and maybe half were wearing the distinctive closed-collar dress uniform reserved for generals. He could make out their ranks by the stars on their shoulders. He counted five major generals, five lieutenant generals, a three-star colonel general, and four wearing the large gold star of a full army general. He wondered who, there being only twelve men of that rank in the entire army, all of whom he was personally acquainted with.

"You can't mean to go through with this," Osip stammered.

"Do you doubt me?"

"Of course not, but—"

"Do you doubt I have the stomach for what's required?"

"Sir, I don't know."

"You could barely hobble up those steps when you arrived," the president said. "I watched you from this very window, struggling with your cane like a feeble old fool."

"I apologize for my—"

"But you're not as weak as you look, are you, Osip? There's grit beneath that scaly skin."

"I've always served in my capacity as a GRU—"

"You're going to serve me in a lot more capacities now, Osip. Those people you see are the ones who got us into this mess. They are the directors and generals and commanders who told me to go to war, who told me to take Kyiv, who advised we roll the dice."

"They were only trying to perform their—"

"They are grasping, snatching, power-hungry swine,

Osip, and they sought to advance themselves at my expense. If the hoods were removed, you'd recognize them all. And you won't regret their deaths. Believe me."

"If you're telling me their deaths are necessary, sir—"

"You go to the front line, Osip. You take this stinking pile of shit we've been handed, and you turn it into victory."

"I'm not sure I can give you what you want, sir, but I will try."

The president ignored his words, turning back to the window and allowing a strange sneer to cross his face. He licked his lips, then rapped with his gold ring against the window pane. The officer of the firing squad looked up at the window. The president gave him a nod, and the officer faced forward and yelled out the order to take aim. Moving as one, the soldiers of the Sevastopol Brigade raised their rifles and took aim. There was a pregnant pause, and Osip thought it was not too late. The officer could look back again. The president could rescind the command. But instead, the officer yelled his order, and in the same instant, the noise of fifty rifles firing filled the air.

Osip watched in horror. There was so much smoke that he couldn't immediately tell what had happened. The first thing he saw was the snow around the prisoners. It had turned crimson with blood. About half the prisoners had fallen to the ground, some dead, others writhing in agony. Some of those who'd not been hit had lost their nerve. With their hoods still on and their hands bound, they ran blindly in all directions, tripping and stumbling to the ground before they'd taken more than a few paces. Others, holding on to what dignity they had left, maintained their position and awaited their fate with resignation.

Some of the screaming was surprisingly shrill, and it dawned on Osip for the first time that not all the prisoners were men.

The officer yelled a second time, and another volley struck the wall of flesh, mowing down the prisoners like a scythe through ripened corn. All those who'd lost their nerve were taken down, as well as all but two of those who'd held fast.

Then came a third volley, followed by less screaming, less writhing, less struggling to live.

When the smoke from the third volley cleared, the officer, accompanied by two soldiers, pulled out their side arms and went forward to finish the job with a single shot to the base of each of the thirty skulls.

The president turned to Shipenko then and said, "I do not like being made a fool of, Osip."

Osip nodded. "No, sir."

"Russia does not lose wars."

"Of course not."

"So go to battle, and bring me back my victory."

"Yes, sir.

"Or I'll put your head on a fucking spike."

18

R itter was seated at the desk in the corner of his hotel room with the lamp on, the coffee machine gurgling, and a pack of chips he'd bought from the vending machine in his hand. He felt like a university student as he leaned back and tipped the crumbs from the chip packet into his mouth. He'd been flipping through the tattered pages of Volga's notebook for some time and felt he was finally getting somewhere.

Every page was covered in numbers—lines and lines of seemingly random gibberish, like something a broken computer might spit out. He had rudimentary training in codebreaking and tried the numbers against some of the most common ciphers. None worked, so he broke the numbers into pairs and checked if any pair exceeded the value of twenty-six. They did. He checked if the pairs were divisible by whole numbers. Not all were. He counted how many unique number pairs there were and realized there were thirty-six, distributed fairly evenly in value between one and ninety-nine.

"Substitution cipher," he muttered and began

counting how often each pair showed up on the first page. Substitution ciphers were not particularly difficult to crack, and he began testing the most common letters in the alphabet against the most common pair combinations on the page. If Volga coded his messages in English, then the most common pairs would correspond to the letters E, T, A, and O. It wasn't long before he saw signs that he was on the right track.

"Not exactly the enigma," he muttered, writing down the first decrypted words. Some of the messages seemed to translate to Russian—at least, they looked that way—but the majority, thankfully, were in English. There were mistakes here and there, letters omitted or incorrectly transliterated, but Ritter had watched Volga at work. He'd encrypted his notes in his head and wrote them out by hand very quickly. It was impressive, and the fact the cipher was simple was not surprising. It was enough to stop ninety-nine percent of prying eyes if the notebook ever landed in the wrong hands, and that was all it was designed to do. Only if the security services found it, and then, only if they'd connected Volga to the CIA in advance, would a concerted attempt ever have been made to make sense of it. Ritter flicked through the notebook, looking for the combination of characters that spelled out the word 'Tushonka.' He found it and tested his decryption on that section.

Tushonka speaking to someone in Washington at highest level. More to follow.

Ritter exhaled through his teeth. It was likely that was

what Volga had communicated back to Langley. Was it the reason he was dead?

He poured himself some coffee and began the laborious process of decrypting the entire notebook from the beginning. On hotel stationery, he systematically translated the whole thing, one letter at a time, skipping any sections that appeared not to be in English.

The first page contained an address in the city. Ritter didn't know what the significance of it was, he'd never been there, but he confirmed that the number pairs he had yet to decipher were, in fact, digits, as suspected. He took note of them and continued to the next page, which was a list of names. Some of the names he was familiar with, some he wasn't. Of those he recognized, most were city officials, local military officers, or federal politicians. Many of the notes were cryptic—a single word or phrase —that were difficult to read much into, but others were very clear. There was a lot of information about military logistics—freight and troop movements, weapons purchase orders, prices and quantities of raw materials. It wasn't anything earth-shattering, but there were dates there too, which allowed Ritter to figure out the symbols for most numbers.

There'd been some numbers he'd skipped, and he went back to them now and figured them out. There were addresses, times, and a phone number that Ritter actually recognized. It was Evgeny Zadorov's, confirming what Ritter already suspected, that they'd both been relying on him for police protection.

When he noticed the sun beginning to rise outside, he skipped ahead to the final pages of the notebook. If there were any clues as to what had happened to Volga, he was most likely to find them there. He wrote out a string of letters and stopped.

Asset in Rostov to kill target. Meeting at 4.15 a.m.

Ritter looked at his watch. It was already after 4.15. He lit a cigarette and got up from his seat. He went to the curtain and looked out. There was a thin line of red on the underside of the cloud in the east, and he pictured Volga's contact sitting on a bench somewhere, waiting for him to show. "Asset," he said quietly to himself. It was a generic enough term, but this one was clearly an assassin. Who was his target? "Me?" he muttered, looking down at the street. "Good luck if it is, pal."

He stretched his limbs and made another pot of coffee. He needed sleep, but he couldn't risk it yet. Not there. He needed to get through the rest of the notebook and make sure there wasn't anything else there that might change his view of things. What he knew so far wasn't painting a very nice picture. Volga was dead, Vilgotsky was dead, and the CIA had moved an asset into the city. The street below was all but deserted, it was still too early for morning traffic, and the sun was struggling to make its mark. It was snowing lightly, and a plow roared by. He left the curtain half open and went back to the desk. The next page of the notebook contained a number string. He worked it out and saw it was a phone number, complete with dialing codes. It was a US number with a 202 area code. Washington DC.

He looked at the landline on the desk. If he used it, he'd have to leave the room. The place would be exposed.

He didn't relish the thought of going out in that cold, especially without having had any sleep, but a phone number was too much not to follow up on. He poured himself more coffee and stared at the phone. There was one final page in the notebook, and he deciphered that before making any calls.

Asset protocol. Rostov-Glavny. Payphone beneath the clock. 7.30 a.m.

He mulled that over. The location was easy enough. Was it today? And what was going to happen there? The assassin would make a call? Report back?

It was no good, he thought. He needed more. He needed to try the number. He picked up the phone and dialed. A series of tones and clicks followed as the call went through a rerouting process and then a woman's voice.

"Hello?"

Ritter hesitated. He didn't know what to say.

"Hello?" the woman said again.

"I'm here," Ritter said, trying to disguise his voice.

"Who is this?"

Ritter said nothing. He was trying to guess who he was speaking to. He had a sense that the voice was familiar, but he couldn't place it.

"Who is this?" she said again. "How did you get this number?"

He cleared his throat.

"Only one person has this number," she said, her tone

suddenly cooling. "If you don't speak, I'm going to hang up."

"The person who had this number is dead," Ritter said. "So is his Russian friend."

"What are you talking about? Who are you?"

"Let's not worry about—"

"Ritter? Is that you?"

"Fuck."

"Craig Ritter. I know it's you."

"How do you know my name?"

"Because I'm the one who recruited you."

He knew he'd heard the voice before. It was the woman from Langley. "Laurel," he said.

"Why are you calling this—"

"Volga's dead."

"What?"

"You heard me."

"How did he die?"

"I should be asking *you* that."

"Surely, you're not suggesting—"

"I told him there was an American mole. Now he's got a bullet in his head."

"Not a CIA bullet."

"You would say that, wouldn't you?"

"Because it's the truth. Why would we kill our own man?"

"Hmm. Why indeed?"

"What are you saying? Did you get the second name?"

"Hmm," he said again. There was no way on earth he was telling her now. "How about you tell me a few things?"

"Like what?"

"Like, who in the CIA did you pass on Volga's last message to?"

She said nothing.

"Interesting," he said.

"I can't tell you who I passed it to, but it's a very select group."

"How small?"

"Three names in the CIA, one of them being mine."

"And who did they tell?"

"No one."

"And now Volga's dead."

"You think one of my people—"

"It could have been you, for all I know."

"That makes no sense."

"Why doesn't it? If he knew something you didn't want him to."

"Whatever he knew, you know," she said matter-of-factly.

"What does that mean?"

"Think. I know your real name. I know where your wife and daughter live. I'm the one who—"

"Are you threatening my family?"

"I would never threaten your family."

"Then why are you—"

"I'm saying, if I was the one who ordered Volga's death, this conversation wouldn't be happening."

He said nothing. She was right.

"If I wanted you dead," she said, "you'd be dead. You're not a difficult man to track down in that city. Not when you know what you're after."

He sighed. He pulled the receiver away from his ear for a second and looked at it. What she was saying was true. It didn't make him feel any better, though. "All right," he said. "Answer me this. Is my family compromised?"

"Of course your family's not compromised."

"Because if one thing happens—"

"They're not compromised. Not because of this. Volga knew nothing about them. He couldn't have compromised them."

"Have you got eyes on them?"

"I can have someone in Bristol within the hour."

"Do that."

"I will," she said, "but we need to figure out what the hell's going on over there."

"I already told you. Someone sold out Volga."

"And his man? Vilgotsky? He's dead too?"

"Yes."

"How do you know someone sold them out?"

"What do you mean? They're dead. Their fingernails were pulled out with pliers."

"Where did you find the bodies?"

"At our meeting place."

"The farmhouse?"

"Yes."

"They weren't taken in, then?"

"In where?"

"In, Ritter. In to HQ. The GRU facility."

"They weren't taken in. But someone was waiting for me."

"You mean an ambush?"

"Yes."

"They were waiting for you at the farmhouse?"

They hadn't been waiting for him. They'd shown up after he'd tried calling Volga's cell. "They showed," he said.

"They were watching?"

"Or monitoring Volga's cell."

"You called his cell?"

"Yes."

"Then of course they showed," she said. "That's standard operating procedure."

"I know."

"There's a million things that could have gone wrong for Volga. You don't know for sure he was sold out, do you?"

"I don't know anything," he said.

"If the Russians had suspected he was CIA, they'd have taken him—"

"Downtown. I know."

"And how did you get this number?"

"I got it from Volga."

She paused a moment. "He wouldn't..." she said, then didn't finish the sentence.

"He wouldn't what?" Ritter said.

"He wouldn't have given you this number. Not willingly."

"Are you suggesting that I killed him for it?"

"No. It's just, he never would have—"

"I got it from his notebook. I found his notebook."

"I didn't know he kept a notebook."

"Well, he did."

"If you found it, that means the Russians didn't."

Ritter said nothing.

She was quiet, too, then she said, "You sound rattled, Craig."

"I'm not rattled."

"Where are you?"

"I'm not telling you that."

"Come on," she said, exasperated. "The call's already being traced. Voroshilovskiy Prospekt."

"There's a lot of—"

"Balkan Hotel."

He sighed. He knew he was being unreasonable, but the truth was, he *was* rattled. He didn't know what was going on. He didn't know why Volga was dead. He didn't know who he could trust. And he'd just found out the CIA had an asset in the city. "I have to go," he said.

"Wait! Don't hang up."

He put down the receiver and stood up. He needed to leave. The location was compromised for certain now, which meant he didn't need to protect it. He took out his cell and powered it up. It took a minute to connect to the network, and he gathered up his few belongings while he waited. Then he scrolled through the messages.

There was one from Zadorov, sent just before he'd gone into the farmhouse.

> Traffic awful on M-4 tonight. Don't go near it.

19

B y the time Valeria got back to her hotel room, she was shivering from the cold. She'd been at the farmhouse for hours, picking over the aftermath of the unmitigated disaster that had unfolded.

"You stupid, stupid, imbecile!" she'd shouted at the police captain. He was the highest-ranked officer from Rostov Oblast who'd made it out to the scene and had therefore borne the brunt of her rage. "Your men barged in like a bunch of—"

"It wasn't my decision to—"

"You fucked me," she'd raged. "You fucked the entire operation. I'm going to have you court-martialed for this. I want the names of every single officer killed in the blast."

"Why?" he'd said.

"Because I'm going to make sure their wives don't receive so much as a single ruble of pension for this."

The man looked like he was going to physically attack her when she said that.

"Oh yeah?" she'd added, almost goading him on. "Their death in the line of duty payout? Forget it. They're getting nothing, and you're going to be hearing from Moscow too."

She'd had half a mind to let rip at Gazzaev, too, even though she knew it wasn't his fault. He'd been operating on Oblast turf, and the paperwork that could have forced them to keep their noses out hadn't been filed. That was on her, which only made her all the more adamant heads would roll. The more of theirs that hit the ground, the less likely hers would.

She needed to report back to Moscow, to give them the bad news, and she was not looking forward to it. She ran the shower and undressed while the water heated up. Then she got in and let the hot water coax her numb body back to life.

When she got out of the shower, there was a message. It was from Gazzaev. She put on the hotel robe, then called him back immediately. "You have some nerve calling me now."

"I'm sorry, boss."

"I still haven't decided what to do with you."

"I know."

"And you're lucky you're still alive, to be honest. If those bumbling idiots hadn't barged in like a herd of—"

"If they hadn't interfered, it wouldn't have gone down the way it did."

"I should hope not. What took you so long to contact me?"

"I got a little burned in the blast."

"Nothing serious, I hope." He said nothing, he knew she wasn't being sincere, and she added, "Anyway, why are you calling?"

"I've got an update."

"Tell me it's something good."

"The phone that was used to call Yuriy Volga earlier. It popped up."

"Where?"

"Central Rostov. Seems to have come from inside the Balkan Hotel."

"Get down there immediately."

"Already on my way. Do you want me to activate a team?"

"That's just what we need, more cowboys with their guns blazing. No. I don't want Center E getting wind of this."

"I'll go in alone then?"

"Put one of our teams on standby. Get a vehicle in the area, but tell them to stay in their van until you call for backup."

"Roger that."

"And go in quietly. Speak to the concierge. Find out who's at the hotel. What interesting characters have shown their face. Anyone who checked in tonight after midnight is automatically a suspect.

She hung up and immediately dialed Moscow, praying no one picked up and she could just leave a message. She gave her clearance code and waited nervously. The girl, the secretary, answered.

"Darya, it's me again. Alpha Four Alpha."

"Go ahead, Alpha Four Alpha."

Her voice was less tense this time, and Valeria figured the boss was no longer present. She said, "Operation at the farmhouse was unsuccessful. Contact approached but got away before he could be apprehended. His identity is still unknown, but we do have a lead. His phone blipped at a hotel in central Rostov. We're investigating."

There was a pause, and Valeria wondered if the boss

was there after all. She heard Darya clear her throat, then she said, "Was the photograph recovered?"

"That's a negative, but once I get hands on the suspect—"

"Just get him what he wants," the girl said suddenly. Her voice was frantic, like she was afraid of being caught speaking. She sounded so vivid Valeria could almost picture her in the office. "Get him what he wants, or get reassigned."

"I'm trying—"

"He'll kill you."

"What?"

"He'll kill you if you don't get him what he wants."

"I don't know how that's supposed—"

"I'm not threatening you. They're killing people here. It's already started."

"What are you talking about?"

"I shouldn't be saying anything."

"Just tell me what's going on?"

The line went dead. Valeria realized she was holding her breath and released it. She had no idea what that had been about, but it wasn't good.

She grabbed her purse and rummaged through it hurriedly for the anxiety pills the shrink had given her. She hadn't found them when the phone started to ring. She froze, then turned and looked at the screen. She expected to see the Moscow area code of Tushonka's office, but it was Gazzaev. She breathed a sigh of relief. "What now?" she barked.

"I'm at the Balkan Hotel. The concierge is here."

"What does he have to say for himself?"

"There are a number of interesting guests checked in, but one of them he thinks will be of particular interest."

"Who?"

"A British arms dealer, new to the city. He's been making friends and throwing around money."

"There are a lot of guys like that skulking about. We're at war—"

"This one checked in tonight, less than an hour after the explosion at the farm."

"Get him in custody. Get him alive. Do you hear me?"

"I can't. He's not here."

"Where did he go?"

"He walked out the front door of the hotel not fifteen minutes ago. He can't be far."

"I want the city locked down like a vise. We need to get this guy, and we need to—"

"He left on foot, Valeria."

"What?"

"His car is still with the valet."

20

L ance got back to the apartment building and unlocked the door. The coffee mug was where he'd left it on the floor, and he picked it up and looked at it. It hadn't been moved. That was something to be grateful for, he supposed.

He climbed the stairs, and when he got inside the apartment, he found Klára up and waiting for him at the counter. She'd dyed her hair. It was still wet, and she had a towel on her shoulders. He looked at her. She looked quite a bit different with black hair. "I see the dye took," he said.

She ignored his comment. "What happened at the meeting?"

He sat down across from her at the counter. There was a fresh pot of coffee, and he poured some.

"Well?" she said.

He shook his head.

"What does that mean?"

He sipped the coffee. "The contact missed the meet. He wasn't there."

"What do you mean, he wasn't there?"

"He didn't show."

She said nothing but kept staring at him like she expected him to say more. "He's probably dead," Lance said.

"We don't know that."

"He's dead," Lance said again, his voice level.

She looked at him a moment. "What does that mean for us? For the plan? What do we do?"

Lance breathed in and let out a long sigh. He was trying not to show his frustration. He'd have liked to light a cigarette but didn't want to get into an argument with her. "We need to leave the city," he said at last.

"Leave?"

He nodded.

"What about our plan?"

"We'll make a new plan."

"We need to speak to the Fixer."

"We can't," Lance said, his voice rising unintentionally. "It's over."

"There's no need to get angry."

"Sorry."

She looked at him more closely now. He felt like she was trying to read his mind. "Fuck it," he muttered, taking out his smokes.

He thought she was going to protest, but instead, she looked away. He lit the cigarette, and she said, "Why do you guys always smoke?"

"What do you mean?"

"Why do you do it? It's going to kill you."

"Probably not," Lance said.

"If a bullet doesn't," she said.

He shrugged. "It's useful for killing time. A lot of this

job is killing time. Waiting. And trying to look like you're not waiting. People believe it more when you've got a habit."

"A vice," she said.

He nodded. "Besides, it's that last bit of pleasure—"

"Oh, come on," she said. He stubbed it out, and she said, "What about the American? The traitor? Are we ever going to find out who that was?"

"No idea," Lance said.

She brought her cup to the sink and rinsed it. "The Brit's still out there," she said.

"If he's not dead too," Lance said.

"If he's posing as an arms trader, he shouldn't be that hard to find."

"He won't be posing as an arms dealer any longer."

"Why not?"

"Yuriy Volga was his only contact. If he's been compromised, the Brit will be scared shitless. He'll go to ground immediately."

"Do you think he'll flee the city?"

Lance took a sip from his mug and put it down harder than was necessary. "Who knows?"

"He could go dark completely," Klára said. "That might be the best option for him, depending on the name of the traitor."

"He can't disappear forever," Lance said. "The CIA's watching his family. He'll show up eventually, in Berlin or Prague or somewhere far from here."

"Too late to help us."

Lance nodded. He drained the rest of his coffee. "There's no use crying about it," he said. "What's done is done."

"Who knows?" Klára said. "Maybe he'll come to us."

Lance shook his head. "He doesn't know we're here. He doesn't even know who we are. We need to move on to the next priority."

"Which is?"

"Finding Shipenko. He needs to pay for the part he's played in all this."

Klára nodded. "I imagine he's in Moscow."

"I need to check in with Langley and find out. They've been trying to track him down."

"How do you contact Langley?"

"There's a procedure. A pay phone at the main train station," he said, pouring himself more coffee. "Rostov-Glavny."

"Then let's not waste any more time," she said, eyeing his coffee. "We should go."

"Hold your horses. We've got time."

"How much time?"

"The phone rings every morning at seven-thirty. If I want to talk to Langley, I just need to be there to pick it up."

"All right," she said, looking at her watch. "Seven thirty. I suppose it would be out of the question for us to go out and get some breakfast in the meantime?"

21

About a kilometer from the CIA compound in Langley, Virginia, a government-issue Cadillac Escalade sped along a quiet tree-lined street. It turned off the road onto a gravel track that looked like a private driveway. After a hundred yards, not visible from the street, there was a military-grade security checkpoint. The guards at the checkpoint had been expecting the vehicle, and it sped by without slowing. It maintained speed, following the road into a reinforced concrete tunnel that looked like the entrance to a mine. The tunnel grew deeper, and the concrete around it grew thicker, to the point that it was capable of withstanding a direct nuclear strike.

When the car stopped, two specially-cleared agents from the CIA's Office of Security approached and opened the back door. Levi Roth stepped out and greeted them with a cursory nod, then put his head back into the car. "I won't be long, Harry."

"Aye, aye, boss."

He followed the guards down a long corridor lit by

fluorescent tubes so bright he had to squint. They stopped at a round steel door that was embossed with the seal of the CIA. The two guards simultaneously placed their fingers on biometric scanners and entered a code into a keypad. The door opened, the guards stepped aside, and Roth passed through it alone into a large elevator. The elevator had no buttons inside, no screen telling him how many floors had been descended. Its doors closed, and it started to move. When it stopped, he stepped out into the bustling lobby of the new, state-of-the-art Emergency Command Center. It was one of the most highly classified facilities in the United States, part of the National Command Authority, and had been built to enact the set of protocols that, under extreme situations, could allow the Director of the CIA to take control of all levers of the US military. It had direct hardline comms with the White House, the Pentagon, and the emergency operations centers for the Army, Navy, and Air Force. It also had direct access to the entire NORAD Alert Network, the Defense Department's Global Information Grid, and the Keyhole Satellite Surveillance Network. The secretive and highly classified Operations Plan, which governed what was to happen in the case of a catastrophic attack against US leadership, invested so much power in the facility and Levi Roth personally that it could roughly be equated with the Dead Hand provisions governing what would happen in the Kremlin under similar circumstances. Not only did it give Roth full executive control, allowing him to issue orders to the National Military Command, the US Strategic Command, and the Air Force Global Strike Command—including the combat-ready units of the US Strategic Nuclear Deterrent at Barksdale Air Force Base in Bossier Parish, Louisiana, and the Strategic Command's

Deterrence and Global Strike Capability at Offutt Air Force Base, Nebraska—it also automatically suspended the judicial and legislative branches of the federal government, so that he could do what needed to be done without fear of interference.

Put simply, it gave Roth full control. He could launch nukes if he deemed it necessary. He could hit the self-destruct button on the planet. The facility was brand new, and now, when the US president spoke of nuclear deterrence, it was the orders issued from within its walls that he was referring to.

Roth looked up at the live feed, as he called it—an enormous, concave, high-definition screen, forty feet wide and over twenty in height. It currently showed the real-time position of every unit of the Russian Army along the vast Ukrainian battlefront, from Orlianka and Lyman in the northeast to Dudchany and Blahodatne north of Kherson. The positions made it painfully obvious just how badly the invasion was going for Molotov. That ought to have made Roth happy, but it didn't. Molotov was now a cornered tiger. It was an uncomfortable position for the tiger but a potentially lethal one for the person blocking his way. In front of the screen, control positions for sixty operators were set out in semicircular arcs. They were currently unoccupied, apart from a skeleton crew of monitoring analysts.

"Molotov's in a tight spot," someone said, and Roth turned to see Tatyana standing next to him, dressed in an impeccably tailored white blazer and an impeccably short matching skirt.

"Tatyana," Roth said, suddenly feeling as if he'd been caught doing something he shouldn't have been. "What are you doing down here?"

"Oh," she said. "I needed to get some things finished. I was just borrowing a desk."

The command center was almost directly below the new headquarters building in the CIA's Langley compound, where Laurel and Tatyana shared an expansive office on the sixth floor. "You couldn't find a desk upstairs?" Roth said.

"Laurel's been sleeping there again," Tatyana said. "Kind of makes it feel like I'm working in a dorm room."

"She needs to get her life sorted out," Roth said. "Find some work-life balance."

"I could say the same to you," Tatyana said, glancing at her watch.

"Oh," Roth said, shaking his head. "I was with the president again. He managed to say a few things that made me restless."

"He usually does," Tatyana said. "Anything I can help with?"

Roth shook his head almost too eagerly. "No, no. You get home. It's very late."

She turned and left, and he remained where he was, watching until he saw her enter the elevator. When he was sure she was gone, he went to the duty officer and told him that under no circumstances was he to be disturbed. Then he went to his office, a glass box that looked out over the control floor, and locked the door and methodically shut each of the half-dozen blinds. The room was fitted with the CIA's most sophisticated digital and analog anti-surveillance devices—signal detectors, frequency jammers, and white noise generators. In a top-secret building hundreds of feet underground whose very existence was classified, Roth's office was a vault within a vault. It was perhaps the most protected space on the planet, fitted with the most secure communications equipment in existence. No one could possibly eavesdrop on what he was about to do.

Which was precisely why he'd made the trip there. He had a very private phone call to make.

He picked up the receiver and dialed a series of codes that routed a number via sixteen analog phone exchanges in twelve different countries, including nine that did not have information-sharing agreements with the United States. He waited—it seemed to take an inordinately long time to connect—then a hoarse, guttural, Russian voice broke the silence. "Da?"

Roth responded in English. "You've got a leaky ship, Osip."

There was a long pause, followed by Osip Shipenko's nauseating voice. "Ah, my friend, I was beginning to think you'd forgotten about me."

"We're not friends," Roth said through gritted teeth.

"Come, Levi. Don't be like that. You know you need me as much as I need you."

"What I need is for you to lock down your operation."

"What are you talking about?"

"There's talk over here of a high-level interaction taking place."

"An *interaction*?" Osip said, and the way he said it made the word sound like something lewd.

"The rumor is that you've got a friend in Washington."

"Me specifically?"

"The intel specifies *Tushonka*. The president had me in his office tonight, saying *Tushonka* this, *Tushonka* that. You said you knew how to keep your shit locked down."

"Hmm," Osip said. "That's a problem."

Roth had known Osip's growing influence would

come with a commensurate uptick in his profile, which for decades he'd succeeded in keeping completely under wraps. It made things more difficult. "You need to close ranks," Roth said. "If Montgomery got wind of this, how long before Molotov does?"

"But I have no ranks, Levi. I trust no one. I work with no one. I haven't made it to where I am by making friends."

"Just tighten up your ship."

"It was your idea to meet. I told you Rostov was unsafe."

"And I told you how to neutralize the threat."

"Yuriy Volga? I had him nabbed. He didn't know a thing."

"Not Volga," Roth said. "The Brit. Ritter."

"Ritter?"

"Yes! I sent the name days ago."

"You sent it? How?"

"How do you think?"

"I never saw that. We must have missed it."

"I thought there was no *we*. I thought you trusted no one."

"I'll have to look into it."

"Your operation's putting us at risk, Osip. If you don't get your shit sorted out, I'm going to have to—"

"You're going to what, Levi? Bet on another horse?" Osip laughed then, and the sound of it made Roth's blood boil. Osip Shipenko was not just the most powerful lieutenant in Molotov's menagerie of psychopaths, he was also the man personally behind the very recent massacre at the US embassy in Prague, as well as countless other atrocities. He was anathema to everything Levi Roth had spent his life trying to build. The things Roth had learned about Osip, the dark corners of his past, his treatment of subordinates, of young women who reminded him of his childhood governess, it was enough to make Roth's stomach turn. Levi Roth abhorred Osip Shipenko and everything he stood for.

But scruples, personal misgivings, twinges of conscience, were all luxuries Roth could not afford. He had a job to do, an unpleasant job, and he knew he couldn't rely on the president or anyone else to get it done. If he was to succeed, if he was to keep the country safe, he had to do what needed to be done, alone when necessary, without the applause or approval of his peers. And without their knowledge. If he had to get onto the wrong side of the law to get that done, that was something he was willing to do. Backroom deals with Kremlin sociopaths, if they furthered his objective, were the least of it. For Roth, the stakes were national survival. If Molotov went off the deep end, as an increasing number of models predicted he would, then he needed a plan to offramp Russia from the path it was on.

In a nuclear confrontation, there could be no winner. War between the superpowers was not an option. That was where Roth was coming from.

"I'm not betting on another horse," Roth said. "I just need you to focus."

"Focus?" Osip said. "Do you have any idea what I've been dealing with?"

"You need to do better."

"He's losing it, Levi."

"I *know* he's losing it. He started a war he cannot win. He invaded the second largest country in Europe, in winter, with an army so woefully under-equipped it couldn't—"

"He's executing generals."

"What?"

"He called me to the palace this morning, and what do you think I found there but thirty of our most powerful and important military leaders lined up like a bunch of criminals? Generals, SVR and GRU directors, even civilian defense officials."

"What are you talking about?"

"You don't know the half of it. Dig out your satellite surveillance of Novo-Ogaryovo from two hours ago."

"Executions?"

"Shot them at dawn, Levi, like he's the villain in a cowboy film."

"On the lawn of the palace?"

"Some of them were women. He gunned them down like rabid dogs."

"Don't tell me that offended your delicate sensibilities."

"If you don't think he's deranged, just say the word, Levi, and I'll forget we ever had a deal."

"We have no deal."

"*Arrangement*, then."

"*Understanding*," Roth said, wincing even at that.

"The head of the Luhansk State Council was among those killed."

"Why? What could he possibly be thinking?"

"He's not thinking. That's what I'm trying to tell you. He's operating on a completely new level. I've known him for decades, Levi. It's all different now. He's changed."

"He was always a paranoid, power-hungry maniac."

"Paranoid, yes. Power-hungry, yes. But he was never a maniac."

"He was ruthless—"

"He was rational. Patient. He knew where his interests lay."

"So what are you saying?"

"We need to accelerate our timeline."

"There's only so much I can do," Roth said. "If we move too fast and make a mistake—"

"Molotov's getting desperate," Osip said. "You're running out of time. He's not going to hold back anymore."

"What are you talking about?"

"Don't make me spell it out."

"He's putting new options on the table?"

"Yes, he is."

"What options."

"Use your imagination."

"Nuclear?"

"Nuclear, chemical, *everything*."

"If you want to accelerate the timeline—"

"It's not a question of what I want."

"I'm going to need to see some proof. Something that shows for sure he's gone over the edge. I'll need it to persuade my own side—"

"You'll get your proof, but I'm going to need a few things myself."

"What things?"

"I'm going to send you a list of names. They're key people close to Molotov. I'm going to need you to get their names on some sort of safe list."

"I'm not offering amnesty to a bunch of your cronies."

"Hold your horses, Levi. These aren't my friends. They're the people who worked with the people Molotov just had executed. They're the people close to the levers of power."

"But there are dozens of names here."

"A hundred and twenty," Shipenko said. "The names in italics are Molotov's personal bodyguards, his elite regiment, his driver and pilot and whatnot. I can't pull off a palace coup without them."

"You want the CIA to bribe them?"

"I want the CIA to guarantee them amnesty in the event they have to leave the country. Safe passage for them and their families. I also want them notified by a Swiss bank that they have access to a numbered account and a balance of five million dollars."

"You're dreaming."

"A few hundred million dollars, Levi. It's a small price to pay to avoid nuclear war, wouldn't you say? The CIA spends more on Post-it notes."

"I don't have access to that kind of cash—"

"Yes, you do, Levi. We both know you do. Make this happen. Handle it personally. And don't shortchange anyone."

"Do these people know this is happening?"

"Of course they don't," Osip said, "but once they accept the banking credentials, which they will, they'll be complicit."

Roth sighed. He didn't like being extorted, and this bore all the hallmarks of a brazen money grab, but Osip was right, six hundred million dollars was a trifle, Roth could have the accounts set up with a single phone call, and it was a hell of a lot less costly than fighting a war against Molotov and his nukes. "Send me the list," he said. "I'll see what I can do."

"You get it done, or you tell the president to start beefing up his missile defenses. It's your choice, because Molotov's about to go nuclear."

"I'll get it done."

"Do it fast, Levi, because I'm about to start putting things in motion. You know how these things go. It's like pushing a locomotive down a hill. Once they get started, they're very difficult to stop."

Roth sighed. He knew that was true, and he was convinced that this plan with Shipenko, this pact with the lesser of two devils, was necessary if nuclear confrontation was to be taken off the table. But the betrayal still left a very sour taste in his mouth. He was committing treason, and he knew it. It might cost him his life. And it might cost his friends' lives too. He swallowed. What he was about to say was sourer still. "There's something else you need to be aware of, Osip."

"Oh?"

"Someone's coming to get you."

"Get me?"

"A CIA assassin. Lance Spector. He's killed a few of your friends."

"I know who he is, Levi. I think I can handle him."

"He's not easy to handle."

"Then call him off?"

"I can't call him off. He's answering directly to the president now. Not me. If he finds you—"

"Then make sure he doesn't find me."

22

Craig left the hotel on foot, ignoring the valet who was snoozing at his post and crossed the street to a café. He found a table by the window and ordered breakfast. From his seat, he could see the front entrance of the hotel, as well as the side street that accessed the hotel delivery bay. He watched both, waiting to see if anything out of the ordinary happened now that he'd given up his location. It was still early, and there was little traffic, a few deliveries at the side entrance and one or two taxis, but no raid, no SWAT team. He sat there for over an hour, and nothing happened. He was relieved. It wasn't proof positive that Langley hadn't turned on him, that they weren't behind Volga's death, but it was always nice when someone you were supposed to trust didn't try to kill you.

He'd finished his breakfast, and the dirty plate was still in front of him. The waitress was an older woman in a thin, cloth dress that was too small to cover her corpulent assets. It seemed at any moment to be in danger of tearing open. She'd brought him his bill sometime earlier and seemed impatient now that he settle it. He looked at his watch. It was almost seven. He put some money on the table and went back across the street to the hotel, where some taxis were idling by the entrance. He got in the first one and told the driver to take him to the train station. Going there wasn't without risk, but he wanted to have eyes on the payphone at seven-thirty. He didn't know what he might be walking into, but it was his only real lead from Volga's notebook.

Asset protocol. Rostov-Glavny. Payphone beneath the clock. 7.30 a.m.

He was familiar with the station, and when the cab arrived, he got it to take him around to the back, where vendors set up stalls beneath the station's large concrete overhang. The market there was useful for any number of things, from counterfeit western CDs and DVDs to counterfeit western fashions and handbags. If you knew who to talk to, you could also get weaponry and military-grade communications equipment. The workers were still setting up for the day, laying out their wares, which they unloaded from vans in large canvas shopping bags. The women were firing up the propane patio heaters that kept them from freezing. A group of them huddled around a man selling hot chocolate, which he scooped from a pot with a soup ladle. The women held the mugs in their gloved hands like precious treasures, and Ritter approached one of them, who looked to be the owner of the neighboring stall. She seemed to specialize in Gucci knockoffs, belts and sneakers mostly, but she also had plain black scarves.

"How much?" he said in his basic Russian, holding up a scarf.

She barely glanced at him and, without interrupting her conversation with the other ladies, held up a thumb and two fingers. Ritter counted out some bills and paid her, then wrapped the scarf around his neck and the lower half of his face.

The main hall of Rostov-Glavny was a cavernous, echoey concourse with ticket booths at one end and escalators down to the commuter platforms at the other. The ceiling was an over-engineered steel-trussed monstrosity that looked strong enough to hold up a bridge. A colony of pigeons had taken up residence on its girders. There was a sort of gazebo structure at the center of the concourse that housed the café, and the seats and tables scattered around it were sheltered from the pigeon droppings by umbrellas. Just off center, hanging from the ceiling on a ship's chain, was an enormous, industrial-era clock, its mechanisms and moving parts visible behind the four clock faces.

It was early, and the concourse was beginning to fill. People entered through the main doors at the front, and there was also a steady stream of commuters coming up from the lower level. Ritter pulled up the scarf and walked to the café, avoiding eye contact with anyone. He picked up a newspaper from one of the stands on the way and sat down at a table facing the pay phones. He raised his hand to get the attention of the waiter, then unfolded the ponderous broadsheet and held it up at an angle that allowed him to look out over the top. The main story was about the US decision to supply the Ukrainians with

Himars. He ordered coffee and glanced up at the clock. It was seven-twenty.

Beyond the pay phones, he could see the mainline train platforms. They were still relatively quiet, but more and more people were coming up on the escalators from the regional and commuter services below. Ritter kept an eye on anyone who approached but couldn't tell much from their faces.

He lit a cigarette.

His position was exposed, approachable from all directions, and overlooked by the entire second-floor gallery of the station, but he didn't think anyone could have expected him to be there. Even if someone figured out he'd found Volga's notebook, they couldn't have predicted he'd be there. In fact, he had no idea if he was even in the right place.

He sucked the cigarette uneasily and tried to keep an eye out in all directions. The clock clicked audibly when the minutes turned. He could hear it above the din of the station. It only added to his feeling of tension.

He watched and waited, waited and watched, and it clicked through the minutes. When it struck seven-thirty, one of the phones started to ring instantly, its metal bell clanging just loud enough to hear. No one in the station paid it the slightest mind, but Ritter reached instinctively inside his coat for the reassuring steel of his gun.

23

L ance and Klára stood next to each other on the street car. It jerked, and she grabbed onto him. Her body pressed against his and their faces were so close they could have kissed.

"Sorry," she said, looking at the ground.

"That's okay," Lance said. She was embarrassed, and, to break the awkwardness, he said, "Try not to attract attention when we get to the station."

"Really?" she said, making no effort to hide her sarcasm. "Don't attract attention? Would that be bad?"

"You know what I mean."

"So, you don't want me to grab onto every man I fall into?"

He said nothing. The tram jerked to an abrupt stop, and again she was forced to grab him. She let go instantly, but as more people crammed onboard, they were squeezed closer to each other, a fact she seemed to resent.

"Sorry," Lance said when his chin brushed against her hair.

"Just tell me we're almost there."

He pressed back against the door to give her more room and said, "It's not far now. Just another few stops."

She nodded. Their cramped confines did have the benefit of allowing them to speak privately, and she said under her breath, "So, what's the plan when we get there?"

"We should enter the station separately," he said. "I'll get off at the next stop and walk the final couple of blocks. You stay onboard until the station. A lot of people will be getting off with you."

"All right," she said.

"The tram lets out on the station's lower level. Just follow the crowd to the escalators and they'll bring you up to the main concourse. You'll see the clock hanging from the roof. You can't miss it. The phones are below it."

"What do you want me to do?"

"Just cover me. One of the phones will start ringing at seven-thirty and I'll pick up."

"Are we expecting any trouble?"

"We're always expecting trouble."

"Anything in particular?" she said impatiently.

"I don't think so," Lance said.

"Did Volga know about this arrangement?"

Lance thought for a second. He knew why she was asking—if Volga was compromised, everything he knew was potentially compromised too, but he didn't think that was the case here. "I don't see why he would have. He had his own methods of communicating with Langley."

"But you don't know?"

He shook his head. "I don't know. I'll ask."

"Okay," she said. "I'll hold back and watch. You speak on the phone. If any surprises come your way—"

"You'll see them coming."

She nodded.

"You won't be tempted to let me meet my fate?"

"You'll have to wait and see," she said. The tram was slowing down, and people began to shove closer to the exit, pressing them even tighter against each other. "We really need to take a cab next time," she said.

"After the call," Lance said, "don't approach me. Come back down to the lower level and get back on this tram. Number forty-four. I'll do the same. We'll regroup onboard."

"All right."

The tram jerked to a halt, pushing them together again, and he felt her breasts against his chest. They both noticed, and it was enough to make her blush. "This is it," he said, ignoring the awkwardness. "My stop. I'll see you on the concourse."

"No you won't," she said. "No one will."

He turned and squeezed toward the exit. The doors opened, and he stepped out onto the street. He stood on the sidewalk for a second, doing up his coat and watching the tram pull away, then walked briskly in the direction of the station. He could see it at the end of the street, an enormous concrete edifice that seemed to have drawn architectural inspiration from every era of Soviet industrial excess. The station had occupied its spot since 1875, but additions and alterations throughout the years made the original structure unrecognizable.

He scanned the front entrance as he approached. From the outside, it had the look and feel of a rundown seventies office block, but once inside, it felt like something from the Victorian era.

It was busy and growing busier by the minute. A

steady stream of commuters came up from the lower level and poured into the concourse, and he made his way through them warily. The crowd provided a sort of safety, a screen in which to hide his activity, but at the same time, made it difficult to see potential threats. He scanned everyone and everything, eyeing every face as it approached. Across the concourse, two trains pulled in and let out their cargo of passengers. By the platforms, people sat on benches, awaiting trains. At the center of the concourse was an open café, and people sat there at the tables, some directly overlooking the pay phones. They were smoking and reading newspapers and sipping coffee, and there was no way of knowing how long they'd been there. Right next to the phones was a cleaner in blue overalls with a large cart holding mops and brushes and garbage bags. Lance imagined the cache of weapons that could have been hidden inside it.

It wasn't a good approach, trouble could come at him from a dozen different directions, and he had no way of heading it off, but it was too late to change the plan now. The place had been decided by some bureaucrat in Langley, probably before the city had even a hint of the strategic sensitivity it held now, and it was what it was.

Lance wouldn't have touched that phone with a ten-foot pole if Volga had shown up for his meet, but Volga hadn't shown, and Lance didn't have the luxury of playing it safe. He needed to make contact.

He looked up at the clock—he had a few minutes to spare—and lit a cigarette to stall for time. He stood near the phones, leaning against an advertising sign, and as the time got nearer, he looked around the concourse for Klára. She should have been there ahead of him, but, as she'd said, he couldn't see her. When the enormous clock struck seven-thirty, he turned toward the phones in the same instant that the one nearest began to ring.

Flicking away the cigarette, he picked up the receiver and said, "Hello?" There was a moment of silence, and he repeated himself. "Hello?"

"Hello," a woman's voice said.

"Didn't expect an answer, did you?"

"Please hold."

Lance glanced around impatiently. He heard the familiar clicks of the call being rerouted and then another woman's voice. "Lance?"

"Laurel. It's me."

"Thank God," she said. "We've got a serious problem."

"Volga missed his meeting this morning."

"Right. He's dead."

"You have confirmation of that?"

"Yes. He missed his meeting last night with the Fixer."

"Ritter?"

"Yes."

"But Ritter is still active?"

"He called me. He shouldn't have had my number, but he did, and he called."

"How'd he get the number?"

"He said Volga kept a notebook."

"Jesus."

"I know. I've had the number disconnected. Everything tied to Volga has been burned."

"He might as well have made the Russians a spreadsheet."

"It's bad. I know."

"Did Volga know about this phone?"

Laurel hesitated just a moment.

"Jesus, Laurel."

"You should go. Get out of Rostov."

"Is Ritter still active?" Lance said, scanning the station with a renewed sense of urgency.

"I don't know."

"What do you mean, you don't know?"

"He was pretty spooked when I spoke to him."

"Did you arrange another check-in?"

"No. He hung up on me. And that's what you should do too. Get out of there."

"What spooked him most?"

"What do you think? He was afraid Langley might have killed Volga."

Lance nodded. "I guess we can't blame him."

"No," Laurel said. "He says there's a mole, then people start dying. It doesn't look good."

"Is there a chance he's right?"

"Lance!"

"Is there?" he said again.

"I'm the only living soul who knows about the leak. I told no one."

"No one?"

"Well, the president."

"You're not the only living soul, by the way," Lance said, interrupting her.

"How's that?"

"Volga knew about the leak."

"I doubt Volga killed himself."

"Not on purpose," Lance said.

"You really should go," she said again. "Hang up now and walk away. We don't know how much Volga spilled."

"When did he call?"

"Volga? He didn't."

"Ritter. When did you speak to him?"

"A few hours ago. After his meet with Volga didn't happen."

"Did you trace the call?"

"He was at the Balkan Hotel, top floor, overlooking the street. I highly doubt he's still there."

"He might be watching, though."

"The hotel? Why would he do that?"

"To see if you send anyone to kill him."

"Which I didn't."

"Might soften him a little."

"You're not thinking of trying to make contact."

"It's our only chance of finding our mole. If Ritter disappears, that name does too."

"He won't still be there. You'll be wasting your time. Time that could be spent making as much distance—"

"It's my only chance."

"If you show up there, he'll think—"

"That I'm there to kill him. I know."

"What if he takes you out?"

"I'll be careful."

"You'll have to be *very* careful."

"I have something we can bond over."

She was quiet for a second, then said, "You mean his family?"

"I've met them. I know where they are. He'll have to listen to that."

"He'll think you're threatening them."

"I don't care what he thinks."

"You wouldn't threaten a man's family."

Lance nodded. That was true. But he still thought he could use the fact he'd met them to force a connection with Ritter. He was about to say as much when a man in a black jacket and scarf stepped up to the phone next to him. His hand was in his pocket, clearly suggesting he was holding a gun. "Put down the phone," he said.

"Lance!" Laurel said. "What was that?"

"Laurel, I have to go."

24

Klára arrived before Lance and took a table in the café not too close to the pay phones. It gave her a somewhat obscured view of the phones, as well as the station's entrance, and she ordered coffee from the waiter and positioned herself to keep an eye on both. No one used the phones, which were battered and vandalized, but traffic entering the station was heavy. She watched for Lance and spotted him as soon as he entered. She didn't think he'd seen her, and she kept her head down and sipped her coffee.

Lance had a few minutes to spare before the phone rang, and he killed the extra time by lighting a cigarette. He glanced at the clock periodically, and she took note of his tells. He actively maintained awareness of his surroundings, positioning himself near an advertisement board so he could see in its reflection. She knew he was using the cigarette as a means of blending in. People paid less attention to someone who was doing something. They'd taught her to do the same.

The time seemed to pass very quickly, and as soon as

the minute hand on the clock struck six, Lance stepped forward and picked up the phone. She watched him. She couldn't hear, but she could tell contact had been made. He was speaking, keeping his hand near his mouth to prevent anyone from reading his lips, watching his surroundings surreptitiously while he tapped the top of the phone with his hand. Klára wouldn't have chosen this location as a contact point, there were dozens of people within a few feet of him, and there was no way of knowing what they were planning. If someone tried something, she'd never be able to intervene fast enough to stop it.

Not that there was much point worrying about that now. She kept her eyes on Lance and tried to interpret what he was saying from his body language. The conversation went on for fifteen seconds, thirty, far longer than she'd expected, given the circumstances. A man in a black jacket who'd been sitting at one of the other café tables got up from his seat and blocked her view. She tried to see around him and noticed that his face was partially obscured by a scarf. That wasn't exactly a smoking gun, but it wasn't that cold inside the station, and the detail caught her eye. She watched him walk around the barrier that enclosed the café tables. When he turned in the direction of the phones, she immediately got up from her seat.

The man walked calmly, taking his time to go around people in his way, but he was definitely headed in Lance's direction. Klára sped up as he got closer, shoving her way through the crowd, but she was still ten feet behind him when he got to the phones. She reached into her pocket for her gun and pulled it out just as she was stepping up behind him. He was at the phone next to Lance, and it seemed he'd said something to him. Klára jammed her gun into his back, concealing it from passersby with her body and leaving the man in no doubt as to what it was. "Do not move a muscle," she said in Russian. The man tried to look back at her, and she dug the gun further into his back. "I said, don't move."

"Easy, tiger," the man said in English, and Klára realized that he had a gun of his own, pointed through the fabric of his jacket at Lance's belly.

"It's all right," Lance said, raising his hands in a gesture of peace. "We're all on the same side here."

"What's going on?" Klára said.

"Craig and I were just getting acquainted," Lance said in his characteristically nonchalant manner.

The man spoke up then, and Klára recognized a strong British accent. "How do you know my name?"

"You're the Fixer," she said.

Lance took a step back from him, keeping his hands visible. "Why don't we all take our fingers off the triggers," he said, "and talk about this in a civilized manner?"

"Why don't you start talking?" Ritter said. "And let us decide what to do with our fingers."

"All right," Lance said. "I'm CIA, the woman at your back is with Czech Intelligence, and you're Craig Ritter, the fixer Langley's been running here in Rostov for the past few weeks."

"Is that so?" Ritter said flatly, and it was difficult for Klára to read his voice. She didn't know if he was angry, afraid, or relieved. She didn't even know if he was surprised to see them, although the very fact of his presence meant he'd known something was going to happen there.

"Look," Lance said. "I was supposed to meet Yuriy Volga this morning. You were supposed to meet him last night. I'm going to go out on a limb and say he never showed for either of us."

"So what?"

"So what? It's unnerving. That's what. He was your handler."

"Volga's dead," Ritter said. "Murdered."

"We figured," Klára said, taking her gun away from his back and giving him some breathing room. "Why don't we all take our hands out of our pockets and keep them where they can be seen?"

Ritter hesitated a second. He stepped back from Lance and turned so he could see both of them at the same time. Klára was holding her gun inside her coat, and she decided to act first. She pulled her hand from her pocket. Lance was still holding his at about chest height, but he lowered them when Ritter took his hands out of his pocket too.

"This isn't the best place for us to talk," Lance said.

"It'll do for now," Ritter said.

"All right," Lance said. "I'll keep this simple. You were going to pass some information on to Volga last night."

"Maybe I was," Ritter said.

"You were," Lance said impatiently. "We're on the same team here."

"I don't know what team I'm on."

"Well, until last night, you were on our team, and you were going to give Volga a name. Volga was going to give that name to me."

"If you say so."

"I *do* say so."

"Well, maybe I wasn't able to get the name."

Lance looked to Klára for help. "Ritter," she said, "you obviously care about the mission."

"I don't care about—"

"You wouldn't be here if you didn't," she said.

"I care about what happened to Volga," he said, then added, "and Vilgotsky."

"Vilgotsky?" Klára said.

"Seems you don't know everything, then."

"Vilgotsky worked with Volga," Lance said.

"Look," Klára said, "if Volga was alive, you'd have given him the name of the traitor, and he'd have given it to us."

"Simple as that?" Ritter said.

Klára shrugged. "We're all on the same side, aren't we? We've been over that."

"I don't know what side you're on," Ritter said. "All I know is that Volga isn't alive, and any name I was going to give him stays with me."

Lance sighed. "This is a waste of time. If you don't want to play ball, then why are you here? To kill us?"

"Maybe you're here to kill me," he said.

"This is nonsense," Klára said. "No one's here to kill anyone."

"Except the traitor whose name you refuse to divulge," Lance said.

"Is that what you were going to do with it?" Ritter said. "Kill them?"

Lance shrugged. "It wouldn't have been my decision, but I'd say that's a distinct possibility. You know the rules."

"I know who I work for," Ritter said.

There was something in the way he said it, Klára thought. Almost as if he loathed the very idea of working for the CIA. "You got a problem with the people we work for?" she said.

Ritter said nothing for a moment, then looked her in the eye. "Depends on who you're talking about."

She shook her head. "This is pointless. If you're just going to play games—"

"I'm not playing games," Ritter said.

"I guess we won't ever find out," she said, turning away. She took a few steps in the direction of the escalator and was surprised to hear Ritter speak up, as if he didn't want her to leave without hearing what he had to say.

"The name," he said. "I think it's the reason Volga's dead."

"But Volga didn't have the name," she said.

"He was about to get it."

"This traitor," Lance said, "you think it's someone with the power to take out an operator like Volga?"

Ritter said nothing.

"You think their reach is that long," Lance continued, "that they could get to him here?"

"All I'm saying is that they could be the reason he's dead."

"Who's the traitor?" Lance said simply.

Ritter shook his head. "Forget it. I thought you had a tight operation. Now, I don't know what to think."

"There could be a million reasons Volga was killed," Klára said.

"For all I know," Ritter said, "you two killed Volga."

"Then why haven't we killed you?" Klára said. "You're the source."

"Maybe you're going to," Ritter said, "once you find out what I know and how I found out."

"Maybe we're getting tempted," Lance said.

"That's not helping," Klára said. Two uniformed policemen were entering the station through the front entrance. "We can't stay here," she said. "We're going to attract attention."

"We have an apartment," Lance said.

Ritter shook his head. "I'm not going anywhere with you two."

Lance rounded on him. "Would you cut the shit? You know we're not here to kill you. We didn't even know you'd be here."

"You knew I'd be in the city."

"I've been in your wife's apartment," Lance said bluntly.

Ritter was taken aback. "What did you just say—"

"You were worried about her. You told Langley."

"What are you—"

"You told Langley to send someone. They sent me. I took care of it. Packed her and the kid into a cab and sent them to her sister's place in Bristol."

Klára watched Ritter's face.

"Why are you telling me that?" Ritter said.

"Why do you think?"

"I hope you're not trying to threaten—"

"I'm trying to make friends."

"You think—"

"That makes us friends? Yes, I do."

Ritter shook his head.

"I didn't just pack them away," Lance said. "I told them I was there because of you."

"You told them what?"

Lance nodded. "You heard me."

"Both of them?" he said.

Lance nodded. "The kid was there. I told them both. I needed them to trust me."

"So," Ritter said, his voice betraying emotion for the first time, "they know I'm alive?"

"I didn't say that much," Lance said.

"What did you say?"

"I said the people who'd sent me owed you a debt of gratitude."

"I see," he said. Klára could already see the change in him. The gamble seemed to be paying off.

"Did you..." Craig said, but his voice trailed off before he finished the question.

"Did I what?"

"Nothing."

"Get with her?"

"Did you?"

"Of course I didn't."

"We're not together."

"I didn't lay a finger on her. I just did what I was told."

Klára looked toward the door. The policemen were making their way slowly across the concourse, getting closer. "We really need to go," she said.

Ritter began walking toward the escalators, and Klára hurried after him, followed a few steps back by Lance.

"Where are we going?" she said to Ritter, rushing to keep up with him.

Ritter waited until they were all standing close together on the escalator, then said, "There's something I need to show you."

"Show us?" Klára said.

"You want to know who the traitor is, don't you?"

"Yes," Klára said.

"Then there's something you need to see."

"Why?" Lance said.

Ritter looked back at him. "Because if I don't show you, you won't believe me."

25

Laurel reached the end of the pool and grasped the ledge. She looked at the clock—she'd managed to shave a few seconds off her target time—and caught her breath before pulling herself out of the water. She turned and sat on the ledge, legs dangling, and looked at the water. It was still choppy from the turbulence she'd created, and she stared at it vacantly until it settled. There was no one else there, there never was at that time, and she lay back and stared at the fluorescent half-domes hanging from the ceiling. She had the entire aquatics wing to herself, possibly the entire sports complex, and she listened to the water lap against the side of the pool. There was something about the place—the way the light reflected on the water, the gurgling of the water filters, the warm, humid atmosphere—that gave it all the feeling of a very large isolation chamber. She found it was the only place she was able to relax.

She got up and grabbed the towel from the rack, then went through to the women's changing room. It was empty also, and she took off her swimsuit and stood naked under the water of the communal shower. Her mind was completely blank, quieter than it was anywhere else in the world, and a whole ten minutes passed before the sound of the cleaner entering the changing area pulled her to the present.

"*Buenas tardes, señora Everlane,*" the cleaner said, lifting her mop with a heave and plunging it into the bucket.

"Evening, María," Laurel said, turning off the water.

She dressed in silence and gave María a brief nod as she left the changing room. She walked down the corridor to the entrance of the sports complex but hesitated before opening the door. It was cold outside. She could tell by the crystalline halo around the street lamps, as if particles of ice were suspended in the night air and were reflecting and refracting the light. She did up the zip on her jacket and looked in her bag for the wooly hat she knew was in there somewhere. She found it and pulled it over her wet hair, then hurried across the quadrangle back to the new headquarters building, where her office was located.

It was almost nine, well past the time she should have been clocking off for the night, but she couldn't bring herself to go to her car. It was a bad habit she'd gotten into, sleeping at the office, but she'd found it more diffi-cult to break than she'd have liked to admit. It wasn't about the demands of the job—though being at her desk at all hours of the day and night did have its advantages— it was something else, something personal, emotional, even. When Roth found out what she was doing, he'd insisted on paying for a suite at the Saint Royal.

"It's rented for the month," he'd told her, "and I want you to go there. I've seen what happens to agents who let the job become their life."

But despite his warning, she'd only managed to get

out to the hotel a handful of times. She just couldn't sleep there, or anywhere, for that matter, other than the top-floor office she shared with Tatyana. She didn't know what it was that made her like that, but she suspected a therapist would have a name for it.

She flashed her ID to the guard at the security desk, and he looked up from his sports section.

"Wizards doing any better?" she said.

"Don't get me started," he said as she passed through the scanner.

She walked across the lobby, where another guard, Bryson, watched her from the counter. "Burning the midnight oil again?"

She nodded and, as she pushed the button for the dedicated elevator, wondered what they all made of her. They must have guessed by now that she slept up there. She was there all hours of the day and night, like a ghost haunting the halls of some old manor in England, she thought, or one of those crazy ladies who never left their apartment complex. She'd read recently about a lady in New York who'd died in her bed. No one noticed until the orders she'd placed for cat food went uncollected at the front desk of the building for two days. Was that what she had to look forward to? She already thought the guards looked at her funny when she came down late at night to pick up her takeout orders. She had all the local delivery places on speed dial. If the Kremlin ever wanted to get to her, all they had to do was create an account on one of the food delivery apps she used.

She stepped out of the elevator to be greeted by the Special Operation Group's empty reception desk. Like much of the rest of the sixth floor, the area had yet to be properly set up, and the only things on the desk were the cables that were waiting to be connected to equipment. There were some Bankers boxes on the floor next to the table, and she stepped over them as she made her way through the rows of empty cubicles that still awaited specialists. The entire floor was still a blank slate, unchanged from how it had been when she first took over. She wondered if, under her leadership, the Group would ever regain the stature it had possessed under Roth. As it stood, the only part of the floor that wasn't empty was the conference room, which she and Tatyana had set up as their office, their desks facing the floor-to-ceiling view over the Potomac that had once belonged to Roth.

She entered the office, ignoring the card Roth had left on the corkboard reminding her to call the Recruitment Services Department. They'd help her get the ball rolling, he'd said, referring to the lists the Agency compiled every year of the best and brightest technical graduates at the nation's top universities. The names on those lists were fully vetted and pre-approved for access to classified information, should a hiring director within the CIA's sprawling bureaucracy decide to pursue them. Laurel didn't know where to begin with it. She couldn't imagine bringing strangers into this sanctum of secrecy she and Tatyana had created. And so, the desks remained empty.

She pushed a button on the expensive Italian coffee machine Tatyana had set up for them, then sat down on Tatyana's seat while a perfect Americano poured into her cup from a chrome nozzle. She leaned back and gazed out the window, watching the traffic flow along the George Washington Parkway, one white ribbon, one red, mirroring the contours of the river. The espresso machine chimed, and she brought the coffee to her desk and logged into her terminal. She should have been asleep, she felt exhausted, but sleep was something she'd been finding harder and harder to come by. Instead, she pulled up the last ten reports she'd received from Yuriy Volga and started to pore over them. She'd read them already a million times, but something had led to Volga's capture, and she needed to find out what it was. Otherwise, everyone still in Rostov was at risk of suffering the same fate he had.

She took a sip of her coffee and was about to look up the name of the agent responsible for Volga's arrest when she noticed a flicker of light coming from the Keyhole Satellite Terminal on Tatyana's desk. It was a green light— the highest level of sensitivity and the lowest level of priority—meaning the alert could have been triggered by virtually anything. From an unannounced missile test in North Korea to an unidentified vehicle parked too close to a US embassy in some far-flung capital, the system was triggered dozens of times every day. Laurel had updated her own alert settings since the latest embassy attack in Prague, meaning every single incident being tracked or monitored by anyone within the CIA, the NSA, or the DoD was simultaneously made available on her terminal.

She put down her cup and woke up the monitor. The alert was local, a wealthy suburb north of DC, and she immediately recognized the address. It was in an exclusive enclave typically reserved for diplomats and senior government officials, and the precise house was one she'd been to a number of times before—Levi Roth's expansive mansion. She could see from the metadata that the alert was already being responded to by the CIA's own internal security team, but she rushed to zoom in on the live feed nonetheless. In her haste, she fumbled her coffee cup, spilling it across the desk and onto her white blouse.

"Shoot," she said aloud, pulling the material away from her skin.

She unbuttoned the blouse with one hand while zooming in on the location of the alert with the other. Security agents were already on the scene, and she could see the flashing blue and red lights of their cruisers in Roth's driveway. Without contacting the specialist who'd triggered the alert, she couldn't see exactly what had caused it. What she could see was that its priority level was still set to low, despite having taken place at the home of the director of the CIA.

She picked up her phone and dialed Roth's number. "Tell me you're not at home," she said the instant he picked up.

"No," he said, the tone of his voice beginning to betray some concern. "I'm on my way, though. I just left the command center."

"With your driver?"

"Yes."

"Tell him to stop."

"Why?"

"Is your security detail with you?"

"Of course it is."

"Just tell them to stop, will you? Tell them to take you back to the command center."

"Laurel! Are you out of your—"

"Something's going on. There are agents at your house."

"My house? Why? What is it?"

"I don't know what it is, but I don't want you pulling up before I find out."

She heard him speaking to his driver then. "Harry," he barked, "you get something about a threat at my house?"

"All clear here, boss."

"Harry didn't get anything," Roth said, speaking to Laurel again.

"It's a Keyhole ping," she said, beginning to lose patience. "Can you, for once, just do as I say?"

26

Osip moved uncomfortably in his seat.

"Everything all right?" the pilot said through the radio.

They were in the cockpit of a Mil Mi-24 attack helicopter, a craft designed in the seventies with precisely zero attention to passenger comfort. That was a fact Osip was painfully reminded of with every vibration of its twin Isotov turboshaft engines. "I've been better," he growled through the mouthpiece on his helmet.

The chopper was an eleven-ton behemoth, affectionately known within the Russian military as the Crocodile due to its distinctive camouflage pattern, and the one they were in had been modified to transport high-value personnel. The upgrades included cabin armor capable of withstanding 12.7-millimeter armor piercing rounds, a thirty-millimeter autocannon that could fire eight hundred rounds a minute, and two racks for carrying 9M120 Ataka-V supersonic missiles. It was a formidable piece of hardware, though not immune to rogue surface-to-air missiles, which was why they were flying at such low altitude. Low enough, in fact, that Osip could make out every detail of the seemingly endless forest beneath them, the trees punctuated only very occasionally by a village or railway line.

Osip had initially requested to fly out on his personal Gulfstream G700. It would have been a lot more comfortable, but the request was "Simply out of the question," according to the Western Military District's Air Defense Division. Instead, his chopper was accompanied by a further two, the three to fly in a defensive V-formation, taking turns at the front to mask which one carried the cargo. They'd also ordered the entire route be patrolled by fighter jets from the 7th Aerospace Defense brigade in Rostov.

The precautions seemed overblown to Osip, but then, this was now technically contested air space.

"Contested air space?" Osip demanded, shocked that any territory inside Russia could ever be regarded as contested. It was one more sign, if any were needed, of just how badly this war was going. It was shameful, he thought, an affront to the prestige of the federation, that an internal flight required this degree of precaution. How could Russia claim to be a super power when it couldn't even control its own territory?

He'd accepted the decision, of course, even though he had the power now to overrule the entire Western District command. He had no desire to be shot out of the sky, for one thing, and Millerovo had been struck three times already by the Ukrainians.

"What riles us most," the commander of the Air Defense Division had said, "is that it's our own missiles they're using against us." What he meant was that they were former Soviet stockpiles, OTR-21 Tochkas, sent to Ukraine by Brezhnev over forty years ago to guard against the Americans.

"Our fathers would be turning in their graves," Osip muttered now at the thought.

"What's that, sir?" the pilot said.

"Ukrainians fighting Russians," Osip said. "It's unnatural."

The pilot nodded, straining to see over the nose of the craft.

"Downright fratricidal," Osip added.

"Agreed," the pilot said.

They were slowing down, which Osip took as a good sign. "How much farther?" he said.

"That's the base there," the pilot said, pointing ahead.

Shipenko peered out at it. Even from a distance, he could make out the signs of missile damage. One of the hangars was scorched black, its roof caved in, and an enormous hole in the larger of the two runways had rendered it mostly unusable.

The pilot brought them around the western edge of the base, doing a quick pass of the facility before zeroing in on a landing pad close to the main administrative building.

"Dismal, isn't it?" Osip said.

"What's that, sir?"

He shook his head. "Nothing," he muttered. "Just mind your landing. The last thing we need now is a mishap."

Millerovo was a Russian airbase in the far west of Rostov Oblast, just ten miles from the Ukrainian border.

On the other side was the territory of Luhansk, one of the provinces Molotov was hell-bent on annexing, no matter the cost. Osip's mind turned to the events at the palace. It was another sign, he thought, of the decadence and rot at the core of Molotov's regime. Russia turning on Ukraine. The president executing his generals. The time was ripe to strike.

The chopper touched the landing pad and powered down. Osip remained in his seat.

"Everything all right?" the pilot said.

Osip sighed and braced himself for the discomfort of climbing out of the craft. He'd traveled without his usual retinue of aides so as to keep his footprint as small as possible. It was essential now that he avoided detection by the CIA's satellites. For one thing, President Montgomery had sent an assassin after him personally—that was hardly ideal—but more importantly, he was worried about Roth. He knew he couldn't seize power in the Kremlin without CIA complicity, and Roth's stomach was pretty strong when it came to doing what was necessary, but even he would balk if he realized what Osip had planned.

Osip pulled himself out of the chopper and immediately raised his cane in the air. It doubled as an umbrella, which was one of the reasons he was never without it—it was invaluable for keeping out of sight of prying satellites. He opened it and growled for the pilot to come around and help him. Then they hobbled, arm in arm, toward the administrative building.

Once inside, they found four Air Force cadets in crisp uniforms standing at attention. An officer issued a command, and the cadets saluted in unison. Osip walked in front of them, eyeing each of them carefully. They made no sign of being surprised by his appearance. They'd been warned in advance, he thought.

He let go of the pilot and closed up the umbrella to use again as a walking stick. One of the cadets was a female, and he approached her. "Look at you in your fancy uniform," he said. She remained still as a statue, eyes fixed forward. She couldn't have been more than twenty. "You look just like the real thing," he added. She made no sign she'd even heard his words, but he could smell the fear on her. "In my day," he said, turning his attention to the officer, "there was only one reason we'd let a girl like that onto the base."

The officer glanced at him, only for a second, then fixed his eyes dead ahead. "Yes, sir," he said stiffly.

Osip patted him on the arm like they were friends and said, "I want to see her after my meeting."

"Yes, sir," the officer said again.

Osip redirected his gaze onto the woman. For the first time, she showed a flicker of emotion. It was just a quiver, the twitch of a muscle at the side of her mouth, but it was enough to give Osip a warm thrill. "Now," he said, turning back to the officer, "has my guest arrived?"

"If you're referring to Kolesnikov, sir—"

"Of course I'm referring to Kolesnikov. Is he here?"

"We had a hard time contacting him. His command post was in the Azovstal Steel Plant."

"Did you reach him or not?" Osip said impatiently.

"We did, sir, but it took time. He's *en route* but has yet to arrive. We've prepared the commandant's office for you in the meantime."

"And where is that?"

"If you'll follow me, sir," the officer said, dashing off down the corridor.

Osip took his time in following, there was no need to hurry, and after a few steps, he stopped and turned back. "Hey, cadet," he said, "put something special on under that uniform for me."

27

Roth hung up the phone and tapped it agitatedly against his leg. The last thing he needed now was some shenanigans at his house.

"We just got the ping," Harry said from the driver's seat.

"Ignore it," Roth said. "I'm sure it's nothing."

"It doesn't look like nothing. They want us to go to ground."

Roth turned and looked out the back windshield at the cruiser behind them. It looked conspicuous with its tinted windows and government plates. There was another in front, as well as two DC Metro police cruisers. One of the cruisers had already pulled into the opposing lane to stop traffic and prepare the convoy for a U-turn.

"We're not going back to the bunker," Roth said firmly. "I don't care if the president himself orders it."

"All I know is what they tell me," Harry said, raising his hands and slapping them back down on the wheel in a gesture of futility. "I take my orders from you." That was what he said, but Roth couldn't help but notice that he was slowing to a stop. "What do you want me to do, boss?"

Roth sighed. "This is some false alarm," he said, shaking his head. "I'm certain of it."

The convoy had come to a halt. They were on a quiet two-lane that wound through thickly forested hills. The police cruisers positioned themselves to stop traffic in both directions.

"We can't stay here," Harry said. "Either we go forward, or we go back."

The radio crackled to life. It was the CIA security officer in the lead cruiser, demanding to know what the hold-up was. Harry picked up the radio mouthpiece and said, "Hold on, Mike. Give us a second."

"We've got an order to go back to the bunker posthaste," Mike said.

Harry looked back at Roth, waiting for his order.

"*Posthaste*?" Roth said, rolling his eyes. "We're not going back for a false alarm. Get me in touch with the Office of Security. I want to speak to the lead at the scene."

The road they were on wasn't a busy one, but there were already a few cars getting backed up. One of them honked, and the car behind it jerked out of its lane and made a u-turn, speeding back the way it had come.

Harry got back on the radio and, after a bit of back and forth, managed to get hold of the lead agent at Roth's house.

"This is Lambercy," the man said.

He was young. Roth could hear it in his voice. He said, "This is Director Levi Roth. I hear you're staging an invasion of my house."

"Well, Director, sir—"

"What's going on over there, Lambercy?"

"We're investigating a flag—"

"What flag?"

"Looks like a lawn motion sensor, sir."

"Do you have any idea how often those things are trig-gered? Rabbits, squirrels, even birds set them off. They're the most over-sensitive pieces of crap I've ever seen."

"We just want to make sure there's nothing—"

"That property," Roth said, "is the most secure piece of real estate this side of Pennsylvania Avenue. If you don't see anything, I assure you, it's because there isn't anything there. Take us home, Harry."

Harry put the car back into drive and proceeded around the cruiser that was blocking the lane. The rest of the convoy had to scramble to keep up.

They drove another seven miles to the manicured lawns and electronic gates that characterized Roth's neighborhood, passing ambassadors' residences and consular offices before turning onto his driveway. They stopped at the gate, a six-foot-high, wrought iron barrier in a neoclassical style that was overlooked by six separate security cameras. Already from the gate, they could see reflections of the red and blue lights at the end of the driveway. Four Office of Security cruisers were parked in front of the house, their agents marching around offi-ciously, trampling Roth's impeccably trimmed shrubs.

Harry drove up to the house, passing the full spectrum sensors and cameras that the CIA had insisted on upgrading after Roth was made director. The house itself was enormous, far beyond the means of even the highest government salaries, and it would have raised eyebrows were it not for the fact that it had been in Roth's family for generations. As they approached, Roth saw more law enforcement vehicles. He was out of the car almost before

Harry had brought it to a complete halt. "What's going on here?" he demanded. "Where's Lambercy?"

A man standing at the open front door of the house came running down the steps. "Director Roth, sir. I'm Lambercy."

"Your men are stomping around like a herd of elephants."

"I apologize, sir—"

"Are they *inside* the house?"

"We had to make sure it was clear—"

"And?" Roth demanded. "Is it?"

"The house is, sir, but we're still checking the grounds."

"I've told the security office a dozen times that it's the sensors."

"I'm just following protocol, sir."

"How many times are we going to go through the same song and dance?"

"We'll be as fast as humanly possible."

"What's that noise?" Roth said. He could hear a faint buzz, and as it got louder, he realized it was coming from the sky. "Don't tell me that's a helicopter."

"They've upgraded the protocols for top level—"

"To hell with it," Roth said, throwing up his hands in frustration. "I'm going inside. I take it you don't have any objections to that?"

"Well, sir, we're still—"

"You said the house was clear."

"But—"

"National security will survive my going inside to feed the dog," Roth said before proceeding without waiting for a response.

Inside the house, two CIA security officers were in the

living room, shining their Maglite flashlights around like burglars searching for a safe. There was a third man in the kitchen, and for some unfathomable reason, he had the door of the refrigerator open.

"All clear, in there?" Roth demanded. The man looked up at Roth like a child caught with his hand in the cookie jar. "I'm sorry, sir."

"Does my milk and canned tuna pass muster?"

"Of course, sir."

Roth's mood was rapidly shifting from irritated to angry, and he wasn't in the mood to hide it. "Then get the hell out of my house!" he said. "You too, all of you. Scram!"

The officers hurried out of the house, but they remained in the driveway, continuing their sweep of the grounds until they were completely satisfied. Roth picked up his phone and called Harry.

"Just wait a few minutes, would you, Harry? Make sure these incompetents clear out before you head off for the night."

"Of course, sir."

Roth took off his coat and threw it over the banister of the stairs, then went directly to his office. It was a stately room off the main hallway with dark wood paneling and green leather furniture. There was a grand mahogany desk, a window overlooking the front lawn, and, across the room, a solid door with a pin pad lock. He went to the door and tapped in his pin. It led to a second office, even more ornately decorated than the first, with a computer on a desk. He sat at the desk and woke up the computer by clicking impatiently on the mouse. As soon as the screen came on, he logged into the house security system and scrolled through the myriad sensors installed on the property, trying to find out what had triggered the alarm.

It took him a minute to figure out it was one of the motion sensors in the backyard, close to the swimming pool, and he opened up its activity log. There was a flag indicating that the incident had been recorded on camera, and he opened the footage nervously.

What he saw almost gave him an anxiety attack—not a squirrel, not a rabbit, but what looked to be a small drone. The drone came down low over the patio and, if he was not mistaken, dropped what appeared to be a manilla envelope into the shrub garden next to the pool. "What in the world?" he muttered, immediately leaping to the only conclusion that made sense—Osip Shipenko was trying to get him executed for treason.

He instantly deleted the footage, deleted the motion sensor log, then got up and hurried to the kitchen, where broad patio doors looked out onto the pool area. Security officers were still out there, rooting around the property like golfers who'd lost a ball in the rough. He pulled open the door. "What the hell do you think you're doing out there?" he yelled at the nearest of them.

"Something triggered a sensor back here, sir."

"Get the hell out of my fuchsias before I have your hide," Roth yelled. "Tell your boss if he has a problem with that, he can take it up with my office directly."

28

Osip sat in the chilly little room that served as the commandant's office at Millerovo Air Base. There was a window overlooking the runway, a single pane of glass that did little to preserve what meager warmth the iron heater emitted, and he stood staring through it. Nothing had been done about the missile damage to the runway other than the erection of some orange plastic cones. It was typical, he thought. The Air Force was depriving itself of a valuable runway ten miles from an actively contested zone because it couldn't arrange for a pothole to be repaired. It was no wonder they were losing.

Things would be different soon.

His mind turned to Roth, and he wondered if his little package had arrived yet. He'd certainly be rattled, Osip thought, not only by the contents but also by the method of delivery. He'd purposely dropped it in a way that would trigger security. He needed Roth to be committed. He needed him to have dirt on his hands. He was about to take steps that couldn't be untaken. He was going to make a move on Molotov that would either end in his accession to the Kremlin throne or his death. The last thing he needed was Roth getting cold feet.

There was a knock on the door, and he turned toward it. "Come in," he said. He was expecting Kolesnikov, but it was the cadet from earlier.

She came in timidly, like a mouse entering a lion's den, and in a voice so quiet as to be almost inaudible, said, "I was told you wanted me?"

"Not now," Osip said impatiently. "After Kolesnikov arrives. Is he here yet?"

"I.... I don't know," she stammered.

"Go and find out," he snapped.

She disappeared, and Osip went over to the desk where Kolesnikov's thick file lay open. He picked it up and reacquainted himself with the highlights of a career that had earned the man the nickname, 'The Butcher of Grozny.' In a military that was already known for its brutality to civilians, its willingness to flout international norms, and its absolute contempt for the Hague Convention, Kolesnikov had managed to forge a reputation for himself as a man who was willing to do anything to get the job done. He was a butcher, if ever there was one.

Osip had first heard his name four decades earlier, when the Soviet Union was so bogged down in Afghanistan that it was threatening to pull down the entire country. It was a time when Osip and Molotov were just beginning their careers in the intelligence service, and already, Kolesnikov was making a name for himself. The file read like something from the Second World War and began with a note from his time in Chechnya and Dagestan on how he'd ordered his men to refer to local civilian populations as cockroaches. He'd been apparently desensitizing his troops, a charge that was supported by reports he'd ordered his men to bayonet farm animals and human corpses to get them used to the sensation. The campaign culminated in mass executions of civilians by Kolesnikov's men. The result was a few raised eyebrows in Moscow and then a promotion.

In Chechnya, Kolesnikov doubled down on his strategy of brutality, ordering that hospitals be targeted with cluster munitions. In Ingushetia, cluster bombs were dropped on fleeing refugee columns. There were also reports of him executing his own men—numerous eyewitness accounts from his own soldiers of men being shot for refusing to carry out atrocities. An investigation was opened by the GRU, and Kolesnikov's career could have ended there and then, but an up-and-coming GRU Director named Evgraf Davidov intervened in his defense. Under Davidov's watchful eye, the investigation petered out, the charges were dropped, and Kolesnikov went on to receive another promotion.

Osip flipped through the file. There were photos, taken by a *Kommersant* journalist but never published, of Kolesnikov's men dousing captured enemy militia members in gasoline and setting them on fire. The same journalist, who mysteriously died a few months later in a tragic car accident, also took photos of the brothels Kolesnikov set up in the Gori District. They clearly showed women and girls being corralled at gunpoint into the brothels.

Osip flipped on. The file was over six inches thick, with the largest section being devoted to Kolesnikov's actions in Syria, where he'd been appointed Group Commander. He flicked through hundreds of pages of UN and Red Cross reports, supported by photographs, showing the degree to which Kolesnikov utterly disregarded all international norms and legal constraints. By that time, Kolesnikov was a powerful force within the Russian military and had ceased even pretending to abide by the Geneva Convention.

He was a man on the rise, and it seemed the more atrocities he committed, the higher on the career ladder he climbed. What had initially been regarded by the Kremlin as an alarming disregard for human life came under Molotov's increasingly violent regime to be seen as an asset—a specialized toolset to be called in when needed. "The only war crime," Molotov told his commanders in an early briefing, "is defeat." No one took that more to heart than Kolesnikov, and in that new climate, and with the mysterious backing of Evgraf Davidov, Kolesnikov seemed on a trajectory for military greatness.

It all came to a crashing halt with Davidov's death. It wasn't clear from the file what, precisely, had gone wrong for Kolesnikov. There were clearly sections of the file that had recently been redacted, and Osip could also see the bent staples and torn fragments of paper where pages had been entirely ripped out, but he hadn't been able to figure out precisely what had gone wrong. All he knew was that Kolesnikov had certainly succeeded in making some powerful enemies during his ascent to the top, and his conclusion was that without Davidof's protection, those enemies were intent on knocking him down to size.

To Osip, that presented an opportunity. There was no dog as loyal as the one in need of a new master, and Kolesnikov had managed, in the space of a few weeks, to go from being one of the most powerful men in the Russian Army to commander of a detachment of Chechen mercenaries primarily known for taking on the jobs deemed 'too dirty' for anyone else. Now he was dodging mortars and eating out of a can in some forward operating base near the Azov Steel Plant.

There was another knock on the door, but this time it opened without waiting for Osip's say so. "This better be goddamned worth it," Kolesnikov bellowed as he entered the room. "Who the hell orders a soldier away from the front at a time like this?"

Osip was still standing at the desk, Kolesnikov's hefty file in his hand, and he threw it down on the desk before looking up. Kolesnikov stopped dead in his tracks when he saw what was before him.

"Anatoly Kolesnikov!" Osip demanded as loudly as his mangled voice box allowed. Like training any new dog, it was necessary to assert dominance quickly. "Do you have any idea who you are addressing?"

"Aye," Kolesnikov growled, eyeing him closely, "the one they call dog food."

"They call me Tushonka."

Kolesnikov waved a hand as if batting away a fly. He was a man who looked simultaneously both older and younger than his sixty-five years. He was strong and lumbering, burdened by what appeared to be an excess of muscle—a bull in his prime, ready and willing to charge —but there was also a grizzled, haggard look to him. A result, no doubt, of the eight wars he'd fought in.

Osip took a step toward him. His frail, hobbled form was dwarfed by Kolesnikov's bulk, but it was already becoming clear which of them would be the master. Kolesnikov was silent, and as Osip regarded him, the only sound in the room was that of Osip's labored, nasally breathing. "Why have we never met?" Osip said.

Kolesnikov hesitated, then said, "We're shadow

dwellers, you and I. We only come out of the dark when there's a reason."

Osip nodded. That much was true. They were both creatures that had evolved to survive in an inhospitable environment. Osip had done so by appearing smaller and less dangerous than he really was. He suspected Kolesnikov of having done the opposite. "You gave Davidov a reason, didn't you?"

There was a flash of surprise on Kolesnikov's face. He tried to hide it but couldn't.

Osip nodded. "I'm a noticer of details," he said.

"What details?"

Osip narrowed his eyes. He took another step forward. Kolesnikov was a far sight from some of the official photographs that peppered his file. He'd been a man who took pride in his appearance before. He wouldn't be accused of being handsome by any stretch, that wasn't the point, but perhaps vain would have been fitting. Now, his hair was matted and overgrown, his uniform filthy, and his fingernails black. He looked more like a Chechen bandit than a soldier.

"Not many people would have the gall to insult me," Osip said.

"To your face," Kolesnikov said bluntly.

Osip wasn't sure how to take this. Most people could hardly string two words together when they first met him. "Not to my face," he repeated quietly. "There's a reason for that," he said after a pause.

He expected a response, but Kolesnikov remained silent.

"Do you know why that is?" Osip said.

Kolesnikov shrugged. "Because it's in their nature."

"In their nature not to insult me?"

"In their nature to cower," Kolesnikov said.

Osip nodded. "And that's not in your nature, I suppose?"

Kolesnikov said nothing.

"If they call me Tushonka—" Osip said.

Kolesnikov cut him off. "They call you dog food."

"Do they say anything else?" Osip said.

"They say you are a puppet master."

"Is that right?"

"That you pull strings from your little hole. Make things happen. Like a spider."

"Is that what you think I'm here for today?"

"It is," Kolesnikov said.

"What strings do you think I'm here to pull?"

Kolesnikov looked back over his shoulder in the direction of the Ukrainian territory he'd just come from. "We're losing a war," he said. "A war against a smaller, weaker foe. It's a humiliation. It makes us look weak."

"So I'm here to turn things around?"

"You won't turn things around."

Shipenko let a grin cross his lips. It forced the scabbed skin around his mouth to crack painfully, but it was a sensation he was used to. "And why is that?"

"Because you won't do what's necessary."

Shipenko raised his hand, quick as a viper, and struck Kolesnikov across the face with his open palm. It was a feminine gesture, a woman's strike, but Shipenko had long ago stopped caring about appearances. "You'll learn your place, Kolesnikov."

"We'll see."

"I'm here to give you back what you lost."

"And what's that?"

"Your position. Your power." That seemed to have

gotten his attention. He said nothing. "You're going to turn the tide of this battle," Osip continued. "You're going to target the schools, the hospitals, the electricity plants. You're going to increase the pain of this war, increase the cost, make them feel it so that they lose the will to keep up the fight. There's no pain that's too much for these animals. No punishment they don't deserve. I want you to bring the fight to their homes, Kolesnikov. Bring it to their hearts. Hit them where it hurts. Their women, their girls, their children. Nothing is off the table."

"I command fewer than a thousand—"

"I'll get you men."

"What men?"

"I'll make you commander of the entire invasion."

Kolesnikov hadn't seen that coming. "Officially?" he said, too quickly to mask his interest.

"Full reinstatement as Army General," Osip said. "The whole shebang."

"There will be mutterings within the Kremlin."

"You leave the mutterings to me," Osip said. "I know how to deal with them."

29

L aurel shifted her weight. She was lying on the sofa in her office and couldn't find a comfortable position. For some reason, the building's heat seemed to be on overdrive. She kicked off her blanket in frustration and sat up.

Her computer monitor was on the desk in front of her, and she got up and looked at it. She'd kept a Keyhole Satellite trained on Roth's house at a cost of over a hundred thousand dollars an hour because the old fool was too stubborn to spend the night in the bunker. She still had no idea what had caused the alarm to trigger earlier and was taking no risks. He'd have been mad if he knew, she thought, but she didn't care. The director of the CIA made sacrifices. Privacy was one of them. She zoomed the camera in on the roof of his house, an expanse of terracotta tile that revealed something of the intricacy of the residence. Apart from the outdoor pool, there was also an indoor gym with its own pool in the east wing, as well as an enclosed courtyard that opened onto a private garden.

Laurel panned to the pool, which was heated all winter and glittered now from its underwater lights like a rectangular sapphire. She wondered, if she was as rich as Levi Roth, would she still work for the CIA? It was ill-paid, thankless, decidedly unglamorous when you got down to the nitty-gritty, oh, and it had the added benefit of putting your life at risk. And yet, once you were in, it was difficult to imagine your life anywhere else. It was like a toxic relationship that you knew you should end but couldn't.

She got up and looked at Tatyana's espresso machine. She'd resigned herself to another night of not sleeping, but instead of making herself a coffee, she grabbed the cardigan on the back of her chair and pulled it on over the tank top she'd been trying to sleep in. She also pulled on a pair of yoga pants and some sneakers, then went to the elevator and took it down to the lobby.

When the elevator doors opened, the guard at the night desk, Bryson, looked up at her. It was late, and there weren't many people still in the building. Sometimes, when it was quiet like this, she felt like an old ghost haunting the corridors of an abandoned house.

"Still working?" Bryson said.

"Trying to," she said, glancing toward the window. It was snowing again, and the parking lot looked as desolate as an ice field. "One of those nights," she added.

"Right," he said, looking at her and then away.

She suddenly felt awkward, painfully aware of the fact that she had no reason to be there. There was a Starbucks kiosk across the lobby, but it was shut for the night. "Any deliveries for me?" she said, certain he would see right through the act.

"I'd have called up if there was. You waiting for something?"

"I thought the Pentagon was sending something," she lied pathetically.

Bryson shook his head. "We don't usually get much from them after the ten o'clock courier." He knew that, and he knew she knew it too. They both also knew that a call to the lobby would have been more than adequate to confirm it. But there she was, standing in front of the elevator like an abandoned pet with nowhere else to go. *Turn around,* she told herself. *Turn around and get the hell out of here, you pathetic idiot.* All she had to do was push the button, recall the elevator, and make her escape, but instead, for some reason that defied all logic, she found herself walking over to Bryson's desk. He seemed to be as surprised as she was and straightened himself up in his seat as she approached.

"What are you watching?" she said, nodding at the cell phone he'd propped against the keyboard of his computer.

"Nothing, really," he said. "Some comedy special. Don't tell the boss."

She waved her hand, then felt stupid, it was obviously a joke, and said, "Any good?"

He shrugged. "Better than staring at the walls all night."

She laughed—too aggressively, like a hyena—then found herself leaning on the desk, boobs forward, nipples visible through the thin cotton of her tank top like two grapes on one of those pancake breakfasts made up to look like a face. "I know the feeling," she said.

He looked up at her like he'd thought he was going to say something, but then no words came from his lips. A second passed in silence, then another, and she was just beginning to panic when he saved them both. "Too much time in this place can really get to you."

It was the worst thing he could have said, an unwitting acknowledgment of how desperate this visit was. There was a gun in the holster at his hip, and she pictured herself grabbing it, putting it in her mouth, and putting them both out of this misery. "Totally," she said.

"When I first started nights," he said, "I thought I was going to lose my nut."

"It might be too late for me," Laurel said, letting her cardigan fall off one of her shoulders. Bryson's gaze dropped immediately to her chest. He caught himself, but not before she caught him.

This was what she'd become, she thought—foisting herself on this poor security guard who was just trying to get through his shift. What was she hoping for? A quick romp in the janitor's closet with the buckets and mops and bottles of bleach? The really sad thing was that the answer was yes—that was exactly what she was looking for—and unless Bryson was a lot more innocent than he looked, he knew it. So what was the holdup? There was no ring on his finger. That didn't mean he wasn't attached, but it was a good start. Did he have a girlfriend? Did he just not want her? Was the comedy special on his Netflix app more appealing than her yoga pants and taut tank top?

"Was there something else?" he said.

She almost felt her body deflate. That was it. Thirty years old and she couldn't even entice this dad bod away from his terminal. He was on the clock, for God's sake. The CIA would have been effectively paying him to do it. She began thinking desperately of an escape plan when she felt the vibration of her phone in her pocket.

She pulled it out and unlocked the screen. It was a ping from the Keyhole satellite she'd put on Roth's house. She opened the alert.

Human motion detected by swimming pool.

There was a snapshot generated by the system. She opened it and made out the turquoise rectangle of water. She couldn't see much else.

She looked up at Bryson and gave him an apologetic shrug, like this was going to be an enormous disappointment to him. "Gotta run," she said.

She hurried back to the elevator, got in, and pushed the button repeatedly in an attempt to make the doors shut faster. When she got to her desk, she pulled up the surveillance feed and zoomed in on the pool.

"Hello," she said to herself when she saw the figure. She rubbed her eyes and zoomed in further. If she wasn't mistaken, it was Roth himself who was standing there. He was right by the pool, dressed in a gray robe and matching pair of slippers, and seemed to be staring into the water. A tiny red ember traced a path back and forth from his mouth, and she could almost smell the cigar smoke.

His security detail was nearby, two cars down by the front gate, and she scrolled through their logs. Nothing out of the ordinary there. The last entry was Roth screaming at them to quit trampling his shrubbery. She panned the camera to them, then back to Roth. It seemed there was nothing to worry about, just Roth strolling around like a Hugh Hefner impersonator. She was about to log off when he, almost as if he was aware he was being watched, glanced up at the sky. The satellite she was watching him through was equipped with a near-flawless ninety-four-inch mirror, capable of resolving images with a diffraction of just 0.05 arsecs. It was like watching from ten feet above his head. When he glanced upward, she felt a shiver run down her spine, as if he'd just looked right at her. He hadn't, of course, the satellite was two-hundred-fifty kilometers above him, but she still felt like she'd been caught spying through the keyhole in his bathroom door.

She had her cursor on the button to close the feed, but something stopped her from clicking. She watched, feeling more like a voyeur with every passing second, as Roth finished his cigar and flicked the butt into the grass next. Then, almost imperceptibly, he looked over his shoulder. Was it her imagination, she thought, or had he just checked that he wasn't being observed by one of his guards? Maybe Bryson was right, and she really was losing her nut. Leaning so far forward her face was scarcely two inches from the screen, she zoomed in as close as the satellite's resolution allowed and watched as Roth walked over to the shrubbery by the pool, reached down into the plants, and picked something up.

It took a photo and started the AI-driven resolution optimization process. A moment later, a crisp close-up began to appear, one row of pixels at a time. It was a brown envelope that he'd picked up—an ordinary manilla envelope, the kind available in every office supply store in the country. It couldn't have been there long, not with the weather they'd been having.

"What have we got here?" she said to herself as Roth tucked the envelope inside his robe and went back up to the house. She had the ability to spy inside the house, there were cameras in every room, but accessing any of them automatically triggered a notification to Roth. It was the one concession the CIA had made to his privacy. She didn't want to do that, so she instead picked up her phone and called the one person who would be as curious about that envelope as she was. "Tatyana, it's me," she said when it picked up.

"Laurel?" Tatyana said. "What time is it?" She didn't sound too happy to be receiving the call.

"Did I wake you?"

"You..." Tatyana said, then, "I was in the middle of something."

"Oh," Laurel said, wincing. "Sorry."

"What is it? Why are you calling?"

"I need you to do something."

"Something that can't wait, I presume."

"You presume correctly."

Laurel heard a man's voice in the background. "It's fine, honey," Tatyana said to him, and Laurel thought maybe she was emphasizing her Russian accent a little more heavily than usual. "It's just my work."

"If it's better—" Laurel said, but Tatyana cut her off.

"Don't worry about it," she said. "We were finished anyway."

"Hey," the man protested, but his voice was already fainter.

Laurel pictured Tatyana in a hotel somewhere, or perhaps the man's apartment, pulling on clothes that had been scattered all over the room in the heat of the moment. She said, "I need you to pay a visit to a mutual friend."

30

Ritter led Klára and Lance to the lower level of the station, and they boarded one of the streetcars.

"Where are we going?" Klára said as she boarded, but Ritter ignored the question.

"We should sit separately," Lance said, which they did —Lance at the front of the car, Klára by the doors at the center, and Ritter farther back where he could watch them both. The tram was almost empty, and Klára kept a close eye on anyone who boarded. Her seat faced the aisle, and she looked back at Ritter. He looked away. At the front, Lance sat motionless, his back to both of them.

Outside, the streets passed by as they left the city center. She did her best not to lose her bearings, but it was difficult, given her lack of familiarity with the city. As near as she could tell, they were headed west, and the farther they got, the more industrial and rundown it became. It was fifteen minutes before Ritter stood up and walked down the aisle toward her. He passed her without speaking and waited at the front set of doors near where

Lance was seated. When the tram stopped, they all disembarked.

"What is this place?" Klára said, looking down a deserted platform. They were at a nondescript tram stop in the city outskirts. There was a major arterial road next to them, and they were separated from the passing traffic by a see-through perspex barrier. The cars and trucks sped by on the road, spraying the barrier with brown slush. A sign above the road indicated the direction of Skazka Park and Sovetskiy Rayon. Neither meant anything to her. Across the road, enormous apartment blocks rose out of the morning mist.

"We're waiting for another tram," Ritter said.

They stood, each a few feet apart, the only three passengers at the station. Lance broke the silence by saying, "How did you know we'd be at the train station?"

Ritter looked at him a moment before saying, "What does it matter?"

"It matters," Lance said.

"I don't see the point of talking right now," Ritter said. "How I knew where you'd be is irrelevant."

"It's not irrelevant," Klára said. "He's trying to figure out how compromised we are so we don't all get our asses handed to us."

Ritter looked at her, she knew he could see her point, but he stubbornly refused to speak. She turned to Lance. The expression on his face was no better.

"It would be nice if you two lightened up a little," she said. "Everything doesn't have to be a sparring match."

"It was Volga's notebook, wasn't it?" Lance said, and Klára thought he could have said it with a little less smugness in his voice.

Ritter lit a cigarette, and when the tram pulled in a

minute later, he threw it away without having smoked any of it. They boarded and sat in the same configuration as before. The second ride was shorter than the first and brought them into an increasingly decrepit industrial zone. They weren't just the only passengers on board the tram, it seemed they were the only people in the entire district. The streets were devoid of traffic. The sidewalks were empty. The driver would remember them, she thought. They couldn't see him, he was in an enclosed compartment at the front of the tram, but she imagined there was a camera or mirror or something.

They got off the tram at the edge of an enormous expanse of concrete that seemed to have once been part of a brick-making operation. There were large stacks of broken blocks, and inset into the concrete pavement, tram lines ran directly to the doors of the largest warehouses. All were abandoned, and around them, a rusted chain-link fence enclosed the yard. "This doesn't look good," Klára said, pulling her coat tighter around her shoulders as a gust of wind whipped up through the snow. "We're sitting ducks out here. We're exposed on all sides."

Lance nodded, eyeing the yard like he thought a tiger might at any minute appear. "Nice spot for an ambush, I'd say."

Ritter lit another cigarette, then began walking in the direction of the nearest warehouse as if he hadn't heard their objections.

Klára turned to Lance. The two of them stood looking at each other for a moment, then Lance said, "Fuck this guy," and followed him into the yard. Despite their concerns, they covered the distance to the warehouse without being taken out by a sniper or, for that matter, attacked by a tiger.

"What's inside?" Klára said when they got to the warehouse.

Instead of answering, Ritter put his weight against the enormous sliding door and pushed. It was stiff, but eventually, it moved. Inside was a white Ford Transit van. It didn't look like it had been driven in a while, and a coating of dust lay on the windshield.

Ritter threw Lance a key. "You drive," he said, and turning to Klára, "you sit next to him."

"Where are we going?" Lance said.

Ritter nodded toward the far end of the yard, where an open gate led to a section of street that looked even more abandoned than what they'd seen so far. The street was lined with old factories and warehouses, and somehow weeds had managed to sprout up out of the cracks in the concrete. Their bare branches reached from the snow like the fingers of skeletons.

"What's down there?" Klára said.

"You'll see."

"We'll see?" Lance said.

"Look," Ritter said, "it's like you said. If I'd wanted to ambush you, that yard would have been the place to do it."

"You're not being fair," Klára said. "You expect us to trust you blindly, but you give us nothing?"

"Oh," Ritter said, raising an eyebrow, "I'm going to give you something."

"What?"

"You'll see," he said, and she mouthed the words even as he said them. She was about to argue with him, but Lance had already unlocked the van and was getting into the driver's seat. "Let's keep moving," Ritter said, going around to the back.

Klára bottled up her frustration and got into the van next to Lance. When Ritter showed up from the back, popping his head through the gap between their seats, she reached out and slapped the cigarette that had been in his mouth, breaking it in half and sending ash and embers onto his legs.

He was about to say something, but Lance turned the key in the ignition, and the van's engine patently failed to fire up. The engine whimpered and died, and Lance turned back at Ritter. "It's the battery," he said.

"It's just cold," Ritter said. "Try again."

Lance tried a few more times without luck. "It's going to flood," he said, but as he said the words, the engine fired up angrily, spouting black smoke from the exhaust and vibrating as enthusiastically as an old washing machine entering a spin cycle. He put his foot down to give it gas, and the engine revved wildly.

"Let's go," Ritter said.

Lance pulled out of the warehouse and turned right toward the gate.

"It's not far," Ritter said. "The fourth factory beyond the fence."

Lance drove down the length of the yard, and when they passed the gate, Ritter said, "That one down there. The brown one. Park next to the door."

Lance drove down the street and pulled up next to the door with a yank of the handbrake.

"Kill the engine," Ritter said.

"I'm afraid it will never start again."

"Suit yourself," Ritter said, then he went to the back of the van and got out.

Klára looked at Lance. "Let's leave him here," she said, only half kidding.

Lance smiled, the first time she'd seen him do so, then opened his door and climbed out. He'd left the engine running. She followed him onto a sidewalk that looked like it had been attacked by a jackhammer, and then they both followed Ritter to a rusted steel door at the side of the factory. It was made of solid steel, and Klára was about to ask Ritter how he proposed getting through it when he gave it a light shove. The bolts in the lock had rusted through, and it opened with a loud creak. It led to what appeared to Klára to have been an overseer's office.

Lance entered, followed by Klára, and she found herself mentally rolling her eyes at Ritter's insistence on being third. The office was a mess, full of old desks and cabinets and overturned chairs. Papers, worn with age, were scattered everywhere. The wall opposite them consisted of dozens of panes of glass, almost opaque from grime and dirt, and Klára walked over to it and looked out. The windows overlooked the factory floor, which was about six feet below the level of the office. It had been stripped of its tooling, but steel brackets were still visible on the concrete floor where the machinery had once been.

"What was made here?" Klára said.

"Ship propellors, turbines, engines," Ritter said, "but it was all pulled out years ago."

They followed him out of the office and down a set of metal steps to the factory floor. When they reached the bottom, there was another steel door that led through a cinderblock wall into the area directly beneath the office.

"Don't tell me you're taking us through there," Klára said, eyeing Lance.

"All right, I won't tell you," Ritter said, inserting a small key into the keyhole. The lock opened with a clank, and the door swung open. It revealed a room in complete darkness.

"We're not going in there," Klára said.

Ritter shrugged. "No one's going to force you," he said, stepping forward.

Lance reached out with his hand and stopped him. "Me first," he said, entering the room in front of Ritter.

Ritter went in after him, and an electric light came on with an audible hum. It wasn't an ordinary light, but fitted with a red-colored bulb like the ones used by photographers for processing film. Klára stopped at the door and peered inside. It took a moment for her eyes to adjust to the light, but the stench hit her immediately. It reeked of chemicals and what she thought might be vinegar. "What is that?" she said, covering her face with her hand.

It was Lance who answered. "Film developer."

She waited until she could make out the contours of the room before going in after them. In the center was a group of draughtsman's desks, angled for drawing, and next to them, some flat work counters. There were plastic trays on the counters, like little basins, and the liquid they contained seemed to be the source of the smell. Above the desks, a string had been stretched from one side of the room to the other like a clothesline. A number of paper sheets hung from it.

"Please tell me this is as far as our journey takes us," she said.

"This is it," Ritter said, walking up to one of the desks and pulling open a drawer.

"Easy," Lance said, reaching for his gun.

Ritter stopped, showed Lance his hands, then, moving very slowly, pulled open a shallow document drawer. It contained a number of twelve-by-six-inch black and white photographs.

"What are these?" Lance said.

"Let me preface them by saying the film negatives are hanging on the lines behind me," Ritter said. "It's Kodak Tri-X film, and I used D-76 developer powder and basic Ilford fixing chemical."

"I'm beginning to think they should have called you the riddler instead of the fixer," Klára said.

"What he's saying," Lance said, "is that the negatives can be examined and shown not to have been tampered with."

"That's right," Ritter said. "The images were burned into the negatives when the photos were taken. Whatever else we end up debating, no one can say these photos were edited after the fact."

"So, let's see them," Klára said.

"If you look at these," Ritter said, "you're going to be in the same boat I am."

"And what boat is that?" Klára said.

"The boat that got Volga and Vilgotsky killed."

"Let's see them," Lance said.

"Don't say you didn't ask," Ritter said, handing the photos to Klára. She looked at the first. It seemed to have been taken through a window, perhaps from a distance, but a zoom lens had been used, and the focus was crystal clear. It showed two men standing in an office, one with his back to the window and the other facing it. The man with his back to the window couldn't be identified, but the man he was speaking to was clearly visible. He was older, good-looking, dressed in a tailored suit.

She looked at the next picture. Same office, same angle, but the men had moved positions. There was another clear view of the man in the suit. The man he was with was out of frame. He'd been partially blocking the view of the room in the last picture, and she could see more details of the office now. It was fairly ordinary. A computer and phone on a desk. Clearly Russian from what she could see of the fixtures.

She flicked to the next photo and then stopped. Her mouth opened.

"What is it?" Lance said.

She looked at Ritter, a knowing look on his face, then, without uttering a word, she handed the photo to Lance.

Lance looked at it and had the same reaction she'd had.

"Recognize him?" Ritter said.

"Osip Shipenko," Klára said. She handed the rest of the photos to Lance. "Did you take these?" she said to Ritter.

Ritter shook his head. "No. I was sent the negatives. I've run some tests, but Langley can run their own if they want. As far as I can tell, these photos are real."

"Who sent them?" Klára said.

Ritter shrugged.

"Oh my God!" Lance said suddenly.

Klára looked at him and was shocked when she saw the expression on his face. He looked like he'd literally just seen a ghost. "Lance! What is it?"

He was looking at the very first photo she'd looked at. The one of the man in the suit.

"How is this possible?" he stammered.

She turned to Ritter, who had that same smug look on his face he'd had earlier, only this time multiplied by a thousand. "Now do you see?" he said triumphantly. "Now, do you understand why I don't know where to turn?"

31

R oth stared into the water of the swimming pool as if he believed he might find some solace in it. He did not. The truth was, he was shaken. Osip should have known better. Coming there, to his house, with all the surveillance the place was under, it was enough to make him wonder if he was trying to get him in trouble. Was Osip purposely trying to scare him? In Roth's experience, fear was a form of leverage GRU officers were very adept at.

He knew where the envelope was, indeed, he could see it from where he stood. It was a miracle the security guys hadn't noticed it. He glanced upward toward the satellites he knew were monitoring the property, then over his shoulder toward the floodlit house.

"Fuck it," he muttered, flicking away his cigar. He walked over to the plants and snatched the envelope from the ground, then stuffed it into his robe and strode back to the house.

He entered the kitchen and shut the patio door firmly behind him. He'd put a Cat Stevens record on the phonograph earlier, but the music had stopped, and he could hear the crackling of the needle on the dead wax. He went through to the sitting room and turned the record over, then poured himself a scotch. With a sigh, he looked around the room. The security officers hadn't disturbed much during their sweep, but he could tell they'd been there. There were scuff marks on the white marble floor in the hallway, and someone had turned over the corner of the eighth-century Persian rug in front of the fireplace. He walked over and corrected it with his foot. There was a fire burning, and he stood next to it for a moment, staring into the flames before taking his scotch over to the sofa.

"All right, Osip," he muttered as he sat down. Then, taking a large swig of scotch, he ripped the top off the envelope and tipped the contents onto his lap. What he found was a collection of documents and photographs, not originals, but hastily made copies. The photos were on ordinary printer paper, the ink dark and blotchy. The first was a scaled-down rendering of a Russian army map. Roth had a rudimentary knowledge of Russian and could just about decipher the place names and grid reference. It was a 1:5000 rendering, detailed enough to show the outlines of individual buildings and topographical features, and seemed to show a large industrial facility with barge access to a dock, as well as a rail connection. In a blank white box in the corner, someone had written by hand, "Taganrog Metallurgical Plant."

Roth read the name aloud. He knew of the place. It was one out of the literally hundreds of industrial facilities across Russia that had been linked to the military. As far as he knew, it hadn't been connected to anything too interesting lately.

He noticed that someone had drawn circles around

some of the buildings on the map, and he flipped through the next few documents. They were grainy black-and-white photographs. The labels had coordinates written in by hand, and he could tell they were detailed shots of the plant. They showed roads muddied by slush and melt, dying plants and trees, and enormous smokestacks billowing fumes into the air. They also showed that security at the plant had been upgraded dramatically. There were pillboxes at the entrances, guard towers watching over chainlink fences topped with razor wire, and between the rows of fencing, armed soldiers patrolled the scrubland on foot, accompanied by dogs.

He continued to flip through the documents. There was a map of the region, showing Taganrog as well as the larger city of Rostov-on-Don. By Roth's estimate, the plant was about twenty miles west of the city along the coast.

Between some blank sheets of paper, he found a collection of photos that had been printed on actual photographic paper. They were clearer, and he saw, on the first, a bird's eye view of a long freight train pulling what appeared to be at least forty or fifty flatcars. Between each of the flatcars were huge, protective bulkheads. It looked like the train was transporting military equipment. The next shot was closer, and he could see that it was military trucks that the train was transporting. He could also see that the train was pulling into the Taganrog facility. It was a strange place to be bringing equipment, he thought, though he didn't know enough about Russian equipment movements in the region to be able to tell for sure. The next few photos showed more of the same, the train cars from different angles, zoomed-in shots of the trucks they were carrying, and detailed shots of the freight station at Taganrog.

There was another pile of copied documents then, and as Roth deciphered the script, he realized they were spec sheets for the Iskander short-range ballistic missile system. There was no mistaking it. It was there as clear as day—9K720 Iskander. Roth was more than familiar with the system, an important element of Russia's mobile missile delivery capability. Its NATO reporting name was SS-26 Stone.

He leaned back on the couch and took a long sip of scotch. The Iskander system was nothing to be scoffed at and had caused more than a few headaches during the Pentagon strategy sessions he'd sat in on recently. The trucks on the flatcars, which he realized now were Iskanders, were capable of launching and guiding rockets with extreme accuracy at ranges of up to three hundred miles. Depending on the missile, hypersonic speeds of up to Mach 5 were not out of the question. They may not have been quite as accurate as the best competing NATO systems, but they weren't far off. The issue that concerned Roth most about them, and that came up time and again in the Pentagon briefings, was the subject of the next photo.

It was a zoomed-in picture of one of the missiles that were being transported with the Iskanders. On the side of the missile, stenciled by hand with white paint, was written 9M723. He'd seen the signature before and got up immediately, and went to his secret office. He reached beneath the desk to where a hidden button had been placed and pressed it. There was a clicking sound from the bookshelf behind him, lined as it was with antique leather-bound tomes, and one of the books moved slightly forward. He pulled the book, and the entire section of the bookshelf came forward and moved out of place to reveal a safe. The safe was accessed with an old-fashioned combination dial, and he turned the dial to enter his code. The door opened, and he took out some files.

He brought the files back to the living room and picked up again the photo he'd been looking at. The stencil in the photo read 9M723, and he flipped through the file until he found it. According to the CIA file, based on the best intelligence available from across NATO, the estimated range of the 9M723 was 415 kilometers. He could see now from Shipenko's spec sheet that the actual range was closer to 500 kilometers. They were also capable of speeds of up to Mach 7, with a flight altitude as high as fifty kilometers or as low as six. The missiles were capable of control at all stages and were not bound to a traditional ballistic flight path. They were stealth capable, as well as capable of intensive evasion maneuvers as they approached their target, making them extremely difficult to intercept with anti-ballistic systems. Roth knew the anti-missile defenses currently in place in Ukraine had little chance of intercepting them. Most worrying of all, the spec sheet confirmed that the 9M723 was capable of delivering a nuclear payload of up to fifty kilotons equivalent.

Roth let out a sigh as he looked at the next photo. It was similar to the one previous, although this time, the stenciled code on the side of the missile was 9M728. He flicked through Shipenko's spec sheets until he found them. These were the 'K' variant of the previous missile, the letter K standing for the Russian word *Krylataya*, or 'winged'. The missile was similar to the previous version, although it flew at lower altitudes and was capable of following terrain relief in flight. That meant it would automatically follow valleys, fly over hills and mountains, and be capable of even more drastic evasion maneuvers. Again, it was designed for carrying a tactical nuclear warhead with a payload of up to fifty kilotons.

Roth threw down the documents and leaned back on the couch. This was about as bad as he could have feared. The Russians were putting themselves in a position to use tactical nukes in Ukraine. From what he could tell from the graphs and charts in the documents, the yields of the tactical nukes would be between five and fifty kilotons. When it came to yields, those weren't very large numbers. The strategic nuclear warheads developed by both the US and the Soviets during the Cold War typically had yields of up to twenty-five thousand kilotons. The largest weapon of all, the Russian Tsar Bomba, tested by the Soviets over Severny Island in 1961, had a yield of fifty thousand kilotons. In comparison to fifty thousand, fifty didn't sound like very much. Five sounded paltry. But the numbers could be misleading. The bombs dropped by the United States over Hiroshima and Nagasaki, Little Boy and Fat Man, were in the five to fifty range. The explosion that had destroyed much of downtown Beirut just a few years prior was the equivalent of just one megaton. If Russia used those tactical nukes, it would change everything. Not only would it prove decisive in the war against Ukraine, but it would also let the nuclear pandora out of a box it had been successfully kept inside since 1945.

It was difficult to see the Ukrainians continuing their fight in the face of tactical nukes. Not only would their battlefield units be defenseless against them, but Molotov had repeatedly shown his willingness, even eagerness, to go after civilian targets. Key infrastructure, residential areas, entire districts of cities would be on the table. The Ukrainians were brave. They'd been fending off the Russian forces successfully. In many ways, they were winning. But no country, at least not since the Japanese at the end of World War Two, had been forced to fight off a nuclear assault. Roth didn't think the Ukrainians would hold up much better than Emperor Hirohito had.

The picture painted by the documents in the envelope was clear. President Molotov was moving vast quantities of equipment, including Iskander launchers and battle-field tactical nukes, to within striking range of the front lines in Ukraine.

Roth drained what was left in his glass and got up to refill it. There was an internal GRU docket stapled to the last page of the spec sheets. It was printed on thin, shiny paper, reminiscent of old fax paper, and Roth noticed that someone had gone to the trouble of writing an English translation on the back with a ballpoint pen.

- Head of Operation: Valeria Smirnova
- Lead on Intercept: Roman Gazzaev
- Target of Intercept: Suspected CIA asset Yuriy Volga
- Status of Target: Dead

Roth read the words and repeated the name Yuriy Volga to himself. He felt a pang of guilt. It was one of the names he'd given to Shipenko. It appeared Volga was the one who'd originally compiled all this data, sourced the photographs, and discovered that the nukes were being transported to the front. The information would have been destined for Laurel's desk had it not been inter-cepted by Shipenko beforehand.

Too bad for Yuriy Volga, Roth thought. The Cat Stevens record had reached the end of the side and was spinning in the run-off again. He got up to turn it over when he felt the vibration of his phone in his pocket. He looked at the screen and saw that it was a message from the security detail at his front gate. He answered and said, "What is it now?" making zero effort to hide his impatience. "It's after midnight."

"I know, sir," the agent said. "I'm sorry to call so—"

"Has something happened?"

"No, not really, sir. Nothing to be concerned—"

"Then out with it, for God's sake."

"It's a caller, sir. She won't take no for an answer."

"A caller?"

"She says she works with you."

"Laurel?"

"No, sir. The other one. The Russian."

"Tatyana?"

"She's saying that you wouldn't turn her away."

"At this time of night?"

"That's what I told her, sir. I'll send her away."

What was going on, he thought. What was Tatyana doing there? A visit out of the blue like this, at this time of night, it was unprecedented. He looked down at the spread of incriminating documents on his coffee table and wondered if it was possible that her unannounced visit was a coincidence. He'd been around the block too many times to give that thought any credence.

"Tell her to give me a second," he said, gathering up the papers and photos, as well as the envelope itself and even the CIA files he'd taken from the safe and bringing them over to the fire.

"Then send her up?"

"Send her up," Roth said with a sigh, throwing the documents one at a time into the roaring flames of the fire. As he watched the flames take hold, he wondered what possible pretense Tatyana could have for this intrusion.

32

Tatyana drove up Roth's driveway and, not for the first time, couldn't help but be impressed by the surroundings. The place was more like an exclusive five-star hotel than a home. Even the driveway, paved in brick and ending in a perfect circle with a fountain at the center, exuded wealth and class. From what she knew of Roth's family, all the pomp had been his grandfather's way of overcompensating for being excluded from the city's elite society of the time. That attitude still seemed fitting somehow, for even though Roth had risen to the top echelon of the nation's intelligence service and met personally with the president on a regular basis, Tatyana knew he still viewed himself as an outsider. At his insistence, his position within the CIA, and his importance within President Montgomery's cabinet, was kept under wraps so he could retain as low-key a profile as possible. Even when she'd gone out for dinner with him —Roth was fond of going to expensive restaurants—the staff never seemed to know he was anything more than a big tipper with a weakness for pretty waitresses.

Tatyana liked him—liked his style, liked working for him. It couldn't have been a bigger contrast from her work at the GRU, where her superiors had been lecherous predators, one and all. There, if she hadn't been worrying about them getting her killed, she was constantly trying to keep them out of her pants. Working for Roth wasn't like that. He treated her and Laurel as equals. He respected them. Or seemed to.

That was why she had such mixed emotions as she pulled up next to Roth's three-car garage. She'd trusted Roth. She'd trusted him implicitly. She'd thought that her days of fearing her superiors were behind her. And now, here she was, sent by Laurel to, as far as she could tell, spy on Roth and find out what he was up to. Apparently, he'd found an envelope in the garden behind the house, and Laurel was sure it was something fishy.

Before getting out of the car, she gave herself a quick glance in the mirror, touched up her lipstick, then opened the top three buttons of her blouse. She knew what she was doing, of course, falling back on the old skills she'd developed in the GRU as a professional honeytrap, and the thought that she was now trying to use those techniques on Roth was mildly nauseating. She closed back up one of the buttons, then stepped out of the car. As she walked up to the front door of the house, she was very aware of the discrete cameras that seemed to hum to life as she approached. The sensors detected her presence, of course, and every camera within range turned silently to focus on her. She did her best to ignore them and rapped firmly on the solid oak door.

She waited a minute, wondering what sort of mood Roth would be in, when the door swung open.

"Boss," she stammered, suddenly at a loss for words.

It was a ridiculous situation. Surely he knew why she was there and would clear up the matter in an instant. That was what she expected at least, looking at his familiar, fatherly face. He looked relaxed, as far as that went—dressed in slippers and a luxurious cashmere robe with a glass of scotch in his hand—but he didn't say anything. "I just came—" she said before he put her out of her misery.

"Tatyana! What a surprise."

"So sorry to drop by so late," she said.

He invited her inside, and she stepped into the hallway. She'd been there on numerous occasions, but the place never failed to impress her, with its checkered marble floor and hundred-bulb chandelier hanging overhead. "I won't pretend this isn't out of the ordinary," she said once he'd shut the door.

"Come," he said as if he hadn't noticed.

She followed him into the living room, where a large fire was raging in the hearth, and a very expensive-looking phonograph was playing a record. "Nice music," she said.

"Are you a fan?"

She didn't recognize the music but nodded anyway. He went over to the machine and turned down the volume, then turned back to face her.

"Well," she began, searching for words. She knew that whatever she told him would ring hollow. If he really was up to something, he would know already that he'd raised suspicions. If he wasn't, he'd think she and Laurel were losing the plot. "The thing is," she started again, still struggling to find something to say that would sound even remotely believable, "Laurel was worried."

"Laurel?" he said, arching an eyebrow in a way that made her even more worried.

"The alarm earlier, they still haven't figured out what triggered it."

"Oh, it happens all the time," he said, waving a dismissive hand.

"Usually, she'd have spotted the culprit on one of the full-spectrum cameras," Tatyana said. "A heat signature or something."

Roth shrugged, apparently uninterested in whatever it had been. "Can I offer you something?" he said. "I have a nice bottle of Chardonnay chilling."

"How about a little of what you're having?" she said.

"Quite right," he said, going to the bar and pouring some scotch from the crystal decanter into a glass. "Ice?"

"Heaven forbid," she said, knowing the answer would please him.

He came over and handed her the glass, then indicated for her to take a seat. She looked around. The room was like the cocktail bar of a fancy hotel, and she sat on a plush purple velvet sofa next to the fire.

Roth took a seat in an armchair facing her, and she looked down at the amber liquid in her glass. It really was an awkward atmosphere. Popping by for a visit like this was not their normal dynamic. Him pouring her a scotch wasn't their normal dynamic. Sexual tension, she was beginning to remember, wasn't part of their ordinary repertoire either. She found herself doing up another of the buttons on her blouse while he leaned forward in his chair and watched her intently.

What could she say, she wondered, that could possibly make this visit seem anything but ludicrous?

Roth spoke first, however. "Whatever triggered the alarm, it doesn't seem to be still around."

"No," she said, nodding. "I think we can safely say the coast is clear."

She thought he was going to ask her then what the real reason for her visit was, but instead, he motioned toward her glass. "You haven't had a sip."

"No," she said, bringing the glass to her mouth, but as soon as she smelled the whiskey, she pulled it away. "Good grief," she said.

Roth let out a little chuckle.

"What is that? Paint thinner?"

"There are men on Islay who'd have your tongue for that."

"Islay?"

"Scotland," Roth said.

"It smells like turpentine," she said, putting the glass on the coffee table.

Roth was amused. "Iodine, I think, would be the more accurate description."

"How do you drink it?"

Roth shrugged and took another sip. "You get used to it."

"Have mine," Tatyana said. "I wouldn't mind taking you up on the Chardonnay if it's not too late?"

"Of course," Roth said, pulling himself out of his seat.

He went to the kitchen, and the instant he was out of sight, Tatyana began scanning the room. She stood up and quickly glanced over the bookshelves, the furniture, the cabinet by the wall holding the exquisite hi-fi system. The speakers were mahogany boxes with tweeters the size of an old gramophone horn. There was no sign of a manilla envelope, though. There was a desk by the window, not Roth's main desk by any means. She'd been in his office across the hall, where he had a much larger desk, but she didn't dare venture that far now. She hurried to the desk and opened the first few drawers. There was a deck of cards and some old candles in the first. A pack of safety matches in the second. She heard Roth returning and hurried back to her seat, making it as far as the fire before Roth entered.

She stared into the flames as if that was the reason she'd gotten up, and he stood in the doorway looking at her.

She looked at him, then back at the fire. She'd thought it was wood that was burning, but she could see now that it was fed by gas, which entered the chamber from a little brass spigot. What she'd thought were logs were, in fact, replicas, and beneath them, on the slate hearth, was the unmistakable gray ash of burned paper.

"Why are you here?" Roth said then, finally deciding to end the charade they'd both been playing at.

Roth was a man Tatyana trusted with her life. Indeed, her life was in his very hands every day that she continued to work for him. There were very powerful men within the GRU who would have liked dearly to get their hands on her throat and squeeze it until she stopped breathing. The only thing between their bony fingers and her neck was Levi Roth. But looking at him now, standing in the doorway in his robe, a glass of wine in his hand, she felt a chill of fear run down her spine.

"I told you," she said, remaining by the fire.

"You said Laurel was worried about the alarm."

"Yes."

His face was unmoving, unreadable. "Is there something else?" he said, stepping forward to offer her the glass.

She was going to reach for it but then didn't. "Perhaps," she said, "I've overstayed my welcome."

He was standing in the doorway, where he remained for an instant before stepping back to let her pass.

"I'll show myself out," she said. She hurried to the door and fumbled with the latch. In her haste, she kept letting it slip, and Roth had to help her with it.

"Such a hurry to leave," he said as she slipped out the door.

"Levi, I'm sorry about all this," she said as she got into her car. He said nothing but remained at the front steps while she drove down the driveway.

She flashed her lights at the secret service guys, but the electrical gate still hadn't opened by the time she reached it. She came to a halt and opened her window.

"Everything all right, ma'am?"

"Fine," she said hurriedly to the agent.

He was holding a tablet, and he looked down at it, no doubt waiting for word from Roth to open the gate. Then he waved at one of the other guards, and the gate began to retract. Tatyana pulled forward onto the road and called Laurel.

"Well?" Laurel said.

"Well, what? That was the stupidest thing you ever sent me to do."

"What do you mean?"

"It was awkward as hell, Laurel. What were you thinking, sending me there?"

"Why was it awkward? There was a security breach at his house earlier. We needed to set our minds at ease."

"He had no idea what the hell I was doing there. There was no sign at all of the breach."

"And the envelope?"

"I don't know," Tatyana said. "It might have been his newspaper delivery, for all I know."

"I saw him picking up a manilla envelope," Laurel said.

"Well, I didn't see any sign of it," Tatyana said, though even as she said it, she pictured the ash in the fireplace.

"I wasn't imagining it," Laurel said. "There's something going on. I can feel it."

"Tell me again what you think you saw?"

"I don't *think* I saw anything. I know I did."

"Saw what?"

"He was in his backyard."

"And?"

"He was smoking a cigar. Looking at the water in the pool. Acting relaxed."

"Did it cross your mind that maybe he was relaxed?"

"He knew exactly where to go—"

"Because he looked pretty relaxed to me, Laurel. He was in his pajamas, for Christ's sake."

"He went to the shrubs by his swimming pool and picked up an envelope."

"Even if he did—" Tatyana said, thinking again of the ash in the hearth.

"He did!" Laurel said, more insistently than Tatyana would have expected.

"It could have been anything," Tatyana said.

"Delivered by God knows who, straight into the bushes behind his kitchen?"

"What do the cameras show?" Tatyana said. "If someone broke in and delivered an envelope, the cameras would have surely—"

"They show nothing."

"What do you mean? How can they show nothing?"

"The cameras start recording when triggered by movement. Birds, animals, leaves, even shadows from clouds can trigger them."

"And you're saying someone came into Roth's backyard and delivered a package without triggering the cameras?"

"I can't be certain," Laurel said, for the first time beginning to sound defeated. She said nothing for a moment, then said, "I don't know. It doesn't make sense, I guess. One motion sensor was triggered. That's all I know for certain from the security logs. Maybe I am losing my mind."

Tatyana was quiet, then she said, "No, I think you saw what you saw."

"What do you mean?"

"There was ash in the fireplace in his living room."

"Ash?"

"I've seen enough hastily destroyed documents in my day to know what it looks like. Ash, and the curled-up plastic film you get when you burn photographs. It was in his gas hearth."

"You're certain?"

"No," Tatyana said, "but that's what it looked like."

"He received an envelope, then burned the contents when he knew you were coming?"

"He could have," Tatyana said, feeling traitorous for even thinking the worst of Roth. Then she said, "So, a single motion detector was triggered?"

"Yes," Laurel said. "Very near where I saw him pick up the envelope."

"But the cameras didn't come on?"

"I guess not. There's nothing there from that time."

"How is that possible?" Tatyana said. "For a motion

sensor to pick up movement, but for a motion-triggered camera not to pick up any visual of the movement?"

"I don't know," Laurel said, then, thinking better of the answer, corrected herself. "Unless the records have been tampered with."

"Could Roth delete footage from the cameras?"

"Yes," Laurel said. "It's his house. He's the director of the CIA. He has access to everything."

"Could you find out if he tampered with the record?"

There was a moment's pause while Laurel typed on her keyboard, then she said, "It's here, Tatyana."

"What is?"

"Roth logged into the database as soon as he got home."

"Can you see what he deleted?"

"No. I can't even confirm for certain that he deleted anything. But I can see he accessed the system."

"That's something."

"Yes, it is."

"Something indeed."

33

Osip was seated at the desk in the commandant's office, he'd commandeered it for the duration of his stay at Millerovo, and he was none too happy. He'd been intending on going back to Moscow as soon as he'd finished with Kolesnikov, but now that Roth said an assassin was after him, he'd decided that staying out in the field was safer. Only his closest circle knew he was there, and he'd been careful to avoid being picked up on satellite.

He picked up the phone and waited for the operator. There was no one there, and he pressed the switch a few times impatiently.

"Mr Shipenko?" a voice said hurriedly. "How can I help?"

"You can pick up the phone, for one thing."

"Terribly sorry, sir, but we don't usually—"

"It's your one job, near as I can tell."

"Yes, sir. Of course."

"If you want to keep it, then be quicker next time."

"Yes, sir. How can I help?"

"Send me in a maintenance guy."

"Is there something wrong with your office?"

"Where to begin?"

"I beg your pardon, sir?"

"The window, for one thing. It's freezing."

"The window? I'll send a crew right away, sir."

Osip hung up, slamming the receiver harder than was necessary, and pulled his coat more tightly around his shoulders. He looked at the mess of papers and maps on his desk and shook his head. The more reports that came in, the worse the picture of the invasion seemed to get. What he was seeing now were firsthand field reports from actual commanders on the ground, not the usual sanitized drivel that was sent to Moscow, and he could see why Molotov was having generals executed on his lawn. The situation was on a knife edge. If things kept going the way they were, it wouldn't be long before Russia was losing ground they'd annexed in Crimea years ago. The Russian Army was bleeding, casualties were mounting at an incredible pace, and Osip was beginning to fear that if he didn't act fast, Molotov wouldn't be in power long enough for him to enact his coup against him.

The latest report said they'd just lost eight more villages on the east bank of the Dnipro. He pulled open a map and found them. The picture was startling.

He picked up the phone again, and this time the answer was immediate. "Sir, a maintenance crew has been summoned—"

"Get me Kolesnikov."

"He's already on his way back to the front, sir. The convoy just left."

"Then get the convoy to turn around," Osip growled and hung up again, slamming the receiver even harder than before.

He looked around the room, then heaved himself out of his seat and went to the window. There were jets on the one runway that hadn't been rendered unusable, and they looked like they were preparing to take off. They were Sukhoi SU-34's, the *crème de la crème* of the Russian Air Force. In the thirty-two years since the first prototypes came off the production line, the Russian aerospace industry had managed to produce just 140 of them at the cost of fifty million dollars apiece. Osip, and every other GRU officer in Moscow, was painfully aware that in the first thirty-six hours of the invasion, thirty of them had already been lost. Even with the expedited production schedule that President Molotov had just approved, the country was on track to produce just fourteen replacement jets over the next twelve months. And the sad thing, Osip thought, was that the damn things weren't even being used for the precision strikes they'd been built for. So much had been made of the aircraft's vaunted tactical capabilities, including its counter-fire and electronic warfare counter-measures, but Osip knew that the planes he was watching now were destined for nothing more than blind, brute force bombing runs. They would be firing raw, non-precision munitions at large, low-value civilian targets such as apartment buildings.

It was yet another sign of Molotov's increasing desperation. Every time the Ukrainians made an advance or successfully targeted an important Russian military target, the president responded by lashing out at easy, low-value targets in Ukraine, such as schools, hospitals, and residential neighborhoods. It was effective at creating fear and terror among the Ukrainians, especially those subjected to an assault, but it was of practically zero military value, and everyone knew it. It was a sign of impotence. A sign of weakness.

Osip went back to his desk and picked up a thin blue document folder. It was the personnel file of the cadet, and he opened it and looked at her photo. The girl's name was Yelena Klishina, and she'd been born in nearby Shakhty just twenty-one years ago. Scarcely more than a child, Osip thought, licking his crusty lips with his brown, withered tongue. She wasn't a perfect match, he thought, looking more closely at the black and white photo in the file, but she would do, especially if she made just a few simple changes. He picked up the phone again and said, "Send in the cadet," then hung up before they could respond.

A moment later, there was a knock on the door.

"Come in," he said, rising from his seat.

The door opened hesitantly, and the young lady appeared.

"Don't be scared, Yelena," he said, beckoning her into the room. "It won't do you any good, in any case."

She flinched when he said her name but did as she was told, shutting the door behind her.

"Yelena," he said again, and again she seemed to flinch. "It's so lovely to see you."

She said nothing, but stood there, still as a statue, her face as white as marble. He looked at her closely, she'd changed little since the photo in her file had been taken, but there were a few details he noticed now that he hadn't before. If he was not mistaken, she had a faint smattering of freckles on her cheeks, and he got up and walked around the desk to get a better look. She wanted to recoil from him—of course she did, they all did—but to her credit, she held her ground. He leaned in close, then licked his finger and rubbed it on her cheek.

She gasped but stood firm, and he wiped the makeup he'd removed from her cheek onto his pants. He'd been right. She did have freckles.

"Sir," she gasped breathlessly, the fear in her voice palpable.

He reached into his breast pocket and removed a very old, aged photograph. It was a photo he'd carried with him almost his entire life. He held it tenderly, then showed it to her. "This," he said, "is a picture of someone very important to me."

Yelena nodded, uncertain of what he was trying to tell her.

"As you can see, she looks not so unlike you."

Yelena nodded again.

"You can't tell from the picture, but her hair leans toward red, just as yours does."

More nodding.

"She's seventeen in this picture, a few years younger than you, but you have that look about you, don't you, Yelena? That coquettish, nymphet look."

"I don't know, sir."

"Oh, you know what I'm talking about. You know exactly what I'm talking about," he said, and he reached up and took her chin in his hand, forcing her to look at him.

She wanted to look away, he could see the fear in her eyes, but she didn't dare do it. She held his gaze, and as their eyes locked, he felt the thrill of excitement rush through his body.

"The bathing suit," he said, "is persimmon."

"Persimmon?" Yelena said uncertainly.

"It's a shade of orange, and it's very important that you find one just like it."

"Find one, sir?"

"That's right, Yelena. I want you to go and transform yourself, as best you can, into a match of this picture."

"Sir, I think there's been some sort of—"

"Misunderstanding? I don't think so. I know what I want, and I know you understand the repercussions that might come about if I don't get it."

"*Repercussions*, sir?"

"Your poor old grandmother, for example. Think how hard it would be for her if the police in Shakhty were to pay her a visit."

"Pay her a visit? My grandmother?"

"I think we understand each other, Yelena."

Her face was panic-stricken, terrified, but she retained her composure and managed to nod her head.

He grabbed her chin again, pinched her cheeks so as to force her plump, red lips to pout, and was about to plant his mouth on them when the phone started to ring.

He looked at it, then back at her. "Go on then," he said. "Find the bathing suit, go to Rostov if you have to, have it made if you have to, but find it. Persimmon orange. I'll come calling on you soon enough."

He waved her away and went back to his desk, waiting for her to leave before raising the receiver to his ear. "What is it?" he said.

"Kolesnikov's convoy is back, sir. It's entering the base now."

"Good," Shipenko said. "Tell them I'll be going with them."

"Going with them, sir?"

"That's what I said, isn't it?"

"But the security situation—"

"Go," he snapped. "Now."

"Yes, sir. I'll let them know right away."

34

Lance chewed his lip and stared blankly across the room at the old four-burner stove. They were back in the apartment, him, Klára, and Ritter, and the photographs Ritter had shown them were on the counter in front of him, sitting in a neat stack. The sun had gone down, and the light in the kitchen was off. The only light came from the window, moonlight, tinged blue by the fluorescent street lamps.

"You look pensive," Klára said, entering the room. She spoke softly, Ritter was sleeping in the bedroom, and she didn't want to wake him.

"I was just thinking..." he started, but let his words trail off.

"That you don't know Levi Roth as well as you thought you did?" she said, completing the thought.

He nodded. "You get used to thinking a certain way," he said. "You take things for granted, like they're part of the furniture of your mind."

"What did you think of Roth?"

"Roth?" Lance said with a sigh. "I thought he was loyal, for one thing. I thought he was a patriot."

"You could count on him," Klára said.

"Yeah," Lance said, looking up at her.

She came over to the counter and picked up one of the photos. "You two were close."

Lance shrugged. "I guess that depends on your definition of close."

"You worked together."

"We did."

"And you took risks together. Faced danger together. Tied your fate to his."

"My fate?"

"You swam or drowned together. If he went down, you went down."

"You could say that."

"There's a closeness in all that," she said, sitting down, "whether you care to admit it or not." She put the photo back on top of the pile. It showed Roth and Shipenko, their faces untroubled, if that could ever be said of a face like Shipenko's, and their right hands gripped firmly as if shaking on some momentous deal. "You feel betrayed," she said.

"I don't know," Lance said, sounding more defensive than he'd intended.

"It's all right if you do."

"It's not personal," Lance said. "It's nothing to do with me, who he makes friends with."

"But he's the one who recruited you. He brought you into this world."

"Yes."

"He made you who you are."

Lance said nothing.

"He made you *what* you are," she added.

"Don't give him too much credit."

She looked at him for a second, and, just to escape her gaze, he got up and went to the stove. "Time for more coffee," he said, filling the kettle.

"You drink too much of that stuff."

"Stops me from chain-smoking," he said, reaching into his pocket for his cigarettes. He lit a cigarette on the flame of the stove, and they watched each other in silence until the kettle began to whistle.

"It might not be what it looks like," Klára said.

Lance made the coffee and brought the pot and two cups over to the counter. "And what does it look like to you?"

"To me," she said, putting a hand over her cup to stop him from pouring her any coffee, "It looks like Levi Roth met with Osip Shipenko."

"In secret," Lance added.

"But we don't know when they met," Klára said. "And we don't know why."

Ritter had received the pictures less than twelve hours earlier, and from the negatives, it was impossible to say when the meeting took place. Maybe the lab at Langley could find out more, but that didn't help them now. There was also nothing in the pictures to suggest the context of the meeting or the content of what was discussed. "It doesn't matter," Lance said. He leaned back in his seat and took a sip of coffee. "Are you sure you don't want any?"

"Positive," she said, shaking her head.

He poured himself some more and said, "Why would he do it? Why would he cut a deal with that creep?"

"There are reasons."

"Not good ones."

"We don't know that."

"Why lie about it?" Lance said. "Why lie to us? If Roth was making a play, why not tell the president?"

"We don't know that he didn't."

Lance nodded. He knew that was true. He knew there were reasons the Director of the CIA might cut a deal with a member of Molotov's inner circle. Pacts with the devil came with the territory. But that didn't mean Lance was bound by them. "After the bombing," he said, looking at Klára, "I got a call directly from the president."

She nodded. "I heard."

"You know what he said to me?"

She shook her head.

"He told me to hunt down Osip Shipenko and kill him."

"Well," Klára said, "given that he'd just blown up a US embassy, I don't think that's very strange."

"Right," Lance said, nodding. "But he also told me not to tell Roth about it."

They both looked down at the photo—the two men shaking hands, Roth and Shipenko. "Do you think," Klára said, "that the president knew Roth was going behind his back? Cutting a deal?" She nodded at the photo as if it was something dirty, something that could defile her just by her looking at it.

"Maybe," Lance said. "I can't be sure of that. What I do know is that if Roth was going to make a play, if he was going to alter the board in some dramatic way, this is how it would have to happen."

"What do you mean?"

"He'd have to go behind the president's back."

"But that would be treason," Klára said, holding Lance's gaze.

"Yes, it would," Lance said.

"Would he really do that?"

"Who knows what a man is capable of?" Lance said. "What I can say is I've heard him argue the point enough times to know he wants to take out Molotov."

"Well, that's not saying a lot. Everyone would like to see Molotov's head on a pike."

"But Roth wants to do something about it. He wants to make a play. In his view, the Cold War should have ended three decades ago."

"It did end three decades ago."

"And yet here we still are," Lance said. "And the war's not over. Because we never delivered the decisive blow."

"That's Roth's view?"

"Roth's been watching the White House back down from the final face-off with Moscow for thirty years, and he's frustrated. Presidents come and go, control of congress shifts back and forth, but nothing ever changes, and Russia keeps growing bolder."

"Well," Klára said, "it's not easy to stand up to the world's largest nuclear arsenal."

"Exactly," Lance said, "and Molotov knows that. He knows we don't have the stomach for a fight. Not for a real fight, in any case. He's tested us time and time again, and every time, we've shown how utterly unwilling we are to take the pain of a real war."

"And Roth wants war?"

"If I had to guess," Lance said, "I'd say yes, that's what he thinks is necessary to end this thing once and for all."

"He wants to unleash Armageddon?"

"If it's a fight that's going to come anyway," Lance said, "then the sooner it happens, the better. Molotov is only getting stronger, and his provocations are only growing. It started the very first year he took power. Remember Chechnya? He began pounding it to rubble, and what did we do? Nothing. Grozny was a city of over four-hundred-thousand people. It's now twenty years later, and it still hasn't recovered that population."

"Chechnya was a long way away—"

"But he keeps getting closer, doesn't he? And he targets civilians. He figured out that if you can't kill the enemy's soldiers in the field, then kill their families, pulverize their towns and villages, target their schools and hospitals and water supplies. The soldiers can't wage a guerrilla war in the mountains when their homes and farms are burning in the valleys. He's led the most brutal wars of the modern era, and time and again, the West has failed to intervene."

Klára nodded. Lance knew he didn't need to convince her of all this. She was a Czech intelligence officer. She'd been born behind the Iron Curtain and was not so young that she couldn't remember what it had been like.

"They did it again in Georgia," Lance said. "They did it in North Ossetia and Abkhazia. They did it in Syria, sinking there to wholly new levels of depravity."

"I know what they did," Klára said.

"And now they're in Ukraine. They took Crimea. They took Donetsk and Luhansk. Now, they're trying to take the rest of the country, and what has the West shown them?"

"We're sending assistance."

"*Assistance*?" Lance gasped as if ashamed of the word. "We should be fighting at their side. They're standing up to Russia for us. For all of us. We should be fighting with them."

"And you think that's what Roth wants to do?"

"Roth's a CIA man, through and through. The CIA

doesn't fight wars. Not in that sense. It doesn't have a military capability. It can't face Russia on the battlefield."

"In the shadows, then?" Klára said. "On the fringes."

Lance thought of Roth, thought of the things he'd heard him say, the actions and objectives he'd watched him pursue, and nodded his head. "Yes," he said. "My guess is Roth's had enough. He's watched Molotov defy us one too many times, and he's decided it's time for the CIA to step up and start fighting the war everyone else is too afraid to face."

"You've heard him say as much?"

Lance nodded and took another sip of his coffee. "Everyone in the cabinet's heard it. Roth against the rest, that's how it goes."

"And you think that's what this is?" she said, nodding toward the photo. "This is Roth's move against Molotov? A pact with Shipenko?"

Lance thought for a second, then nodded his head. There was nothing Roth could possibly be hoping to gain from a meeting with Shipenko other than a coup against Molotov. "You want to know what I think?" he said, looking up from his coffee. "I think Roth's calculated that the only way the CIA can fight in this war is to go after Molotov personally."

"A decapitation strike."

"Exactly. Just go for the jugular. The top dog. Directly."

"That's a dangerous game."

"Yes, it is," Lance said, " but that's what Roth's thinking. He's going to hit where it hurts. He's going to take out Molotov. Because no one else will."

Klára's eyes widened at the thought. She picked up the pot of coffee and said, "Perhaps I will have some."

"Think about it," Lance said, watching her pour.

"Molotov is so entrenched in his power, so protected by the Dead Hand and Russia's nuclear deterrent, that there's no way Montgomery can go after him with the military. Not without risking a nuclear response."

Klára nodded. It had become orthodoxy within the CIA and the other NATO intelligence agencies that Russia's nuclear deterrent was no longer focused solely on the defense of Russia but also on the defense of one man —Vladimir Molotov. If anyone tried to take him out, he would take down the world with him. She took a sip of her coffee and said, "You really think Russia would launch its nukes if we went after Molotov?"

Lance shrugged. "That's the risk," he said, "and the men with their fingers on the button, they're Molotov's creatures, one and all. Without Molotov, they're nothing."

"They'd blow up the world to protect one man?"

"If they saw us go after him," Lance said. "If they saw NATO take him out."

"Which is why Roth needs Shipenko?"

"An inside job?" Lance said. "One of their own? Maybe it would work."

"This creature here?" Klára said, pointing to Shipenko's disfigured image on the photo. "Isn't that just exchanging one monster for another?"

Lance shrugged. "That's above my pay grade," he said. "But I'd bet dollars to donuts that Roth's calculus."

She leaned back in her seat and sighed. "So Roth's going to attempt a regime change?"

It was a big leap, Lance had to admit, but looking at the photo, weighing the alternatives, if he had to make a bet, that was where he'd put his money. "Yes," he said after a long pause. "I think so."

Klára said nothing. The information was sinking in,

and she didn't look happy about it. When she spoke next, there was a sharpness in her voice that hadn't been there before. "What makes him think he can get away with that?"

Lance looked at her. He could see she was getting angry, and he could sense that, perhaps because of his proximity to Roth or perhaps because he was the one explaining his logic, some of that anger was getting directed at him. "The war," he said simply.

"The war?"

"Molotov was secure before. He was untouchable. Now he's losing a war. That creates weakness. It creates fractures in the upper echelon. If Roth's been watching for a time to strike—"

"Then this is it?" Klára snapped.

"This is it," Lance said quietly. He felt he should explain to her that he was only articulating Roth's motives, not defending them, but she spoke again before he could.

"But Shipenko is such a *monster*."

"They're all monsters," Lance said, immediately regretting it. It sounded like he was defending Shipenko now.

The words set Klára off in an instant. He saw the flash of anger in her eyes. When she spoke next, her voice was unsettlingly calm. "They're all monsters?" she repeated, mulling over the words as if trying to pick out the meaning of a riddle. "So that's it?"

"Klára," he said.

"They're all monsters, so we should just let this happen?"

"Obviously," he said, "in an ideal world—"

"Excuse me?"

He knew he was in trouble. He'd seen that expression on a woman's face and heard that tone enough times to know what it meant. "In an—"

"*Ideal world*?" she said again, her voice growing louder.

"I've upset you," he said, seeking to backstep.

"You're actually considering this now, aren't you?"

"Considering what?"

"Don't give me that. You're thinking about Roth's plan. What if this? What if that? What if Molotov was dead and we had a puppet in the Kremlin?"

"I don't know what you're talking about."

"You're thinking that this monster might be a good move."

"A good move?"

"In the grand game."

"I'm not thinking anything."

"I can see it on your face, Lance. I *know* you're thinking it."

"I know what this man did," Lance said, planting his finger squarely on Shipenko's face.

"But Molotov's done *so* much worse, hasn't he?" she said, her voice growing louder by the second. "I mean, how can this guy be a worse bet? At least he'd be our puppet. At least he'd owe us."

Lance drained his cup and rose to his feet.

"Oh, did I offend you? You're leaving now?"

"I'm not leaving. I just don't want to argue with you about this. It's pointless. Neither of us knows what Roth's up to, and neither of us is going to decide who the leader of Russia is. We don't get to make those decisions."

"But the CIA does," Klára said. "It's practically your *modus operandi*. You've done it countless times before, deposing leaders and installing new ones in their place like it's all a big game. Let me tell you something, Lance. It's not a game, and it doesn't work out how you expect. Installing one monster in place of another never works out as predicted."

"I know that, Klára."

"They have a way of taking on a life of their own."

"We don't even know if that's what's going on."

"What was it that Roosevelt said?"

"I have no idea," he said.

"Yes, you do. That quote about sons of bitches."

"What are you talking about?"

"He may be a son of a bitch, but he's our son of a bitch? Roosevelt said that."

"I don't know anything about it," Lance said.

"As long as they scratch our back," Klára said, "as long as they take their cues from us and do as we say, then it doesn't matter how evil they are."

"Klára, come on."

"No, *you* come on, Lance. How's your history? South Korea, Taiwan, Zaire, Egypt, Nicaragua, Iran, Guatemala, Chile, Argentina, Saudi Arabia, Afghanistan, Iraq—"

"Enough," Lance said, raising his hand. "I get it. I get your point."

"It never works."

"I'm not saying it does," Lance said.

"The attack in Prague," Klára said, getting emotional, "that was *my* home. That happened in *my* town. On *my* watch."

"It wasn't your fault, Klára."

"It was personal."

She looked him in the eye but said nothing. The silence seemed to grow and grow until Lance broke it. "Maybe we should get some sleep."

35

Osip looked up at the cab of Kolesnikov's Ural-4320 truck, then heaved himself into the passenger seat before his doubts got the better of him. Darkness had fallen, and the temperature had dropped precipitously.

"Are you sure you're up for this?" Kolesnikov said, looking over from the driver's seat.

"Of course I'm up for it."

"I thought perhaps you were the kind of man who liked to lead from the rear."

"What's that supposed to mean?" Osip said, well aware of the point Kolesnikov was making.

"Once we get into Ukraine, how should I say? The *facilities* are crude."

Osip slammed shut his door and ignored the remark. It was just the two of them in the cab, and the one thing it seemed to have going for it was that it was spacious. It was enormous, actually, an off-road-capable six-by-six-wheeler that had been produced continuously at the Ural Automotive Plant in Miass since 1976. As far as Osip was concerned, it was one of the few pieces of Russian military equipment that could be relied on to do its job, no matter what. Kolesnikov turned the ignition, and its fifteen-liter, V8 diesel engine started growling reassuringly.

It was so loud that the two men had to raise their voices to be heard over it. "You always drive your own truck?" Osip said.

"Always," Kolesnikov said. "It's that or ride in the back like a sack of potatoes. That's no way to get to a war." He fidgeted with the heater dial, which didn't seem to be responding, then slammed his fist down hard on the steel dashboard. There was a whirring sound, like a wheezing animal coming back to life, and some warm air finally began to flow from the vent. "That's better," he said.

Osip looked in the wing mirror at the rest of the convoy—four 4320s, recognizable from their headlights, each loaded with supplies, munitions, and a dozen men. Their own truck, rather than carrying men, was fitted with a BM-21 'Grad' multiple rocket launcher. Its tubes had been loaded with forty M-21OF rockets. The system was dated, having been introduced during the Sino-Soviet border clashes of the late sixties, when Brezhnev and Mao Zedong flirted with the idea of bringing the world's two largest communist countries into an all-out war. Osip wondered grimly how it would fare now against Ukraine's US MI42 Himars, British M777 howitzers, and Turkish Bayraktar TB2 drones. "How long to get there?" he said.

"The border," Kolesnikov said, heaving the enormous gear stick into first and jerking the truck's seventeen tons into motion, "is just a few miles away. We'll be there in a matter of minutes."

"Good," Osip said.

"But," Kolesnikov continued, "the Luhansk side has been shelled heavily. It's going to be tough."

"How tough?"

Kolesnikov looked at him. "Really," he said, "we can arrange something more suitable for you. A car, maybe, like the ones they have in Moscow."

"That won't be necessary," Osip said, adjusting his position in a vain attempt to get comfortable.

"It'll take most of the night to get to headquarters."

"Then we better get going," Osip said, thinking with dread of what lay ahead.

The first leg of the journey wasn't so bad, and they crossed the border into Luhansk at the small village of Novorusskii, the bridge over the Derkul River miraculously still intact. As Kolesnikov had warned, however, things got harder after that. The road was in bits, and when they weren't plowing through rubble and crashing headlong over potholes, they were leaving the road entirely to get around stretches of asphalt that had been rendered unpassable. The trucks were well up to the task, but the jerking around caused Osip no end of pain. By the time they reached the village of Metalist on the outskirts of the city, Osip was oozing so much blood his clothes were beginning to stick to his skin. "Is that artillery I hear?" he said, breaking a long silence.

"It is," Kolesnikov said.

"Ours?"

"Both sides." The explosions formed a steady thrum in the distance, and Kolesnikov added, "We'll lose the city if we don't do something about it."

Osip had been intending to sound out Kolesnikov's political leanings during the drive, and he said now,

"Molotov wouldn't be very happy to hear you talk that way."

"If Molotov doesn't like it," Kolesnikov said, wiping his nose on his sleeve, "he can come here and kiss my fat ass."

Osip took note of the sentiment.

As they entered the city, he was surprised by the degree of devastation. It was plain even in the darkness. He'd seen the reports, of course, but Molotov, eager to snatch whatever signs of progress he could, had painted the taking of Luhansk as such a victory that even Osip had been taken in by the propaganda. The rows and rows of bombed-out apartment blocks they were passing now didn't exactly suggest victory. "There's not much left," he said.

Kolesnikov steered the truck around some charred vehicle carcasses and said, "You sound surprised."

"I was at the celebration," Osip said, referring to the grand ceremony just a few days earlier, where Molotov had announced in front of a stadium full of ecstatic supporters that the annexation of the four Ukrainian oblasts of Luhansk, Donetsk, Zaporizhzhia, and Kherson was complete. "They showed footage of the city."

"Pre-war footage," Kolesnikov said. "It's all rubble now. In the central park, there's not a single tree left standing."

"Doesn't bode well for an incorporated region of the country, does it?"

"When I first got here," Kolesnikov said. "It was still possible to have a good time."

Osip nodded.

"There was a restaurant we used to go to. Across from the Dal House."

"Dal House?"

"Vladimir Dal?"

Osip shrugged.

"A writer of some sort," Kolesnikov said. "The house was a museum, but my men turned it into a brothel. Good times."

"And Molotov says this is a new regional capital?" Osip said, shaking his head. "It's madness." He was watching carefully for Kolesnikov's response. What he needed was for the man to betray himself—to say something against the president's strategy.

But Kolesnikov turned to him and said, "Don't tell me you've suddenly grown a conscience."

"No," Osip said, shaking his head. "War is war."

"That it is," Kolesnikov said, "and if I understood you correctly earlier, things are going to get a whole lot worse around here. You want Ukraine to look like Chechnya, do you not?"

Osip took a moment to respond. He needed to choose his words carefully. "Are you familiar with the phrase, pyrrhic victory, Kolesnikov?"

"Don't start that crap with me," Kolesnikov said. "You know who I am."

"What crap?"

"I know what you're doing. I'm not a complete imbecile."

"I'm not doing anything."

"You Kremlin cretins never stop, do you?"

"Stop what?"

"Playing your little games. I want no part of it, Osip. I'm a soldier. I obey orders. If you told me to shell the Kremlin, I'd pulverize it for you and not hesitate a second."

Osip made to respond but stopped himself. For once, he wasn't sure what to say. Kolesnikov's phrasing, his choice of words, was it the nod he'd been looking for? "Pulverize the Kremlin," he said softly. "You paint quite an image."

"I do what I'm told, Osip."

Osip nodded. That had never been in doubt. What was in doubt, and what was critical to Osip and his plans, was whose orders, precisely, Kolesnikov was willing to obey. They drove on, and Osip regarded Kolesnikov very closely—the way he drove, the way he sucked on his cigarettes, one after the other, and squished the butts between the dash and his calloused thumb to put them out. He needed him, or someone very like him, to push things over the edge. He'd been intending on tricking, of making him believe the orders he was going to give were all authorized by Molotov, but now he found himself wondering if the relationship could become something a little bit more robust. More reliable. More *quid pro quo*. "You did what you were told in Syria, didn't you?" he said.

Kolesnikov eyed him suspiciously. He could sense something was afoot. "I did what I was told everywhere."

"But in Syria, you really went above and beyond."

Kolesnikov said nothing to that. He was well used to such talk, Osip imaged, well used to people implying he was a monster, and Osip doubted he lost much sleep over it. What Osip needed to do, however, and what he was seeking to insinuate into the conversation now, was a certain piece of unused leverage he'd been holding in reserve—something he'd been keeping in his back pocket in case Kolesnikov got cold feet later on.

"Because," Osip continued, "Ukraine is a Christian country, isn't it? It's in Europe. There are people who would say that puts it a long way away from places like Chechnya and Syria."

"There are people who say a lot of things," Kolesnikov said dryly.

Osip nodded. "That's true," he said. "That's true." He looked at Kolesnikov again and said, "People were saying a lot of things about what happened in Syria."

Kolesnikov eyed him carefully. "Were they?"

Osip reached into his pocket and pulled out a sheet of paper. It was something he'd brought with him from Moscow, a computer printout neatly folded into thirds as if it had once been in a letter envelope.

"What's that?" Kolesnikov said.

"A letter."

"What letter?"

"About the BZ."

"The BZ?"

"The Chlorine Benzilate." Osip said nonchalantly, watching closely for a reaction. "In Syria. You remember?"

"I remember a lot of things," Kolesnikov said after a pause.

"Do you remember using chlorine? Sarin gas? Sulfur mustard?"

Kolesnikov seemed to have something caught in his throat, and he fell into a fit of coughing.

"Are you all right?" Osip said, unable to hide the smugness in his voice.

"I'm fine."

"I'm bringing back too many nasty memories."

Kolesnikov looked at him like he wanted to strangle him, then slowed the truck to a halt and pulled over. They were the lead vehicle of the convoy, smack in the middle of contested ground, and the trucks behind wouldn't be too happy at the prospect of stopping. Osip leaned forward to look at them in the wing mirror.

"Status?" one of the other drivers said through the radio.

Kolesnikov didn't answer but coughed some more as if trying to bring up a lung.

"Are you quite sure you're all right?" Osip said.

Kolesnikov raised a hand in answer but kept coughing.

"If I didn't know better," Osip said, "I'd say you were trying to get out of a difficult conversation."

Kolesnikov finally got his coughing under control and looked up at Osip. "Look, Osip," he said, "if you've got something to say, you best spit it out."

"This letter," Osip said, unfolding it carefully as if it was very valuable to him, "was intercepted by my men in the Hague. It was drafted by Joseph Miller. Have you heard the name?"

Kolesnikov shook his head.

"Interesting," Osip said. "He's heard of yours."

"Who is he?"

"A member of the Chemical Weapons Joint Investigative Committee."

There was a honk from one of the trucks in the rear, and Kolesnikov picked up the radio mouthpiece and grunted into it, "Wait a minute."

"Would you like to know what it says?"

"Why would I give a flying fuck what a bureaucrat in Holland has to say?"

"Well," Osip said coyly, "it is about you, after all."

Kolesnikov said nothing.

Osip looked at him a moment, then began reading. "The following eighty-four incidents are confirmed violations of the International Convention on the Prohibition of Chemical Weapons. They were orchestrated by General Anatoly Kolesnikov of the Russian Army and were carried out in secret by units of the FSB's Spetsgruppa K, as well as paid mercenaries from the Wagner Military Group. They took place between October 2012 and were still ongoing as late as May of 2019. The chemicals used include Chlorine Benzilate, 3-Quinuclidinyl Benzilate, Agent 15, Sarin, Phosphorous, Chlorine, and Mustard Gas, and ranged in scale from single grenade or missile attacks to concerted and sustained campaigns over prolonged periods, from multiple directions and involving multiple units. The larger attacks frequently resulted in hundreds of deaths. Children, being less resilient to the chemicals in use, were particularly singled out as targets, with kinder-gartens, elementary schools, and children's hospitals constituting the bulk of the most lethal attack sites. In some cases, children were corralled or herded into more confined spaces to increase lethality." Osip looked up to make sure Kolesnikov was listening, then continued, "It goes on to specify the details of each of the eighty-four separate instances and provides drafts of the individual indictments for use by the International Criminal Court."

Kolesnikov remained silent.

"Nothing to say?" Osip said.

"Whatever I did," Kolesnikov said, "I did with the backing of Moscow."

"So many of these," Osip said, running his finger down the page, "went out of their way to target children. Was that Moscow's idea, or did you come up with that yourself?"

"All I did was follow orders."

"Seven hundred," Osip said with a whistle, turning over the page, "women and children mostly. Even our own analysts aren't sure what the military objective was of that one."

"The military objective," Kolesnikov said, "was terror. Moscow knew the strategy very well and not once, in seven years, sought to stay my hand."

"I'm just wondering," Osip said, folding the letter neatly and putting it back into the envelope, "what steps Moscow has taken to beef up your personal security?"

"What are you talking about?"

"Bodyguards. New identity arrangements. Safe houses."

"I've been a bit busy, as I'm sure you can see," Kolesnikov said, waving his hand in front of the windshield, "to worry about foreign indictments that have zero chance of being enforced against me."

"All right," Osip said, as if the issue had no interest to either of them whatsoever, as if they were discussing whether or not to stop for lunch, "As long as you're satisfied—"

"Satisfied with what?"

"Well," Osip said, "as I said, my people intercepted the letter in the Hague. But it wasn't addressed to the International Criminal Court."

"Who was it addressed to?"

"CIA Director Levi Roth."

"Roth? So what? The CIA always knew what we were up to there, and they didn't do anything to stop it either."

"They didn't at the time," Osip said, and then, as if the effort was a great burden, he took the letter back out of the envelope and found another section. "In answer to the Director's specific request, and in light of Russia's continued noncompliance with the provisions of the Convention on the Prohibition of Chemical Weapons, as well as those of the Rome Statue on the creation of the International Criminal Court, it is recommended that an extraordinary rendition of the above named Anatoly Kolesnikov be executed by the CIA forthwith."

"Extraordinary rendition?" Kolesnikov said.

"I take it I don't have to explain the term."

Kolesnikov said nothing.

"It looks like the CIA is sending someone to come get you, which is why I was asking about the bodyguards."

"Let them come," Kolesnikov said.

Osip shrugged. He looked again in the truck's wing mirror and saw that the other trucks were beginning to pull forward to pass them. "Looks like they're getting restless," he said.

Kolesnikov put the truck back in gear, and they began to move once again. They were approaching Kolesnikov's makeshift command center, which was based in the same building that had, until a few days earlier, housed the office of the People's Governor of Luhansk—the Kremlin-installed puppet in charge of the so-called People's Republic—and was now supposedly being converted into the seat of the new Russian administration. Osip looked up at the fifteen-story concrete edifice. Not a single window remained intact, and most had been boarded with plywood. Rubble and debris littered the road.

Sitting on a low wall, soldiers in a patchwork of makeshift uniforms—one of them seemed to be wearing the armor of an ice hockey goalie—were smoking cigarettes.

"All I'm saying," Osip said as Kolesnikov pulled up the handbrake, "is that, regardless of the outcome of this war, it's going to be important for all of us to know who our friends are." Kolesnikov opened his door, and Osip added, "Oh, and Joseph Miller, I've taken care of him for you."

36

Klára woke with a start. It was the sound of the door, she thought, that had woken her, and she hurried out of bed. In the living room, Ritter was standing by the window, looking down at the street below. In the moonlight, his skin was ghostly blue. "He's gone, isn't he?" she said.

Ritter nodded.

She went to the window and looked out. There was a man down on the street, silhouetted against the snow, and there was no question it was Lance.

"Where's he going?" she said.

Ritter shrugged. "I was asleep."

Klára rapped her knuckles hard on the window, and Lance turned and looked up. She thought, in the moonlight, that he was looking right at her. Then, he turned away and continued down the street.

"Where does he think he's going?" she said, almost angrily, and without thinking, she crossed the apartment and ran out to the hallway.

"Wait!" Ritter called after her, but she was already at

the stairs and had no intention of letting this happen without a fight. She dashed down the steps and was out on the sidewalk, her bare feet stinging in the snow, in a matter of seconds. She gasped as the cold air swept around her, cold as ice water. "Lance!" she called.

He was fifty yards away, and he stopped and turned back. "Klára, what are you doing out here? You're going to catch your death."

"Where are you going?"

"Go back inside."

"Not until you answer me."

He looked in the direction he'd been headed, then turned and hurried back to her, ushering her into the building before she caught hypothermia. It was only then that she realized how absolutely frozen she was. Her bare feet were red and already beginning to swell, and her body was shaking frantically under the thin cotton shirt she'd been sleeping in.

Lance took off his jacket and tried to put it on her shoulders, but she pushed it away.

"Calm down," he said, keeping his voice low to avoid disturbing the other residents of the building.

"Don't tell me to calm down," she said, surprised at how panicked she'd gotten at the sight of his walking away. "Tell me where you were going right now."

"To the train station."

Ritter appeared at the top of the stairs and said, "Why didn't you tell us?"

"You were sleeping."

"Sneaking out in the middle of the night," Ritter said, descending the rest of the steps, "forgive me for thinking that smells a bit fishy."

"Tell us what you were doing," Klára said.

"I told you."

"Going to the train station. But why?"

"Laurel's call. That's still my only active comms protocol, and I need to talk to her."

"What about the number from Volga's notebook?" Ritter said.

"Already deactivated."

"But what do you want to talk to her about?" Klára said.

"We need to find Shipenko."

"*We* never decided that," Ritter said.

"I did," Lance said.

"Oh, you did, did you?"

"This isn't a democracy," Lance said. "I'm here to follow an order, and that order is to kill Osip Shipenko."

"We're all here for the same reason," Klára said.

"Speak for yourself," Ritter said.

"I don't have time for this," Lance said, turning toward the door.

"Lance!" Klára said. "You can't just go back to the train station. What if there's a trap."

"I can trust Laurel."

"You don't know who you can trust." Lance hesitated just a second, and Klára said, "Think about it. Ritter told Volga there was a mole, Volga passed that information to Laurel, and within days, Volga was dead, and soldiers were waiting for Ritter."

Lance looked at her, and she thought for a second he was going to agree with her. Then he said, "Klára, I have to give her a chance."

"Why?" Klára said, locking eyes with him.

"Because he's got a hard-on for her," Ritter said.

Lance looked away.

"Lance!" she said again, and there was more pleading in her voice than she'd intended.

Lance just shook his head. "I've got to go," he said quietly. "I've got to put the question to her."

"And you'll know if she's lying?" Ritter said skeptically.

Lance sighed. "I don't know what I'll know."

"But you're willing to risk our lives," Ritter continued, "based on that?"

"I'm coming with you," Klára said.

"No," Lance said.

She looked at his face. It was blank. Cold. He was unreadable at the best of times, but up until that moment, she'd at least felt that they shared a common cause—that they were working for the same thing. Now, she suddenly wasn't so sure.

"If he wants to walk into an ambush," Ritter said, "let him. I'm not sticking around to watch the fireworks."

"No," Klára said. "I came here for you, Lance. I'm not letting you drop me now, like this, because of her."

"Klára," Lance said, "no one's dropping you, but if Laurel's somehow in on this with Roth, if they're both involved with whoever killed Volga—"

"Then they'll have a sniper watching that phone at this very moment," Ritter said. "Just on the off chance we're idiot enough to go back to it."

"Maybe," Lance said, "but one way or another, I have to find out, and I'm not bringing you with me, Klára. It's my risk to take."

"Lance!" Klára said again, and when he looked at her, she wasn't even sure what she wanted to say. Everything he'd said made sense, up to a point. If she'd thought some of the people she trusted had double-crossed her, she'd want to find out too. But she wasn't sure she'd risk her life for it. He was looking at her, waiting for her to speak, and she said, "If you leave, I have a terrible feeling I won't ever see you again."

Lance said nothing for a moment, then, "If I'm not back by eight a.m., cut loose. Both of you. Walk away. Don't look back."

"You're seriously going to do this?" Ritter said, "Knowing what you know now?"

"I have to."

"Someone killed Volga," Ritter said. "If Laurel's working with Roth, and if they're mixed up with this whole thing with Shipenko—"

"I have to know," Lance said.

Ritter shrugged, then turned to Klára. "His funeral," he said, then reached into his pocket and handed something to Lance.

"What's this?" Lance said.

"Day scope and thermal imager," Ritter said. "If you're going to use yourself as bait, the least you can do is try to protect yourself."

Lance looked at the equipment, a Schmidt & Bender 25x magnification day scope and a Qioptiq Sniper Thermal Imager. British standard issue. "Thanks," he said.

Klára shook her head. She couldn't believe she was letting him go. "If you're not back by eight," she said.

"Then walk away."

"No," she said. "If you don't come back here, then I'm going to go to the payphone on the embankment where we first met. I'll be there tonight at midnight. We can regroup then." She turned then and brushed past Ritter to go back up the stairs. At the top, she looked back at Lance. He was still standing there, the door open. "Go," she said.

37

Try as he might, Osip could not find a comfortable position. He was in a Luhansk hotel room, sprawled across the room's expansive bed, lying on top of the blankets. His feet were right next to an enormous iron radiator mounted to the wall. No matter how much he shifted his weight, he couldn't get comfortable. His body was too sore and agitated, his skin too inflamed from the truck ride he'd just endured with Kolesnikov. He placed his feet, still in their woolen socks, onto the radiator directly and realized it wasn't even hot.

"Curse this blasted place," he muttered, looking at his watch. It was about an hour since they'd arrived in the city, and Kolesnikov had insisted on getting him checked into the hotel—Luhansk's finest, if that was saying anything—before leaving to inspect his troops.

Osip was wearing a hotel robe and, apart from the socks, nothing else. He'd sent the rest of his clothes to be laundered. The robe was a heavy old thing, brown and worn thin at the elbows. The crest of the Luhansk People's

Republic was sewn onto the breast pocket. He pulled it tighter and went to the window.

The sun was just cresting the horizon, lighting up Luhansk's main square in all its dismal glory. It might have been something once, but now, the buildings were all shuttered, their windows blown out or boarded up. Scraps of lace curtain fluttered from some of them, blowing in the breeze like tattered flags of surrender. The cobbled square was strewn with debris, bits of old barricades, and the remains of what had once been a large stone fountain.

It was a doleful, woebegone place, and he was not one bit happy to be there. He craned his neck to see down the side street, then looked away. The view utterly depressed him. No light, no life, no comfort. To a man in his condition, the modern amenities of Moscow were more than just luxuries. They were essential. If he remained in this place for much more than a day, he would become ill—life-threateningly so.

He consoled himself by remembering it would all be over soon. Molotov's position was deteriorating by the hour. With what Osip had planned, it was going to become untenable. Osip was going to act fast, strike at the very heart of Molotov's power from multiple directions, and topple him before anyone even realized it was happening. It was a risk, but all of life was a risk, and he'd lined up the pieces just the way he needed them.

The first step had been getting the Americans on board. Not the president *per se*, the White House would never have the audacity for something as bold as this, but the CIA. No plan could succeed without their tacit backing, and to that end, Osip had been feeding Roth a steady stream of chicken feed to keep him fattened up. He'd already sent him photos of the tactical nukes being transported to the front. Soon, he would have chemical weapons to point at too. Osip didn't need the CIA to do anything, he would take care of the palace coup himself, but he did need to know they wouldn't scupper his plans and step in to save Molotov at the last moment.

Domestically, Molotov was pretty much doing Osip's work for him. The man, who for decades had maneuvered with such political skill, had all of a sudden whipped up the perfect storm to undermine himself. Before the invasion, Osip would have thought Molotov was completely unassailable. Not that he hadn't been plotting from the sidelines, but he'd thought he would have to wait years to put his plans into motion. Now, it was as if Molotov was almost begging for someone to step up and challenge him.

The only way for a dictator like Molotov to remain in power was through fear, and that required a constant projection of strength. Losing a war was kryptonite to that, and Molotov wasn't just losing, he was losing spectacularly. In a matter of days, his vaunted military machine had been exposed as a complete and utter shambles. A paper tiger. A chimera. The troops were failing on the battlefield, their morale was abysmal, their discipline was nonexistent, and their equipment was falling to pieces. They couldn't even manage to keep fuel in their tanks. Casualties were mounting so rapidly that the most dangerous constituents in the country, the Russian Mothers, were already gathering in the streets in protest. It didn't take too many bodybags to get mothers worried about their sons—now being forcibly conscripted—and Osip knew the country was about to start seeing bodybags by the trainload.

There would be unprecedented unrest, and not just from the usual ragtag protestors. This time, everyone was hurting—the mothers whose sons were dying, the workers whose jobs were going up in smoke, even the military hardliners. No one was happy, and it was about to get a whole lot worse. Osip had come up with a cunning little plan, he thought, that would pour rocket fuel on all the discontent that was brewing. It would be a performance worthy of a Hollywood Academy Award, a tragedy of such epic proportions it would sour the mood of the entire country in a heartbeat. And all he needed to pull it off was a puny local politician, a former schoolteacher named Petro Bulavin, who was already on his way.

He pulled a cigarette from the packet in his pocket and lit it, then leaned his head back and exhaled a plume of smoke into the air above. After years of preparation and patient waiting, he was about to snatch the prize, claim the title, and perhaps, become one of the most powerful men ever to set foot on the earth.

In the distance, the loud rumble of an artillery strike shook the ground. There was an old landline phone on the side table next to the bed, and he picked up the receiver. The phone wasn't secure, it went through the hotel switchboard on the ground floor and anyone could listen in, but he'd replaced the operator with one of Kolesnikov's men and he didn't plan on using it for anything too sensitive. He dialed now for the operator and waited.

"Yes, sir?" the operator said.

"I'm still waiting for Bulavin," Osip said. "Where the hell is he? It's been almost an hour."

"He took some time to track down, sir. I understand he's *en route* now."

"He better be."

"I'll have him sent to your room the instant he arrives."

"In the meantime," Osip said, opening the belt of his robe and letting it fall open to expose his withered genitals, "send up that cadet."

"The cadet, sir?"

"The girl. What's her name?"

"Yelena Klishina?"

"Exactly. I want her sent up immediately."

"About that, sir...."

"What is it?"

"She's...."

"Don't tell me she's not there."

"Oh, no, sir. She's here. She's sitting in the lobby right now."

"Then what's the problem?"

"She's... *crying*, sir."

"Crying?" Osip said, letting out a quick laugh. "Of course she's crying. Do you have any idea what I have planned for her?"

"Sir?"

"Just send her up." He hung up the phone and adjusted the robe, making sure it revealed his manhood in its full glory. The girl was in for a rude awakening, he thought, licking his crusted lips. There'd been a time when the revulsion on a woman's face had caused him dismay. Those days were long past. Now, the revulsion, the fear, was the point of the entire thing. He liked people to squirm, especially women.

There was a knock on the door, and he stubbed out his cigarette. "Come," he said regally.

The door moved an inch, then opened hesitantly to reveal Yelena's wary face.

"Come in, come in," he said, beckoning her with his hand. She did, and when she saw him lying there, naked, exposed, spread out like a Roman emperor on a bed, her eyes widened in terror. Osip felt the throb of desire running through his blood. This was the moment of maximum pleasure for him, the tears in the eyes, the quivering, trembling hands, the abandonment of hope. A single touch would have been enough to make him climax. "Shut the door," he said. "Turn on the light. Let me get a look at you."

She stepped forward and turned on the light, and he saw how different she looked now from what she'd been at the air base. Her hair had been dyed, for one thing, and she'd done a reasonably good job of matching her makeup to the photo he'd shown her. He could also make out her freckles now, which he loved.

"Take off that blasted coat," he said. She was wearing her heavy, army-issue overcoat, and he could see that her legs were bare beneath it. "And the shoes, too," he added. Her shoes were the black leather clunkers also issued by the military.

She slipped out of the coat, revealing a thin, cotton dress, very like the one Anya had worn in the photo. She shivered from the cold, and Osip leaned forward, like an old man straining to see through his glasses, and could just about see the goosebumps on her arms. "Are you cold, dear?"

She shook her head. She was still wearing the shoes, they looked foolish now with the dress, but he didn't tell her again to remove them. "What did you do to your hair?" he said.

"Is it wrong?" she said, reaching up to touch it. "The photo was black and white."

"It's not *wrong*," Osip said, "but it's not quite right. It was better before when I first met you. I didn't tell you to change it."

"You told me to mimic the picture."

"*Mimic*?" Osip said, taking exception at the word. "You're not mimicking anyone, my dear."

"Sorry, sir?"

"You're *becoming* her."

"*Becoming* her?"

"That's correct. It will take time, perhaps years, but you'll get there." A look of terror crossed her face, and a corresponding twitch of pleasure crossed his. "The first step is your name. It's no longer Yelena. It's Anya now."

She said nothing. She'd been holding a shopping bag when she entered the room, a paper bag bearing the logo of the main department store in Rostov, and he said, "Did you find what I asked for?"

"I did my best," she said timidly. "It wasn't easy to find bathing suits in the city. Not at this time of year."

"Let me see," he said, moving his hand to his lap.

She reached into the bag and pulled out an orange bathing suit. It was similar in cut to the one in the picture, but the color wasn't quite right. "I wouldn't call that persimmon, would you?"

"It's the closest I could find. I searched everywhere."

"Put it on."

She looked down at the bag, then up at him. His meaning was clear, but it appeared it would take a little time for it to sink in.

"Sir?"

"Put it on," he said again. "What do you think this is all for?"

She looked around the room as if there might still be

some means of escape. There was a private bathroom, and perhaps she thought she might use it as a changing room. He decided to disabuse her of the notion. "Where you are."

"Here?"

"Yes," he said. "Where you stand. Hurry up."

She glanced in the direction of his groin, her eyes falling for just a second on his swelling member, and she let out an almost inaudible gasp. Then she stood deathly still for about ten seconds.

"Strip," Osip said, his tone growing more forceful. "I won't say it again."

Forcing herself to action, she pulled the thin cotton dress over her head and let it fall to the floor.

"Good," Osip said quietly. "Very good."

She was down to her underwear, plain white panties and bra, and the two discordant black shoes rooted to the ground like anchors. They had the effect of making her look faintly ridiculous, and he was about to tell her to take them off when another knock on the door disturbed them.

"What now?" Osip growled.

A man's voice answered. "It's Petro Bulavin, sir."

Osip sighed. "Work, work, work," he muttered, then, "Come in, for God's sake."

The relief on the girl's face was palpable. Osip vowed to make sure it would be only temporary.

The door opened, and Bulavin entered the room, a sturdy-looking fellow of about forty-five with ruddy cheeks and thick black hair. Osip said, "Make room for him. Get out of his way."

The girl shuffled aside, and Bulavin's eyes widened

when he saw her standing there, in her underwear, looking like a child on a diving board too scared to jump.

"Don't stop," Osip said to her, "Continue."

"Sir?"

"Continue undressing. Put on the swimsuit."

She looked from him to Bulavin, and for an instant, he wasn't sure if she was going to obey or not. Then she reached behind her back and opened the clasp of her bra. It fell to the ground.

Osip wasn't looking at her, though. He was looking at Bulavin, regarding the man through his beady eyes as if he was some strange new species. The thought crossed his mind that he could play with both of them, or rather, force them to play with each other. In his condition, watching was more practical than participating.

The girl stepped out of the cotton underpants she'd been wearing and stood stark naked but for the clunky shoes. There was something about how the shoes looked, how comical they were, that prevented Osip from telling her to take them off.

He looked from Bulavin to her and back again. "I know what you're thinking, Bulavin. You're wondering if you're going to get your beak wet."

"Sir?"

Osip laughed, then to the girl, he said, "You greedy slut. You want us both, don't you?"

She was so terrified she couldn't respond. Her eyes seemed fixed on the pile of clothes on the floor before her.

"Get out!" Osip barked at her. "The men have business to discuss."

38

P etro Bulavin was a man whose rise in rank had been as fast as it was unexpected. Just three years ago, he'd been a high school teacher in Alchevs'k, an industrial town about forty kilometers from Luhansk, living on a meager teacher's salary and sharing a cold, drafty apartment with an elderly mother whose main occupation, it seemed, was criticizing his achievement in life. Not that Bulavin had ever sought to improve things in that regard. Not once had he sought the position he now possessed. Not once had he set his sights on greatness. And yet, here he was, standing in a small hotel room in front of one of the most powerful men in all of Russia.

There was an almost naked woman there too, and he glanced in her direction before she'd had the chance to make her departure. He should have been shocked, he supposed—she was young, clearly terrified, and completely naked but for a pair of clunking black shoes— but war had a way of making even the strangest things seem commonplace. Just a few minutes earlier, on his way to the hotel, he'd passed a dozen soldiers making their way to the front riding on donkeys. He'd almost have said that after so many years of war, he'd lost his ability to be shocked at all.

But then there was this... this man, this *creature*, on the bed in front of him, luxuriating like some strange lizard sunning himself on a rock. He was doing up his robe now, but he'd had his member in his hand when Bulavin first entered the room, and if he wasn't mistaken, it was bleeding.

"My name is Tushonka," the man said. "Not my real name," he added, "but there you have it."

Bulavin nodded. He was nervous. He knew the man was from the Kremlin, and he'd been warned ahead of time that he was not one to be trifled with, but other than that, he had no idea what to expect. Bulavin would always be a fish out of water in this world, no matter what titles they foisted upon him, and he suspected that if this Tushonka character had any idea who he really was, how utterly unqualified he was for everything that had come his way, he would not have wasted his time requesting a meeting with him.

"Though I suppose," Tushonka added, "that you might as well know my real name. Soon enough, the whole world will know it."

Bulavin searched for somewhere to set his gaze. They'd warned him in the lobby not to stare.

"It's Osip Shipenko," the man said.

Bulavin nodded.

"I understand," Shipenko said, "that you're an efficient administrator."

"I've been called as much," Bulavin admitted, "though I highly doubt I'm what you're looking for in this instance."

"And how do you know what I'm looking for?"

"I mean no disrespect. It's just you're a top-level Kremlin official—"

"I'm a Director of the GRU, Bulavin, and I speak with the full authority of the president."

Bulavin gulped. "Yes, sir."

"And my people tell me that the situation here in Luhansk was improving under your stewardship before this," and he waved a hand to take in everything before him, "this *invasion* turned everything back to chaos."

Bulavin felt completely bewildered. He had no idea why he was there, and if he could have had his way, he would have turned around and never found out. "I'm sure your advisors are being too generous, sir."

"And what do you make of it? The invasion? Good idea?"

Bulavin shook his head. The only thing he wanted to say was whatever this man wanted to hear, and his sense was that the man was a critic. "It's certainly created its challenges," he stammered.

"Challenges? Now who's being generous?"

"Big challenges."

"We're losing ground, isn't that correct? Ground we'd previously secured from Ukraine almost a decade ago."

"If you mean in this oblast, sir—"

"Of course that's what I mean."

"It's being contested—"

"We're losing it."

Bulavin swallowed. It seemed his mouth was suddenly having difficulties producing enough saliva. "I'm no military expert—"

"Are we going to lose this city?"

Bulavin hesitated just a second before saying, "Heaven forbid."

"Let me make something clear," Shipenko said. "I'm not looking for someone to blow smoke up my ass. If I'd wanted that, I'd have stayed in Moscow. What I want from you is a true assessment of the situation."

Bulavin nodded but said nothing.

"From Kolesnikov's reports," Shipenko continued, pulling a creased map from the table next to his bed, "the Ukrainians are shelling our positions in Svatove and threatening to rout our forward line."

"If that's what Kolesnikov is saying—"

"But what are you saying?" Shipenko snapped.

"I ordered the razing of all villages on the east bank—"

Shipenko raised a hand, and Bulavin stopped speaking. "Just give it to me straight," he said. "The true situation."

"The true situation?" Bulavin said, wondering if this was some sort of trap. It was not unheard of for Molotov to send out officials just to see if they could get politicians in the provinces to say things that would compromise them. When he looked at the man in front of him, however, Bulavin had a strong feeling this was not a trick. This was the real thing. This was a man seeking to find skeletons. He took a breath, then said, "The true situation is that this invasion is an unmitigated disaster. Our forces lack discipline, they lack supplies, and frankly, they lack fighting spirit. The only men even close to showing themselves combat-ready are the Wagner mercenaries, and even they're being squandered, thrown at the front like so much cannon fodder. If we don't turn the fight around soon, or get out of it altogether, we're at risk of losing all territory gained in Ukraine since 2014, including Crimea."

Shipenko nodded his head. He must have known that was the situation already, or he wouldn't have been there —Moscow bigwigs were not in the habit of visiting the Danubia Hotel in Luhansk. Nonetheless, he seemed to Bulavin pleased to be hearing a voice critical of Molotov's actions. Shipenko put down his map and said, "Is that something you'd be willing to testify before the Duma?"

Bulavin almost swallowed his tongue. "Testify?" he gasped.

"Is it?"

"I think..." he stammered, "that is to say, sir, I'm really not—"

"You're not what?"

"Not... the *heroic* type."

"I said nothing of heroics."

"To criticize the invasion now, sir, at a time like this, in a forum like the Duma, would be tantamount to signing my own death warrant."

Shipenko nodded, and Bulavin wondered desperately what the hell he'd managed to get himself into. He'd had a lucky run these past few years, there was no doubt about it. By all accounts, he was lucky just to be alive. Perhaps, he thought, that luck was finally running out.

The way Shipenko was looking at him, Bulavin was reminded of a lizard before it devoured its prey. There was definitely something new in his beady eyes when he said, "Remind me, Bulavin, what was it you used to do before all this."

"Before politics, sir, I was a school teacher."

"A humble school teacher," Shipenko said. "And what, pray tell, is a school teacher doing in charge of a frontier district in the middle of a war?"

"It was.... I mean."

"It just happened, Bulavin."

"You could say that, sir. Yes."

Shipenko smiled, a sickly, nauseating sneer, and said, "We all have to play the hand we're dealt, don't we?"

"We do, sir," Bulavin said. This was it, he thought. His meteoric rise had come to its inevitable conclusion. He'd always known it would. Shipenko was right. What the hell was a school teacher from Alchevs'k doing ruling a territory as strategically vital as Luhansk? It was ludicrous, and he knew it would come crashing down as suddenly, and violently, and randomly as it had begun.

For his career was all of those things—sudden, violent, and random. It had started with a bang. An explosion, no less. A misdirected Russian cruise missile, later blamed on the Ukrainians, that slammed into the building that just happened to be hosting the first annual Luhansk National Teacher's Convention. Over three hundred teachers died in the blast, including all serving members of the Board of Education, and Bulavin, one of the few survivors, was chosen more or less at random to take over as Head of Education of the new People's Republic.

He spent two nights in the Alchevs'k hospital recuperating from the blast, and when he got home, he was surprised to find a police car already waiting for him outside the building. The cops, armed with AK-47s, refused to leave without him, and so, almost before he knew what was happening, Bulavin found himself in a Luhansk courthouse being sworn in as a fully-fledged member of the new puppet regime. From there, the police drove him directly to the government administration building, where they unceremoniously dropped him off outside the building's front entrance. Bulavin looked up at the imposing building, then spent the better part of the next hour wandering its corridors in a bewildered and futile search for an office with his name on the door. His first official action, he later realized, was being escorted to his office like a lost child by a security guard.

To Bulavin, the situation was farcical. He knew he had no business being in government. He didn't know his ass from his elbow and would have been the first to admit it had anyone asked. But no one did ask. And, in fact, his ascent only accelerated—first to minister, then to head of the Luhansk Governing Council, and then to Head of State of the entire Republic. This rise was not the result of a sudden increase in competence, ambition, or even intrigue. It was from the same simple process of elimination that had put him in government in the first place.

Luhansk, then as now, was not a place where politicians enjoyed long or happy careers. Merely being associated with the regime was enough to make them a target.

Bulavin's current title was Head of Republic, and every predecessor who'd held the role in the last two years, twenty-three men in total, had died by assassination. Some after only a matter of hours in office. Whether killed by the Ukrainians, by rival Donbas factions, by Russian mercenaries with competing interests, or by the government in Moscow itself, holders of the office found themselves on the wrong side of a bullet with such alarming frequency that no one in their right mind was any longer willing to take the job. Bulavin, the only idiot in government so lacking in guile that he couldn't dodge the promotion, had found himself in the hot seat just thirteen days ago. He was certain that the only reason he was still alive was that he was viewed by all sides as so utterly inconsequential that killing him wasn't worth the effort it would take. That, and the fact that the recent annexation of the oblast into Russian proper meant that no one was even sure if his position still existed.

Certainly, Bulavin didn't know.

"You've shown yourself to be a good administrator," Shipenko said, "and it just so happens that an administrator is what I'm in need of."

Bulavin wanted to say something, but no words came from his mouth.

"I won't do you the indignity of threatening you if you fail," Shipenko continued. "I won't threaten your little old mother in that dismal flat in Alchevs'k. I won't threaten that sweet, married secretary in the government office that you've been secretly diddling every time her husband's back is turned."

"Sir!"

Shipenko raised a hand. "I know you, Petro Bulavin. I know you have four sisters, one here in Luhansk, one in Donetsk, and two in Alchevs'k. I know they have families, children, happy lives. I won't threaten any of that because I believe in you."

Bulavin didn't know what to do. He couldn't speak. He couldn't move. He was the type of creature whose fight-or-flight mechanism had evolved more in the direction of paralysis than anything useful. He knew very well what was being threatened and eventually managed to stutter, "I assure you, sir, that I will do everything and anything to avoid punishment."

The answer seemed to be satisfactory, for Shipenko only said, "Good man, Bulavin. What I need is a man who can carry out orders. A man who can do as he's told without raising objections and difficulties, is that you?"

"It is, sir."

"I don't want to deal with roadblocks and barriers at every turn."

"Of course, sir."

"You're going to be named governor of the new Russian Province of Luhansk. The province is being placed under martial law, and you will have full legal authority to carry out the orders I'm about to give you."

Bulavin nodded.

"You are used to acting as an official in a small, break-away pariah state, Bulavin. Now, you are a governor of the Russian Federation, and the status of martial law is a very serious thing. You will be acting with the full authority of the Kremlin in everything you do, and your actions will be judged as such."

"I'll do everything in my power to make you satisfied," Bulavin said.

"Good," Shipenko said. "The first order of business is a new battalion."

"A battalion, sir?"

"I want eight hundred men."

"Eight hundred men? To fight?"

"And I need them by tomorrow. Is that a problem?"

"Tomorrow?" Bulavin gasped. "I... I don't know if it's possible."

"You must make it possible."

"There aren't eight hundred free men in the province, sir. We've been at war for almost a decade. Everyone who could fight is either dead or already at the front."

"There are men in this province, Bulavin, and your job is to find them."

"But where?"

"Where? Where do you think?"

Bulavin racked his brain. He genuinely didn't know.

The prisons, the shelters, the public works departments had all been drained of men long ago. "I'm sorry, sir, but I really don't know."

Shipenko looked at him, and a slow smile crept across his broken, fractured lips. He said, "I see here there are four high schools in this city,"

"Schools?"

"Have military recruiters been to the schools?"

"The school system has collapsed, sir."

"The students must be somewhere."

"They've fled. They've evacuated."

Osip shook his head. "They haven't all fled."

"The ones old enough to fight have all been recruited."

Shipenko shook his head.

Bulavin felt as if the walls were closing in on him. "I don't know what you're telling me to do, sir."

"Go to the schools, Bulavin, and get me my men."

"But—"

"If they're old enough to hold a rifle, they're old enough to fight."

"There are only children left in the schools."

Osip looked at him closely. "Fourteen," he said, enunciating the syllables very clearly.

"Fourteen, sir?" Bulavin said, the horror of what he was being told to do only now dawning on him.

"Fourteen years and up. That's who I want. I want eight hundred of the little brats by tomorrow."

"I can't, sir. I won't—"

"Don't worry, Bulavin. They're not going to see conflict."

"What do you mean, sir?"

"You'll see soon enough. Just sign them up. Tell them it will be an adventure."

"They won't see conflict, sir?"

Shipenko was opening back up his robe. Bulavin looked away from the sight of his erect penis. "It's for a publicity stunt," he said. "Nothing more. Now call the girl back in and take off your pants."

39

L ance lit a cigarette and looked up at the enormous facade of the Rostov-Glavny station. It wasn't yet five. Laurel's call would be at 7.30, giving him plenty of time to get a lay of the land. He was standing next to a bus stop, and he watched the station for a minute before walking down the Ulitsa Deputatskaya toward the long bridge over the Temernik River. The bridge was narrow, with two car lanes, a tram lane, and a concrete pavement all crammed too close together. There was little traffic, just a few freight trucks carrying logs, and they sprayed slush up onto the sidewalk as they passed. Lance cursed them every time.

Beneath the bridge, a light industrial zone sprawled along the banks of the Temernik. The river was little more than an open drain, a filthy sludge-filled channel lined on both sides with concrete banks. It was less than twenty feet wide, frozen solid, and fed into the Don River beneath Prospekt Siversa.

When Lance reached the center point of the bridge, he took out the scope and imager Ritter had given him. He checked that no one was approaching, then raised the scope to his eye and scanned the rail yards and freight platforms that lined the east side of the river. He saw nothing out of the ordinary.

He continued to the far side of the bridge, turned right onto Prospekt Siversa, followed that a few hundred yards in the direction of the Don, then crossed back over the Temernik on the Krasnoarmeyskaya bridge. The bridge gave him the same view of the train station and freight yards, but from the south now instead of the north. He scanned the freight yards hurriedly, and also the bus station and passenger train platforms that he now had a better view of. The Temernik was even narrower here, almost narrow enough to jump across, and he made a note of that as a possible escape route if things were to go badly later on.

Once across the bridge, he cut through a parking lot to get to the front of the station. The area was rundown, the pavement cracked and potholed. The apartment buildings were cheap and dilapidated, and covered in graffiti. There was a lone car in the center of the parking lot, and it had been stripped of its wheels.

Across the street from the train station, there was a grimy old diner overlooking the front entrance. Lance looked at his watch—he still had over an hour before Laurel's call—and went inside. A loud bell clanged over his head as he entered. There was no one inside except an older woman in a brown waitress uniform standing behind the counter. She looked up, startled by the bell, then watched Lance as he found himself a table, eyeing him like a bird of prey watching a mouse.

Lance gave her a nod, then took a seat by the window. She continued watching him, as motionless as the portrait of President Molotov that was hanging from the wall behind her. An omen, Lance thought, looking away from it.

There was a single-page menu on the table, and he glanced over it before ordering coffee and a specific pastry that he'd never heard of until his arrival in the city. It was a local staple, it seemed, and he'd had one at the station the day he arrived. He had a feeling it was one of those products invented by the Soviets to use up excess corn starch. When it arrived, he saw that the frosting, which wasn't so different from Cool Whip back home, had been dyed pink.

"Thank you," he said, taking a sip of the coffee. It tasted like it had been cut with chicory.

The woman went back to the counter without acknowledging his words and stood with her arms crossed, watching as if afraid he might try to run out on his bill. Lance sat where he was for the better part of the next hour, keeping watch over the front entrance of the station while the waitress kept watch over him. During the hour, the diner steadily filled with its usual morning traffic. Someone came in with a newspaper, and Lance saw on the cover a headline announcing that Molotov had just ordered a mandatory partial mobilization. It was one more sign, if any was needed, that things weren't going according to plan.

At a quarter after seven, Lance put some money on the table and left the diner. He crossed the street and entered the main passenger concourse directly. Only a day had passed since he'd last been there, but already the place felt different. War changed things, and this war was doing so quickly. There were some men with clipboards standing by the escalators, and they were accompanied by armed soldiers in uniform. They hadn't been there the day before and were stopping people as they got off the escalators and asking to see their identification documents.

Lance pulled up his collar, kept his head down, and hurried across the concourse. Ordinarily, he wouldn't have come back to the same spot twice in a row. It was poor tradecraft, sloppy, especially in a place as exposed as a train station. But he needed to speak to Laurel. He needed to know he could still trust her.

He scanned the crowds of passengers coming up from the escalators, the waiters in the café, the soldiers and policemen. No one was paying him any attention. He leaned up against an advertising display near the pay phones and scanned the raised gangway overlooking the platforms. It would have been an excellent spot for a sniper, and there was a part of him now that almost expected to hear the loud crack of a sniper shot at any moment.

He glanced at the clock. It was just a few minutes until the call. Over by the escalators, an argument seemed to have broken out among the men with clipboards and some passengers who were refusing to show their documents.

Lance caught the eye of the waiter in the café and said, "What's going on there?"

"They're calling up men to the front," the waiter said. "They'll be coming for us all soon enough." Lance nodded, wondering how he would be able to keep a low profile if the mobilization drained the city of men. Then the phone started to ring, its metal bell seeming as loud as a fire alarm in his mind.

He eyed the commotion across the way—the soldiers

and policemen were not remotely within earshot—then stepped forward. This was it, he thought—the moment of truth. If he'd ever wanted to test Laurel's loyalty, he wouldn't get another chance like this. He picked up the receiver and held his breath. Nothing happened. No bullet. No splattering of his brains. No betrayal. "Hello?"

He heard the same voice as the day before. "Please hold."

He tapped the side of the phone impatiently and waited. Then Laurel's voice came on. "Lance?"

"Yes," he said, breathing a sigh of relief.

"I was worried."

"I'm fine," he said.

"You shouldn't have gone back to the phone. We don't know what Volga gave up. The GRU could have been all over it."

"It wasn't the GRU I was worried about."

She said nothing for a few seconds, then, "What do you mean?"

"You know what I mean."

"You're getting paranoid in your old age."

"I'm not that old."

"You've been with Ritter, though, haven't you?"

"Yes."

"And he gave you the name of the mole."

Lance said nothing.

"You really don't trust me?" she said.

"I never said that."

"After everything we've been through?"

"If I didn't trust you, I wouldn't have come back to this phone."

"Well, isn't that enough? You came back. We're talking. No one was waiting for you."

"That I know of," he said, scanning the gangway. Just because he couldn't see anyone didn't mean he wasn't being watched. There were a million places someone could have been spying from. And, now that he thought about it, that would have been the smarter play. Watch and wait. Follow him back to Klára and Ritter. Clean up the entire mess at once. Take out everyone who'd seen the photo.

"Lance," Laurel said, "are you still there?"

"I'm still here," he said with a sigh.

"It's Roth, isn't it?"

"What?"

"The mole. It's Levi."

"How do you know that?"

"I don't. Not for certain."

"Then why did you say it?"

"I'm not certain, but you are. You know it's Roth, and you don't know who else is involved. That's why you're scared of me."

"What makes you suspect it's Roth," Lance said.

She hesitated before saying, "Things."

"What things?"

"Things have been happening here. Signs. Tatyana and I have been watching him. He's up to something."

"Like what?"

"He received documents."

"What sort of documents?"

"We don't know. When Tatyana paid him a visit, he'd already thrown them in a fire."

"That doesn't say much. He's a spy. Destroying documents is in his DNA."

"I think he's been tampering with the security logs at his house."

"Doesn't mean—"

"Just tell me, Lance. Is it Roth? It is, isn't it?"

"Well," Lance said, "Ritter showed me a photograph."

"Of Roth?"

"Yes. He was shaking hands with Osip Shipenko."

"That's pretty damning."

"Yes, it is."

"Almost too perfect."

"I think it's real."

"Where was the photo taken?"

"I don't know."

"And when? And how'd he get it?"

"He's got the negatives, Laurel. If I could get them to a lab, we'd know for sure, but my gut tells me they'll hold up to examination. The photo is the real thing."

"So Roth's in cahoots with a Kremlin terrorist?"

"Wouldn't be the first time a director of the CIA tried to cut a deal with the devil."

"No, it wouldn't," Laurel agreed. "Particularly if he thought he could get himself a puppet out of it. Is that what you think this is?"

"You've heard the way he talks. Getting rid of Molotov is the only thing that will move the needle. He's said it a thousand times."

"I didn't think he'd go ahead and plot it," Laurel said.

Lance was distracted. The argument by the escalators was getting more heated. Some men were refusing to show their identity cards, and it seemed the men with clipboards were trying to hand out draft notices on the spot. There weren't enough soldiers to keep the crowd under control, and police were beginning to get involved.

"Is everything all right there, Lance?"

"I might have to make myself scarce."

"If you need to leave—"

"I'll let you know. In the meantime, you know what I've been thinking about?"

"What?"

"Who got to Yuriy Volga?"

"It could have been a hundred things."

"He was here for years, operating under the radar, not so much as a hiccup."

"And then he passes on info on a mole."

"And gets himself a bullet in the head. The timing's very bad."

"Do you think Roth would ever sell out one of our own?"

Lance said nothing for a moment, then, "Do you?"

Laurel cleared her throat. She sounded like she was going to say something, but then she went silent too.

"I'll tell you one thing," Lance said. "If he did, it sure as shit isn't what I signed up for."

"No, it's not," Laurel said. "Neither is replacing one monster with another, if I'm honest."

"The president, when I spoke to him, he told me my mission was to hunt down Shipenko and make him pay."

"Is that still what you plan to do?"

Lance thought for a moment. He tried to grasp the big picture, the grand strategy, the game he knew Roth was playing, but he couldn't do it. How could replacing Molotov with a known terrorist, a cold-blooded killer like Osip Shipenko, ever be worth the risk? It was like Klára had said. Monsters had a way of taking on a life of their own. How did Roth think he was going to control him? He said, "Hey, do you know if Roosevelt ever said something about guys being our son of a bitch?"

"What's that?"

"He's a son of a bitch, but he's our son of a bitch, something like that?"

"Right," Laurel said. "Yeah. I think I've heard that."

"What do you make of it?"

"It was about a South American dictator, I think."

"But installing puppets like that? Trying to control the strings?"

"It's a pretty cynical game, Lance. I don't think anyone would say it wasn't."

"Yeah," Lance said, eyeing the police by the escalators. "Yeah, it is."

"And I'm guessing, from your tone, it's not a game you're too keen on playing."

"You know me," Lance said. "I'm a simple guy."

"Sure you are."

"Shipenko attacked our embassy. He spilled a lot of blood. And the president told me to find him and kill him."

"Well, that sounds pretty simple to me," Laurel said.

"It's a lot simpler than whatever game Roth's playing," Lance said.

"So you're sticking with the original plan? You're going to do what the president said?"

"You bet your ass I am."

"You don't care about Roth's plans?"

"Roth's plans?" Lance said. "Fuck Roth's plans."

"Well," Laurel said, "then it looks like you called the right girl."

"I was hoping you'd say that."

"There was an unscheduled military flight into Millerovo Air Base yesterday. VIP transport. Straight from Moscow."

"And you think Osip Shipenko was onboard?"

"The flight was tracked, but we never got a visual of the passenger."

"Then how do you know who it was?"

"It was near gale force winds when the choppers landed at Millerovo, but the passenger was escorted off by the pilot holding an umbrella. Shipenko's been next to impossible to track, he's been keeping off our radar since long before we were aware of his importance, but the one thing I've been able to gather about him—"

"Is that he uses umbrellas to avoid detection," Lance said.

"It's his MO. Always the same black umbrella. It's a tell."

Lance was listening but also watching the situation by the escalators. Some guy in a navy jacket was fighting off three police officers who were struggling to get him restrained. A crowd was growing and getting rowdy. People were trying to pull the cops off the man.

"Is everything all right there, Lance? It sounds like—"

"It's fine," Lance said, turning away from the commotion so as not to draw attention to himself. He had little doubt the age written on his Russian ID card fell within the terms of Molotov's draft order.

Just then, the doors at the front of the train station flew open, and eight police, dressed in the kevlar armor and black balaclavas of the Center E counter-extremism unit, stormed in and lined up in a crowd control formation.

"It's not just satellites he's hiding from," Laurel was saying. "He's sensitive to sunlight too."

Lance could tell there was more commotion brewing in the corridors that led to the two side exits. People were rushing into the concourse from them in a panicked fashion. The station was being locked down. Things were about to get out of hand. "Laurel," he said, "I've got to go."

"Is everything all right?"

More police poured in through the front entrance. Lance looked over to the escalators and saw the cops there had gotten the better of the man in the navy coat. He was on the ground now, his hands cuffed behind his back, and one of the cops was beating him with a baton. A few members of the crowd were trying to stop it, but the soldiers held them back. People were beginning to panic.

Lance looked toward the police at the front entrance. A second squad of Center E men had just arrived and was lining up behind the first, distributing riot shields and batons. Inadvertently, Lance caught the eye of one of them.

"You," the cop called out instantly, pointing a finger in Lance's direction.

Lance turned away, pretending not to have heard, and hung up the phone. With the exits cut off, he made his way toward the train platforms at the far end of the concourse. Between him and the platforms were some waist-high turnstiles, guarded by some relatively harmless men in the navy and gray uniform of the Oblast Transit Police.

Lance walked briskly toward them, resisting the urge to run. He also resisted the urge to look back over his shoulder. As he passed the glass of a newspaper kiosk, he saw in the reflection that some riot cops were definitely coming after him.

"You," one of them called out again, "you in the jacket!" Lance kept moving, and as he approached the turnstile, the cop yelled to the transit police, "Stop that man."

Lance was about to reach the turnstiles when his path

was blocked by three transit cops. He slowed his pace and glanced over his shoulder for the first time. Three Center E cops, better trained and better armed than the transit cops, were hot on his heels.

Lance stopped and raised his hands. "What is this?" he said in Russian to the transit cops.

They didn't know and looked past him toward the Center E guys. They were the ones calling the shots, and Lance turned around to face them. He didn't think the transit cops would jump him from behind.

"I'm not looking for trouble," Lance said.

"Not looking for trouble?" the cop closest to him said. "Let's see your ID?"

"I don't have it."

"He's a draft dodger," the second cop said. "He doesn't think he has to fight for his country."

"Maybe he's a pacifist," the third cop said, grinning.

Lance adjusted his stance, shifting his weight to his front leg, and said, "I wouldn't say that."

The cops came in closer, drawing their batons. The first said, "I think he wants to go to the front in the back of an ambulance."

Lance looked at each of them. "I hope you've already called the ambulance."

"What's that?" the first said.

Lance moved suddenly, like a pouncing cat, leaping forward and jabbing the lead man in the neck and then the rib cage. He buckled, and before he hit the ground, Lance stepped around him and hit the second man in the groin with his knee. When the man doubled over, Lance landed an elbow on the back of his head, sending him to the ground on top of the first. The third cop hesitated, backing slightly as he drew his pistol. Lance picked up a baton and, with a rapid jerk, knocked the gun to the ground. The cop looked at his hand, shocked to suddenly find it empty, and Lance followed the blow with another to the side of his temple. When he turned to face the transit cops, they backed away immediately.

The police back in the main concourse were being distracted by the crowd, which was swiftly turning riotous, but at least one of them had seen what Lance had done. Lance turned to the turnstile and leaped over it as the sound of a gunshot rang out in the air. It missed its mark, and Lance ran for the nearest platform and jumped down onto the track. He made his way then toward the freight yards that he'd scoped out from the bridge earlier. He was running fast and didn't look back to see if he was being followed. When he got to the freight yard, he crossed a hundred yards of open track to get to the concrete bank of the Temernik. He didn't hear any more gunshots, and when he looked back, no one was following. He looked down at the frozen river and tried to judge the thickness of the ice. The weather had been more than cold enough to freeze a river of that size, but it was always possible heated water was getting leaked into the stream from the surrounding industries.

He looked toward the station again. There was still no one coming. If there had been, he might have risked the ice, but as it was, he didn't think he needed to. Instead, he ran along the riverbank until it narrowed, then leaped across it to the brushy scrubland on the opposite side. From there, he climbed the slope to a six-foot-high chain-link fence. He scaled that and, a moment later, was disappearing down a side street toward the nearest tram stop. Somewhere in the distance, he heard sirens.

40

B y the time Bulavin stepped out of Shipenko's hotel room, he was scarcely able to breath. What had he just done, he thought. What had just happened? It was like something from a nightmare, him and the girl, the two of them, on the bed, blindly obeying Shipenko's callous commands like two automatons. He hadn't even been able to perform physically until he took the pill Shipenko offered him.

"I'm sorry," he whispered to the girl before leaving the room.

She said nothing.

Osip said nothing, either. By that time, there was so much blood on his robe it looked more crimson than white.

Two guards, one very tall and the other unusually short, were waiting for him outside the door. Bulavin brushed them off. "Give me a minute," he growled, almost unable to speak. He shut his eyes and when he opened them, realized that his hand was shaking. He couldn't feel it shake, but when he looked at it, there was no doubt that it was. A performance he'd watched of the play *Macbeth* suddenly came to mind. He'd seen it at the Alchevs'k Drama Academy, and all he could think of now was the actor on the stage, scrubbing his hands, trying to wash off blood that no one but he could see. That was what a fall from grace looked like, he thought. That was what happened to a mind racked with guilt.

After a minute, the guards took him by the elbow and ushered him down the corridor. He'd assumed they were going to escort him as far as the hotel lobby, but they remained with him all the way outside, where a black car was waiting. The taller guard went around to the other side and got in the back seat while the shorter held the door for him.

"My car is round back," Bulavin said.

"Get in," the guard said, ignoring his words.

Bulavin got in, sandwiched between the two of them.

There was a third man in the driver's seat, and when he started the engine, Bulavin said, "What is this? Where are you taking me?"

"Relax," the shorter guard said.

"I've just been named governor. This isn't necessary."

"We're here for your protection. We're taking you to your office."

Bulavin eyed the three men suspiciously. The government administrative building was just a few blocks away, and he went there every day. He didn't require an escort. "Stop the car," he said suddenly.

To his surprise, the driver stopped.

"Let me out," Bulavin said.

The driver shook his head. The car started moving

again, and the short guard said, "Just play along, pal. This will go a lot nicer."

"Am I a prisoner?"

The guards said nothing, but a minute later, the car pulled up in front of the government administration building. The short guard got out and held the door again. Bulavin followed him and looked up warily at the enormous building. His office was on the fifteenth floor, not far from where the war criminal, General Kolesnikov, was in the process of setting up his command center. Miraculously, all the offices on that floor still had their windows intact.

The guards followed him into the building, walking about a foot behind, one on his left, the other on his right. They ushered him through the lobby and Bulavin realized that, to anyone else, there really was no way of telling if he was leading them or they were leading him. As they stood courteously aside to let him enter the elevator, he almost didn't know himself.

They seemed to know where they were going and brought him up to the fifteenth floor and stopped outside his office door.

"Not coming inside?" he said to them.

"We'll be in the hallway if you need us," the short guard said.

Bulavin nodded and opened the door. Before stepping in, he said, "Am I under arrest?"

The guards looked at each other awkwardly, as if he'd just managed to say something very embarrassing to them, and the short one said, "Not as long as you stay where you're supposed to be."

"Which is inside this office?"

"Exactly."

He entered and shut the door. There was a blind on the window, and he shut it for privacy. Then he turned his back to the door and began immediately to hyperventilate. He was having a panic attack, and he doubled over and grabbed his knees, struggling to catch his breath.

It took him a few minutes to calm down, and then he went to his desk and searched frantically for some cigarettes. He was one of those people who was constantly in a state of half-having-quit, and there were none. He went back to the door and opened it.

"I need cigarettes," he said to the guards.

The taller of them took a pack from his shirt pocket and offered him one. Bulavin lit it and went back into the office. He shouldn't have been so surprised, he thought, that things had turned out this way. He'd always known they would, ever since he first set foot in the office. That day, and every day since, he'd had the feeling that his position in the government was an illusion, that it wasn't real, and certainly that it would be short-lived. He'd always felt like one of those poor sods you read about who miraculously won the lottery, but then, when the press went back to check in on them a few years later, they were back to being broke. It happened time and time again, like their luck was an aberration, a deviation from the mean that had to be corrected. His rise in the Luhansk government was a similar aberration, he thought. It was an aberration from reality, from what was supposed to be. Indeed, the very existence of Luhansk as a state separate from Ukraine, its creation as a Kremlin-backed puppet, imposed at gunpoint, and regarded by the entire United Nations General Assembly as an *Illegal Entity,* felt like a break from what was supposed to have been. Bulavin, in his bones, knew it would be ill-fated. None of it would end well for any of them. An overwhelming aura of futility hung over everything.

He sat down at his desk and stared at the blank wall in front of him. He'd never decorated the office, never even unpacked a computer or set up a telephone. It had the same bare walls, the same empty desk and plain chairs as it had when he'd first set foot in it. It was all a sham. He hadn't been expected to do real work there, and no one had ever attempted to provide him with the means to do so. He was a figurehead, a *stuffed shirt*, as the administrators in Moscow constantly put it, and he was there solely to lend credence to the Kremlin's claims that the region was autonomous.

He stubbed out the cigarette in an old coffee mug and was about to go ask for another when there was a knock on the door. It opened before he said anything, and he was surprised to see Anatoly Kolesnikov's grizzled old face peering in.

"Oh," he said, unable to hide the dismay in his voice. Bulavin didn't know Kolesnikov well, but he was vaguely aware of who the man was, of the kind of thing he stood for. The man was a war criminal, to put things bluntly. A cold-blooded killer implicated in countless atrocities. Bulavin felt distinctly uneasy whenever he found himself in his presence.

"Don't sound too excited," Kolesnikov said, entering the room and shutting the door firmly behind him.

"General Kolesnikov," Bulavin said, trying too late to regain his composure. He rose to his feet, an endeavor that required more effort than he would have imagined, and extended his hand. "I hear congratulations are in order."

Kolesnikov shook his hand vigorously, almost pulling

his arm from its socket in the process. "I hear you've received a promotion yourself," he said.

Bulavin shrugged. They both knew what promotions under the current circumstances meant. "Let's hope we're both alive long enough to enjoy them," he said weakly.

Kolesnikov pulled over the cheap plastic chair Bulavin kept for guests and sat down. He took some cigarettes from his coat pocket and stuffed one in his mouth. He turned away as he lit it, like a man more accustomed to lighting cigarettes in the wind than indoors. When he offered one to Bulavin, Bulavin snatched it eagerly.

"So," Bulavin said, "to what do I owe—"

"Read this," Kolesnikov said, pulling a creased envelope from inside his jacket.

"Oh," Bulavin stammered, looking at it. "What is it?"

"It's your script," Kolesnikov said.

"For what?"

"A press conference."

"I don't understand."

"Shipenko didn't tell you?"

"Tell me what?"

Kolesnikov shrugged. "We're all taking orders on the fly these days, I suppose."

"What are you talking about?"

"You'll see when you read the note," Kolesnikov said. "No one really knows what's going on right now. All I know is that he doesn't want you to become alarmed."

"Alarmed? It's a bit late for that, I'm afraid."

"Well, try not to read too much into the speech. It's just a publicity stunt, nothing more. Your job is to read the words exactly as written. Apparently it's a bait-and-switch with the media. "

"Bait and switch?"

"You know? Get their emotions going, get them all riled up, then alter the dialogue at the last minute for maximum effect. It's an old propaganda stunt."

"I'm not sure I'm the right person for a publicity stunt," Bulavin said.

"You're the face of the administration now," Kolesnikov said. "A full-fledged governor of an incorporated Oblast. They need you to be out in front of this thing. To give it credibility."

Bulavin couldn't even muster a smile. He sucked on his cigarette and ashed in the coffee mug.

"You don't believe me?"

"It's not that—"

"Look," Kolesnikov said. "Man to man, you don't want to fuck this up. Take my word for it. Osip Shipenko is not a man to be trifled with."

"No," Bulavin agreed, the images flashing across his mind of what he'd been forced to do in the hotel room. He'd have to find a way to live with those memories, to live with what he'd done.

"I mean," Kolesnikov continued, sucking hard on his cigarette, "the man's own face looks like it was put in a blender. Imagine what he'd be willing to do to yours."

Bulavin nodded. He needed no convincing on that front. He was already terrified of Shipenko. He was terrified of Kolesnikov, too, for that matter. He was so scared of so many things that the only reason he could still function was that he'd been stunned into a sort of numbness. "I understand there was some sort of industrial accident," he said.

Kolesnikov scoffed. "*Industrial*," he said sarcastically, and Bulavin got the impression there was a lot more to

that story that he didn't know. The truth was, he didn't
want to know. He didn't want to know any of it.

"Aren't you going to read it?" Kolesnikov said, nodding
at the envelope sitting on the desk.

Bulavin looked at it, then picked it up reluctantly and
opened it. As Kolesnikov had said, it was the script of a
press release, and as he read the words, his hands began
to shake again. "How am I..." he stammered. "How am I
going to read this?" His hands were shaking so badly he
could barely hold the sheet.

"I already told you," Kolesnikov said, "it's all a ruse.
Don't take it literally."

"This is going to cause an outrage."

"That's all been accounted for."

"It's going to get me killed," he said.

Kolesnikov shrugged as if that were scarcely a
concern. "I think Shipenko will have impressed upon you
already that there are worse things than getting killed."

"You can't be serious about this," Bulavin stammered,
letting go of the paper. "The people will riot."

"Let me show you something," Kolesnikov said, and
he got up and went to the window. Reluctantly, Bulavin
followed, already certain he wasn't going to like whatever
it was he was about to see.

The window overlooked the central square of the city. It
was not quite the sight it had been before the war, but it still
played the same role as a place of congregation. Bulavin
had noticed earlier that there were more soldiers than usual
milling about, but now he saw why. The entire area was
being prepared for an event. A crew was erecting a stage
with a podium at the center, and technicians were setting
up the stands and cables for lights and loudspeakers.

"They're setting up for the press conference," Kolesnikov said. "It's going to be a big one."

Bulavin could see that. The press, if that was even the correct word for the rabble of sellouts who purported to report news for the Kremlin's censors, was out in force. Dozens of cameramen and reporters, and not just from the local outlets but from the big Moscow outlets too, had clearly been told to expect something.

Bulavin looked back at the paper on his desk, the words typed out on it in some strangely anachronistic font, like it had been printed by a teleprinter, and thought of everything he'd seen since the start of the war. For most of the world, the Ukraine war had started just a few days ago, but for him, and the rest of the people of the Donbas, it had been raging almost a decade. He remembered, of course, how it had all been before, when he'd been a simple history teacher teaching kids. He'd enjoyed that life. He'd enjoyed exploring the sins of the past, the excesses of the Soviet era, the crimes of Stalin and the rest of them. He used to tell his students that all crimes eventually found the cold light of day. The truth always came out in the end, and the perpetrators, if they weren't caught and punished during their own lifetimes, eventually found their way to the place they belonged—the ash heap of history. The words he'd just read, he realized, would make him a part of that heap.

"I don't think I can do this," he said plainly.

"You just have to say the words."

"I can't. I just can't."

Kolesnikov nodded. "Shipenko was afraid you'd say that," he said. "That's why he's had your mother and sisters brought into custody."

"What?"

"He also said to tell you, whatever happened in the hotel room this morning, that was just a foretaste of what will happen to your family if you fail to deliver this message."

"I can't do this," Bulavin stammered. "I'll jump from the window."

Kolesnikov shrugged. "Do whatever you like," he said, "but it won't save your family."

41

Klára was sitting at the kitchen counter, watching Ritter scurry around the kitchen, opening and shutting drawers, searching cupboards. She was tense, and his constant movement was getting on her nerves. He'd checked the refrigerator and left the door partially open, which added to her frustration.

"What are you looking for?" she said irritably as she shut it.

"There must be something to eat in this place."

"There isn't," she said, and from the look on his face, it felt as if he was perhaps planning on blaming her for the fact. "Sorry to disappoint," she added dryly.

"No, no," he said, turning to the coffee pot. He poured himself a cup and joined her at the counter. "It's fine."

She watched him take a sip of the coffee. She'd made it over an hour ago and was sure it was cold. He swallowed it with a grimace and put the cup down a little harder than was called for. "Not up to your standards?" she said.

"How can you drink this?"

"If you'd like to lodge a complaint with the manager—"

"How does he live like this?" Ritter said, cutting her off.

"He doesn't," Klára said, feeling suddenly defensive of the place, like it had somehow become her responsibility since Lance's departure. "It's not his home."

Ritter took out his cigarettes and looked at her. From his moment's pause, she knew he knew she didn't want him to light one. He did it anyway. She wanted to say something but bit her tongue. Instead, she got up and went to the rickety window overlooking the yard behind the building. She tried to get it open, but its wooden frame was so old she couldn't get it to budge. Ritter watched her struggle with it, making no offer to assist. "Thanks," she said.

"What's that?" he said, looking up suddenly.

"You're a real gentleman."

He got up and yanked the window for her. It squeaked loudly and budged about half an inch, letting a sliver of ice-cold air into the room. They went back to the counter, and he grimaced again as he took another sip of his coffee.

"Feel free to make a fresh pot," she said. "If it's that bad."

He shook his head. She glanced at her watch, and he said, "It's not my fault, you know."

"What's not your fault?"

"You're upset because Lance is not back."

"There's still time," she said.

Ritter shrugged, and something about that really irked her. She rolled her eyes.

"What?" he said, catching the gesture.

"Nothing."

He puffed his cigarette, then looked at his watch and raised an eyebrow. It was after nine. "I'm sorry, Klára."

"Don't apologize."

"He should have been back by now."

She knew he was right. "Give him another hour."

Ritter looked at her like she had two heads. "An hour?"

"He'll be back."

"We need to get out of here. We should have gone already."

"I'm not leaving. Not yet."

"Every extra minute we stay—"

"If you want to go, go. No one's stopping you."

He looked at her, then went to the living room window and looked down at the street below.

"See anything?" she said, knowing the answer.

He shook his head.

She looked in the other direction, toward the kitchen window, as if ignoring him might somehow change the facts. He reminded her of some of the guys back at the BIS who'd been recruited from the military. They all had a certain bearing.

There was an old television in the living room, and Ritter turned it on. "I take it you speak Russian," he said, using the dial on the front to flip through the channels.

"Do you really think there'd be something on the news?" she said.

He kept flipping until he found the local news channel, then stood back. "What's that?" he said. "What are they saying?"

She couldn't believe her eyes. There was a news reporter speaking into the camera, and there was no mistaking the backdrop behind her. It was the enormous façade of Rostov Glavny.

"What are they saying?" Ritter said again.

"Shut up," she snapped, waving her hand at him. The reporter was talking about a disturbance at the train station without specifying what it had been. Clearly, though, it had led to dozens of riot police being called in. They could see them running around in the background.

"It was him, wasn't it?" Ritter said.

"I don't know what it was."

"What's she saying?"

"There was an incident. Gunshots were fired."

"That's a lot of ambulances," Ritter said. "A lot of police cars."

They watched until the end of the segment, then Klára said, "You can leave if you want, but I'm staying."

Ritter shook his head. "That's crazy. The GRU could be on their way here this very second."

"Even if that was Lance," she said, "there's no way he'd lead them back here."

"We're leaving right now," Ritter said, grabbing the few things he'd brought with him.

"No," Klára said defiantly.

"Klára!"

"I mean it, Craig. I'm staying right here."

"I can't exactly leave you here alone, can I?"

"You don't have a choice," she said, "unless you plan on carrying me out by force."

He shook his head. "I don't believe this."

"Believe what?"

"You're sweet on this guy, aren't you?"

"I'm not sweet—"

"He's off calling his girlfriend in America," Ritter said, "and you're here waiting for him like some abused housewife."

"I'm waiting because I know he's coming back."

"What if he isn't? I mean, look at that."

She looked at the TV screen for a moment, then said, "Switch it off."

Ritter left it on but went to the coat rack and started putting on his coat. "Come on," he said.

She shook her head.

"You're kidding me," he said, shaking his head incredulously.

"I'm not coming."

"But why? You made a plan—"

"Because I can't," she said, her voice rising. "I can't. Not yet."

"You've lost it."

"Just go," she said. "If you want to see me again, I'll be at the pay phone at the embankment at midnight."

"I don't believe this," he said.

"I'm sorry."

"Once I leave—"

"Just leave," she said, her voice colder and harsher than she'd intended.

"You're not acting rationally," he said, opening the door. And then he did it. He left. He walked out and shut the door behind him. She stared at it for a minute after he left, then went to the window and watched him walk away down the street.

She was torn. She knew he was right. She wasn't acting rationally, and it wasn't too late to run after him. But she didn't. She stayed put.

42

A sneer crossed Kolesnikov's face as he left Bulavin's office. He liked seeing other men squirm, and Bulavin had been squirming so badly he could barely read the words on the printout Kolesnikov gave him. Weakness, Kolesnikov thought as he waited for the rickety elevator to appear, was something he had a knack for detecting. Even as a boy, he'd had a sixth sense for ferreting out the weakest child in a classroom. He seemed to have an innate understanding of what made a person vulnerable. He could sniff it out like a truffle pig rooting around for a mushroom. And he smelled the stench of it on Petro Bulavin. There was no way a man like that was going to survive the maelstrom that was coming his way.

The elevator arrived, and he descended to the lobby. There were more soldiers in it than usual. A few of them stood to attention as he passed, but many didn't bother. Discipline was abysmal.

Rumors were flying, though. News had spread among the ranks that someone new from Moscow had arrived to shake things up. Shipenko was an intensely secretive man, even more concerned with security and keeping a low profile than the other politicos Kolesnikov had come across, and he imagined it was a result of his severe disfigurement. Even still, everyone seemed to know *something* big was coming. The preparations brewing for the press conference only added to that energy.

Kolesnikov found the captain of the riot control unit he'd assembled earlier and made sure the men were in position, then he left the building and walked across the square, stepping over the piles of rubble and detritus that lay strewn everywhere. By the old fountain, some wounded soldiers lay on the ground, bandaged, huddled under military blankets that were sodden wet from the melting snow. He looked back toward the building, up at the window on the fifteenth floor that was Bulavin's, and wondered for a moment if the man would take the leap. He didn't think so. It wasn't *that* bad, what he'd been asked to do—simply read an announcement. Kolesnikov had certainly seen worse.

He walked past the news crews and reporters, shielding his face from the cameras. He was surprised at how many of the national outlets had made a showing—there were newspapers and TV stations from Moscow, Saint Petersburg, even Rostov—and he wondered if Shipenko had circulated advance notice of the announcement before his arrival.

If so, he was even more cunning than Kolesnikov had realized—a true grandmaster, playing his game four or five moves ahead. Kolesnikov knew to be careful of men like that. Those were the ones who were underestimated. They were the most dangerous.

Kolesnikov thought of himself as one of them. He was used to being underestimated by his rivals, of being viewed as a mere brute, a sledgehammer in a world where precision tools were all the rage. He had a feeling that was about to change. His time, he felt, was about to come. This Osip Shipenko was the real deal, and Kolesnikov was already on the inside track.

He reached the steps of the courthouse on the opposite side of the square and sat down. A few hundred people were standing in the square, soldiers and press mostly, but passing civilians were beginning to be drawn in by the promise of some excitement. Most of them had no idea what they were waiting for. Someone had started playing music through the loudspeakers, and Kolesnikov recognized the plodding, orchestral tones of the anthem, *Glory to Luhansk*. He wondered if it was appropriate to still play it now that the state had been formally annexed.

He lit a cigarette and waited. He was flicking away the butt when the noise of the crowd began to change. The music was cut off abruptly, and some guards began clearing a path from the administration building toward the stage. Kolesnikov rose to his feet, expecting to see Bulavin, but instead, he saw someone in a cadet's uniform climbing the steps onto the stage. It was a woman, a redhead, no less, and if he was not mistaken, he recognized her from the air base back at Millerovo. She was too far away for him to be sure, but once she reached the podium, her image was projected onto a screen, and he saw that it was indeed her. Strangely for someone about to make an announcement in front of a crowd, her hair was disheveled, and her makeup smeared around the eyes. It looked like she'd been crying, and Kolesnikov guessed that she was being forced there against her will, as Bulavin was. He must not have been the only one who noticed because the atmosphere in the crowd began to feel darker, and the people stopped talking and grew silent.

The cadet stood at the podium and leaned into the microphone, her eyes darting around the crowd as if searching for an escape. The photographers clicked and flashed wildly. She cleared her throat, then began, timidly, to speak. She was interrupted instantly by a loud whistle of feedback from the speakers. She leaned back, startled, and Kolesnikov thought she was going to burst into tears. She looked at the sound engineer, waited a moment, then tried again.

"Ladies and gentlemen of Luhansk," she started, her voice quivering timidly. It was a very strange choice, he thought, to have her open the speech. She was too young, too helpless-looking, hugging herself as if for protection, and speaking so faintly it was as if she didn't want her words to be heard. "Thank you," she quavered on, "for showing up for this momentous announcement on such short notice. I know many of you have had to travel." She was reading from a notecard in her hand, and it was shaking so much Kolesnikov was afraid she'd lose hold of it. "It is my immense honor," she continued, "to introduce to you the new Governor of Luhansk, the honorable Petro Bulavin."

There was a smattering of applause. One of the onlookers, a lout in a pair of rubber farming boots, booed. Most stood still and watched in silence, glued to the unfolding scene like the passersby of some terrible car accident. The crowd grew quiet again, and there seemed to be an uncomfortably long pause before Bulavin appeared on the steps of the administrative building. He walked toward the stage, moving with the demeanor of a man who was being marched to his execution. Everything about him spelled weakness and fear. The two guards who'd been standing outside his office were escorting him now, and Kolesnikov wondered if it was as obvious to everyone else as it was to him that they weren't there to protect him but to prevent his escape.

Bulavin, to his credit, didn't run. He gave the cadet a quick look of acknowledgment—she looked away as if he were her vilest enemy—then stepped up to the microphone and cleared his throat. He glanced around the crowd, his face every bit as terror-stricken as the cadet's had been, then pulled a piece of paper from his pocket and began to speak.

"People of Luhansk, of the Donbas, and all of Mother Russia," he began haltingly, clearing his throat almost between every word. "I address you today not as the governor of a peaceful and prosperous province but as the leader of a land at war." He looked up. The crowd remained silent. "We are today, locked in a battle for our lives, our future, our very right to exist. From every direction, the forces of Nazism, Satanism, and Western Imperialism are trying to wipe our people from the face of the earth. This is a battle for national survival. A fight for our right to exist."

It was a punchy speech, Kolesnikov thought, looking at the camera crews and photographers. The media really had made quite a showing. There was little doubt that the eyes of the entire nation, if not the entire world, were on them. He hoped, for Shipenko's sake, he hadn't overplayed his hand.

"This is a time for heroes if ever there was one,"

Bulavin continued. "Like the heroes of old, the heroes of the Soviet Union, the men and women who gave their lives to defend our nation in times of existential crisis, this is a time to put our names in the history books. This is a time for heroes of the battlefield. It is not going to be an easy war. It is not going to be a quick war. Not only are we battling the treacherous Ukrainians, but we are battling all of their Western puppet masters too, the countries of NATO who are pulling the strings, and especially, we are fighting the United States."

Kolesnikov kept his eye on the crowd, but they were giving very little sign of what they thought. He looked up at the sky. The mood was so somber, and as if nature was conspiring to make it more so, some low, dark clouds appeared to be rolling in from the west. The breeze, too, seemed to be picking up.

"It is no secret," Bulavin continued, "that the opening salvos of this war have not gone our way. Our forces have been repelled. We've suffered casualties. Our initial attack on Kyiv, our attempt to cut the head off this evil serpent before it had a chance to respond, was unsuccessful. This failure is not the fault of our soldiers."

The man in the rubber boots gave a brief whoop of support, but for the most part, the crowd was too rapt to make any noise.

"It is the fault of traitors," Bulavin added, pausing again. Kolesnikov didn't know if he was pausing for effect or because he needed to breathe, but he had to admit, for a man who was acting with a gun to his head, Bulavin was doing a halfway decent job. "The reason for our setbacks, despite the noble leadership of the Kremlin and the brave sacrifices of our soldiers, is the direct result of sabotage. That is correct, people. We are in the midst of traitors, and we have been stabbed in the back. It is this murderous, cowardly scum who sold out their country and got fat off the good graces of our people who are to blame for our initial setbacks. These people lied to President Molotov about our preparedness for war. They lied about the quantity and quality of our arms and munitions. They pilfered and stole our supplies, raided our public coffers, and falsified the records and reports that said our vehicles were maintained and ready for action. They stole bread from the mouths of our children and sold the boots from off the feet of our soldiers. They got rich on the backs of our laborers and workers. And now, I announce to you that President Molotov has started to make them pay."

There was another pause. It was still impossible for Kolesnikov to judge the sentiment of the crowd, but there was one thing he could be absolutely certain of, the people were listening. In fact, not only were they listening, they were hanging on Bulavin's every word. Kolesnikov's instinct, from the moment he'd met Shipenko, was that the man was a skilled tactician, a plotter who knew what he was doing. If he was planning a coup, Kolesnikov saw that it was not beyond the realm of the possible that he would be successful. From the way this speech was going, he was only becoming more convinced of that impression.

In Russia, the people were used to political debate being scripted, false, merely giving the appearance of dissent. They knew that their politicians were puppets of the Kremlin, mouthpieces for Molotov, regardless of the part they played. Some spoke in favor of the president, others against him, but in the end, they were all actors reading their lines, playing a role that had been scripted in advance. People were used to hearing the chatter in the background, but they'd long ago stopped actually listening to it. Every debate was a rigged fight, the outcome foreordained.

This speech was going differently. The people could sense something real was being said. They could sense there were genuine stakes.

"I have just received notice from the Kremlin," Bulavin said, "that as of today, the president will be listening to the soldiers, not the generals, and will be coming down hard on those people who betrayed our fighters. Measures are already being taken to hunt down and punish those responsible for our battlefield struggles. In every branch of the armed services, at every level of the army, the air force, the navy, and the intelligence community, amongst the leaders, the elites, and the ruling class that has for so long gotten fat off the backs of Russia's hardworking people, the punishments will be meted out harshly and swiftly. I am not talking about fines and jail sentences. I'm not talking about slaps on the wrist. I'm talking about executions."

For the first time since he'd started talking, Bulavin's words met with noise from the crowd. He took a moment to look at the people, then continued. "This is the moment of reckoning. If you stole from our soldiers, if you let your own greed and corruption take precedence over the lives of our fighters, you are going to pay with your life."

On cue, footage came up on the screen behind him of a firing squad shooting a row of hooded prisoners outside the president's Novo-Ogaryovo Palace.

There was a long moment of stunned silence then, before a quiet round of applause broke out. Kolesnikov watched Bulavin closely now. This was the time when he might show his true colors. What he'd said so far had been the easy part. Now was the time to see what he was really made of. Kolesnikov had seen men do strange things when their families were at stake. Most men liked to think they would do the right thing, take the hit, save their loved ones. Kolesnikov knew, however, that a surprising number were too cowardly and ended up saving only themselves.

"With these punishments," Bulavin said, clearing his throat again, "comes the recognition that more must be done by all of us. We have been wronged by these traitorous criminals, but now we must redouble our efforts to make up for those wrongs. Once again, it falls on us, the Russian people, and our tireless president, to rectify the faults of others. Just as we did not ask for this war, just as we did not ask for NATO and the criminal fascists who run the United States and Europe to bring their military alliance to our borders, so have we not asked for the next sacrifice that I am about to announce."

"What sacrifice?" one of the journalists called out.

Kolesnikov braced himself for what was about to be said. He'd read the speech in advance, Shipenko had given it to him in an unsealed envelope, and he knew the words were going to cause an outrage. In fact, it would have been hard for him to imagine a more incendiary speech. It would cause riots, he knew, and not just in Luhansk, which was the only oblast that would be directly subject to the order, but across the entire country.

He lit another cigarette and began walking toward the far side of the square, where he'd had the foresight to arrange for some riot control troops. He estimated there were almost a thousand people in the square now. He'd assembled two-hundred troops, which should be more than enough to handle any upheaval that was about to break out.

"The sacrifice I've been asked to announce," Bulavin said, his voice for the first time threatening to fail him, "is an amendment to the partial mobilization order that was announced by the President today across the rest of Russia."

He paused, and the murmurs in the crowd grew louder. Kolesnikov kept walking. What Bulavin was about to say, if Shipenko's calculation was correct, could very well be the words that toppled President Molotov.

"I hereby declare the Oblast of Luhansk under martial law. My office will take on the maximum powers afforded under the constitution to protect our territory and, with the help of the military, enforce a new mandatory mobilization order."

The murmur grew louder.

"This order applies to every male in the oblast over the age of fourteen."

Kolesnikov smiled but did not look back. He didn't need to. He rounded a corner and saw that the men were standing at the ready, armed with riot shields and batons. A squad of riflemen had loaded their weapons with rubber bullets, and there were six armored vehicles fitted with water canons.

"Ready for action, men?" he roared, walking swiftly toward them. Back at the square, the sounds of an upheaval were already beginning to rise into the air.

The men looked at him expectantly, ready for their order.

With a flick of the wrist that he'd fashioned after Captain Jean-Luc Picard of the *USS Enterprise*, he said, "Roll out!"

43

After leaving the apartment, Ritter went directly to the café on Voroshilovskiy Prospekt that overlooked the Balkan Hotel. He wasn't going to risk going back to the hotel room—although it was still rented under the name he'd given—but there were some things in the Škoda he needed. He'd left the car with the valet, and as far as he knew, it was still in the underground parking lot beneath the hotel.

He entered the café and sat at the same table as last time, with the same view of the hotel entrance and side delivery bay. The waitress, the same corpulent lady in the same thin cotton dress, seemed just as irritated by his presence as she had the day before. He ordered coffee and looked out at the hotel, watching the comings and goings while he waited for it.

It all looked normal. There were two valets, and they took turns picking up or parking cars. To access the lot, they either drove or used the dedicated elevator in the lobby. Ritter had seen it many times but had never used it.

He lit a cigarette, and the waitress instantly brought

him an ashtray, as if afraid he would ash on the floor. She started talking to him in Russian, and he assumed she wanted him to order more than coffee. He pointed at an item on the menu, and that seemed to satisfy her.

She left, and he watched a taxi pull up to the hotel. Nothing out of the ordinary. He played through in his head the different methods he could use to get to the Škoda. He could present his ticket to the valet and ask them to bring it up, he could go down to the parking lot himself, or he could try something more creative if he could think of something. In any case, it didn't look like that would be necessary.

The waitress brought him his food, some kind of potato pancakes with a fruit compote. He didn't eat it, and before leaving, just to bug her, he stubbed out his cigarette on the plate. Then he exited the café and crossed the street to the hotel, pulling up the hood of his coat to give himself a little cover. He walked past the valets into the lobby and went to the bar, where he took a seat facing the entrance.

The bartender came up, and he asked for a scotch and soda. When the bartender returned with the drink, Ritter handed him enough money for the drink and a handsome —though not suspiciously so—tip. He also gave him his valet ticket and asked in English if he wouldn't mind having the car brought up.

He watched the bartender go out to the valet, then, leaving his scotch untouched, he got up and went to the parking lot elevator. He pushed the button, and while he was waiting, the valet showed up and waited with him. Ritter didn't speak to him, scarcely acknowledged him, and when the elevator arrived, they got in and stood next to each other awkwardly. It was mostly the valets who used that elevator, but it wasn't unheard of for customers to do their own parking. When the elevator doors opened, Ritter let the valet go first, then followed him out. He stood by the elevator, holding the door open with his foot, and watched the valet use the key to find the Octavia. The valet got in, fired up the engine, and drove off toward the exit.

Ritter watched and waited. The car disappeared, and nothing unusual happened. No GRU agents jumped out of the shadows. No police sirens wailed. The parking lot was still and empty. Ritter got back into the elevator and rode it to the lobby, then went to the valet stand and asked for his car.

He got into the car and pulled out onto Voroshilovskiy Prospekt, where he drove three blocks, turned onto a side street, and pulled over in front of an old tenement building. He checked his mirrors to make sure no one was watching, then unlocked the glovebox and took out the four passports he'd left there. Then he got out of the car and popped the trunk. There was a bag full of weaponry and ammo, and he took two Glock 17 pistols, as well as extra magazines, and stuffed them into his coat. There was also a briefcase full of cash in a number of different currencies, and he took that too.

Then he reached down and removed the cover over the spare wheel. He pulled up the wheel and reached under it to where he'd placed the car manual. The manual was in a leather binder with the Škoda logo embossed on the front, and he flicked through it until he found what he was looking for—a list of phone numbers, about fifty in total, all written backward and labeled with incongruous names like Mr September, Mr Marseilles, Ms Pimlico, and Mr Mars Bar. All meant something to him, and he scanned the list for Mr Garfield, memorized the number, then tore out the page and put it in his pocket.

The street he was on was quiet enough, but if he left the car there, someone would get suspicious soon. Then the police might be called. He got back into the driver's seat and drove it around to the lot behind the apartments, parked in the corner farthest from the building, got out, locked up, and walked away.

He was in the Bogatyanovka neighborhood, and he entered the October park, throwing the paper with the numbers, as well as the key to the car, into a small, concrete culvert as he crossed over it. There was a Ferris wheel in the park, out of use, with some pay phones nearby, and he went up to them and dialed the number he'd memorized.

"Allo?" a man said in Russian.

Ritter hesitated.

"*Kto gavarit*?" the man said.

Ritter cleared his throat. "Zadorov?" he said.

"Wait," came the terse reply in English.

Ritter waited. He could hear Zadorov excuse himself hastily, leave a room, then shut a door. When he came back on the line, he was livid. "What the hell are you doing calling this number? Are you trying to get me killed?"

"Volga's dead," Ritter said bluntly.

"I tried to warn you not to go out there."

"Well, I didn't get the message in time, and I didn't feel like conducting this conversation over text message."

"You should get out of the city," Zadorov said. "It's too dangerous now. The GRU is everywhere."

"Are they looking for me?"

"They're looking for a lot of people. I'm telling you to get out while you still can."

"I want to know what happened to Volga."

"But you were at the farmhouse. You must have seen."

"Yes, but how did he get picked up? Who sold him out?"

"I don't know. All I know is that someone requested his file from me, and I gave it to them."

"Who requested it?"

"The GRU."

"And you didn't think to warn Volga?"

"Of course I did, but then I'd have been under suspicion. I tried to warn you, though."

"The least you could do," Ritter said.

"Look, I need to go. Don't call me again."

"Not so fast," Ritter said. "You took Volga's money. You took mine. Now you can earn it."

"That was before. We're at war now. Everything's different. All bets are off."

"Tell me who in the GRU took over the file," Ritter said.

"Trust me, you don't want to know."

"If I want your advice, I'll ask for it."

"You're going to get yourself killed."

"You didn't see them there," Ritter said. "The least they deserve is revenge."

"I don't know who requested the file. It was a generic GRU jurisdiction slip. That's all I know."

Ritter sighed. He thought back to what he'd seen at the farmhouse. "Three was a shoe print out there," he said. "A woman's shoe. A heel."

"A high heel?"

"Yes. Have any female GRU officers been flown in?"

"If there were any, trust me, I'd have noticed."

"So that's a no?"

"It's a no, Craig, and trust me, even if I had, these are not the type of people you want to get mixed up with."

Ritter glanced around the park. He thought he saw some movement near the bushes by the concession stand, but there was no one there now. "I've got to go," he said.

44

L ance was extremely careful in returning to the apartment. He took all countermeasures, detouring through busy tram stations to drop any tails, backtracking on himself multiple times to make absolutely certain he wasn't being followed. It meant it took far longer than it should have to get back, and he was sure Klára and Ritter would no longer be waiting when he got there.

When he reached the street the apartment was on, he stopped at the corner and watched the entrance. He lit a cigarette and stood at the corner for the time it took to smoke it, the cold gradually penetrating his coat and boots. No one had entered or exited the building while he'd been watching, and there was no sign of anything suspicious except for one small thing—a light was on inside the apartment. He wasn't sure if it was an issue. Klára and Ritter could have left it on when they'd left. Certainly, if the Russian security services were waiting inside for him, they'd have turned it off. But it was unexpected.

He rubbed his hands together and stamped his feet, wondering what to do. Another few minutes standing around, and his fingers would be too numb to hold a gun. The safest thing would have been to turn his back on the place, but his things were inside, and, in any case, he needed to know if something had happened.

He approached the building cautiously, acting as if he was going to walk past it, and as he got closer, he examined the front door for any sign of tampering or damage. It all looked normal, and he stopped at the door, unlocked it, and slipped inside the hallway. He knew the stairs would creak on his way up, and he drew his gun before climbing them. When he got up to the landing, he peered at the crack of light beneath the apartment door. There was no sign of movement, but he did think he could make out the faint sound of voices. He looked up the stairwell, scanned the other apartments on his floor, then stepped forward, creeping silently up to the door. He was about to put his ear to it when, unexpectedly, it swung open. In an instant, his gun was out in front of him, his finger on the trigger, ready to fire.

"Lance!" someone gasped in shock, raising her hands.

"Klára!"

"I heard you on the stairs."

"What are you still doing here?"

"Waiting for you."

"You shouldn't be here. You should have left."

She gave him a blank look, like his words made no sense to her, then retreated into the apartment. He followed her in, locking the door behind him, and scanned the interior for any more surprises. The voices he'd thought he heard turned out to be the TV, tuned to a local news channel.

"Where's Ritter?" Lance said.

"He left."

"He had sense."

Klára shrugged. She looked mildly offended. "I told him to be at the embankment tonight. We can regroup there."

"You can regroup," Lance said. "I've got somewhere else to be."

"What are you talking about?"

He walked past her to the bedroom and began rooting through a box in the closet.

"What are you doing?" she said, and when he didn't answer, she repeated herself more loudly. "Lance! Talk to me."

"It's better if you don't ask," he said, checking a gun and putting some spare ammo into his inside coat pocket.

"Better if I don't ask?" she said, following him back into the kitchen. "What's that supposed to mean?"

"We should split up. You should meet up with Ritter and get out."

"Get out?" she demanded, her voice getting louder by the second.

"Out of the country," he said, realizing that his words had a more emotionally charged impact than he'd intended.

"Lance, what are you even talking about?"

He stopped what he was doing, giving her his full attention for the first time since his return. She was sitting at the kitchen counter, two empty coffee cups in front of her and an empty cigarette packet. She was very angry. Livid would be the word, he thought. "I got some intel," he said. "From Langley." He realized he'd avoided mentioning Laurel by name.

"Intel?"

"Actionable intel," he said.

"You got a location on Shipenko?"

He looked at her but said nothing. She'd stayed there, waiting for him. She'd stayed long beyond the agreed time. "You should have left with Ritter," he said.

"I wanted to make sure you were okay."

"And what if I wasn't? What would you have been able to do? The GRU could have come here and killed you."

"Only if you told them where to come."

"You don't know that I wouldn't."

Her eyes flashed back at him as if he'd just slapped her in the face. "You wouldn't have," she said, her voice uncertain for the first time.

"Everyone talks eventually, Klára. Your waiting here was a needless risk. It was a mistake."

She said nothing. The news reporter on the television was talking about the disorder at the train station, and she got up and turned it to mute.

"You knew something was happening at the train station," he said, "and still you stayed."

She didn't respond, her face as still and cold as a statue.

"You knew all that was happening," he said, nodding toward the screen, which was showing dozens of riot police lined up on Ulitsa Deputatskaya, "and still you stayed."

"I thought you'd be glad."

"That you risked your life—"

"I stayed for you."

He made to respond but stopped himself. He didn't know what to say.

"The only reason I'm here is that you told me to come," she said.

"To go after Shipenko."

"Exactly."

"But I know where he is now."

"*Really?*"

"Yes."

"Because Laurel told you?"

"Yes," he said, feeling distinctly out of his depth, as if he'd been leading her on, and she was only now realizing it. As if he'd been using her, manipulating her. And perhaps, he thought, she was right. Maybe he had been. It certainly had suited his purpose to have her there. "If I let you believe there was anything more to this than the mission—"

"Oh, fuck off," she said suddenly.

"Excuse me?"

"Get over yourself, Lance."

"You shouldn't be nearly this angry—"

"I'm here for Shipenko, and Shipenko only."

"Okay," he said, raising his hands as if trying to calm a barking dog.

"Laurel told you where to find Shipenko. What did she say, exactly?"

Lance hesitated, but from the look on her face, he thought better of it. "Millerovo," he said.

"The air base?"

"Yes. It's about two hundred kilometers from here."

"I'm well aware of where Millerovo Air Base is," she said, "and I know it's a complete backwater. There's zero reason anyone important would be there."

"They saw him there," Lance said, suddenly feeling defensive.

"Who did?"

"Langley. They spotted him by satellite. He arrived by chopper."

"They saw his face? They got a positive ID?"

"No," he said weakly.

"So a chopper arrived, and they assumed he was on it?"

"They have their methods, Klára."

"Did any choppers leave?"

"Nothing left, choppers or planes."

"And what about ground vehicles?" she said. He could detect a hint of defiance in her voice now but wasn't certain where it was coming from. "Any trucks or cars leave the base?"

"What are you trying to say?" he said. She was facing the television, looking over his shoulder at it, and he turned to follow her gaze as she unmuted the volume. The newscaster was reporting on some speech that had taken place in the last hour. Apparently, it had led to an outbreak of protest similar to the one he'd just witnessed at the train station. "What's this?" Lance said.

"Langley didn't tell you?"

He looked at the screen closely. A man was speaking to a crowd in Russian, reading a prepared speech, and the building in the backdrop had its windows boarded up with plywood. Draped from two of the windows was the Russian flag. "Ukraine," he said. "Donbas."

"Luhansk," Klára said. "Millerovo is less than ten miles from the border there."

From the looks of things, the protests had turned violent, and troops had been called in. The newscaster said in Russian, "The announcement by Governor Bulavin of the new province of Luhansk, that martial law had been declared and that a compulsory draft was being ordered for all males over the age of fourteen, sent the assembled crowd into a frenzy."

"What?" Lance said, looking at Klára.

She motioned toward the television for him to keep watching. The view had switched to the news studio back in Moscow, where a number of supposed experts had been assembled to interpret the events. Lance recognized most of them, all chosen from a reliable roster of hawkish Molotov supporters that were permanent fixtures of the Kremlin's tightly controlled news cycle. "If Molotov knew about this," one of the commentators, a bald, former Olympic boxer named Girkin, was saying, "then I honestly don't know what to make of it. I mean, we all want to crush Ukraine," he continued, "but boys of fourteen? That's...."

"It's barbaric," another commentator chimed in. "It's barbaric, and I'm not afraid to say it."

"It's not confirmed this order was approved by the Kremlin," the host said.

"I can't see how it was," Girkin said. "I mean, who is this new governor? What do any of us know about this Petro Bulavin? From what I've heard, the man was a schoolteacher before the war."

"I would guess he's maybe out of his depth with these issues," the host said. "My guess is the Kremlin will come down on this announcement like a ton of bricks."

Lance turned to Klára. "What happened?"

"What they said," Klára said, turning the television volume back down. "The new governor of Luhansk announced a draft of all males aged over fourteen."

"That's suicide," Lance said. "For any politician, that's ludicrous. He'll lose his head."

"What could have persuaded him to do such a thing?" Klára said, her tone almost triumphant.

"You think this was Shipenko's doing?"

"If he's planning a coup, this would be a pretty nice way to start it off, wouldn't it? Enrage the mother's all across Russia who are already up in arms over his draft order."

"But Molotov won't stand for this," Lance said. "If Shipenko got someone to say this without permission, it will be his head Molotov will be after."

Klára only shrugged. "Definitely something worth considering, though, isn't it? Something that might be worth the time of a man like Osip Shipenko, who is not known for his penchant for long, uncomfortable helicopter rides."

"You think Shipenko's in Luhansk?"

"What do I know?" Klára said. "I mean, Laurel has access to more satellites than Cape Canaveral."

Lance said nothing. He knew she was right.

"I mean, all this did happen after you spoke to her...."

"Can you stop talking about her like she's some sort—"

"Some sort of what?"

Lance didn't know what to say, so he satisfied himself with a frustrated shake of the head.

"I just thought," Klára said, "that you'd want as much information as possible before making the four-hour trek up to Millerovo Air Base for no good reason."

45

Osip stood by the window of his hotel room, looking down on the street below. The outcry resulting from Bulavin's speech had exactly the effect on the populace he'd thought it would, and from his room, he could see the smoke rising from the protests in the central square.

On his television, disorder seemed to be spreading across the country like wildfire, with crowds gathering outside government buildings in all major cities. The unrest had been simmering beneath the surface even before Osip's little stunt—he'd seen footage of a riot breaking out at the Rostov train station that had only been put down when riot police were called in—but Bulavin's speech had definitely put it into overdrive. In Moscow and Saint Petersburg, it was worst, with students, mother's groups, and political activists taking to the streets, their placards reading 'Death to the Dictator' and 'End the War.' He had the TV on, and it was showing footage from Red Square of police dragging an elderly woman into a van, her face covered in blood. The placard she'd been holding was a picture of Leonid Brezhnev. The caption, stenciled in red ink below the image, read 'Still fighting for Freedom.' Osip couldn't have asked for a better outcome. This was how coups began, it was how regimes were toppled, and it was only going to get worse for Molotov. When the news spread to all corners that boys of fourteen were being drafted, the chaos would be uncontainable.

Molotov had never been so vulnerable.

Which also meant he was going to be angry. Very angry. And when Molotov got angry, heads tended to roll. Lots of heads.

Osip had put himself right in the firing line, and he was well aware of the fact. The president's people had already been in touch, and an urgent phone call was being set up. It was a risk, certainly, but it was a calculated risk, a measured move of a chess piece. You couldn't pull off a coup without putting your neck on the line, and Osip had spent years planning for this moment. He was not about to lose his nerve now that it had arrived.

There was a door connecting his room to the one next to it, and he opened it to check on the progress. It had been Yelena's room, and she was still there, sitting on a chair near the window with a look of complete shock on her face—he was beginning to think he'd pushed her too hard—but she was far from the top of his priority list. There were a dozen other people in the room, soldiers, bureaucrats, and a military comms team that was working furiously to set up a secure line to the Kremlin. "What the hell is taking so long?" Osip growled.

"It's complicated, sir," one of the technicians said. "The Kremlin has requested top-level security for the call, and it's not something we were set up to accommodate."

"Did you let them know that?"

"They're aware of our situation, sir, but the order came from Molotov himself. He's convinced the CIA has infiltrated his comms, and he wants everything done by the book."

"Well, get it sorted," Osip said, lighting a cigarette, "and fast. It is not wise to keep an angry man waiting, and I assure you, at this moment, President Molotov is a very angry man." He remained in the doorway, leaning on his cane, and watched as they wheeled a rickety old AV cart into the room. The cart was loaded with old electronic equipment, and he said, "Don't tell me all this is necessary for just one phone call."

"I'm afraid so," the technician said. "The Ukrainians aren't making it any easier, jamming the airwaves and tapping any lines that go through their territory."

"It's our territory," Osip corrected. "They're squatting on it, but not for much longer."

"Of course, sir."

He watched the team scurry around the room, setting up power cables and searching for electrical outlets to plug them all into. He came closer and picked up what looked like a cell phone handset from the nineteen eighties. "What the hell is this?" he said, holding it up as if he'd just found a dead rat.

"It's a DyanTAC 8000X, sir."

It was connected by cable to another handset that had its make and model number written on a military storage sticker. The sticker was beginning to turn brown with age and said, 'OKI 900 - Rostov Central Depot - 1991'. It had been wired to an old desktop PC that was, in turn, connected to an Icom PCR-1000 radio receiver. An engineer was typing furiously on the PC's keyboard.

Osip looked at the mess of cables and wires with a growing sense of unease. It wasn't normal for this level of precaution to be taken for a single call. He'd always known this would be one of the key moments of his plot, but now that it was drawing nearer, he could feel his heart thumping in his chest.

"Hello? Hello?" the technician was saying into the receiver, and Osip had to retreat into his bedroom just to get away from it. "Tell me when you're ready," he said before shutting the door.

This was it, he thought, lighting another cigarette. He'd known Vladimir Molotov for more than forty years, and in all that time, he'd endeavored to give the man precisely zero reason to ever suspect him of posing a threat. It had been a long wait, requiring inhuman levels of patience, but it might yet pay off. There were no guarantees, of course. Like so many Russian leaders who'd preceded him, Molotov was prone to bouts of such intense paranoia that they frequently manifested themselves in leadership purges. There had been days during his reign when literally hundreds of military officials, senior bureaucrats, and intelligence officers were executed at the stroke of a pen. Everyone, in every department, in every government building in Moscow, knew they were always just a single signature away from losing their lives. It maintained a level of control among the upper echelons that was hard to imagine for those who'd never experienced it. Osip knew men who refused to order soup at the GRU cafeteria on a Monday because someone who'd once done so had died. Others avoided specific elevators or swore by a certain brand of aftershave they were convinced Molotov was partial to.

As for Osip, the man who so frequently incited horror

and revulsion in the people he came across, the president seemed to have a blindspot—some species of loyalty, forged in the very earliest days of their careers in the KGB, that kept Osip safe where so many others had perished. Osip was, by necessity, uniquely well-versed in the more unusual survival tactics provided by nature. It appeared as if he'd somehow figured out a way to become the cuckoo egg in Molotov's nest, the intruder that, for some reason known not even to the president himself, would be nurtured and protected, even as it hatched and grew and plotted to devour him.

Osip was pulled from his musings by a knock on the door. A technician opened it and said, "We're ready, sir."

He took a deep breath. The moment of truth had arrived. There was no turning back now. He was about to find out if the machine he'd fired up was going to continue cranking its gears or if the whole thing would blow up and get him killed.

He walked into the room and told everyone to get out. "All of you," he snapped. "You too, Yelena. This is completely private." As the technicians hustled out of the room, he followed them to the door and made sure no one waited behind in the corridor. "If I need you, I'll call," he said to the technicians who continued to tweak the equipment. "Now get lost, the lot of you. If I find anyone within earshot of this conversation, I'll have his head on a spike."

He left the door open so that he could make sure the corridor remained empty, then went back to the contraption the technicians had set up and picked up the receiver. "Hello," he said, then, clearing his throat, repeated louder, "Hello, this is Osip Shipenko."

It was a female voice that came back to him,

sounding strangely warped through the layers of tele-
phony that had been set up. "Please hold for the President, sir."

He was surprised that the voice was familiar. "Darya?
Is that you?"

There was the briefest of pauses, it was always the
same with her, and then her timid voice, as if making a
confession, said, "It's me, sir."

"They routed the call through you?"

"Through your office, sir, yes."

The line clicked then, and she was gone. Osip sat on
the bed next to the receiver and took a deep breath. He lit
another cigarette—he was chain-smoking, a sure sign of
nerves—and waited. In a surprisingly short time—the
president loved making people wait—Molotov's thun-
derous voice came on the line. "Osip, is it you?"

"It's me, sir," Osip began. "I can explain everything."

"What the devil are you playing at?"

"You sent me to get results—"

"And you've lit a fire under all of Russia. Half the
country is up in arms. Who in their right mind would
order the mobilization of children?"

"It's a ploy, sir. A tactic."

"They're rioting outside my very gates. I'm calling you
from the Kremlin bunker."

"It's all a publicity stunt, sir. You have to trust me. This
is what I do."

"I trust nothing and no one. You know that."

"This will have the country eating out of your hands,
sir. In a matter of hours. I swear it."

"They were already up in arms over my mobilization
order."

"Exactly, sir. An order that applied to eighteen-year-olds. Grown men. They should have been eager to fight for their country."

"But your order pushed it too far."

"My order will put shame on any grown man who refuses to fight, sir. These Luhansk boys, they're going to be ready, willing, and able. I'll make sure of it. They're being handpicked."

"But we can hardly send boys onto the battlefield."

"We won't have to, sir. The whole thing's a stunt, as I said. And every moment of it will be caught on camera. The eyes of the entire nation will be watching."

"And what are those eyes going to see?"

"They'll see Luhansk boys, our nation's newest citizens, who are not only willing but eager to spill their blood in defense of their new Motherland. I'm going to line them up for the cameras, put them in freshly pressed uniforms, and drive them to a nearby base where they'll be greeted by their comrades who are already fighting."

"And?" the president said impatiently.

"And then, that's when you step in, sir."

"Me?"

"You call the whole thing off. Countermand the order. Execute the governor here if you have to. You'll be the one who steps in to save the day."

"And all the while...."

"All the while, the people will be seeing brave boys who were willing to give their lives for you, sir. You'll be merciful. The heart of every mother in the country will be filled with gratitude, with pride that her son was chosen to fight in this war. It will make you look magnanimous."

Molotov was quiet for a moment, surely a good sign, Osip thought, then he said, "How long?"

"How long, sir?"

"Until I call it off. Until I release the tension? Because I don't know how long my police can keep these protestors in line."

"Hours, sir. Just a few hours. It'll all be over before the end of the day."

Molotov went silent again, then said, "You should have discussed this with me."

"We had to preserve deniability, sir. You knew nothing of this. And now, with the entire nation watching, you're the one man who can set it right."

Molotov sighed.

Osip had him. He could sense it. "It's a risk, sir. But it's a controlled risk. And it will pay off very soon."

"It better."

"And the media coverage? It will be the biggest drama the country has watched in years. It will distract from everything else."

"Hmm," the president said.

"Sir?"

"It's *everything else*, Osip, that I'm worried about. It's all very well having the nation behind us, but if we don't win in Ukraine, it's all for naught."

Osip sucked hard on his cigarette. One hurdle cleared. One more to go. If the president said yes to what Osip said next, his plot was about to transition from something that was perhaps remotely possible to something that was not just possible but probable. "On that front, sir, I have another proposal."

"Oh, do you?" Molotov said.

"Something that will get NATO off our backs for good."

"You've cooked up some magic fairy dust, have you?"

"Without Montgomery, sir, the western coalition will

evaporate. Support for Ukraine will dry up immediately. They'll have to fight alone."

"Fighting alone," Molotov said, "is a fight they cannot win."

"Precisely, sir."

"And how, pray tell, do you propose getting them to do that?"

"It's another risk, sir, but again, a calculated one."

"You're having a fine time at the casino today, Osip. Placing your bets with my chips."

"We need to call Montgomery's bluff, sir. He's spineless as a jellyfish. He's proved it a dozen times. If we go bold, he'll run with his tail between his legs. I promise you."

"You know what they say about people who make promises they can't keep."

"This one, I can keep, sir. If...."

"If what?"

"*If* we put the nuclear card on the table."

"We've been spouting off about nukes for weeks, Osip. They don't buy it."

"We need to put the fear in them this time. The real fear. We need to walk up to them with our hounds off their leash."

"I've already given you the Iskander-M brigade, Osip. I gave you the 9M723s and 9M728s. I let you move them to Taganrog in broad daylight, letting everyone and his dog see where they were going."

"But they still don't believe we'll use them, sir."

"What are you suggesting, Osip? That I nuke Kyiv?"

"No, sir. But there is a way to make the Americans know we're for real this time."

"Short of actually using the damn things?"

"Yes, sir."

Molotov waited for a second, then said, "Are you going to spit it out, Osip, or make me guess?"

"You can transmit a launch code, sir," Osip said, holding his breath as soon as the words escaped his lips. His heart pulsed in his chest like an engine piston.

When Molotov responded, his tone had changed dramatically. "You want me to give you the keys to the fucking kingdom, you sly piece of—"

"Not to me, sir. Don't send it to me. Send it to Taganrog. A single code for a single nuclear-capable Iskander."

"A real code?"

"The Americans will know the difference, sir. Their spies are all over our launch apparatus. If you send a live code, they'll know you've done it, and Montgomery won't be able to live with it. Mark my words, he'll back off like the mutt he is."

"You've lost your mind. If I do that, some halfwit in the Western Military District could end the fucking world."

"Which is precisely why Montgomery will shit his pants."

"I'll shit my own pants, Osip."

"But the missile won't be fired, sir. There's not a man in Russia who'd fire without your say-so."

"You want to bet the entire farm on this one gambit."

"With all due respect, sir, that bet's already been placed. We're in play now. The stakes are real. They couldn't be higher. And we're losing."

46

L aurel pulled up to the sumptuous entrance of the Saint Royal Hotel and stepped out of a cab. The hotel was one of the most prestigious in Washington, located on Lafayette Square just a block from the White House. It was one of the few places in the city where Roth still thought it safe to be seen together. "If we're not on friendly territory here," he'd once said, "then the entire thing's a lost cause."

Laurel hadn't asked him to elucidate, but she had to admit, the place did give a sense of security. The ushers in their hats and tailcoats, greeting her by name and remembering her favorite brand of tequila, the absolute discretion that was guaranteed by signed contracts between the hotel's board of directors and the federal government, even the flag over the entrance that was made of Napoleonic-era ciselé velvet, all breathed safety.

She walked up to the polished brass doors, held open by the maître'd, and entered a lavish lobby replete with marble floors, brass art deco fixtures, and crystal chandeliers that hung from the vaulted ceiling on long, razor-thin chains.

"Ms Everlane, how lovely to see you again," he said. "Your guest is already waiting in the private bar."

She walked through the famed Library Bar, where some of the most expensive spirits ever produced could be seen in their crystal decanters, and through a set of oaken doors. There, Tatyana was seated at a high-top table by the fire, looking eminently pleased with herself. She'd taken off her coat and gloves to reveal an elegant black evening dress that exposed her shoulders, back, and an exquisite pearl necklace. In her jeans and blazer, Laurel suddenly felt decidedly underdressed. "I hope this isn't for my benefit," she said, indicating Tatyana's outfit as she took her seat.

"Oh," Tatyana said, "I was on my way out when you called."

"I see," Laurel said, careful not to show any hint of judgment. Tatyana was sensitive about such things, and Laurel had to admit if she lived the same lifestyle, she would have been too.

Not that there was any danger of that. The more time the two women spent together, the more their social lives seemed to diverge toward two opposing poles. While Tatyana got ever more promiscuous, ever more willing to take risks to fill the void that accompanied their life of secrecy, Laurel seemed intent on imitating the life of a nun, complete with all the solitude and celibacy one might imagine.

"You know," Tatyana said, sensing her thoughts, "it wouldn't do you any harm to get a little yourself from time to time. It relieves stress, for one thing."

Laurel ignored the comment and got the bartender's

attention. "Whatever she's having," she said. The bartender left, and she looked around to make sure there was no one else in the room. "Okay," she said, once she was certain they were alone, "what have you got for me?"

"You're the one who called the meeting," Tatyana said.

"Which I wouldn't have had to if you bothered to show up at the office every once in a while."

"I only avoid it because you've made it feel like a college dorm room. Honestly, I don't know how you can live like that."

Laurel paused, thinking of a reply, but everything she thought of only made her sound jealous of Tatyana's social life. "Fine," she said, "I'll go first."

"Please do."

"Roth's been in contact with Osip Shipenko. It's confirmed. Lance has seen photographic evidence." She waited, watching Tatyana's reaction. She wasn't sure exactly what she'd expected—the news pretty much confirmed what they both already suspected—but what she got was something akin to boredom. Boredom mixed with skepticism.

"Is that why you cut my date short?" Tatyana said.

Laurel glanced at her watch. It was after midnight. She wondered how Tatyana found the time to fit it all in. "I'm sorry," she said irritably, "if confirmation that the director of the CIA is meeting secretly with a known Kremlin terrorist is not worth cutting into your hectic dating schedule."

"Photographic evidence?" Tatyana said. "Let me guess. It was verified against the negative on a roll of Kodak Tri-X film?"

Laurel was surprised. She didn't have that detail to hand and had no idea how Tatyana did. She wondered if

Lance had been reporting back to her too. A pang of jealousy caught in her throat. "If you knew that, you should have told me. It's an issue of national security which could affect—"

"Hold your horses," Tatyana said, raising a hand. "I don't know as much as you think."

"You knew Roth was meeting Shipenko."

"I suspected."

"And you suspected that Lance had a roll of Kodak whatever you call it? Triplex?"

"Tri-X. I knew there was a roll of film, but I had no idea what it showed."

Laurel looked at her. The expression on her face was so smug she was finding it difficult not to imagine herself punching it. Their relationship had always been somewhat competitive, but recently, she felt it was getting downright catty. And she didn't know if that was Tatyana's fault or her own. "Well, go on," she said. "Tell me how you knew. I can see from your face you're dying to."

Tatyana shrugged nonchalantly, and Laurel felt her hand clench into a fist. She put it in her lap to hide it.

"After you sent me to Roth's house," Tatyana said, "I saw him again at the Command Center. He was acting so suspiciously that I decided to do a little digging of my own."

"Why were you at the Command Center?"

Tatyana shrugged. "Contrary to what some people may think, cooping yourself up in our little office isn't the only way to get work done."

"And you didn't think to tell me about this... this *digging*?"

"I didn't know what I was going to find."

Laurel was about to respond but stopped herself. She

wasn't sure what to say. Was there an implication there that Tatyana didn't know if she could trust her? When she spoke, there was more emotion in her voice than she wanted there to be. "You're saying you didn't know if I was involved?"

"I didn't say that?"

"When I found out about the photo," Laurel said, "the first thing I did was call you."

"You and Roth are close, Laurel. I'm an outsider. What would you have done in my position?"

"I'd never be in your position."

"I'm a Russian in Washington. I don't have the luxury—"

"The only reason you even suspected Roth was because I sent you to his house. The instant you found something, you should have told me."

"I'm telling you now."

"Too little, too late."

"But that's the thing, Laurel. It's *very* little. Almost not worth reporting. I'm still not sure exactly what I found."

Laurel threw up her hands. "Oh, come on. You knew there was a photo of Roth and Shipenko."

Tatyana was shaking her head. "No," she said. "I didn't."

"You just told me—"

"I knew there was a roll of film. A roll of Kodak Tri-X. Unprocessed."

Laurel sighed. She didn't know what Tatyana was saying, and she was beginning to feel like she didn't want to know. She was about to say as much when the bartender appeared with her drink, a cocktail in a coupe glass that looked very citrusy. She took a sip and tried to let the alcohol cool her nerves. "Strong," she said.

Tatyana nodded.

"You can play your games if you want," Laurel said, "but I'm going to proceed on the assumption that we're still working as a team."

"Laurel! Of course we are—"

Laurel raised a hand to stop her. It was too late for all that. "Here are my cards, on the table, plain as day," she said pointedly. "Ritter got his hands on some film. How I don't know, but one of the pictures purports to show Roth and Shipenko shaking hands."

"Is that it?"

"That's it for now," Laurel said, insulted that what she'd given wasn't the bombshell she'd expected. "You go."

Tatyana sighed. "Okay," she said, "but let me preface by saying what I have is circumstantial. There are a lot of different ways you could read it."

"Are you going to spill the beans or not?"

"I'm just trying to explain why I didn't come to you sooner."

Laurel rolled her eyes. She wasn't in the mood. She was going to say nothing, but then her curiosity got the better of her. "Have you been communicating with Lance?"

Tatyana was surprised by the question. "Oh my God. That's why you're so pissed off."

"No, it's not."

"I haven't got any way of contacting Lance. I haven't spoken to him once."

Laurel hated to admit it, but she felt relief. "Okay," she said.

"That's why you're upset," Tatyana said again.

"Just get on with it, will you?"

"Okay," Tatyana said. "You know I encountered Shipenko before, right? In Moscow?"

"I know, yes."

"And he made an impression."

"You didn't like what you saw."

"I got the sense from him that, well, let's just say, if there's a man in Moscow that my instinct tells me is more dangerous than Vladimir Molotov, if there was to be one man I'd like to see in charge less—"

"It's Osip Shipenko," Laurel said.

"Right," Tatyana said.

"Well, that's unfortunate, isn't it?" Laurel said, sounding snide even to herself.

Tatyana ignored it. "So," she continued, "I started digging. I'd read the CIA file on Shipenko already, of course, and I know the rumors I heard back in Russia. He's an opaque character, intensely secretive. He even stays out of sunlight when he gets the chance."

"His condition makes him light sensitive."

"Right," Tatyana said, "but it's more than that. The secrecy is ingrained in his DNA. It's in everything he does. He's a black box. Our file on him is wafer-thin, which is crazy when you think about how long he's been active and how much power he likely holds."

"So what did you dig up?" Laurel said.

"Very little. Like I said—"

"He's a black box. Yes, I heard you."

Tatyana sat up. "Fine," she said. "I tracked some medical appointments. There's a clinic in Moscow. Tsar Nicholas II Medical Laboratory. It's used exclusively by elites."

"And Shipenko uses it?"

"The whole place shuts down for two hours twice a

week, and security is ramped up to the max. At the same time, like clockwork, a convoy leaves Osip Shipenko's residence near Novo-Ogaryovo. Our satellites were only ever to track him as far as a depot where we concluded he switched vehicles. But the time lining up with the clinic closures—"

"You think they shut down the clinic so they can treat him?"

"He's obsessed with secrecy, obsessed with security, so yes, I think so. I cross-checked the patient logs of the clinic, and I found one patient whose entries matched the closures."

"And what did that lead you to?"

"I told you this was all kind of tenuous," Tatyana said. Laurel said nothing, so Tatyana continued. "It led to this," she said, pulling a computer printout from her purse. It was a picture of a girl. "A nurse at the clinic. A child, really. She's barely eighteen."

"A redhead," Laurel said.

"Right. I presume you know from the file—"

"His governess," Laurel said. "Yes. He's got some sort of—"

"Fetish," Tatyana said, enunciating the word like she was uttering a curse.

"Right."

"So, this nurse," Tatyana said, "her employment at the clinic was terminated right after Shipenko's last visit."

"He got her fired?"

"I'm not sure, but I ran her name, Darya Kovalchuk, through the NSA database. I wasn't sure what I was looking for."

"And what did you find?"

"The same name, that very same day, showed up on

the GRU central personnel database, listed as a secretary in some obscure unit in the Sixth Directorate. Unit 0324."

"Which is what?"

"No idea," Tatyana said, "but I'm thinking it's to do with Shipenko."

"So you think Shipenko took a shining to her at the clinic and brought her with him to the GRU to act as some sort of... what?"

"Secretary?" Tatyana said, refusing to say aloud what they were both thinking.

"Right," Laurel said, a shudder running down her back at the thought of what was really happening to her.

"And he hid her in this Unit 0324, deep in the bowels of the organization where no one would ever pay her any mind."

"We should put that unit on a watch list."

"Yes," Tatyana said. "It's the first concrete thing we've found on Shipenko's true role inside the GRU. If you read his file—"

"There's nothing in it," Laurel said. "No meat."

"It's all smoke and mirror," Tatyana said. "He's been hiding in the shadow so long I doubt even the Russians know what he's up to anymore."

"So, how does this lead back to the photo?" Laurel said.

"Well, you have to do some reading between the lines. I have no clue really where Shipenko put Darya. No clue what he's been using her for. She's an eighteen-year-old nurse, so I imagine her position is...."

"Ceremonial?"

"That's one way to put it."

"I shudder to think what it's like," Laurel said.

"Well, whatever it is, she's a fighter."

"How so?"

"I'm thinking Shipenko let his guard down, or he left her somewhere he shouldn't have. In any case, I came across this." Tatyana pulled another printout from her purse and laid it in front of Laurel.

"What is it?"

"A mail log."

"A mail log?"

"Soon after her arrival, a package was sent from Unit 0324 to a small hotel in the theater district of Rostov. A place called Park Central."

"A package?"

"Read the log."

Laurel scanned it for the relevant item. Then her eyes widened in surprise. "It was sent care of Craig Ritter?"

"Yes, it was," Tatyana said triumphantly.

"She sent him something?"

"Sure looks that way. The log lists the content of the package as 'One roll Kodak Tri-X film. Unprocessed'."

"But how did she know what was on it?"

"I don't know," Tatyana said.

"How did she get Craig Ritter's name?"

Tatyana said nothing, and Laurel's mind ran through the permutations. "Oh, no," she said.

Tatyana nodded. "That's where you have to be careful what conclusions you jump to."

"Roth!" Laurel said quietly. "He sent the name to Shipenko. They've been sending information back and forth."

"I don't know that," Tatyana said. "All I know is some nurse in Shipenko's office got access to the name."

"This is my worst nightmare," Laurel said. "Roth, plotting with Shipenko. No, not just plotting but actually giving him names. Selling out our own people. Clearing the path for him. This is how Yuriy Volga got caught. Vilgotsky too. You know that, right?"

"It crossed my mind."

"That blood is on Roth's hands."

"I mean," Tatyana said, "we already suspected Roth was willing to cross the line to get rid of Molotov."

"But this is more than crossing the line, Tatyana. Who else is he selling out? Lance is over there right now. Has he warned Shipenko about him too?"

"I don't know."

Laurel picked up the printout of Darya Kovalchuk and said, "If this girl's name is in the log, Shipenko's going to find out."

Tatyana nodded.

"It's going to cost her her life," Laurel said.

"I think that was a risk she was willing to take."

Laurel nodded. "Brave girl."

"She fought back," Tatyana said. "She did the one thing she could do."

"Have you told anyone else this?" Laurel said.

Tatyana smiled. "Come on, Laurel. Who am I going to tell? Levi?"

"You did good work," Laurel said. "This is really...."

"Good?"

Laurel nodded. "*Really* good." She looked around the bar as if suddenly wary of being overheard. There was still no one there, but she leaned in closer to Tatyana anyway. "You know what the question is now, right?"

Tatyana shrugged. "I would say, the question now is what are we going to do about all this?"

47

Osip sat in the back of a twenty-year-old S-Class Mercedes. The car had once been a taxi, an old meter was still sitting on the dash, and it seemed to have an engine problem that made it sound like a lawnmower, but it was the best the concierge at the hotel could rustle up on short notice. The cadet, Yelena, was seated next to him, her face ashen, her eyes motionless, staring straight ahead as if she was being transported to her own execution. Outside, the devastated Luhansk streetscape flitted by. The road, pocked and battered and strewn with rubble, would have been hard on the best of vehicles, and the Mercedes bounced and jostled mercilessly.

He turned to look at Yelena. She didn't look back. She hadn't spoken in hours, and he figured he'd traumatized her. That was a disappointment. The timing really wasn't good for him to have to find a new plaything. "If it's any consolation," he said, seeing if he could coax a little more life from her, "it gets easier with time."

She remained silent.

"Nothing to say?"

She turned to look at him then, something he could see from her face she found unbearably difficult to do, and she said, almost in a whisper, "Please, let me go."

A sly grin cracked across his lips painfully. This was what he liked the most. He liked to see them beg. He liked to see them get what they deserved. "I don't think I can do that, Yelena."

"You could get anyone you want," she whispered. "You could get a hundred girls, a thousand—"

"Is that what you'd like? For me to get a thousand other girls just so you could go back to your comfortable life?"

"I'm a soldier in the Russian army," she said. "Doesn't that buy some—"

"Some what?"

She said nothing and only shook her head.

"Some what?" he insisted, nudging her with his foot.

"Respect?" she said, her voice quivering like a frail, frightened animal.

He turned away and looked out the window. "I could talk to you of respect," he said. "I could talk to you about the things people have sacrificed to make this country what it is. What you're seeing," he said, turning back to face her, "when you look at me, is the result of a century of sacrifice. Of pain. Generations of Russians have suffered, have starved, have perished in Gulags to make this country what it is. I myself was a casualty. My life is a sacrifice on that altar."

Yelena said nothing. She wasn't listening to him. If she was, she wasn't hearing him. No one ever heard him. How could they? How could they understand? He'd suffered unimaginable torments, he'd become a monster so hideous even his own mother couldn't stand to look at him, and all so that his country might have more powerful, more destructive weapons. That was what he was. He was a sacrifice on the altar of destruction. A sacrifice on the altar of his nation's need to kill more effectively, more mercilessly. Who was she, this girl, this *cadet*, to speak to him of respect? No. She would pay. They all would.

She looked up at him, tears streaming down her face, and whispered, "I'm begging you."

He shook his head. "I'm sorry, Yelena, but it can't be done. You're going to have to remain with me. I just got some very disappointing news about a traitorous secretary back in Moscow. You're going to have to take on her role."

"But I can't."

"Yes, you can," Shipenko said. "And you will." He pulled a handwritten note out of his pocket. "This is the number of a courier company in Moscow. I need you to call them, give them this client number, this account code, and tell them to dispatch the one-hundred-twenty registered letters that my office sent them earlier this morning."

"Registered letters?"

"It's mail, Yelena. Tell them to send my mail. I take it you can handle that?"

Without warning, Yelena threw her head between her legs and began vomiting violently onto the floor of the car.

"Stop!" Osip cried. "Stop the car!"

"Sir, this is a high-risk—"

"Stop the car, you idiot," he bellowed.

They were traveling as part of a convoy of four vehicles, with Bulavin in the car behind and the two others containing soldiers for their protection. It was a laughable arrangement, the soldiers crammed into a Hyundai Solaris and a Kia Rio with zero military modifications, but there was nothing better at hand. If they were attacked, it wouldn't have been like shooting fish in a barrel so much as sardines in a can.

The driver stopped, and the rest of the convoy did likewise. "Get the umbrella," he said to the driver. "I'm switching cars." He waited for the driver to get the umbrella from the trunk, then climbed out of the car with his help, not even looking at Yelena. "Get that mail dispatched," he muttered, leaving her behind.

In his experience, the only way to maintain control, and avoid being stabbed in the back, was to keep himself surrounded by weak people who knew nothing. It was safer than using professionals, who inevitably got greedy. Darya had been an exception. Usually, these women he pressed into his service lived and died on his whim without ever getting the courage to challenge him. It had served him so far, and it would continue to do so. The letters he was getting her to dispatch were vital. They contained precise instructions for each of the one-hundred-twenty key people in Moscow that he needed in order to isolate Molotov. All of those people would have already received notice from Levi Roth's Swiss banking friends that they were millionaires. That wasn't just a bribe. If Molotov ever found out about it, he'd have them killed. There would be no amount of explaining that would save them. These people were his now. They'd been bought. They'd have known it the moment the bankers called and notified them. What these registered letters would tell them was who they'd been bought by and for what purpose.

He made his way to Bulavin's car and ordered

everyone but Bulavin and the driver out. Then he got into the backseat next to Bulavin and opened the window. "Take the girl back to the hotel," he said to one of the soldiers, "and guard the room. See to it, she doesn't get any ideas." He made a gesture like someone hanging themself, then shut the window and told the driver to move on. They got moving again, and it didn't take long before they were pulling up to their destination, the renowned Lysychansk Gymnasium. Before the war, it had been one of the best schools in the city, and now, it was one of the few that was still operating. The police were already lined up in front of it, holding back the crowds who'd gathered in opposition to what was being done. There were mothers there, family members of the students, and the usual rabble of political protesters.

The driver honked and pressed forward, almost knocking someone down.

"There's going to be a riot," Bulavin said, looking out at the mob with dread.

The police had come prepared, armed with batons and riot gear, but from the look of the crowd, Osip thought he might be right. "You're going to be addressing the crowd," he said to him as the car inched forward. They'd been forced to slow down, and the people were coming closer now, slapping their hands angrily on the windows and hurling insults.

"This crowd?" Bulavin said, a look of terror on his face.

"Don't be worried," Osip said. "I've had the speech prepared for you. All you have to do is read it."

"What sort of speech?"

"The usual drivel," Osip said. "Honor, glory, victory and sacrifice for the Motherland. You know what they like to hear."

A woman in a headscarf threw herself onto the hood of the car before the police pulled her off and dragged her away. "These are the boys' mothers," Bulavin said. "Their families. Half of them still believe they're Ukrainian. They're not going to respond kindly to a political—"

"Fill them with patriotism and courage, Bulavin. Tell them they're heroes."

The car proceeded into the school's central courtyard, a rather grand structure of red brick, and Bulavin saw that the television crews and journalists were lined up and recording the scene as he'd ordered. "They're all here," he said as the car came to a halt. "The eyes of the nation, Bulavin. Play this right, and you could become a real star."

"I'm not sure this is going to be remembered kindly," he said.

"It's perfectly orchestrated," Osip said, turning up the collar of his coat and putting on some sunglasses. "You'll see."

"Are we certain it's a good idea to have it all on film?" Bulavin said.

Osip gave him a withering look. "Oh ye of little faith," he said with a shake of the head. "Just read the words as they've been written for you. A monkey could do it." He took a sheet of paper from his jacket and handed it to him.

Bulavin took the speech but made no move to leave the car. Outside, the entire male student body, over three hundred boys in all, ranging in age from fourteen to eighteen, were standing in long, single-file lines. There was one line for each grade, and at the front was a table manned by draft officers, medical officers, and an army captain. Soldiers were standing around the perimeter, making sure no one tried to escape.

"You did well here," Osip said to Bulavin. The school

had been his suggestion. "It's one of the oldest buildings in the city, isn't it?"

"Survived both wars," Bulavin said.

"Let's see if it survives this," Osip said, letting a sneer cross his face. It cracked his skin painfully, but the look of horror on Bulavin's face was worth it. The man was pale with fright.

Osip looked out at the lines of boys. There were more draft officers walking amongst them, picking out individual boys and asking them to show their teeth, checking their height with a yellow tape measure, and making a show for the cameras.

The lines were moving forward at a decent pace. As each boy reached the front, he stepped up to the desk where he was asked to show his identification card, confirm his name, age, and address, and the names of both his parents. Then, an admission officer handed them a small pile of folded clothing, like the bundles given to prisoners on intake, and a draft card. The boys then went to an area behind the desks where they stripped down to their underwear, right there in the snow, and received the briefest of medical exams. Shivering then, hugging themselves for warmth, they put on the uniforms they'd just been handed as the television cameras captured it all. It couldn't have been more perfect, Osip thought, if it had been orchestrated by a film director. The country was going to ignite like a tinderbox.

As if on cue, a woman's voice rose out from the angry mob outside the courtyard. "This is a crime," she shouted. Osip turned to see one of the mothers break through the police cordon. She was racing toward the lines of schoolboys, and then, out of nowhere, a soldier stepped out and blocked her path. She slowed down, still scanning the crowd, no doubt searching for her son. Osip saw the soldier rear up his rifle, then glanced at the television crews to make sure they were capturing everything. They were, and right in front of them, before the eyes of a nation that was on the very precipice of revolt, the soldier jammed the butt of his rifle into the woman's face, sending a splatter of blood onto the snow as she collapsed to the ground. The blow was so brutal even Osip found himself wincing. The cameras of the newspaper photographers clicked with the ferociousness of a swarm of hornets.

Osip turned to Bulavin and saw the doubt on his face. He wondered if the poor fellow was up to the task. "You better get going," he said. "You don't want to keep your audience waiting."

"I don't know if I can read this," Bulavin said, scanning the printout Osip had given him.

"Well," Osip said, "it's going to be a terribly bad day for your poor mother and sisters if you don't." He saw the quiver of Bulavin's lip and added, "You're so close, Bulavin. You're almost home free. Read those words, and you'll never have to set eyes on me again." Bulavin took a deep breath, then opened the door and stepped out of the car.

A good number of the schoolboys had been processed now, and Osip had to do a double take when he saw them coming forward for the cameras in their new uniforms. If the situation hadn't been so serious, they'd have almost looked comical in their oversized pants and jackets. What added the macabre note was the fact that the clothing was so badly damaged, so covered in blood and mud, that the fates of their previous owners were blatantly apparent. Osip saw bullet holes and blood on one boy's chest. A tattered sleeve and more blood on another. Some of the boys were hastily being issued marginally better replacements, but the effect on the crowd, who could just barely see what was happening from outside the courtyard, was immediate. As a single voice, the women began to scream and wail.

As Bulavin stepped up to the microphone, some more mothers broke through the police line.

"You will not take our boys like this," one screamed.

"Snatched from their mother's arms," the other cried.

"Perfect," Osip whispered to himself, watching it all unfold. For it was perfect. The boys, as young as fourteen, their acne and uniforms only highlighting their youth, couldn't have been more incendiary. There was no way, he thought, that Molotov would come back from this.

48

V aleria Smirnova lit another cigarette and leaned back in her seat. It was one of those cheap, plastic chairs they used in high schools, and every time she leaned back on it, she was afraid it would buckle beneath her. She looked around at the place and thought she'd never actually worked in an office so singularly unsuited to its purpose. For a supposedly elite unit, the Center E headquarters on Budonnovskiy Prospekt lacked even the most basic communications infrastructure and equipment she'd have expected to see. There was no satellite overview of the city, no live feeds from CCTV and traffic cameras, no hard links to the city police or federal security bureaus. It was like a place transported from thirty years ago, with most of the officers, as far as she could tell, whiling away their morning flipping through newspapers or buying the deplorable coffee dispensed by the machine in the hallway. The little plastic cups it gave out were everywhere, on every desk, in every garbage can.

There was a TV on in the corner, the news anchors

going apoplectic about the fourteen-year-olds who were being drafted, and Valeria herself wondered what the hell the Kremlin's strategy had been there. It was a public relations nightmare. She couldn't think of a worse time for such an announcement. Even before the already infamous speech in the square, people had been protesting the general mobilization order, and that only applied to grown men. The Luhansk order was specific to just that one oblast, and as far as most Russians were concerned, it was still a war zone there, but the response to the speech had been immediate, universal, and electric. It was a lightning rod.

"Turn that off, would you?" she said to Zadorov, whose desk was next to hers. "It's impossible to concentrate."

He gave her a disappointed look but got up from his seat and switched it off. "You want anything from the machine?" he said, reaching into his pocket for change.

"Please, no," she said, watching him scuttle off, scratching his ass in the process.

She sighed and looked down at her desk. A single page, freshly faxed through from Moscow, was in front of her. It was supposedly classified, but she'd found it on the floor in front of the office fax machine that morning when she got in. It had arrived an hour earlier and could have been seen by anyone in that time, a shocking breach of protocol if ever there'd been one. But then, she supposed, what could you expect when people insisted on selecting their secretaries based on their skill in the bedroom rather than knowledge of office procedure?

She doubted it mattered anyway. The information was a dollar short and a day late, as far as she was concerned. It confirmed that Craig Ritter, the British arms dealer, black marketeer, and general *bon vivant,* was the man she was after. What bugged her was that, according to the watermark, Shipenko's office had been in possession of the information when the hit on Volga and Vilgotsky was ordered. If it had been transmitted to her then, she could have picked up Ritter immediately and avoided the entire mess they were in now. Instead, she was getting it now, which was too late. Fatally so. She had her men scouring the city, but she doubted they'd come up with anything. The Brit was in the wind, doubtless with a fake passport and enough cash to get anywhere in the world. If they ever set eyes on him again, she'd be very surprised. She wondered if she should notify Shipenko—his little secretary had just screwed up a major operational objective—but there was probably no benefit in doing so. It was more a criticism of him, the man who'd put an eighteen-year-old nurse in that position, than anything, and one did not get ahead in the GRU by criticizing superiors.

Zadorov returned, sauntering over, holding his little coffee cup like a snifter. "What are you working on?" he said.

"If you needed to know, you'd have been informed," she said flatly.

He shrugged, then turned the TV back on.

"I told you I couldn't concentrate—"

"Come on, look at this," Zadorov said. "It's the story of the year."

With a sigh, she looked up at the screen. She had to admit she was finding it difficult not to follow the story. The schoolboys had been loaded onto buses now, and the talking heads in the studio were debating furiously where they thought they were being sent.

"Are they singing?" Valeria said.

Zadorov turned up the sound, and they saw that the

boys were indeed singing. There they were, sitting in buses like a troop of boy scouts, singing camping songs. Their spirits had certainly picked up since the earlier scenes of wailing mothers and protestors throwing rocks at riot police.

"Maybe it's a smarter play than we thought," Zadorov said.

"Always playing to the cameras," Valeria agreed.

"That's it, the whole thing, it's got to be a stunt for our benefit. Otherwise, why would the cameras be following their every move? It's like a grand production."

"It is," Valeria agreed.

"My bet," he said, "is that if one of these boys sees actual combat, if they get so much as a scuffed knee, I'll eat my hat."

"Makes sense," Valeria said. "I can't see otherwise why they'd be letting it get this round-the-clock coverage."

She listened to the commentary. An 'expert' had a map up of Luhansk, and he was pointing out the major battle zones west of the city. They were just thirty miles from the front.

"Our forces are being pushed back all around Bakhmut," the expert said. "It's a critical strategic point. Also, the entire area east of Kramatorsk is being contested. If Ukraine starts retaking territory inside Luhansk, the humiliation will be difficult to stomach."

"Can you believe this?" Zadorov said, shaking his head. "It's a farce, talking about these boys as if they're actually going to help hold a front. We've had Wagner in the district, and even they can't hold it."

"At least it's shifted the conversation," Valeria said. "No one's talking about the protestors. Everyone's eyes are fixed on this." She was about to tell him she'd changed her mind and would take a coffee if the offer was still open when her cell started to ring. She looked at the screen. It was Gazzaev. "What have you got for me?"

"You're not going to believe this."

"You found him?"

"He went back to the Balkan for his car. We've got eyes on him as we speak."

49

Kolesnikov stepped out of his Chinese-built Haval H9 SUV into a puddle of muddy slush six inches deep. "God damn it," he muttered, looking around the bleak industrial wasteland of the enormous Taganrog Metallurgical Plant. The facility was an iron and steel plant, one of the largest in Russia, and had been operating since the nineteenth century. He could see the lights of the newer electric furnaces in the distance, but the section he was in, with its old open-hearth blast furnaces, had long been abandoned. The buildings were ramshackle and decrepit, and whatever was not black with soot was covered in mud and rust.

"You there, halt," a soldier shouted, coming out of an enormous corrugated iron warehouse with a rifle stretched before him. He was accompanied by a slower, fatter man who followed behind, a gun slung carelessly on his shoulder, apparently doing up his fly.

Kolesnikov turned to face them, revealing his uniform.

"Sorry, sir," the fatter soldier said. He was the more senior man.

"My name is Kolesnikov," Kolesnikov said. "You should have been expecting me."

"Of course, sir. I thought you'd be traveling accompanied."

"Just me," Kolesnikov said, spitting into the snow. "Now take me to the facility commander."

The two guards led him through a series of shockingly lax checkpoints to a warehouse where another six men sat at a table playing cards. They looked up at Kolesnikov but didn't stop their game.

"Call Oleshko," the fat soldier barked at them. "This is General Kolesnikov."

The men got their act together then, putting down the cards and stubbing out their cigarettes. One of them rushed up a set of steel steps toward the old foreman's office.

Kolesnikov watched him go, then glanced at the assembled vehicles. They'd been notified in advance of what to prepare, and he saw they'd pulled out an entire Iskander-M brigade, over twenty vehicles in total, that comprised one of the most mobile and dangerous units in the entire Russian military. It was certainly the one NATO feared most, he thought, inspecting the nearest TEL, or transporter-erector-launcher.

The TEL's frame was based on the old MZKT chassis from the Minsk Tractor Plant in Belarus. Referred to by the Russians as the Atrolog, it was essentially a standard-issue, eight-by-eight transport truck powered by a 500-horse-power YaMZ-846 diesel engine and capable of speeds of about forty miles per hour.

What put these trucks in their own league in terms of the threat they posed NATO was the launchpad built into their cargo bed. Those pads could carry, erect, and launch

rockets, essentially making each truck a miniature Cape
Canaveral, capable of launching virtually any missile-
borne warhead the Russians were in possession of. And
the Russians were in possession of a dizzying array of
nasty warheads.

They were fast, mobile, and very difficult to keep track
of, being essentially identical from the sky to any other
Astrolog transport truck. They usually traveled in a
brigade formation of between four and twelve TELs,
along with the support vehicles necessary to carry extra
rockets and special loaders that could re-arm them after
each launch. The brigade also had a command post
vehicle for targeting and communications and an information processing vehicle, which was necessary for high-
precision targeting using drone or satellite imagery.

In general, a brigade was something NATO was
equipped to track from the sky. An individual TEL,
however, without the support of its brigade, was a
different matter. A lone truck could carry two rockets and,
if it did not need to reload or use high-tech targeting
support, was perfectly capable of traveling and firing on
its own. That was what made them so utterly terrifying.
With an official range of five-hundred kilometers but a
suspected range of twice that, although that couldn't be
admitted because it breached the Intermediate-Range
Nuclear Forces Treaty agreed by Ronald Reagan and
Mikhail Gorbachev in 1988, a single truck could, in theory,
threaten all of Western Europe. It could drive off a base, as
Kolesnikov proposed doing now, go virtually anywhere,
undetected, and within minutes of pulling over, it could
launch a missile that, for all anyone knew, could be armed
with a nuclear warhead.

"General," a taut-looking man in an oversized coat said

from the door of the foreman's office. "Forgive me for keeping you waiting."

"I take it you've received the authorization code," Kolesnikov said, ignoring the platitudes.

"Perhaps we should speak in my office, sir."

Kolesnikov looked at the assembled soldiers, none of their uniforms compliant, some again smoking cigarettes, and decided it was a good idea. "Very well," he said, hauling himself up the steel stairs to the office. At the top, he brushed past Oleshko to enter the grubby little room. It contained a single metal desk and matching chair, and there was a large window overlooking the shop floor, so dirty now as to be completely opaque. He stepped up to the desk and saw a small stack of pornographic magazines on it. They were Ukrainian.

"You didn't think to put these away before I arrived?" he said, picking one up and thumbing through the well-worn pages.

"Sorry, sir. The men like them."

"I have no doubt," Kolesnikov said, throwing it back onto the desk. Then, proceeding to the matter at hand— he had no wish to be in that place for any longer than was necessary—he said, "I take it my vehicle is ready?"

The vehicle he was referring to was a single TEL that had been altered to remove all signs that it was part of an active Iskander-M battalion. The identification markings had been painted over, two of the tires had been removed to give it a different profile, its roof had been painted black, and the cargo bed had been covered by a tarp. The idea was the make it look like a civilian truck, at least to American and NATO satellites. Kolesnikov had been ordered by Shipenko to drive it personally, without bringing anyone with him and without stopping along the way, from Taganrog to an empty hangar near the Millerovo Air Base. It was a three-hundred-kilometer distance, and he was to cover it before nightfall, avoiding highways. He had a long drive ahead of him.

"It's ready, sir, but there was some confusion about the armament."

"*Confusion*?" Kolesnikov said, sensing the doubt in Oleshko's voice. It didn't surprise him that there would be some resistance. An Iskander, armed with two chemical weapons warheads, was not the type of thing you came across very regularly, especially when it was going to be driven off by a lone man without support. "Is there going to be a problem?"

"Of course not, sir. It's just...."

"Yes?"

"We've never been ordered to arm a chemical warhead like this. At least, not inside Russia."

"I didn't realize President Molotov was required to discuss these things with you before making his decisions."

"No!" Oleshko said hastily, raising his hands. "Of course not, sir. I didn't mean to suggest for a second—"

"This authorization has been cleared by the highest levels, has it not?"

"It has, sir."

"I imagine you called for verification the moment you received it."

"I did, sir."

"And?"

"They confirmed it, sir."

"So what's the problem?"

"There's no problem, sir."

"Then arm the fucking thing. Two warheads, 3-Quinuclidinyl Benzilate, triggered for a manual launch." Kolesnikov turned to leave, it would take about thirty minutes to carry out the order, and he had no intention of spending that time in that little office with Oleshko, but Oleshko cleared his throat as if to say more.

Kolesnikov turned back to him. "Something more to say, Oleshko?"

"Sir, it's just...."

"I'd advise you to think very carefully before you start voicing your own ideas," Kolesnikov said.

Oleshko seemed unable to stop himself. "It's just," he said again, "I have a duty to the...."

"To the what?"

"The Motherland."

"The Motherland?" Kolesnikov scoffed.

"Yes, sir."

"Obeying a confirmed authorization from the Kremlin doesn't fall within your duty?"

"I'm required to make sure these launchers don't fall into hands that would...."

"That would what?"

"I'm sorry, sir," Oleshko said, backing down.

"Surely you're not suggesting that the Kremlin isn't to be trusted with its own weapons."

"Some of these weapons, our doctrine is to use them—"

"You speak of doctrine?" Kolesnikov scoffed. "*You* speak to *me* of doctrine?"

"I'm sorry, sir."

"You worm."

"I apologize."

"Arm the fucking TEL," Kolesnikov growled.

Oleshko hurried off, and Kolesnikov breathed out

slowly through his teeth. He'd never witnessed such insubordination in his life. Shipenko was right. Molotov's iron grip was beginning to show signs of strain. There were riots in the streets. Soldiers were deserting the battlefield. Men of conscript age were refusing the draft order. And now this bullshit.

50

Ritter strode briskly through the October Park, watching over his shoulder for any sign he was being followed. It was a cold morning, and a thick mist hung over the empty amusements across the pond. There were a million places for someone to hide, and if they were trained professionals, he'd never see them coming. He exited the park onto Pushkinskaya and kept walking.

The street was wide, with a neat line of poplars lining the sidewalk. As he approached each tree, his pulse quickened at the thought that someone was waiting behind it. He glanced over his shoulder again and could have sworn he saw a figure ducking out of sight. He gripped one of the Glocks in his coat, keeping it concealed in his pocket.

When he reached a side street, he turned onto it, glancing again toward the park. Visibility was terrible, and he saw nothing but the two round glows of a pair of approaching headlights. He walked on, passing the medical faculty of the university, and stepped into a recessed service entrance that was shielded from view by a dumpster.

A moment later, a car drove by. It was a slow-moving, black BMW, and it stopped a few yards ahead, its red brake lights glowing in the fog. Ritter drew his weapon as the passenger door opened, and a figure stepped out—a man in a heavy coat. The man looked both ways, then headed onward up the street in the wrong direction. The car followed him.

Ritter gave them a few seconds to make some distance, then stepped out of the recess and headed back in the direction from which he'd come. He was just reaching the corner of Pushkinskaya when he felt a heavy thud against the back of his left shoulder, as if someone had just punched him with all their strength. It was the noise, the loud crack of a gunshot, rather than the pain, that made him realize what it was. In the time it took his brain to process that information, another crack filled the air, and chips of brick flew into his face as a bullet struck the wall in front of him.

Acting purely on reflex, he drew his gun, fired off a single shot into the opaque fog, then backed around the corner for cover. There were pedestrians on Pushkinskaya, already running from the gunfire. A car jammed on its brakes and was immediately struck by the car behind it. Ritter reached back and touched his shoulder, feeling the familiar sensation of wet blood on his fingers.

He looked around frantically, checking for more threats, then glanced back around the corner. There was a crumpled heap on the sidewalk about thirty feet away—his assailant. Ritter had no idea if he was dead or alive but fired another bullet—which hit the heap with a dead thump—then began striding back toward the October

Park. He looked back and saw no cars and no one following on foot. He broke into a jog anyway, cradling his left arm in his right as pain shot through his body. As he reached the gates of the park, he heard the revving of an accelerating engine and broke into a sprint without looking back to see it.

He hopped over the low chain that crossed the foot-path and veered off it onto a sloped patch of grass that led toward the pond. There were some trees at the bottom of the slope, and he stopped when he reached them to catch his breath. He stood then with his back to one of the trees, his breath billowing into the cold air before him.

The car had entered the park, breaking through the chain to do so, and he could see the glow of its lights back up at the top of the slope. The car stopped, some car doors slammed, and he heard the shouting, in Russian, of men who'd spread out and were conducting a search. There were three of them, as far as he could tell.

One of them was coming his way, and he put his arm in front of his mouth to muffle the cloud billowing from his breath. A figure emerged into view slowly, just an outline, and Ritter wondered how long he would have after firing a shot before the other two showed. He gauged the distance to the wall of the park. It was about six feet high and would have been easy to climb over were it not for the bullet in his shoulder.

The man was coming closer, within earshot but out of visibility of his companions, and Ritter rounded the tree trunk to remain out of view. As the man passed the tree, Ritter trained his gun on his head and broke the silence. "Drop the weapon," he said in English.

The man froze.

"Drop it," Ritter said again, wondering if the man understood his words.

The man leaned down and placed his gun on the snow very slowly.

"Turn around," Ritter said. The man did so, and Ritter got a look at his face for the first time. There was a bandage on the left side of it, but even with that, Ritter thought he looked familiar. "I've seen you before," he said.

The man said nothing.

"You were at the farm." A sneer crossed the man's face, and Ritter added, "You were calling the shots out there."

The man turned his head slightly and spit on the snow.

"You were the interrogator, weren't you? You're the one who killed them."

"So what if I was?" the man said defiantly. "What difference does that make now?"

"You tied them to their chairs, pulled out their finger-nails, and put a bullet in their skull. It makes a difference to me."

"I did what I was ordered to do. You'd do the same."

"Who ordered you to do it?"

The man spat on the ground again. It didn't look like he had much intention of talking.

"Hmm," Ritter said, nodding. "We'll see how tough you are when I pull this trigger."

"Pull that trigger, and half a dozen men will be down on you in a second."

"Half a dozen?" Ritter said, arching an eyebrow. "That's a lot of guys for one car." The man said nothing. There was some shouting in the distance, and Ritter said, "Don't even think about answering."

The man did think about it, Ritter saw it on his face,

but he decided against it. He was looking at Ritter's feet. The blood from his shoulder was dripping, and it had formed a crimson stain about the size of a quarter on the white snow. "You're fucked either way," the man said. "You're not going to get far like that."

Ritter nodded. "You're probably right," he said, then depressed the trigger twice, sending two shots into the man's gut. They rang out into the frigid air like the cracks of a whip, sending a flock of cawing crows out of the trees. The man reached for his belly, then slumped to his knees, his head bowed forward as if in reverence. He seemed to want to say something, but when he opened his mouth, only blood came out. Ritter could have given him a final *coup de grâce* and put him out of his misery, but he didn't. A slow, painful death, that was what he deserved. It was what Volga and Vilgotsky deserved.

Ritter looked up the slope—there was still no sign of the man's companions—then turned and fled.

51

Roth was standing before the main live feed of the Emergency Command Center—an enormous, forty-foot-wide concave array of high-definition screens, which was currently showing a live satellite feed of the Taganrog Metallurgical Plant. His people, a full team of thirty specialists and analysts, were seated at their stations around the screen. Some were clacking away at keyboards, but most had their eyes fixed on the image on the screen before them. They'd been there for hours, and they were watching for one thing—proof that President Molotov was preparing to use tactical nukes.

Roth had directed the attention of the entire Command Center to Taganrog. Not only that, but he'd also requisitioned two Keyhole Satellites, which up to that point, had been monitoring the Russian advance into Ukraine. Diverting them from the battlefield was a decision that had raised a few eyebrows. The satellites were absolutely vital to the Pentagon's efforts to support the

Ukrainians in real time. Calling them off the field would cost lives.

Keyhole, or more precisely, Evolved Enhanced Keyhole/CRYSTAL, was the crème de la crème of global surveillance. From one-hundred-fifty miles up, satellites piloted by operators at the National Reconnaissance Office in Chantilly, Virginia, watched precise locations on the earth's surface with cameras built from the most perfect mirrors ever created. The mirrors made it possible to resolve wavelengths of 500 nanometers at a diffraction resolution of 0.05 arcsecs, making them powerful enough to identify a human face. If that human was holding a newspaper, the operators in Chantilly could have read the headlines. And they could do it not only from directly overhead but at an angle. At that power, however, the area under focus was very small, no more than a few square meters in focus at any one time, which was why Shipenko's coordinates were so vital.

Shipenko had told Roth not only where to look but what to look for. And Roth was not about to miss it.

He was nervous, though. He wasn't in the habit of doing things behind the president's back, and he certainly wasn't in the habit of opening himself up to a charge of treason. In this case, however, he'd decided that the threat justified the risk he was taking.

In his view, it was a threat that was unprecedented since at least the Cuban Missile Crisis. He was convinced that Molotov was prepared to use tactical nukes. His forces were already floundering. As that got worse, which it undoubtedly would, he would have no choice but to use every weapon at his disposal. And when that happened, even if just a single nuke was detonated, and no matter how limited it was in terms of payload, it would open up a Pandora's box that had not been toyed with since Hiroshima and Nagasaki. It was a box that threatened all of human existence, and Roth wasn't going to let that happen, even if it meant there was a price he would have to pay personally. He'd already decided that he had to get Molotov out of the Kremlin, and he was going to stop at nothing to make that happen. But in order to convince the president, he needed evidence, irrefutable evidence, of what Molotov was preparing to do. It was for that reason, and that reason only, that he'd temporarily allied himself with Osip Shipenko.

And it was working. It was Shipenko who'd told him Molotov was preparing to use tactical nukes in the first place. Not only that, but Shipenko had backed up the claim with the coordinates of the units that would launch them, as well as verifiable photographic evidence that the units were nuclear-armed. What Roth needed now was some sort of smoking gun, a threat that was utterly irrefutable, a threat that posed a real and immediate threat. That would be something no president could countenance, no matter how fearful he was of igniting a Third World War.

When that happened, Roth would go straight to the president and come clean. He would prove to him not only that Molotov had gone over the edge but also that there was a plan to replace him with Shipenko. It wasn't a perfect plan by any means—Roth had no doubt Shipenko was every bit as evil as Molotov—but at least he was a man the CIA could do business with. He'd already proved that fact. He wouldn't throw away his chance over Ukraine. He'd back down. And he was also someone the CIA had leverage over. His coup would only be possible with the CIA's help, and if that fact ever came to light, he would be ousted by his Kremlin rivals in a heartbeat. That gave America power over him. It gave Roth power over him.

Roth hoped that would be enough to justify what he'd done. If it wasn't, he was willing to accept the cost. He would go to jail, suffer disgrace, even face execution for treason. Some things were worth dying for.

An alarm started to ring at one of the specialists' stations, and everyone turned to it.

"What is it, Anderson?" Roth said.

Specialist Meghan Anderson picked up the flashing phone on her desk and was listening to someone on the other end. "Sir," she said, putting down the phone, "we just received confirmation from the NSA that a live code has been transmitted."

"A what?" Roth said, already feeling his pulse quicken.

Anderson looked around the room. All eyes were on her. "A live code, sir."

"A live code?"

"That is, a top-level launch code clearance, sir."

"From the Kremlin?"

"From the Kremlin to an unidentified unit of the Western Military District stationed at Taganrog."

Everyone looked back at the screen. It was suddenly very clear to them all why Roth had requisitioned so many resources to watch a single steel plant in the middle of Rostov Oblast. "Top-level?" Roth said, trying to keep his voice steady.

"The code's been filtered through Backdoor already," Anderson said, referring to an algorithm the NSA had come up with to confirm the validity of intercepted Russian launch orders. "It's real, sir. Whoever is inside that steel plant is authorized to strike."

"Strike with what?" another specialist blurted out of turn.

"Strike with whatever the hell they have," Roth said, his voice suddenly growing very hoarse.

He realized his hand was trembling and stuffed it hastily in his pocket. He couldn't believe it was actually happening. This was it, the moment he'd been waiting for his entire career, the smoking gun that no US president, however reluctant, could countenance. Molotov had taken off the safety. He'd primed the trigger. He'd issued an active nuke launch code. And, if everything went according to plan, he'd just signed his own death warrant.

Roth's phone started to vibrate in his pocket, and he pulled it out impatiently. It was Laurel. He'd already missed a number of her calls, she was with Tatyana at the Saint Royal, and he had no difficulty in trying to imagine what it was they'd been discussing. They were on to him. They might not have pieced together everything, but they were sharp, and they knew he was up to something. If he could just stall them a little longer, until after he'd had a chance to show his evidence to the president, then it wouldn't matter.

There was another alarm on the desk of one of the specialists. "What is it now?" he croaked, for some reason having a difficult time swallowing.

"Would you like some water?" his aide said, but he waved her away.

"I'd like to know what the hell that alarm is?" he said.

"It's on the screen now," another specialist said, and all eyes turned to the screen.

Roth watched for a moment, processing what he was seeing, then said quietly, "My word."

"This is it, sir. This is what we've been waiting for. We're in play."

The image zoomed in very close, and what they saw was a single vehicle, a truck with a tarp-covered bed, coming out of one of Taganrog's many warehouses. "I want confirmation that's what we think it is," Roth said. The aide had returned with a glass of water despite his refusal, and he took it now and drained it. "I want to know what that truck is, and I want to know what warhead it's carrying."

"SS26 Stone, sir," another analyst said. "Confirmed."

Roth's pulse quickened. It was exactly as Shipenko had said and as his photos had purported to demonstrate. 'Stone' was the NATO designation for the Iskander system, which was capable of carrying and launching tactical nukes with mere minutes of notice.

"So it's Iskander," Roth said. "What's it carrying?"

"The bed's covered," an analyst said, referring to the screen, which clearly showed a white tarp over the cargo bed of the truck.

"I can see that," Roth said irritably. "What I want from you people is to find out anyway. I mean, a fifty-billion-dollar budget should let me know what's behind a tarp, shouldn't it?"

"The vehicle is definitely 9M723 and 9M728 capable, sir," another analyst said. "Range of at least five hundred kilometers. Breach of Intermediate Nuclear Forces Treaty highly likely."

"Highly likely?"

"But not confirmed. I'm sorry, sir."

"I want to know what that thing is armed with," Roth said, practically breathless as he spoke the words. There was an awkward pause. "What are they?" he snapped more loudly.

"We don't know, sir."

"Payloads designation M possible," another analyst said.

"Enough with the possibilities. I need to go to the president with proof." The images zoomed in closer.

"Speed, seventy km/h, sir."

"Where are they going?"

"We don't know, sir."

"Fifty kiloton payloads possible," another analyst said.

"Fifty kilotons," Roth repeated, suddenly finding it necessary to hold on to the edge of the desk to steady himself. This would do. It was enough. He had his smoking gun. A nuclear-ready vehicle with a nuclear-level launch clearance, driving toward an active battle line. Molotov was moving tactical nukes onto the battlefield. If this didn't get the president to green-light the coup, he didn't know what would.

"I need to get to the White House immediately," he said. "And tell the Pentagon to scramble a jet."

52

Valeria was just getting into her car when her phone started ringing again.

"Gazzaev? Did you get him?"

It was not Gazzaev's voice that answered. "I'm sorry, ma'am. This is Safanov. Agent Gazzaev is dead."

"Dead?"

"Along with another agent."

"I take it the Brit hasn't been brought into custody, then?"

"I'm afraid not, ma'am. He slipped through our fingers at the October Park. We're scouring the area—"

"God damn it," Valeria said. "So he's in the wind?"

"We need to call in more support."

"You mean Rostov PD?"

"Yes, ma'am. They have the manpower we need to lock down the area."

"You want to call in the guys who botched this thing from the start? You better be kidding me."

"We're just not set up for this type of retrieval, ma'am. He's a professional. He knows how to evade surveillance."

"Just stay on the line," Valeria said, getting out of the car and storming back into headquarters.

"There's another thing, ma'am."

"Let me guess. More bad news."

"He's hurt, ma'am."

She walked briskly through the lobby and lost her cell connection in the elevator. When she got to her floor, she called him back immediately. "If he's hurt," she said, "he can't have gone far. I'm going to see if we can get some help from Moscow. The systems here are too out of date." She hung up and sat down at her desk.

Almost instantly, Zadorov appeared. "I thought you'd gone out," he said.

She ignored him and used the landline on her desk to call GRU headquarters in Moscow. "Was there something else?" she said, glaring up at Zadorov.

"Oh," he said as if he hadn't noticed he was staring.

"This is private."

"By all means."

She watched him leave, then bit her lip. She was beginning to suspect there was more to his constant pestering than just lust. He was watching her. It wouldn't be surprising—of course, Center E would put her under surveillance, she was an outsider in their house—but that didn't mean she had to make it easy for them.

She got through to Moscow and asked to be transferred to a facial recognition team. "One with the new Chinese algorithm," she added.

She was put on hold, and it took an inordinate amount of time for someone to pick up. A very bored-sounding voice eventually came on the line and said, "Code, please?"

"Code?"

"Clearance code. I haven't got all day."

"I don't have to give a code for a facial search, do I?"

"New tech. New procedure."

"On whose authority?"

"It's a Chinese requirement," the operator said. "If you don't like it, take it up with someone who can actually do something about—"

"Alpha Four Alpha," she said impatiently. "And did I mention this was urgent?"

"Hold."

She waited again, another five infernal minutes, then the same man came back on the line. "You're supposed to put these through the system yourself now."

"If I could do that, I would have. I don't have access to a terminal."

"If you're in the field, you're supposed to—"

"I'm in Rostov-on-Don, posted with local law enforcement, and this is a matter of national security. If I lose my man because of your dilly-dallying—"

"Whoa! Hold on. I'm just doing my job."

"Then run my search. Start with central Rostov. We're looking for a suspected British citizen named Craig Ritter. He was logged at Center E as a person of interest by lieutenant Evgeny—"

"Zadorov," the operator butted in. "I see him in the database. Do I have a source file? Yes, I do. And," a slight pause, as if to build suspense, "search is running, ma'am."

"How long will it take?"

"It will take as long as it takes."

She sighed. She was about to ask him how long that was likely to be when he said, "Hello, what have we got here?"

"Do you have a match?"

"It's your lucky day. I've got one hit six, maybe seven minutes ago. My bet he's still there."

"Where?"

"Hang on. Ticket desk. Rostov Glavny."

"Did he board a train?"

"Let me re-run the station cameras. There's been some sort of riot there. The request log's been jammed up with—"

"Just tell me if he's still there," she said, firing off a text to Safanov telling him to go to the station.

"Cameras are running. He's definitely not still at the ticket counter."

She tapped her fingers impatiently on the desk. "Anything?"

"Your man is a professional. He should have been picked up dozens of times."

"So nothing?"

"All I have is the one hit at the counter."

"Where'd he buy a ticket to?"

The operator laughed. "I'm afraid it's not that type of camera, ma'am."

"Well, what counter was he at? Local? Regional?"

"It's hard to tell—"

"Oh my God, can you just do your job?"

"Getting pissy won't make this any faster."

Valeria bit her tongue and made a mental note to get the man's operator number later. If Ritter got away because of his incompetence, she would personally make sure his life became a living hell.

"International ticket desk!" he announced at last as if he'd just made the discovery of the century.

Valeria hung up the phone instantly, turned to the old desktop she'd been given by Center E, and pulled up the international departures schedule at Rostov Glavny. The war had hit Rostov's connections hard, there wasn't a single train headed west, and the only international departure that day was a train leaving in ten minutes for Tbilisi.

Ten minutes, she thought. Safanov had said he was two men down. That left only two, and she didn't fancy their chances against someone like Ritter. Even injured. She dialed Safanov's number on her cell, and he picked up instantly.

"Are you *en route* to the station?"

"We're just pulling up outside."

"Ritter's on the Tbilisi train, scheduled to leave in ten minutes. Go to the platform and stay out of sight. Don't make a move on him without my say-so. I'm going to see if I can get the train stalled."

"How are you going to do that?"

"I have a few tricks up my sleeve," she said, picking up the landline. She hung up on Safanov and dialed the number she had for Osip Shipenko's office. If he was as big a deal as he made out, his office would be able to hold up one train departure.

The receptionist picked up, Valeria gave her clearance and then waited for Osip's office. As she was waiting, Zadorov reappeared, looking intent on making another approach. Valeria suddenly lost her patience. She rose to her feet, pointed right at him, and said, "Zadorov, back off," loud enough for everyone in the office to hear. They all turned to look at her. Zadorov stopped in his tracks as if she'd just pointed a gun at him. "Tell your boss, whoever it is, to back off and let me do my job."

He looked like he was going to say something, but at the same moment, Shipenko's office picked up the phone, and Valeria turned away. "Darya," she said breathlessly. "It's Valeria. I need urgent assistance on Alpha Four Alpha. Can you get a requisition through to the rail authority in Rostov in the next ten minutes?"

There was a brief pause, then a different female voice said, "Darya Kovalchuk no longer works at the Prime Directorate."

"What? What happened to her?"

"My name is Yelena Klishina. I'm her replacement."

"Are you in Moscow, Yelena?"

"I'm not permitted to say."

"This is a disaster," Valeria said. "I need someone with access to the rail authority in Rostov. I need to halt a train. This is mission-critical. I need a professional GRU administration—"

"I don't think I can help you," Yelena said, and from the sound of her voice, Valeria guessed the girl was no different from Darya. She guessed she would last about as long, too. She hung up the phone and turned back to the room. Zadorov was standing right over her. She clenched her hand into a fist and was about to fling it at him when he spoke.

"I can get a departure delayed," he said.

"What?"

"Rostov Glavny. I've got contacts there. What train is it?"

"The Tbilisi departure. It's supposed to leave in a matter of minutes."

53

Five days earlier, Lieutenant Colonel Chris Mauler had been living in England, deployed with the 48th Fighter Wing based at Royal Air Force Lakenheath. He'd liked it in England. The tempo of life suited him there. The winter days were a lot shorter, darker, and damper than he was used to in Nevada, but England had always been a place he'd wanted to live. Being there made him feel more connected to his father, who'd flown with the F-15 Eagle Squadron out of the same base thirty years earlier. He'd enjoyed driving around the Suffolk countryside during his downtime or spending his evenings off in the cozy old pubs of Mildenhall or Thetford.

Now, he suddenly found himself stationed at the Šiauliai Air Base in northern Lithuania. Šiauliai was a fine city, he supposed, but it didn't exactly do it for him the way Suffolk had. The pubs weren't as snug, the country roads weren't quite as windy, and his father had never served there. He wouldn't have chosen the reassignment, which was a small consideration, he supposed, given what was going on in the world.

It was another gray, dismal day outside the window of the cafeteria. He was sitting at a table, sipping his fourth cup of deplorable instant coffee, and rereading for the third time a chapter of a book about Winston Churchill that he just couldn't seem to get his teeth into. Across the table, Colonel Griffith, a Bostonian with a ridiculously strong accent who talked about nothing but hockey, was playing a game of solitaire with the same well-worn deck he'd played with in England.

For the first four days after their arrival, NATO's Quick Reaction Alert had been sitting at DEFCON two. That meant their F-35 Lightings were required to maintain a state of readiness of just two minutes. They'd spent the entirety of their first four shifts sitting in the cockpits of the planes, on the runway, ready to go. Today was the first day the threat level was at DEFCON three. They'd been notified by the local Control and Reporting Center when they arrived, and that was the reason they had the luxury now of sitting in a cafeteria. DEFCON three was still a heightened readiness level, though, and their jets were sitting on the tarmac just a few hundred yards away, their engine idling, ready to scramble within five minutes.

Mauler was contemplating another cup of coffee when the entire room lit up in red, and a deafening alarm began to clang above their heads. Moving as a single man, he and Griffith rose to their feet and began running for the garage door that opened directly onto the runway.

Less than two hundred seconds later, both pilots were airborne, and the runways at Šiauliai were disappearing into the mist behind them at a rate of a thousand miles per hour. With afterburners ignited, they were flying at maximum acceleration, and within three and a half minutes, they'd covered the hundred-kilometer distance to hostile Belarusian airspace.

"Looks like the target is inside Russia," Mauler said on his radio. "On the ground."

"Copy that," Griffith said. "This could be the real deal, pal."

"Let's hope not," Mauler said. He could feel the rush of adrenaline in his veins as he processed what was happening. It was the first time since takeoff he had a chance to think. Their stealth capability meant they could enter hostile territory undetected, but he still prayed they wouldn't have to cross the line into Russian air space. Judging from the targeting coordinates, and armed as they were with an array of air-to-surface missiles, it didn't appear like that would be necessary. There were no guarantees, though.

There was no fire order as of yet, but he checked the codes, and the target was confirmed live. A few short minutes passed, and they were entering Ukrainian airspace.

"We're in range," he said into his radio.

"Hold," was the response from the Control Center. "Do not fire."

No fire. That was something. Still, a target inside Russia, that was the type of thing nightmares were made of. It was the type of thing they practiced for in drills— drills rehearsing the end of the world.

54

Roth's motorcade ripped through the nighttime streets of the capital. Its police escort tore ahead, rushing through red lights and intersections, holding back traffic on side streets, and ensuring the convoy could move through the city without slowing for anything.

"Are we taking the back door, Harry?" Roth said to the driver.

"That's affirmative," Harry said over his shoulder as they tore through another intersection. "The president wants no one to know this meeting is taking place."

It only took a few minutes for them to reach the White House, and Harry jammed on the brakes at H Street, swinging the car sharply into the narrow alley next to the Federal Claims Courthouse. A ram-proof metal pole quickly retracted into the ground, just in time for them to avoid crashing into it. It re-emerged behind them immediately. To hide its destination, the police escort continued without stopping, speeding down Fifteenth Street toward Pennsylvania Avenue and onward toward the Capitol.

Before the Escalade had even come to a complete halt, secret service agents were running out to it, opening the door for Roth and escorting him down the alley and through a set of steel doors into the Treasury Annex. From there, they descended a set of steel steps into a tunnel that passed beneath Pennsylvania Avenue. A moment later, they were beneath the White House itself. They passed rooms filled with computer servers, audiovisual equipment, and security monitors and reached a large service elevator. Two agents accompanied Roth into the elevator, which descended briefly before opening to a hardened concrete corridor.

Roth strode down the corridor to a set of tinted glass doors that led directly into the White House situation room. He could already see Schultz, Schlesinger, Winnefeld, Cutler, and the President, as well as their staffers, sitting at the long oval conference table. Behind them, a large high-resolution screen showed a live satellite feed of the Iskander TEL he'd alerted them to. With a gasp of relief, Roth saw that it was still on the move.

He pushed through the doors and said, "Looks like I'm late to the party."

Elliot Schlesinger, the Chairman of the Joint Chiefs, had been speaking, but he stopped when Roth entered. Everyone in the room turned to look at him, and a silence grew up. "What?" Roth said, feeling like a schoolboy who'd just been called into the principal's office. "What is it?"

Schlesinger cleared his throat but looked to the president instead of continuing what he'd been saying.

The president shook his head.

Roth spoke again. "What's going on?" It was only then that he noticed the row of four secret service agents standing against the wall behind him. The meeting was supposedly top secret. Those men didn't belong there. "What is this?" he said.

"Levi," the president said, at last breaking his silence, "you brought this crisis to our attention."

"You're damn right, I did."

"If you're right about that TEL, it's a nuclear-armed vehicle capable of firing a fifty-kiloton tactical nuke on Ukraine in a matter of minutes."

"What do you mean, *if* I'm right? Of course I'm right."

The president looked around the table at the assembled faces. He said, "You can't be certain of that, Levi."

"I also got confirmation that Molotov transmitted a top-level launch code to Taganrog right before that TEL left the hangar. The NSA has confirmed that the code's the real thing."

"That doesn't confirm that the TEL is nuclear-armed," the president said.

Roth threw up his hands in disbelief. "What is this? What are you saying? Why would anyone transmit a nuclear-level launch code to a unit that's not nuclear-armed?"

"To frighten us," Schlesinger said.

"Well, it's pretty fucking frightening, wouldn't you say?" Roth said.

"I've also been informed you scrambled fighter jets," the president said.

"Because of *that!*" Roth said, pointing at the screen. "This isn't a simulation, Mr President. That's live real-time footage you're looking at."

"The CIA doesn't scramble jets," the president said. "I do."

"I didn't order them into the air," Roth stammered. "I sent the order to the Pentagon."

"And we acted on it," Schlesinger said, turning to the president. "Given the circumstances, sir, I do have to say the decision is justified."

"If you don't want the birds in the air," Roth said to the president, "call them back. They're your planes. They fire on your command."

The president suddenly slammed his fist on the table. The sound was so loud it made Roth jump. "You're pushing me into World War Three," he shouted at Roth.

Roth's eyes widened. He hadn't seen this coming. He felt blindsided. Unprepared. "I don't know what to say," he stammered.

"Well, you'd better say something," the president said through gritted teeth.

"With all due respect," Roth said, "I'm not the one flinging nuclear launch codes around. This situation is not of my making, sir. I'm simply trying to put options before you so that you can make the best decision for all of us."

"The best decision?" the president said. "The best decision for all of us? That's all you're doing?"

"What is this?" Roth said, looking at the secret service men. "Are you going to have me arrested?"

"It's too late to play coy now," the president snapped, and Roth was certain he'd never heard the man sound so angry in his life. "If you get out of this room without being charged with *treason*, you'll be very lucky."

"Treason? Ingram!"

"Treason," the president repeated.

"I don't know what you're talking about."

"Really?" the president said, almost petulantly. He

pressed a button, and another screen came on, showing a grainy, black-and-white photograph.

Roth felt his blood run cold. It was a picture of himself and Osip Shipenko shaking hands. He'd had no idea it existed. He made to speak, but his voice failed him.

"Nothing to say?" the president said.

"It's not what it looks like."

"The negatives have been authenticated. This photo is real."

"Where did you get it?" Roth said.

Another screen came on, and this time it was a live link to Laurel and Tatyana. They were back in their office at Langley, sitting next to each other like a couple of kids sharing a webcam. "It was probably taken by someone on Osip Shipenko's team during the meeting," Laurel said. "Probably to blackmail you."

Roth shook his head. He couldn't believe Laurel and Tatyana would betray him like this. He'd thought he'd had more time.

"Why didn't you come to me with it?" he said. "I could have explained."

"You left us with no choice," Tatyana said. "Especially once our own people in Rostov started showing up dead."

Roth tried to swallow, but his throat was so dry he couldn't. Everyone in the room was staring at him in silence. This was bad. It wasn't at all how he'd wanted things to unfold.

"What were you planning?" the president said. "Tell me now before I have these guards take you away in handcuffs."

Roth shook his head. It was no use lying any longer. He had no choice but to come clean. "You know what I was planning," he said weakly.

"With *him*?" the president spat. "With Osip Shipenko? The man who has more blood on his hands than anyone else in Moscow?"

"Anyone other than President Molotov."

"You've overstepped," the president said gravely.

Roth knew this was it. This was everything. He was fighting for his life. "As much as it pains me to say this," Roth said, "that man is our only hope, and I'm the only one in this room with the guts to admit it." The instant he said the words, he realized he'd sealed his fate. Every face around the table changed. The words might very well have earned him a place in front of a firing squad.

"The last time I checked," Elliot Schlesinger said, "the commander in chief of this country was the president."

"If we don't cut a deal with Shipenko," Roth said, "we might not have a country."

"You've lost your mind," the president said, nodding to the secret service agents, who stepped forward and grabbed Roth by both arms.

"Wait," Roth gasped. "Zoom in on the TEL. Let me show you."

The guards looked to the president, who waved them back, and the satellite image on the main screen zoomed in on the TEL. It was still on the move, trudging along some lonely country road, completely unescorted. It was almost inconceivable that such a small thing could pose such a threat to the world, but Roth's job now was to convince everyone in that room that it did.

"That truck," he said, trying not to lose his breath in his haste to get the words out, "make no mistake, it's the closest we've come to nuclear annihilation since the Cuban Missile Crisis. That truck has the power to unleash

Armageddon. It has the power to light the spark that ignites World War Three."

"You don't even know for sure it's nuclear-armed."

"Yes, I do," Roth said. "I've seen the proof that tactical nukes were being moved to Taganrog."

"Proof from where?" Schlesinger said.

"From Shipenko. He sent incontrovertible photographic evidence that tactical nukes, 9M723 and 9M728 missiles, were shipped into Taganrog in the last few days. My team has also verified that a live nuclear launch code was transmitted to Taganrog less than an hour ago. What more do we need? This is it? This is a gun that's being locked, loaded, and pointed at our head."

"You should have come to us with this sooner," the president said.

"Maybe," Roth said, "but the fact now is that we're minutes from a nuclear strike against Ukraine."

"And you know this because Osip Shipenko told you?"

"Look at that screen!" Roth gasped. "Look at that TEL. It's armed, it's got a verified launch code, and once it stops moving, we're going to have mere minutes to decide what to do about it. That's why we needed to scramble jets."

"To take it out?" Frederick Winnefeld, the Navy Chief of Operations, said. "Don't you think that's a decision for the president to make?"

"He couldn't make it if the birds weren't in the air, ready to launch the strike."

"So the option you've given me," the president said, "just so we're all very clear, is to launch a first strike against a Russian military unit inside Russian territory before it fires anything?"

"It's an option," Roth said, trying desperately to hold his ground. "And if it prevents the nuclear seal from being broken, then isn't that worth the price? I don't need to remind anyone in this room that no nuclear weapon has ever been used in anger since Fat Man and Little Boy were dropped on Japan in 1945. Those two bombs killed half a million people instantaneously. They showed the world something so terrifying that the genie was put back into its box, the box was sealed, and no one had dared open it for almost a century. And those bombs were between fifteen and twenty-one kilotons. The weapons Russia currently has deployed, and there are thousands of them, are not even measured in kilotons anymore. They're three orders of magnitude more destructive. What happens if we let Molotov unseal that box? What happens if we let him use even a single tactical nuke in Ukraine?"

He looked around the table. No one was saying anything. He took that as his cue to continue. "Molotov is acting increasingly irrationally. He's invading his neighbors. He's assassinating his generals. He's transmitting live nuclear launch codes to remote steel factories that we know contain tactical nukes. How can we say we're still dealing with a rational actor?"

"You're making a lot of assumptions," Jared Cutler, the president's National Security Advisor, said.

"Of course I'm making assumptions," Roth said. "Assumptions and evidence, that's all I have to make this calculus. I admit that if I'm wrong, the repercussions will be catastrophic, but I believe the evidence I've presented here shows that we can no longer afford to sit back and assume that if we act reasonably, if we avoid escalation, President Molotov will do the same."

"He's always acted in his own interest," the president said.

"But he's become unhinged," Roth said. "He's crossed

the line. The fact that TEL is armed with a launch code proves it."

"We know the Russians have measures in place to ensure nuclear war doesn't break out accidentally," Cutler said.

"I'm not talking about an accident," Roth gasped, ignoring Cutler and addressing himself to Winnefeld, Schlesinger, and the President. "We're talking about a nuclear first strike. We know Molotov can't lose this war. It would be the end of his regime. It would be the end of his life. The Russians have a nasty habit of killing their rulers when they have a revolution."

Roth paused. The president was at least listening.

"To a man like Molotov," he went on, "a brutal dictator who's shown that he believes in nothing but his own grip on power, how can we doubt that he'd tear the whole world apart to remain in the Kremlin?"

"So you groomed Shipenko to take his place?" the president said. "Even though I said no?"

"My job is to give you options, sir."

"Your job is to obey its constitution."

Tatyana spoke up. "You sold out your own people," she said. "Volga, Vilgotsky, Ritter, you told Shipenko how to find them."

"Look," Roth said, looking at each person in the room before concluding his defense, "if you want to take me down for this, I can't stop you. I did what I did because I believed it was necessary. I don't like Shipenko any more than the rest of you. Believe me when I say that. The man is pure evil, and I've dedicated the better part of my life to fighting monsters like him. It was my job to see him coming in Prague, and I missed it. We lost lives that day because of my failure, and that's something I'll take to my grave. But if the choice is between Shipenko and nuclear annihilation, it's my duty to push for the former. I believe that's fully in keeping with my oath to protect this nation." He turned to the guards behind him and held up his hands, wrists together, to accept their handcuffs. "I won't fight you," he said. "I don't deny the charge. Arrest me if you must."

"Hold on," the president said, looking at the screen. The TEL had stopped moving.

55

Roth stared at the screen. The secret service men were still standing behind him, and he wasn't even sure yet if he was off the hook, but for the time being, everyone in the room seemed more interested in the rogue TEL than they were in him.

"It's stopped moving," the president said again. "The tarp on the back's coming off. What does that mean?"

"Are you asking me?" Roth said.

"It's preparing to launch," Laurel said.

"We don't know that for certain," Cutler said.

"Yes, we do," Laurel said. "I've got the infrared data in front of me. The TEL's increasing in temperature."

"Which means?" the president said.

"It's preparing for launch," Roth said. "Order the strike, sir. Now."

"How long before the TEL's ready to launch?" the president stammered.

"Shoot it," Roth cried. Everyone turned to look at him. "You've got birds in the air. Take it out. Before it's too late."

"If we take out that TEL—" the president said.

"If you take it out, it can't launch a missile."

"If I take it out, I start a war. A war that could end us all."

"Sir, the clock is ticking. We have no idea how long—"

The president raised his hand, and Roth stopped talking. "How much time do we have?" he said to Laurel.

"There's no way of knowing for certain," Laurel said. "Minutes at most."

"SS-26 Stone requires sixteen minutes to launch," Winnefeld said.

"On paper," Laurel said. "We have no idea how long it will actually take. Judging from the rate at which that launch pad is increasing in temperature, I would say it's going to launch any second."

"Fire on it," Roth said again.

"Stop," the president said, but Roth could see from his face that he was wracked with doubt. It was exactly as he'd feared. The moment was on them. A missile was heating up on a launch pad, F-35 Lightings were in the air within range, and the president still couldn't make the order that was needed. He was too timid. Too weak. Too scared of prodding the bear.

"I can see the smoke on the TEL," Roth gasped. "It's going to fire any second. Sir, you need to take that thing out before it ends us all."

The president was staring at the screen in complete paralysis. He couldn't move. He couldn't speak.

"Take it out," Roth yelled. "Order the hit. Schlesinger, Winnefeld, tell him."

"If I make that order—"

"You have no choice," Roth gasped.

"Where's it targeting," the president stammered, glancing around the room.

Laurel answered first. "There's no way of knowing that, sir. Not until the missile's airborne, at least."

"What about the missile? What's it armed with?"

The satellite was zoomed in close enough to read markings, but there were no markings. There was just a single rocket, painted white, completely without identification. "I can't say," Laurel said.

"So we don't know what it's armed with," the president said, "and we don't know where it's aimed."

"We know enough," Roth gasped. "For the love of God, we know enough."

"F-35s are within range and ready to fire," Schlesinger said, a phone receiver at his ear.

"If they fire," Cutler said, "it could trigger a response of unprecedented proportions."

Roth couldn't believe it. He could see the smoke on the launch pad, and still, the president and his men were talking, debating, hesitating.

"Any change in the status of the intercepted launch code?" the president said.

"The launch code was already verified," Roth said. "It won't change."

"I want it rechecked."

"Sir," Roth said, "the missile's smoking like a firecracker. It's going to launch. Please order the strike."

There was so much smoke around the TEL that it was getting difficult to see what was going on. The satellite zoomed out, and Roth looked at the surrounding forest, the lonely logging road. The scale of the view spread to a kilometer, and there were no other vehicles in view. There was nothing that was going to stop that missile other than the F-35s he'd scrambled. Looking at the screen now, he felt so utterly powerless, so helpless. Everyone's eyes were glued to the screen in horror, but no one was doing anything about it.

"Do the F-35s have the targeting coordinates?" Roth said to Schlesinger.

"Yes, they do," Schlesinger said.

"Are they within strike range?" the president said.

"They can fire," an analyst said from behind them.

"Get the pilot on the line. I want clear comms on this."

The analyst looked to Schlesinger, who nodded immediately. There was some static on the line and then a crackly voice. "This is Lieutenant Colonel Chris Mauler, 48th Fighter Wing."

"This is the president of the United States, Colonel."

"My gosh."

"Just keep your cool, son. I need you to tell me if you can take out that TEL."

"That's affirmative, sir."

"No question?"

"It's a truck on the ground, sir. I couldn't miss it if I tried."

"Order the shot," Roth said.

"Not yet," the president said, seemingly regaining control of his faculties. "Do we have comms with the Kremlin?" he said to another analyst.

"Mr President—" Roth protested.

"Do I have a line?" the president said to the analyst.

"I'm checking, sir."

"Time's running out," Roth said.

"I'm not about to order missiles fired into Russian territory without at least trying to get the Kremlin on the line," the president said.

"That's a negative on Kremlin comms, sir. I can try to open a line, but it will take time."

"What's the range of the Iskander system?" the president said.

"Good God," Roth said. "It's too late for all this."

"It could hit Kyiv," an analyst said.

"What else? What targets inside NATO?"

"Mr President!" Roth gasped.

"Tell me," the president shouted at the analyst.

"No significant NATO targets are within range. It could technically hit some rural parts of Turkey, but all likely targets are in Ukraine east of the Dnipro. Kharkiv, Kherson, Zaporizhzhia—"

"Kyiv," Roth gasped. "That thing could drop fifty kilotons on Kyiv."

"Its official range is—" the analyst began.

"Do you know how much damage fifty kilotons will cause?" Roth shouted over the analyst.

"Levi," the president gasped, and Roth could see the fear on his face. "If I strike that TEL, we are at war with Russia."

"If they nuke Kyiv, the world as we know it is finished."

"No," the president said, and Roth could see nothing but terror in his eyes. "If we go to war with Russia, the world as we know it is finished. If that thing fires a missile at Ukraine, that's a continuation of the *status quo*."

"*Status quo?*" Roth gasped. He couldn't believe what he was hearing. The president was going to back down from this.

"Colonel Mauler, if it fires a missile, can you shoot it down?"

"If it gains enough altitude," the pilot said.

"If it fires at Kyiv?" the president said.

"Most likely," the pilot said. "If it's firing at any major

city in Ukraine that's still outside Russian control, I have a good chance of intercepting the missile."

"What's a good chance?" the president said.

"Over fifty percent," the pilot said.

"Fifty," the president said to himself.

"It depends on the trajectory. The higher the missile goes, the easier it is to shoot down," Schlesinger said.

"Any word from Moscow?" the president said.

"Negative," the comms analyst said. "Nothing."

"They don't want to talk to us," Roth said.

"Or they weren't expecting us to call."

"Sir," Roth said, unable to hold back any longer. "The clock is ticking. That thing could fire at any second, and it is significantly more difficult to bring down a missile in the air. For the love of God, order the shot."

56

Kolesnikov's phone buzzed, and he looked at the message. It was the targeting coordinates and the order to fire sent by Shipenko. He was on an isolated logging road, and he stopped the TEL at the next clearing and retracted the tarp covering the launch pad. Then, he immediately got to work entering the targeting information and clearance code necessary to launch a missile. If there'd been a second person in the vehicle, they could have done all that while he drove, but he was alone. His fingers flew over the keys on the keyboard, entering the coordinates and code, and with every passing second, he was painfully aware that his entire existence could disappear into the inferno of a NATO-fired air-to-surface missile.

He knew that the moment his TEL was spotted, it would take NATO just a few minutes to scramble jets and get them into firing range. If the jets were already in the air, a missile could strike even sooner. In any case, at any second, the world could disappear, and he'd never see it coming. Everything would just go black, like a power cord being yanked from a television set.

He had no doubt he was a target. He was on his own, completely undefended, in one of the most dangerous battlefield weapons systems in the entire Russian arsenal. He had no support. No air defenses. He was as vulnerable as a fish in a barrel. If NATO knew he was there, and if they saw him preparing to fire, they'd have no way of knowing what kind of payload his missile was armed with. For all they knew, he was carrying a live tactical nuke.

He finished entering the targeting information and initiated the missile launch sequence, painfully aware that such a move was detectable by the most advanced NATO satellites. The countdown information came up on his screen. Two-hundred-forty seconds to missile ignition. The number began decreasing.

Anyone watching would be expecting him to attack Kyiv, he thought, which was a lot farther away than the target Shipenko had sent. Shipenko's target was, in fact, just over the border in Luhansk, scarcely forty miles away. The missile would barely be airborne before it struck. Kolesnikov tried not to think about who was there, but he knew what was planned. Those schoolboys were no mere publicity stunt. They played a crucial part in Shipenko's planned coup.

He looked through the windshield at the sky. No sign of any incoming missile, not that he'd see it coming. He wondered if there would even be a shot. He was in Russian territory, and President Montgomery was too much of a coward to strike Russia first. All American presidents were. They'd proved it time and again. They were afraid to stand up to Russia. They were afraid to spark off a World War. It was the single most predictable aspect of their geopolitical strategy. They were rich, soft, and comfortable, and they could no longer countenance the levels of casualties that a major war would involve. It was the first and last thing they taught at all Russian military academies.

He was firing a chemical weapon. The Americans called that a red line, but it was a red line Kolesnikov himself had crossed many times in Syria. What had the Americans done then? Nothing. Sanctioned a few oligarchs, maybe, confiscated a few yachts, but nothing really. America was too weak, too disunited, and too soft to fight.

The clock on his screen counted down to zero, and he felt the vibrations of the missile leaving the launch pad. It was so loud he thought the TEL would explode, but it didn't.

He leaned forward and watched the sky again. It was a sight to behold, the missile arching forward on a low-altitude trajectory. It would be striking its target in a matter of seconds. He pushed open the door and stepped out of the vehicle. His foot touched the ground, and then, without a sound, without realizing or seeing anything coming his way, his entire existence was reduced to the deafening sound of an explosion. And then he felt the blast of heat. And then a searing, immense, immeasurable pain of oblivion.

57

Roth leaned forward, his hands on the conference table, his eyes riveted to the screen.

"Did we hit it?" the president gasped. "Did we hit it?"

"Target destroyed," the pilot said, and they could see confirmation of the fact on their screens. A flash of light from the TEL, then a cloud of black smoke. There was a round of applause from the people in the room.

"Thank God," Roth said, his eyes still on the screen.

"God help us," the president said. "This will mean war."

"Not if Molotov is out of the picture," Roth said.

The president looked at him, and for the first time since entering the room, Roth felt that perhaps his plot with Shipenko was going to get a warm reception.

"We'll have to see about that," the president said.

For now, that was something Roth was willing to accept. It was a lot better than leaving the room in hand-cuffs. And with the TEL gone, the immediate threat of a nuclear strike was off the table. Whatever Molotov made of it—and Roth had little doubt the man was willing to go to war over something like this—if they could get Shipenko into power, it wouldn't matter.

The president was looking at him, and Roth didn't know if the look on his face was one of fear or gratitude.

"Wait a minute," the pilot said through the comms. "We've got a problem."

Roth looked back at the screen. He could see the problem before the pilot even said it. The TEL had launched its payload. Its missile was in the air.

"Missile airborne," the pilot said. "Missile airborne."

"Intercept it," the president gasped. "Shoot it down."

"Can you take it out?" Schlesinger said.

"Air-to-air launched," the pilot said.

But Roth could already see a problem. The missile had no height, no altitude. It was on a trajectory that would take it no distance at all. Everyone watched the screen, the blipping red dots on their various paths, and then, boom, the Russian missile made contact with its target.

"What happened?" the president gasped. "What just happened? Was it a nuke? Somebody tell me."

"The missile hit its target," Roth said.

"What was its target?"

"A small village," Laurel said through the comms. "In Luhansk, near the battle line."

"Why did they hit it?" the president said.

"I don't know," Laurel said, "but the missile was not nuclear. That much is for certain. I repeat, the missile was not nuclear."

"What?" the president said.

He, and everyone else turned toward Roth. "You told me you knew what it was," the president said.

Roth shook his head. "I saw the warheads myself. They were clearly marked as nukes. And the launch code was for a nuke."

The president shook his head. "I just ordered a first strike against Russia because you told me that missile was nuclear. God help me. What have I done?"

58

Bulavin played with the buckle of his seatbelt nervously. The bus driver had told him to put it on before leaving Luhansk, and Bulavin had said back to him, "Is that really necessary?"

"Of course it's necessary," the driver, a pudgy fellow from Donetsk, said. "We may be entering a battle zone, but believe it or not, I'm far more likely to kill you than any stray Ukrainian shells."

"How comforting," Bulavin said dryly, clipping the belt shut. That had been three hours ago, and they'd traveled less than a hundred kilometers in the time since, much of it along a road so battered and broken that Bulavin would have sworn it was unpassable. As they crossed ever more devastated countryside, taking long detours to get around damaged bridges, uncrossable stretches of road, and areas flooded by blown-up dams, he quickly learned why the driver had been so adamant he wear the belt.

They were approaching their destination now, an utterly destroyed village just south of Lysychansk, not far from the railway junction at Lyman that had been the scene of so much fierce fighting. The surrounding landscape looked to Bulavin like a scene from a different planet. There was nothing but rubble and destruction, and he breathed deeply to calm his nerves.

He was sitting at the front of the bus, just behind the driver, like a school teacher on an excursion. It could almost have brought back memories of such trips in the past were it not for the constant signs of death.

"This is it," the driver said.

Bulavin undid his seatbelt and stood up. "All right, boys," he said. "Off the bus. Everyone. Watch your step."

He got off first and stood by the door watching the boys disembark. The bus had traveled in a convoy of five buses, escorted by police on motorcycles, and behind them, they'd been followed by a veritable flotilla of news trucks and other media vehicles. He'd never seen anything like it. There were cars carrying journalists and reporters, vans for the crews and their equipment, and even some trucks that carried antennas and satellite dishes on their roofs. If he'd been in any doubt that this whole thing was a publicity stunt, their presence was enough to put those doubts to rest once and for all.

There was clearly also some sort of welcome ceremony planned. Not only were there electricity generators and lights for the benefit of the news cameras, but there was also another podium ready and waiting for yet another blasted speech. Shipenko had given him the text of it before the departure from Luhansk. It was printed in a large, bold font, ready to be delivered. "Not another one," Bulavin had protested. "You told me the one at the school was the last one I'd have to give."

"I told you you'd never have to set eyes on me again," Shipenko said. "That's not exactly the same thing."

Bulavin had taken the script reluctantly, and he read over it a few times during the ride. It was more of the same bullshit he'd been spouting off since the beginning of this whole sordid affair—honor, and duty, and sacrifice, and glory to the Motherland. It was a wonder the viewers kept tuning in to see it. But that was exactly what they were doing if the reports were to be believed. According to Bulavin's assistant back at his office in Luhansk, this was the story of the year, getting round-the-clock coverage on every major network from Moscow to Vladivostok.

Bulavin watched the boys assemble, they were being shepherded by a number of soldiers who'd joined the convoy a few miles back, and from the looks of the soldiers, they were fresh from the battlefield. Some had blood on their clothes or smeared across their hands and faces. Others were covered in mud and dirt. All carried weapons that they seemed very familiar with.

"What's happening here?" Bulavin said to one of the soldiers as another bus approached.

"Oh, God," the soldier said, shaking his head. "You don't want to know."

It was true, Bulavin didn't want to know, but he watched anyway while the bus came to a halt, and one by one, the members of a brass band, decked out in full parade regalia, got out of the bus and began unloading their instruments.

Bulavin turned away and saw that a man in a tailored suit, carrying a briefcase, was approaching him. "Mr Bulavin," the man said, "everything's in order for the ceremony."

"What ceremony?" Bulavin said with dread, wondering what fresh hell he was in store for.

"Very funny," the man said, "but seriously, the cameras and satellite uplinks, the sound and lighting for your speech, the music, it's all good to go."

Bulavin didn't know what to say. He settled for, "And who, may I ask, are you?"

"I'm Sobyanin," the man said, "Dmitry Sobyanin, the Kremlin press secretary."

"What are you doing here?" Bulavin said, shocked that someone of that level was out there in the middle of nowhere.

"I was flown in this morning," Sobyanin said, "to orchestrate the coverage."

"But what's going on?" Bulavin said, looking around at the unfolding scene. "What have they got planned for us out here? They do know there's a war going on, don't they?" Someone could be forgiven, he thought, for thinking that preparations were being made for a three-ring circus. The brass band, the media people, the crowd of schoolboys in their farcically ill-fitting uniforms. All that was missing were the clowns and elephants.

"From where I'm standing," Sobyanin said, "what you're looking at is the most significant propaganda endeavor of the last decade. Perhaps of the entire Molotov era."

"Propaganda endeavor?" Bulavin said.

"This is the biggest show since Khrushchev put a dog in space."

"And we all know how that ended," Bulavin said grimly.

"The first living creature launched into orbit?" Sobyanin said. "It was a monumental success."

Bulavin nodded but said quietly, "Not for the dog, it wasn't."

Sobyanin looked at him. "You need to get your shit together before your speech. The eyes of every man, woman, and child in the country are going to be on you. You're not going to want to screw it up."

"At this point, I doubt anything I do or say is going to make the slightest difference—"

"Don't underestimate the importance of this moment," Sobyanin said, cutting him off. "This story is a perfect storm. It has polarized the nation. I don't care where anyone stands on the political spectrum. We've got their attention."

Bulavin noticed that some of the reporters had begun approaching the boys. One, with a microphone in her hand and a camera crew following closely behind, was speaking to a lanky boy with freckles who looked like he was still a few birthdays shy of his first shave. "What's your name?" she said to him. "Where are you from? What do you make of the decision to send boys like you into battle?"

The questions were coming faster than the boy could answer, but he honed in on the last one and said, "We're not boys anymore. We're men. And we're ready to fight for the Motherland."

"So you're going to battle willingly?" the reporter said.

"Boys a lot younger than us have died fighting for this country," the boy said, and Bulavin, despite himself, found himself nodding in agreement. "I'm willing to do my bit. So are my friends."

Some other boys had gathered around, eager to get their faces on camera, and they all cheered in unison.

"War is not a game," the reporter said, raising her voice over the cheering to be heard. "People get killed."

"Tell that to our enemies!" a boy from the crowd shouted out.

"Have you received any training?" the reporter said.

That was Sobyanin's cue. He ran over to halt the interview, tapping the cameraman on the shoulder and telling him to stop recording. No one wanted to hear about such banalities as training, it seemed.

There were other interviews being conducted, but Bulavin didn't listen in to any of them. Sobyanin returned and led him up to the podium. There was another interview taking place on it when they got there, not with a boy but with one of the soldiers who'd shown up. He looked so fresh from the front that the mud on his boots still hadn't had time to dry.

"What's your opinion on all this?" another fresh-faced female reporter was saying. "What are we witnessing?"

"Witnessing?" the soldier repeated as if he didn't understand the word. In fact, judging from his accent, which Bulavin thought sounded Central Asian, it could well have been that he didn't.

"What are we going to see?" the reporter said.

The soldier nodded. "We're going to see a big mistake," he said bluntly. "A big mistake."

Sobyanin went straight to the cameraman to get him to halt recording, but not before the reporter said, "Who do you think you are to say a thing like that?"

Sobyanin paused for a moment, perhaps curious as to the answer, and the soldier said, "Who am I?" as if dumbfounded by the question. He tugged at the patch on his sleeve of the Russian flag. "This is who I am?" he said. "I'm a soldier in the Russian army. Who are *you*?"

"It looks like I caught you off guard," the reporter said, beginning to retreat.

Sobyanin got the cameras to stop recording, and the moment she had confirmation that she was off the air, the reporter turned on the soldier and said, "What the hell do you think you're doing? This is going out live."

"I don't give a rat's ass where it's going," the soldier said. "I watched two friends die this morning while you were still styling that hair."

"Oh, you'll care when the GRU comes calling at your door,"

The podium was cleared, and Sobyanin's people began preparing it for the main event. When they were ready, Bulavin stepped up onto the stage and waited for the crowd to come to attention. It took a few minutes, and while he waited, he had to admit, on some level, the entire scene before him was quite remarkable. Shipenko had succeeded in turning the war into some sort of reality television special. It wasn't surprising that the entire country was watching, and there was no doubt it would sway the conversation. Molotov's power base, the conservatives, the right-wingers, the military bloggers and pro-war nationalists, would eat it up like flies on honey. But even his opponents, the pacifists and malingerers and traitors who wanted to see him ousted from power, would have to shut their mouths after watching this. How could they continue to refuse to fight when they'd watched these young boys go to the front willingly. In some terrible way, it was genius.

When the crowd finally settled, Bulavin leaned into the mic. He cleared his throat as the lights zeroed in on him, and the cameras began filming. Sobyanin gave him the signal to begin, and then he said, "We are here on this momentous day not to celebrate victory but to honor the patriotism, the bravery, and the self-sacrifice of those who are determined to bring it to us." The applause was immediate. Whether it was a true reaction or a choreographed part of the performance, he didn't know. "The young men we see here today," he continued, "are an example to their countrymen, for they are making the greatest sacrifice any young man can ever be asked to make for their country. They are going to battle." There was more applause, and it was so fervent, so rapturous, that he began to think it must be the real thing. He even felt himself warm to his topic. If there was one thing a politician knew how to get behind, it was the adoration of a crowd.

He was about to continue when he saw a bright flash in the sky. It was followed by a shout in the crowd. "What was that?"

"Is that?" someone else cried. "Is that a... rocket?"

Before Bulavin fully realized what was happening, the crowd surged in terror, knocking over the podium he was standing on and sending him flying back to the ground. He hit his head hard and struggled to get to his feet as people began running in every direction, shouting and screaming in fear. Somewhere not too far in the distance, he heard an explosion, but his more immediate fear was that if he didn't move soon, he would be trampled to death. He was only just getting his bearings when he heard a second explosion. He turned toward it to see a burning bus, and billowing out of it, as thick and potent as if it were coming straight out of a smoke grenade, was a mustard-yellow cloud of gas.

What happened next was almost too fast to register. Instantaneously, the crowd went from panic to absolute terror. Boys began to collapse on the ground, scrawling at their faces, grabbing their throats, struggling to breath as blood poured from their mouths. Reporters and cameramen, soldiers, even Sobyanin began coughing and gasping for air. Bulavin saw it, and then, before he knew it, he was part of it. It was as if the oxygen had suddenly been sucked from the world. He looked around in confusion and terror. The sky was still there. The trees and fields and railway line were still there. But there was no air. There was nothing to breathe. Only agony.

And then, out of one of the trucks that had accompanied the soldiers, men began pouring out of the back. There were eight of them, and they made even less sense than the explosion. They were holding cameras and sound recording equipment like what the media crews had carried, but these men were wearing gas masks.

59

Ritter made his way through the train station, careful to avoid looking like he was injured or that he was rushing. He'd patched up his shoulder as best he could in a washroom on the station's lower level, but it was a temporary job at best. The bullet was still in there, and even now, he could feel the blood seeping into the wad of fabric he'd stuffed over the wound. He would have to see to it again soon, and there was a high likelihood there would be an infection to deal with in the not-too-distant future.

For now, though, getting out of the city was the priority. He'd killed the man who'd killed Volga and Vilgotsky. That was enough for one day. He felt bad for leaving Klára behind, but staying had been her choice. He'd tried to change her mind, he'd tried to warn her that staying was futile, but she'd been adamant she wanted to wait for Lance. He prayed, for her sake, Lance was still alive.

He looked up at the departure board and found his train, the only international departure for the entire day, and checked the platform. It was platform eight, all the way across the concourse, leaving in just ten minutes. He made his way toward it, wincing with each step and keeping his collar and hood up to avoid being picked up by the numerous CCTV cameras that were all over the station. When he was passing beneath the enormous hanging clock, he heard a commotion coming from the direction of the café and turned toward it, certain that he would see a bunch of police officers running toward him.

He was ready to flee but realized it was something else that had caused the commotion. There was a newspaper stand next to the café, and in the corner of the stand was an old thirty-inch TV screen. A crowd had gathered around it, watching the news, and for some reason, the people were getting very angry.

Ritter found himself walking over, and as soon as he got close enough to make out what was going on, he could barely believe his eyes. There was an infographic on the screen, one of those battlefield maps the news channels were so fond of. The map showed an area north of Rostov just east of the old border with Ukraine. There was a graphic on the Russian side of the border of a soldier, and on the Ukrainian side, clearly marked with an American flag, was a little icon representing a plane. An icon appearing to represent a missile was being fired by the American jet and hitting the Russian military unit. Ritter had to do a double take to make sure the target was inside Russian territory. It was.

If he understood what he was looking at correctly, and it seemed to be pretty simple, then the US had just launched an airstrike against Russia. That was unprecedented. It would likely lead to war. It certainly explained why the crowd was so angry.

Ritter couldn't make sense of it, it went against everything President Montgomery said he stood for, but then, just when he thought the news couldn't get any stranger, the coverage shifted to a live scene from some sort of disaster site. Ritter was aware of the schoolboys in Luhansk, it was the biggest news story in the country, and he'd passed enough TV screens since leaving the apartment to get the gist of it. He'd assumed it was some Kremlin media manipulation—all news in Russia was government propaganda of one kind or another—but what he was looking at now seemed to be something completely different. He'd seen scenes like it before, not on TV, but on the battlefield, and never in Europe. This coverage looked like it was in Russia, and he recognized the flashing icon in the corner of the screen that indicated that it was live. To his eye, based on what he'd seen before, it looked like live coverage of a chemical weapons attack. How was that possible? Who would broadcast such a thing? And how was the cameraman not suffering the same fate as the people in the footage? He wanted to ask someone in the crowd what was going on but didn't dare draw attention to himself by speaking English. Instead, he just stared at the screen, dumbfounded, as the footage showed a journalist walking across the frame, dressed head to toe in a Russian military hazmat suit.

His jaw dropped, and he wasn't the only one. The growing crowd around him was every bit as shocked as he was. Right there, live and in living color, the schoolboys the entire country had been following and falling in love with and rooting for were choking to death. It was like a scene from a disaster movie. If it was real, and not some stunt by the Kremlin, it was one of the worst disasters he'd ever seen. The boys were on their hands and knees, choking, coughing up blood. Pretty journalists in tailored blazers and expensive hairstyles were dying next to them. It was horrible. And for some reason, the camera crews seemed intent on capturing the gory scene as vividly, and in as much detail, as possible.

If this was the result of the attack that the previous graphic had purported to show, it would mean war. Potentially nuclear war. Ritter couldn't see how it was real. No US president would order an attack of this nature. But that wouldn't matter. If the Kremlin said it was an attack by the West, enough people would believe it. Besides, who else could have done such a thing?

The time had definitely come for Ritter to get out of the city. The crowd was growing angrier by the second. There'd already been riots in the station, the signs of the damage they'd caused were everywhere, but it looked like there were about to be more. As the news percolated through the station, Ritter kept his head down and went straight to the international platform, showing his ticket to the guard as he passed the turnstile. The train was already there, but as a precaution, he sat down on the bench on the platform before boarding and lit a cigarette. There were still a few minutes before departure, and he wanted to get his bearings and get a feel for the layout of the train and the people who were boarding. If there was anyone suspicious, any groups who looked armed or like they knew how to handle themselves, anything at all, he wanted to know sooner rather than later. He was in no condition for surprises.

As he watched the people board, everyone seemed preoccupied with the news. Some were watching it on their phones. Others were calling loved ones. Everyone was shocked, or distraught, or angry. Ritter hoped he wouldn't have to do much talking, it didn't feel like a good time to announce he was a foreigner, and he flicked away his cigarette and got on board when there were just a few minutes left to departure.

He was in the third carriage, and his seat was one of four, facing a small melamine table. The other three seats were unoccupied, as was most of the carriage, and he sat facing the turnstile on the platform so that he would see anyone else who got on board. No sooner had he made himself comfortable than the train driver made an announcement. There was a groan from the few passengers in his car, and he saw the departure time on the platform disappear to be replaced by a word in red lettering. He didn't have to be a language professor to guess that it meant there was a delay.

It was bad news, and he wondered if it had anything to do with what he'd just seen on the news. It was, after all, the only international departure from the city.

Ritter sat tight and counted the passing minutes. A few more passengers boarded, and he watched each of them closely, as well as anyone who appeared on the platform but didn't board. He looked at his watch. The original departure time came and went. Five minutes passed, and then ten, and he began to get impatient. The other passengers were still waiting, which told him the train hadn't been canceled, but he considered getting off anyway. Perhaps the train wasn't the easiest way to make his escape. Perhaps he'd be better off resting up in a hotel room somewhere, giving his shoulder time to heal.

His plan was to take the train as far as Vladikavkaz, the capital and largest city of Russia's North Ossetia region. Vladikavkaz was about seven hundred kilometers away, and it would take at least fourteen hours to get there. It was also the last stop before the Georgian border, and the train would be boarded there by soldiers who would check passports. Ritter had a number of passports, but they were all from English-speaking countries. Also, Russia and Georgia had suspended relations due to the war, and the border was notoriously difficult to cross, even at the best of times. With what was happening now, there was a good chance it would be closed completely. To avoid all that, he'd already decided to cross the border illegally on foot. That meant getting off at Vladikavkaz and crossing the last few miles through the mountains on foot.

The mountain terrain was treacherous, but it was also poorly guarded. Bootleggers and black marketeers crossed it all the time. He doubted he'd have much trouble, and even if he was caught, a few well-placed bribes would probably be enough to get him over the border and into the Georgian town of Stepantsminda.

The only hiccup in the plan was the bullet painfully lodged in his shoulder. Still, he had fourteen hours to rest up. Perhaps he could even remove the bullet in the little toilet at the end of the carriage. It would leave a suspicious mess of blood, but if the water was running, he'd be able to wash it up well enough.

There was a couple out on the platform, a man in a soldier's uniform and a woman in a white dress, and Ritter watched them. If the train had left on time, they'd have missed it, but that didn't seem to have caused them any undue worry. The man was carrying two suitcases, and he put them on the ground so that he could hug the girl. It seemed she was the only one leaving. They kissed, not overly passionately, and he helped her get the suitcases on board. She entered Ritter's carriage, and he looked down the aisle to watch her stashing the suitcases. Outside on the platform, the man stood dutifully, waiting for the train to leave. He looked at his watch once and waved when she peered out one of the windows on her way to her seat.

As she got closer, he reached into his jacket and gripped his gun, keeping one eye on her, one on the soldier on the platform. After what felt like an eternity, he heard the conductor's whistle. He glanced up and down the aisle, then stood up and leaned against the window to make sure no one boarded at the last minute. He waited, counting the seconds until he felt the lurch of the train grinding into motion, then sat back down in his seat. There was a no smoking sign, but there was also an ashtray built into the table, and he was wondering which of the two he should obey when he felt the train brake.

It came to a halt, and he saw that out on the platform, two men were running toward the train as if their lives depended on it. They were dressed casually and carried no luggage. He watched them with a growing sense of dread as the conductor stepped off the back carriage and waved them onboard.

The train started up again, and Ritter got up and made his way down the aisle to the back of the train, where the two men had boarded. The back car also happened to be the bar car. Ritter took a breath before entering, reached into his pocket for the reassuring steel of his gun, then opened the door. The car was thick with smoke, despite the same no-smoking sign as the one posted in his own car, and the two men were there, sitting at a table, smoking and drinking vodka. They didn't look up at him when he entered, and it appeared as if they were settling in for a long ride. One of them had removed his boots. Ritter went up to the bar, looking at them closely as he passed, and ordered a tea which was served to him in a paper cup. He brought it back to his own car and, as he approached his seat, noticed that the woman in the white dress was no longer sitting in her seat.

He was about to turn around when a female voice directly behind him said in English, "Hands up."

He froze.

"In the air," she said. "Now, or I shoot." He made to turn, and she said, "Don't try it."

He put his hands in the air. He couldn't see her, but he had no doubt a gun was pointed at the back of his head. The other passengers in the car were alarmed, but none moved. The woman made an announcement in Russian, probably identifying herself as law enforcement, then said to Ritter, "The seat on your right, sit on it." He did so, and she said, "Put your hands on the table."

He did that, too, and heard her taking the seat directly behind him. He still hadn't seen her gun—for all he knew, it didn't exist—but that wasn't a bet he was going to take. A bullet would have little trouble passing through the back of his seat.

"No sudden moves," she said. "I know you're armed. If you so much as sneeze, I'm going to pull the trigger."

"I'm not going to move."

"We'll see," she said.

"I've been waiting to meet you."

"You had no idea I existed until this moment."

"Not true," he said. "There was a woman's shoe print at the farm. A fancy shoe. Could that, by any chance, have belonged to you?"

She said nothing. He heard the sound of a cigarette lighter flicking and wondered if she'd done that with one hand. He smelled the smoke. "I don't see what difference that makes now," she said.

"I suppose not," he said. "It's just something I was wondering about."

"Oh?"

"I had a kind of premonition," he said, "when I saw the shoe print. Something told me I'd come across its owner sooner or later." He was stalling for time, which he knew she knew, but that was how these things went. He would stall. She would let him. Until she didn't.

"I was out there for a reason," she said. "I was sent to retrieve some photos. A roll of film. I don't suppose you still have them."

"I hope you haven't gone to too much trouble on that account," he said. "That ship sailed long ago."

"I thought it might have," she said nonchalantly.

"That doesn't seem to bother you very much."

"It is what it is. Can I ask how you came across the film?"

"You can ask," Ritter said, "but I can't answer."

"Why not?"

"I don't know where it came from."

"That didn't make you curious? Suspicious?"

"Sure it did," Ritter said. "In fact, I had a feeling, as soon as I opened the envelope, that the contents were about to change everything."

"I bet you didn't think they'd lead to this," she said.

"I don't know."

"So it came to you in an envelope?"

"Through the mail," he said, "with a Moscow postmark, no less."

She said nothing.

"That doesn't come as a surprise, does it?"

"Not really," she said.

"I'm guessing from the fact you're here that it was the real thing."

"It was the real thing," she said, "and I have a feeling it's going to cause some very powerful men an awful lot of trouble."

"You don't seem bothered by that."

She was quiet for a moment, then she said, her voice suddenly quieter, "Between you and me, I'm not very fond of my boss."

They were getting to the end of the conversation. He could hear it in her voice. Outside, the cityscape had given way to dense forest. They were headed south, and he was aware that they would be passing through a tunnel at some point soon. The sudden darkness might be an opportunity to make a move, he thought. "I don't suppose you know who sent it?" he said.

"You wouldn't believe me if I told you."

"Try me."

"She's dead now," the woman said. "For her troubles."

"She?" Ritter said.

"Does that surprise you?"

He thought about it for a second, then said, "I suppose not."

"Just count yourself lucky you're not going to see the shitstorm it's going to lead to," she said, and then, all the world went black. He never heard the bullet.

60

Yelena Klishina was standing with her back to the wall, as erect as a lamppost. In her hands, she held a heavy crystal ashtray, and Osip Shipenko, when it pleased him, tapped his cigar ash into it. A piece of human furniture, that was what he'd made of her, she thought. Or at least, that was what she would have thought if her mind wasn't so petrified, so absolutely paralyzed, with fear.

They were in the government building in Luhansk, and Osip was seated at his desk, looking at a computer screen. He'd just received a video file and had the sender on his cell. He pressed play, making sure Yelena could see too. It was of a young woman chained by her wrists to a wooden stake. She was in a basement somewhere, she was naked, and she was surrounded by a pack of rabid, frenzied dogs. It looked like the dogs were intent on devouring her, and they growled menacingly. The only thing holding them back were long leashes held by men dressed entirely in black, their faces covered by balaclavas.

"They have the nerve to call me Tushonka," Osip said,

looking up at her. "She's the Tushonka. She's the fucking dog food." He picked up his cell and said, "Release the hounds."

A moment later, the men let go of the leashes, and instantly, the dogs leaped on the girl. What followed was a scene of such horror that Yelena had to shut her eyes. That didn't block out the sound of the final, blood-curdling screams of the girl as she was ripped to shreds by the dogs.

"You see what happens?" Osip said. "You see what happens to people who betray me?" Yelena did see. She saw very well. The girl on the screen was Darya Kovalchuk, Osip's former secretary and Yelena's predecessor, and Yelena knew she'd earned her spine-chilling demise by sending a secret package to a CIA informant. "It's nothing compared to what I'm going to have done to her family," Osip said. "But you'll get to see all that as it unfurls."

He turned on the TV, the sound on mute, and watched the news coverage. It was live coverage, from a helicopter flying over the Kremlin, of a mob that looked like it was going to overrun the security forces.

There was a knock on the door, and one of the technicians who'd organized Osip's prior call with the president appeared. "Sir," he said, "your call with the Kremlin is ready."

"Come in then," Osip said. "Hurry up."

Two technicians then wheeled in the same AV cart as last time, and Yelena breathed a silent sigh of relief. "Should I leave you, sir?" she managed to say, her voice scarcely louder than a whisper.

The response was immediate, a back-handed blow across the face so hard she almost fell to the ground. She lost hold of the ashtray, and it fell, shattering on the floor into a thousand pieces.

"You do not move," Osip growled at her, his tone darkening as quickly as a winter storm. "You do not speak, you do not think, without my say-so, do you understand?"

She said nothing.

"Now, hold out your hand," Osip said. She hesitated a split second, then obeyed. "You idiots, clean up her mess." Osip watched them do it, then tapped the ash from his cigar into Yelena's open hand. "You're lucky I'm not using your mouth for this," he said.

The technicians hurried about their work, then retreated from the room. Osip looked at her as he picked up the clunky receiver. "Are you ready to see a man become king?" he said.

Yelena found herself holding her breath. She said nothing.

"You had a part to play in it," Osip said. "You sent those letters for me. I hear they were received quite warmly."

The phone Osip was using was very old technology, and the speaker in the earpiece was so loud that Yelena heard the president's voice when he came on the line. "You sly, ungrateful mongrel," the president screamed. "You've fucked me. The moment you televised those boys choking to their deaths—"

"I didn't fuck you—"

"You fucked me!" the president roared. "The riots have already started. There's a mob outside my gates now. They're practically holding pitchforks, Osip. Not just here but everywhere, right across the country. But don't you think I don't see you coming, you cretin. You're going to pay for this with your life."

"Sir!" Osip said, obviously feigning shock. "Whatever are you talking about? It was Kolesnikov who did this."

"You're going to die for this, Osip Shipenko. I'm going to have you hung, drawn, and quartered. But not before I come up with some special torture that will make all those years you spent in medical laboratories feel like a summer camp. Who knows, maybe I'll get the boys at the lab to help me. I'm sure they could be persuaded to come up with some ideas."

"Is that what you called me to say?" Osip said, still sounding awfully smug, to Yelena, for someone whose life was being threatened by the president. He was looking at the TV, and he said, "I must say, I'm surprised you found time to call me, what with that angry mob threatening to scale your walls."

"I wanted you to know what's in store for you," Molotov said. "I should never have trusted you, and you've put me in a right mess, you weasel, but you must know it's not going to be enough. I'll quell these riots. I'll make these mothers forget about the boys you killed. I'll blame it on NATO, and I'll use it, and their violation of our air space, to justify new wars of aggression."

"I see," Osip said, and Yelena knew he'd foreseen all this. He was toying with the president now. He was enjoying this moment that he'd spent a very, very long time building toward. "Let me ask you one thing," Osip said.

"What is it?"

"Are you in your office?"

"I'm not telling you where I am."

"If you are, have a look outside your window. The one facing the helipad."

"Why?" the president said, but Yelena could hear in his voice that he was already on his way to the window.

"Tell me," Osip said, "do you see your chopper out there?"

There was a briefest of pauses, and then, for the first time, she thought she detected a hint of doubt in the president's voice. "Where is it?"

"That's a good question," Osip said. "You might ask the same of your chauffeur and your personal guard."

"Osip, what are you playing at?"

"Go to the door," Osip said, unable to contain the glee in his voice any longer. "Go on. Try to go for a walk."

They heard the sound of a door opening, someone speaking, and then the door slamming. "Osip? What is this?"

"They're all my people now," Osip said. "Your driver, your pilot, your bodyguards, your palace security."

"Surely you know that it would take a lot more than a few servants to seize control of the country—"

"Oh, don't worry about that, Vladimir. I thought of them all. The head of intelligence. The head of the armed units around the capital. The phone operators and IT engineers. Even the television station heads."

"You couldn't have. Not without me getting wind of it."

"Oh, you know, you kind of made it easy for me when you started having their bosses executed on your palace lawn. I mean, it wasn't too hard for them to imagine themselves on that lawn."

There was a sound of an explosion somewhere in the distance, followed by shouting, and they saw on the TV screen that there was a lot of smoke coming from the outer walls of the Kremlin. "I should let you go," Osip said. "It sounds like you've got your hands full there."

"I'm going to have your neck for this, Osip Shipenko," the president spat, but Yelena could hear clearly now the fear in his voice.

"One more thing," Osip said, leaning back comfortably in his seat, "the best part about this revolt is that you'll go down in history as having been overthrown not by me but by the people."

"I thought you were smarter than this, Osip. Do you really think the people will want to follow a monster like you?"

Osip hung up the phone. On the screen, more explosions rocked the Kremlin walls, and it became apparent that some of the security forces had abandoned their posts and were joining the crowd. It really did look like the end, Yelena thought.

Osip's gaze was fixed on the screen. "It doesn't matter what the people want," he said quietly, more to himself than her.

61

Lance pulled over at a gas station and got out of the car. He'd rented it back in Rostov, a gray Lada Vesta, and had spent the last two hours driving it as far as the border. On his way, he'd listened to the radio, switching back and forth between stations, doing his best to keep abreast of the news reports that were coming through thick and fast. The radio's AM band had been disabled, so he only had Russian media reports to go on, but he thought he had a pretty clear idea of what was happening.

He stopped at the last gas station before the border. He could see the border checkpoint a few hundred yards up ahead but needed to fill his tank before making the crossing. He pumped the gas, then went into the little kiosk to pay.

"You heading across?" the clerk said to him in a thick local accent.

Lance nodded.

"Don't envy you," the clerk said.

"Do they give much trouble at the checkpoint?"

"No idea," the clerk said. "Probably wouldn't hurt if you had a little...." He rubbed his thumb and forefinger together to indicate a bribe.

Lance nodded. "I'll take some cigarettes, too," he said.

He went back to the car and drove up to the checkpoint warily. If they asked to search the car, there would be trouble. He had a number of documents in the glove box, false passports, and other paperwork that he wouldn't be able to explain. In the trunk, he had a few thousand dollars in hard currency, a burner phone for communicating with Klára, a Czech CZ 75 9mm, a Russian PYa, and ammo.

"Documents," the soldier said, beckoning him closer to the barrier.

Lance handed him a Russian passport and began opening the pack of cigarettes he'd just purchased. The soldier thumbed through the passport and called over one of his companions. There seemed to be four guards in total, all Russian. From their point of view, they shouldn't even have been there, Lance supposed. It was Russia on both sides of the line now, as far as Molotov was concerned. He didn't say as much, though. He watched the other guard get off a plastic chair and come over. The first guy told him to go to the guardhouse and check if there had been any bulletins.

The other two guards watched disinterestedly from across the road, where they were leaning on the barrier, smoking. There didn't seem to be any dogs.

"You just come in from Rostov?" the soldier asked. He was a burly guy in his forties with bristly stubble and a black patch on his jacket where his name patch should have been. He seemed to be the one in charge.

Lance nodded.

"And you're headed to?"

"Luhansk."

"Luhansk," the man repeated thoughtfully as if the answer might have been any different.

The man took a step back and looked the car over. "Purpose of visit?"

"I'm an assassin," Lance said, as plainly as if he'd just asked for a light for his cigarette.

The soldier looked at him a moment, then made to grab his gun. Lance shook his head. "Don't do that," he said.

"What is this?"

Lance was watching the two men across the road, who hadn't noticed anything was up, and said, "I told you. I'm an assassin. A contract killer."

"Is that...."

"Is it what?"

"Legal?"

"Depends on who you're doing it for."

The man glanced around. His companion in the guardhouse gave him a thumbs up, indicating that there were no active bulletins. The soldier looked Lance in the eye for a few seconds, reading him the way a dog might read an intruder. Lance lit a cigarette, keeping his eyes mostly on the other three men.

"You're a contract killer?" the soldier said.

"That's what I said."

"Whose side are you on?"

Lance thought for a moment, then said, "You know, the more I do this, the harder it gets to keep that clear in my head."

The guard pursed his lips. He seemed to know Lance was telling the truth. Who would lie about such a thing?

He seemed smart, too—at least, smart enough to know he didn't have to die for no good reason.

"Are we good?" Lance said.

The man hesitated a few more seconds, then let out a brief sigh as if he'd just remembered something he'd forgotten. "All right," he said, handing back the passport and waving Lance on through. "We're good."

Lance nodded and pulled forward. "Thank you, officer," he said, flicking his butt out the window.

"And drive carefully," the guard added. "The road could be mined."

Lance was rolling up the window. "I always do, officer."

AUTHOR'S NOTE

First off, I want to thank you for reading my book. As a reader, you might not realize how important a person like you is to a person like me.

I've been a writer for fifty years, and despite the upheavals my industry has faced, the ups and downs, the highs and lows, one thing remains constant.

You.

The reader.

And at the end of each book, I like to take a moment to acknowledge that fact.

To thank you.

Not just on my own behalf, but on behalf of all fiction writers.

Because without you, these books simply would not exist.

You're the reason they're written. Your support is what makes them possible. And your reviews and recommendations are what spreads the word.

So, thanks for that. I really do mean it.

While I have your attention, I'd like to give you a little

bit of background into my opinion on the events portrayed in this book.

Writing about politics is not easy, and I hope none of my personal thoughts and opinions managed to find their way into this story. I never intend to raise political points in my writing, and I never intend to take a stand. I'm one of those guys who stays out of politics as much as possible, and I would hate to think that any political ideas raised in my book hampered your ability to enjoy the story or relate to the characters.

Because really, this is your story.

These characters are your characters.

When you read the book, no one knows what the characters look like, what they sound like, or what they truly think and feel, but you. It's your story, written for you, and the experience of it is created by you when you read the words and flip the pages.

I write about people who work for the federal government. The nature of their work brings them up against issues of national security and politics, but apart from that, I truly do try to keep any views I might have to myself. So please, don't let any of my words offend you, and if you spot anything in my writing that you feel is unfair, or biased, or off-color in any way, feel free to let me know.

My email address is below, and if you send a message, while I might not get back to you immediately, I will receive it, and I will read it.

saulherzog@authorcontact.com

Likewise, if you spot simpler errors, like typos and misspellings, let me know about those too. We writers have a saying:

To err is human. To edit, divine.

And we live by it.

I'm going to talk a little about some of the true facts that this book is based on, but before I do, I'd like to ask for a favor.

I know you're a busy person, I know you just finished this book and you're eager to get on to whatever is in store next, but if you could find it in your heart to leave me a review, I'd be truly humbled.

I'm not a rich man. I'm not a powerful man. There's really nothing I can offer you in return for the kindness.

But what I will say is that it is a kindness.

If you leave me a review, it will help my career. It will help my series to flourish and find new readers. It will make a difference to one guy, one stranger you've never met and likely will never meet, and I'll appreciate that fact.

Now that those formalities are out of the way, let's talk about some of the events in this book.

As I write these words, the world watches in shock and horror the war of aggression President Vladimir Putin has unleashed on Ukraine. These events were on the horizon when I started writing the book, and there is no doubt they influenced my thinking as I developed the plot, but I could scarcely believe my eyes when Russian troops actually crossed the border and started shelling Ukrainian cities. It is a strange feeling for a person in my profession when the events on the nightly news are more dramatic and alarming than the plots of my novels. All I can say is that, like everyone else, I had no idea that Russia was actually going to invade Ukraine, and my thoughts and prayers are with every person affected by that unjust and illegal conflict. While the plot of the next book will certainly have to take account of the events that are unfolding before our eyes, the true events that were included in this book are more historical in nature.

The first that comes to mind is Valentina's use of the PSS silent pistol and the NRS-2 Scout Firing Knife. Both are real weapons developed by the Soviet Union for use by assassins. The PSS, also known as the MSS "Vul," was developed in the early 1980s for assassinations and reconnaissance and was issued to KGB Spetsnaz units beginning in 1983. It is still in development and was updated in 2011 to use a more powerful silent 7.62x43 mm SP-16 cartridge. Today, elite units from the FSB and MVD in Russia, as well as similar units in Georgia, are known to use the weapon.

The firing mechanism in the PSS was reproduced for use in the NRS-2 Scout Firing Knife, which was manufactured during the 1980s at the Tula Arms Plant. Soviet Spetsnaz units were issued the weapon, and it remains in use today among special law enforcement units in Russia. The knife can be used for stabbing or throwing, and a single shot can be fired with a twenty-five-meter range.

It hardly needs to be said, but any country that commissions weapons for assassins probably has assassins, and probably carries out assassinations. At the very least, it keeps that option on the table.

The depictions of the US and Russian embassies in Prague are accurate, and the history of the Russian embassy, including its use by the Gestapo during the Nazi occupation of the Second World War, is also true. The tunnels that the Gestapo built were indeed used by the Soviets to house KGB Line X officers. Today, the building is widely suspected to be a hub of Russian intelligence activity in Central Europe.

Perhaps the most disturbing thing my research uncovered are the events that took place at the Pitești Prison between 1949 and 1951. Known today as the Pitești Experiment or the Pitești Phenomenon, this chapter is a truly shocking example of the pain and degradation that man can inflict on his fellow man. The words written in the book are no exaggeration, and in fact, I forced myself to hold back and tone down the more disturbing events that I unearthed. For those who are interested, there is ample material available publicly that I will allow you to look up for yourself. Even here, in this author's note, I cannot bring myself to go into it in more detail.

The other incident that is based on history is the Iași Pogrom, in which Romanian government forces under the command of Marshal Ion Antonescu killed 13,266 Jews, a third of the city's Jewish population, during the first week of July 1941.

I draw from such true events for no reason other than to emphasize, as we are being forced again to witness with Putin's invasion of Ukraine, that the truth is often worse than anything that occurs in fiction. It is a sad fact, and one that many people do not realize, but what we read in today's espionage thrillers or see on the silver screen is nothing compared to what has actually happened, and continues to happen.

I am told from time to time that events in my books are unrealistic or far-fetched, and while I wish that were the case, any reading of history tells us otherwise. There is a famous quote from the Roman playwright, Terence.

Homo sum, humani nihil a me alienum puto.

It is translated in English to:

I am a man, and nothing human is alien to me.

While I remain an optimist on the direction the world is taking, and while I believe people are more good than bad, the truth is that terrible things have happened in the world, and we do ourselves no favors in pretending otherwise.

Finally, I'd be remiss if I didn't tell you that Book Four in the Lance Spector series, *The Sleeper,* is now available for pre-order.

So grab your copy now. I promise, if you enjoyed the first three, you're only going to be drawn into these characters more deeply!

God bless and happy reading,

Saul Herzog

Made in United States
Orlando, FL
08 February 2023

29718017R00286